The Captai

and

A History of Pugachov

The Captain's Daughter
and
A History of Pugachov

Alexander Pushkin

Translated by Paul Debreczeny

Series editor: Roger Clarke

ALMA CLASSICS

ALMA CLASSICS LTD
London House
243-253 Lower Mortlake Road
Richmond
Surrey TW9 2LL
United Kingdom
www.almaclassics.com

The Captain's Daughter first published in Russian in 1836
A History of Pugachov first published in Russian in 1834
This edition first published by Alma Classics Ltd in 2012

Printed in Great Britain by CPI Group (UK) Ltd, Croydon, CR0 4YY

Typeset by Tetragon

ISBN: 978-1-84749-215-9

Contents

The Captain's Daughter
and
A History of Pugachov

Publisher's Foreword

This is one of a series of volumes, to be published by Alma Classics during the coming years, that will present the complete works of Alexander Pushkin in English. The series will be a successor to the fifteen-volume Complete Works of Alexander Pushkin published by Milner and Company between 1999 and 2003, the rights to which were acquired by Oneworld Classics, now Alma Classics. Some of the translations contained in the new volumes will, as here, be reprints of those in the Milner edition (corrected as necessary); others will be reworkings of the earlier translations; others again will be entirely new. The aim of the series is to build on the Milner edition's work in giving readers in the English-speaking world access to the entire corpus of Pushkin's writings in readable modern versions that are faithful to Pushkin's meaning and spirit.

The Milner edition volumes were only available in hardback and as a set. Alma Classics, however, are offering the new Pushkin in English paperbacks for purchase individually.

In publishing this series Alma Classics wish to pay a warm tribute to the initiative and drive of the late Iain Sproat, managing director and owner of Milner and Company and chairman of the original project's editorial board, in achieving the publication of Pushkin's complete works in English for the first time. Scholars, lovers of Pushkin and general readers wishing to gain knowledge of one of Europe's finest writers owe him the heartiest admiration and gratitude.

– Alessandro Gallenzi

OTHER WORKS OF ALEXANDER PUSHKIN ALREADY AVAILABLE FROM ALMA CLASSICS:

Ruslan and Lyudmila, a dual-language text
trans. Roger Clarke, 2009

Boris Godunov and *Little Tragedies*
trans. Roger Clarke, 2010

Eugene Onegin, a dual-language text
trans. Roger Clarke, 2011

The Queen of Spades and Other Shorter Prose Fiction
trans. Paul Debreczeny, 2011

Alexander Pushkin (1799–1837)

Abram Petrovich Gannibal,
Pushkin's great-grandfather

Sergei Lvovich Pushkin,
Pushkin's father

Nadezhda Osipovna Pushkina,
Pushkin's mother

Natalya Nikolayevna Pushkina,
Pushkin's wife

The Imperial Lyceum in Tsarskoye Selo, which Pushkin entered in 1811

Pushkin's manuscript of the penultimate stanza of his ode 'Liberty'

An 1891 illustration for *The Captain's Daughter*
by Pyotr Petrovich Sokolov

Catherine II at Tsarskoye Selo, painted in 1794
by Vladimir Lukich Borovikovsky

Yemelyan Pugachov, painted by N.D. Vakurov.

Note by Series Editor

This volume, which corresponds to Volumes Seven and Fourteen of the Milner Edition of Pushkin's Works in English, contains Pushkin's one full-length prose novel, *The Captain's Daughter*, and his only completed historical work, *A History of Pugachov*. The pairing is a natural one, the novel being set in the context of the history. It was Pushkin's intense interest in history that drew his imagination to the genre of the historical novel; and it was his assiduous research into the events of the Pugachov uprising and its background that enabled him to develop the plot and characterization of his novel so accurately and realistically.

Although the novel was Pushkin's original idea – he started planning it in 1832 – his research into the historical background soon engrossed him so much that he decided to concentrate first on an account of the facts. He wrote the *History* during 1833, and it was published with the Tsar's permission in St Petersburg in 1834. The published edition consisted of two volumes, the first containing Pushkin's narrative and extensive notes, and the second transcripts of some of the documents, memoirs and other material that he had used as sources. In this edition we give translations of Volume One only – that is, of the material authored by Pushkin himself or cited by him as an integral part of the work – appending for the reader's information a list of the contents of Volume Two.

Pushkin did not finish writing the novel, *The Captain's Daughter*, until 1836. It was published in his literary review, *Sovremennik* (*The Contemporary*), at the end of that year, only a few weeks before his death.

The late Paul Debreczeny's edition of these works was first published by Stanford University Press in 1983. I should like to record my own and Alma Classics' gratitude to Stanford University Press for their permission to reprint Professor Debreczeny's material. For this edition I have made a minimum of revisions and corrections to

Professor Debreczeny's prose translations. I have revised his notes and supplemented them with some of my own, including, in the case of the *History*, my translations of nineteen unpublished notes by Pushkin that he submitted privately to Nicholas I in 1835 and that have not, to the best of my knowledge, appeared in English before. The verse translations in the epigraphs and text of *The Captain's Daughter* are my own, as is the translation of Pushkin's published notes to the *History*, which Professor Debreczeny omitted from his edition. Professor Debreczeny's introduction to *The Captain's Daughter* (here slightly shortened) and Professor Paul Dukes' introduction to *A History of Pugachov* were first published in the relevant volumes of the Milner edition in 1999 and 2000.

Dates of events in Russia and Eastern Europe are Old Style.

Asterisks in the text indicate editorial commentary to be found at the end of each part, while superscript numbers in *A History of Pugachov* refer to Pushkin's own notes to the work.

– Roger Clarke

Part One

The Captain's Daughter

Introduction

The Captain's Daughter is the fictional twin sister of Pushkin's scholarly *A History of Pugachov*. The Emperor Nicholas I took Pushkin into government service as a historian in 1831, and gave him access to archival collections, except for a few sealed, confidential ones. A year later he sent Pushkin a set of the recently published *Complete Collection of Russian Laws and Edicts*, Volume 20 of which contained the sentences meted out to participants in the Pugachov Rebellion of 1773–74. Pushkin, who had always been interested in rebellions and their causes, read through these sentences with fascination. What caught his eye, among other cases, was the trial of a nobleman who had been captured by the rebels and eventually joined their ranks. The unusual story of a man fighting against his own class and interests struck him as a good subject for fictional psychological exploration. So it was that from the summer of 1832 Pushkin started planning a historical novel about the rebellion, which was eventually to become *The Captain's Daughter*.

In order to gather material for his projected novel, Pushkin spent much of the early part of 1833 delving into documents relating to the period and completed the first draft of a historical study by the end of May: later that summer he even travelled to the Volga and Orenburg regions, in the eastern part of European Russia, where most of the military clashes had taken place. Stopping at his estate of Boldino in the autumn of that year he wrote up a second draft of the *History*, which was published, with the Emperor's encouragement, in December 1834.

Yet Pushkin was not satisfied with a dry factual account of the rebel leader's military actions and atrocities. Judging by the eventual *Captain's Daughter*, it is reasonable to speculate that he saw something heroic, even affectionate and poetic, in Pugachov's larger-than-life historical character, qualities that could not be sufficiently documented in a scholarly work. The intuitions of fictional writing were clearly called for, and Pushkin turned back to his original idea of a novel. The last chapters of the complete manuscript reached the censor on 24th October 1836. The censor required a few minor changes (some of which are indicated in the notes), and the novel appeared without the author's name on 22nd December in Volume 4 (1836) of Pushkin's literary journal *Sovremennik* (*The Contemporary*), a little over a month before his death.

What makes Pushkin's historical novel an outstanding work of art is the complexity that is almost imperceptibly woven into its texture. By letting Pyotr Grinyov, a little-educated nobleman of moderate means, tell the story in first person, Pushkin gives the narration a misleadingly naive tone. The young Grinyov has romantic expectations, which are invariably frustrated. He thinks his father will send him, when he is of age, to serve in the elite Semyonovsky Regiment in St Petersburg, a service he imagines must be the height of bliss. But in fact the elder Grinyov, fearing that his son will be caught up in the corrupting whirlwind of social life in the capital, dispatches him to Orenburg, asking an old comrade to post him to a fort where he will smell real gunpowder. The young Grinyov is disappointed, but as he is sent off from Orenburg to Belogorsk, he expects to see "fearsome bastions, towers and a rampart," constantly exposed to danger and commanded by a stern captain who will put him through his paces. What he finds is a simple village surrounded by a palisade and commanded not so much by its captain, Mironov, but rather by Mironov's wife, Vasilisa Yegorovna. The fort's single cannon has not been fired for years, because the couple's daughter, Masha, would be frightened by the boom. Mironov drills his ageing garrison in his dressing gown; the soldiers still cannot tell left from right, despite years of training, and the drill has to be finished because Vasilisa Yegorovna is putting dinner on the table. The humorous description of the fort turns into downright farce when we learn that the day's main event in Belogorsk was that a Cossack had a fight with a woman over a bucketful of hot water in the bathhouse.

All romantic notions about the gallant life of a young officer are dashed against the mundane details of everyday life. Pushkin manages to construct a story that is not only full of humour, but is also infused with affection for the simple characters.

Frustrated expectations, as they accumulate, strike us more and more as the basic technique of plot development. Grinyov falls in love with Masha, and prepares to fight a duel over her with Shvabrin, a St Petersburg rake sent to the remote fort in punishment for a previous duel. Tensions rise, but Vasilisa Yegorovna gets wind of the two young officers' plan, has them arrested and orders her maid to lock away their swords in the cubby hole. When the two finally get round to fighting in secret, it looks like Grinyov is gaining on his opponent, but his old servant, Savelich, arrives on the scene, hurrying to save his young master's life, distracts Grinyov with his cries, and Grinyov is wounded by Shvabrin. Masha nurses him back to life, and he writes to his parents for permission to marry her. However, his father not only refuses to give his consent, but threatens to see to it that he is transferred to another post. This does not happen, because the Pugachov rebellion breaks out, and Belogorsk is besieged. On the eve of the expected assault, Grinyov is awaiting "danger impatiently, with a feeling of noble ambition." As the rebels approach, he grasps the hilt of his sword, remembering that he received it from Masha's hands the evening before, and he sees himself as "her knight-protector." When the actual charge against the enemy comes, however, Captain Mironov's intimidated soldiers dare not follow him; Grinyov is hurled to the ground, and when he is on the point of rushing to his Captain's side some hefty Cossacks seize him and bind him with their belts. When Pugachov orders the officers to swear allegiance to him, Mironov and his old comrade Ivan Ignatich defiantly refuse and are hanged for it. Grinyov is about to utter the same defiant words, but it turns out that Pugachov was the man to whom he had once shown kindness by giving him a hare-skin coat. Pugachov decides to return the favour and lets Grinyov go.

Another instance of Grinyov being on the point of doing something truly martial occurs when he is in Orenburg and participating in a sortie: he is about to strike a Cossack, when the man takes his hat off, reminds him that he is Maximych from Belogorsk, and hands him a letter from the orphaned Masha. Grinyov's encounters with both Pugachov and Maximych imply that personal relations, individual sympathies, are far more important than military feats.

If the series of frustrated expectations strikes one as parody, so does the conspicuously conventional love plot. First a love triangle, followed by a duel with a jealous rival; the maiden nurses her chosen one back to life; and when the young couple openly declare their love, there arises an impediment to their union – the objection of Grinyov's father. Later, the hero, exposing himself to danger, comes to rescue the maiden from the clutches of the evil Shvabrin. The first impediment to their union is removed, once the Grinyov parents get to know the angelic Masha, but a new one arises when Grinyov, falsely accused by the same villain Shvabrin of having joined the rebels' forces, is tried and sentenced to permanent exile in a distant part of Siberia. Only Masha's accidental meeting and pleading with the Empress saves him, after which the couple live happily ever after. An element of plot that conspicuously imitates the romantic historical novel is Grinyov's chivalric refusal to explain to the investigating commission why he left Orenburg, since it would entail bringing Masha's name into the sordid business. Finally, Masha's meeting with Catherine II is a deliberate wink at Jeanie Dean's meeting with Queen Caroline in Sir Walter Scott's novel *Heart of Midlothian*.

In the course of all this action, Masha's behaviour is simply angelic; Pushkin refuses to endow her with any individual features. This is ironic, yet there is an element of Pushkin's empathy with different periods and lifestyles. By creating Masha as she is, he accepts the simple, though idealized, perceptions of the preceding century, as though bowing to the memory of his ancestors.

The young Grinyov, despite his naive style, is not quite so simple. He is shown in what we would call today "teenage rebellion". His bold game at billiards with the older officer Zurin, leading to the loss of a hundred roubles, is a lame attempt to assert his independence. In ordering Savelich, a substitute father figure, to pay the debt, he is showing him who is the master. Deciding to press forward despite the threat of a blizzard, he asserts the right to make a decision like a grown-up. The most curious detail from this point of view, much commented on by psychoanalytical critics, is the dream he has while his guide, the future rebel leader Pugachov, is leading his sleigh in the blizzard to the safety of a tavern. In the dream his father is dying, but Grinyov is afraid to enter the room because the old man might disapprove of him returning home without his permission; when he kneels down to receive his dying father's blessing, the elder Grinyov is suddenly replaced in his dream by a black-bearded muzhik, much like his guide, who fells people with his axe, but saves Grinyov, showing affection for him. The affinity between him and Pugachov also becomes apparent in the morning, after the night spent at the inn: the Cossack has no coat because he had pawned it in the course of a drinking bout – behaving just as irresponsibly as Grinyov had done with Zurin. This endears him to Grinyov and makes him all the more determined to give him his hare-skin coat. Finally, the agent that brings about Grinyov's eventual marriage to Masha, despite his parents' original opposition, is the Pugachov Rebellion, for without it he would have been transferred elsewhere and might never have seen her again. Moreover, Pugachov not only indirectly changes the young man's circumstances, but offers to feast at his wedding as they ride to Belogorsk to rescue Masha from Shvabrin. Grinyov's adoption of Pugachov as a substitute father, despite his opposition to the rebellion, shows an ambivalence in him that makes his character much more complex than the naive tone of his narration would make us expect.

Grinyov's character in *The Captain's Daughter* gains additional colour and complexity from certain parallels to the heroes of folk tales. Grinyov sets out in quest of maturity and meets a "helper", a wild beast that he assists, not suspecting that the beast will rescue him later. Like the hero of an old tale, he has to pass many tests and go through many tribulations before the fairy godmother grants him his wishes.

The qualities that draw the young Grinyov to Pugachov are those that Pushkin had sensed, but could not empirically document, in his scholarly account of the leader of the rebellion. Pugachov is seeking affection from Grinyov not just because he is grateful for the hare-skin coat, but also because he is lonely and in need of a kindred spirit to whom he can feel truly close. He is close to his own "generals", fellow ring-leaders in the rebellion, but it is clear from several passages that their reverence towards him is sham. Pugachov himself tells Grinyov that these people will be the first to betray him if he runs into bad luck and they think they can save their own necks by handing him over to the tsarist authorities (a correct prediction). Grinyov, as Pushkin did, grows to admire Pugachov for his daring challenge to fate, best expressed in the Kalmyk tale that Pugachov tells Grinyov. According to the tale, the eagle asks the raven why he, the eagle, is given only thirty-odd years to live, when the raven can live to three hundred. The raven's answer is that he lives so long because he feeds safely on carrion, while the eagle needs to have fresh blood. Trying to adopt the raven's habits, the eagle joins him in tearing into a dead horse; he pecks at it a couple of times, but leaves it alone, saying, "No, friend raven: rather than live on carrion for three hundred years, I'll choose one drink of living blood, then take what God brings." The notion that the quality of experience is dearer than life preserved for its own sake had been voiced many a time in Pushkin's previous work. It is one of the central themes of his poetry. Perhaps it is most clearly articulated in the prose fragment 'We Were Spending the Evening at Princess D.'s Dacha', when a character asks: "Is life such a treasure that one would begrudge sacrificing it for happiness?"

Savage as he is, Pugachov turns out to be the most engaging character in the novel. The strange incongruity of the stylistic devices Pushkin employs are evidently designed to bring home the deep contradiction and ambiguity inherent in such a portrayal. The greatest tension between the generally humorous tone of the narration and the events' unmitigated tragedy builds up in the scene at the commandant's house, where Grinyov is visiting Pugachov. Vasilisa Yegorovna's body, slashed by a sabre, is lying just outside, and it is emphasized several times how the bodies of Ivan Kuzmich, the Captain, and Ivan Ignatich, his old comrade, are looming over the square on their gallows. Yet this is the first scene in which Pugachov is seeking Grinyov's affection, which the latter cannot help noticing. When Pugachov is ready to retire for the night, he asks his comrades to sing a barge-hauler's song, which turns out to be about a robber sent to the gallows. Grinyov comments: "I cannot describe what effect this folk song about the gallows, sung by people destined for the gallows, had on me. Their fearsome faces, their harmonious voices and the doleful intonation they gave to the song's already expressive words – all this stirred me with a kind of poetic dread."

Bearing all this in mind, where can we place *The Captain's Daughter* within the history of literature? Pushkin was an avowed admirer of Sir Walter Scott, and indeed we can find traces of the British novelist's influence in his historical fiction. Yet to the modern reader Pushkin's terseness is far preferable to Scott's prolixity. The comparison, of course, is not fair, because the two authors had different purposes in mind. Pushkin's is a poet's prose, whose aim is to gather the narrative's various strands into a heightened emotional focus. The playful use of fictitious narrators was common currency in Pushkin's era, and its combination with incongruous pathetic elements was not entirely new either. In Russian literature, Nikolai Gogol is the best practitioner of mixing disparate modes of presentation. But Gogol, although he tried in *Dead Souls*, was never able to achieve the "poetic dread" that *The Captain's Daughter* inspires in scenes like Grinyov's meeting with Pugachov after the siege of Belogorsk. Pushkin's great Russian successors admired his prose style and came under its influence, but once more they were each pursuing different aims, and left to Pushkin the unique achievement of joining a bemused tolerance for the human condition with a clear view of its tragic side.

– Professor Paul Debreczeny

THE CAPTAIN'S DAUGHTER

(1836)

Take care of honour while you're young.
– An old proverb

Chapter I

A Sergeant of the Guards

"He could be captain in the Guards tomorrow."
"Unnecessary that. The ranks will be enough."
"You're absolutely right: he needs a life that's tough…
. . . .
*And who's his father?"**

– Knyazhnin

MY FATHER, Andrei Petrovich Grinyov, served under Count Münnich in his youth.* He retired with the rank of lieutenant colonel in 17—.* From then on, he lived on his estate in Simbirsk Province,* where he married the young Avdotya Vasilyevna Yu——, daughter of an impecunious local squire. There were nine of us children, but all my brothers and sisters died in infancy.

I was still in Mother's womb when they registered me as a sergeant in the Semyonovsky Regiment, thanks to the good offices of Major of the Guards Prince B——, a close relative of ours.* If – against all expectations – my mother had delivered a baby girl, my father would simply have informed the appropriate authorities that the sergeant could not report for duty because he had died, and that would have been the end of that. I was considered to be on leave until the completion of my studies. But in those days schooling was not what it is today. At the age of five I was entrusted to the care of the groom and huntsman Savelich, who was appointed my instructor in recognition of his sober conduct. Under his supervision I had learnt to read and write Russian by the age of twelve, and could make a sound assessment of a wolfhound's qualities. Then Father hired a Frenchman for me,

Monsieur Beaupré, who had been ordered by mail from Moscow along with our annual supply of wine and cooking oil. This man's arrival greatly displeased Savelich.

"Praise God," he muttered under his breath, "the child's been kept clean, well-combed and fed. What need is there to throw away money hiring this *m'sewer*, as if there weren't enough of our own folk?"

In his homeland Beaupré had been a barber; then he did some soldiering in Prussia; and finally he came to Russia *pour être tiouteur*, though he did not quite understand the meaning of that title. He was a good-natured fellow, but irresponsible and dissolute in the extreme. His main weakness was a passion for the fair sex; his amorous advances frequently earned him raps and knocks that would make him groan for days. Moreover, he was (as he himself put it) "no enemy of the bottle" – that is (in plain speech), he loved to take a drop too much. In our house, however, wine was served only with dinner, a glass at a time, and they usually forgot to offer even that to the tutor. For this reason he soon grew accustomed to home-made Russian vodka, eventually even preferring it to the wines of his homeland as a drink incomparably better for the stomach. He and I hit it off immediately. Although by his contract he was supposed to teach me "French, German, and all the sciences",* in practice he chose to learn Russian from me, soon acquiring enough to prattle after a fashion; and from then on we each went about our own business. We lived in perfect harmony. I certainly wished for no other mentor. Fate, however, soon separated us, through the following incident.

The washerwoman Palashka, a fat and pockmarked wench, and the one-eyed dairymaid Akulka somehow decided to throw themselves at my mother's feet at the same time, confessing their blameworthy weakness and complaining in tears against the *m'sewer* for seducing their innocence. My mother did not treat such things lightly and lodged a complaint with my father. With him justice was summary. He immediately sent for the *canaille* of a Frenchman. When he was told that *m'sewer* was giving me one of his lessons, he came to my room. Beaupré at this time was sleeping the sleep of the innocent on my bed. I was engrossed in work. It must be mentioned that a map had been obtained for me from Moscow and had been hanging on the wall of my room without being of the slightest use to anyone; it had been tempting me with the breadth and quality of its paper for a long time. I decided to make it into a kite and, taking advantage of Beaupré's sleep, had set about the task. At the time my father entered the room I was just fixing a bast tail to the Cape of Good Hope. Seeing me thus engaged in the study of geography, my father pulled my ear, then stepped up to Beaupré, woke him none too gently, and showered reproaches on him. Beaupré, all confused, tried to get up but could not: the hapless Frenchman was dead drunk. "Seven problems, one solution", as the saying goes: my father lifted him off the bed by the collar, shoved him through the door, and that very day banished him from the house, to Savelich's indescribable joy. Thus ended my education.

I lived the life of a young oaf, chasing pigeons and playing leapfrog with the serving boys. Meanwhile I had turned sixteen. Then the course of my life changed.

One autumn day my mother was making preserves with honey in the parlour, while I, licking my chops, was watching the boiling froth. My father was seated by the window, reading the Court Almanac, which he received each year. This book always had a strong effect on him; he could never leaf through it without absorption, and reading it never failed to rouse his spleen. My mother, who knew all his habits inside out, always tried to tuck the unfortunate book away in some hidden corner, so that the Court Almanac sometimes did not catch his eye for whole months. But if he did chance to come across it, he did not let it out of his hands for hours on end. This time, too, he kept reading it, occasionally shrugging his shoulders and muttering:

"Lieutenant general! He used to be a sergeant in my platoon! Decorated with both Russian crosses!* It was only the other day that he and I..."

At length Father tossed the almanac on the sofa, and sank into a reverie that augured little good.

Suddenly he turned to Mother. "Avdotya Vasilyevna, how old is Petrusha?"

"He's just sixteen," answered Mother. "Petrusha was born the same year that Auntie Nastasya Gerasimovna lost an eye and when—"

"Very well," interrupted Father. "It's time for him to enter the service. He's had quite enough of hanging around the maidservants' quarters and climbing up to the pigeon lofts."

The idea of soon having to part with me upset my mother so much that she dropped the spoon into the saucepan, and tears started streaming from her eyes. By contrast, my rapture would be hard to describe. The thought of entering the service was connected in my mind with notions of freedom and the pleasures of St Petersburg life. I imagined myself an officer of the Guards – a status that to my mind was the summit of human happiness.

Father did not like either to alter his decisions or to postpone their implementation. The day for my departure was fixed. The evening before I was to leave, Father declared his intention to furnish me with a letter to my future commanding officer, and he asked for pen and paper.

"Don't forget to give my regards to Prince B——," said Mother. "Tell him I hope he'll take Petrusha under his protection."

"What nonsense is this?" Father answered, frowning. "Why should I be writing to Prince B——?"

"Well, you did say it was your pleasure to write to Petrusha's commander."

"Well, and so what?"

"But isn't Prince B—— his commander? He is, after all, registered with the Semyonovsky Regiment."

"Registered! What does it matter to me that he's registered? Petrusha is not going to St Petersburg. What would he learn if he served there? To be a spendthrift and a rake? No, let him see some service in the army, let him learn to sweat and get used to the smell of gunpowder, let him become a soldier, not an idler. Registered with the Guards! Where is his identity certificate? Give it here."

Mother searched out my certificate, which she kept in a box together with my baptismal shirt, and gave it to Father with a trembling hand. He read it carefully, put it on the table in front of him, and began his letter.

Curiosity was tormenting me; where was I being sent if not to St Petersburg? I could not take my eyes off Father's pen, which was moving rather slowly. At last he finished and sealed the letter in an envelope along with my certificate. He took his glasses off, called me over to him, and said, "Here's a letter to Andrei Karlovich R——, my old comrade and friend. You're going to Orenburg* to serve under his command."

So all my bright hopes were shattered! Instead of a merry life in St Petersburg, boredom awaited me in some remote, godforsaken region. The army service, which I had contemplated with such enthusiasm even a minute before, now seemed like a burdensome chore. But there was no arguing with my father. The next morning a covered sleigh was brought up to the front porch, and the servants piled into it my trunk, a chest containing a tea service and parcels of rolls and pies – last tokens of a pampered domestic life. My parents blessed me. Father said, "Goodbye, Pyotr. Serve faithfully the sovereign to whom you swear allegiance;* obey your superiors; don't curry favour with them; don't volunteer for duty, but don't shirk it either; and remember the proverb, 'Take care of garments while they're new; take care of honour while you're young.'"

My dear mother admonished me in tears to look after my health and exhorted Savelich to watch over the "child". They helped me into a hare-skin coat and a fox-fur overcoat. I got into the sleigh with Savelich and set out on my journey, shedding floods of tears.

That night I arrived in Simbirsk, where I was supposed to stay for a day while various necessary items were procured – that task having been entrusted to Savelich. We put up at an inn. Savelich left for his shopping expedition in the morning. Bored with looking at the muddy side street from my window, I went wandering about the rooms of the inn. Reaching the billiard room, I spied a tall gentleman, about thirty-five years old, with long black moustaches, wearing a dressing gown and holding a cue in his hand and a pipe between his teeth. He was playing against the marker, who received a glass of vodka each time he won and had to crawl under the table on all fours every time he lost. I stopped to watch their game. The longer it lasted the more frequently the marker went crawling, until at last he remained under the table. The gentleman uttered a few pithy phrases over him by way of a funeral oration, and asked me if I would like to have a game. I refused, since I did not know how to play. This evidently struck him as rather strange. He cast a pitying look at me; but we nevertheless got into a conversation. He told me that his name was Ivan Ivanovich Zurin, and that he was a captain in the —— Hussar Regiment, had come to Simbirsk to receive new recruits,* and was staying at the inn. He invited me to take potluck with him as a fellow soldier. I agreed with pleasure. We sat down to the meal. Zurin drank a great deal and treated me generously too, saying that I had to get used to the service. He told me anecdotes of army life that made me roll with laughter; by the time we got up from the table we were bosom friends. He offered to teach me how to play billiards.

"It's essential for the likes of us in the service," he said. "Suppose you're on the march, you come to a small village: what's there to do? You can't be beating up the Yids all the time. Willy-nilly you end up at an inn playing billiards: but for that you must know how to play!"

I was entirely won over, and embarked on the course of instruction with great diligence. Zurin encouraged me vociferously, marvelled at the fast progress I was making, and after a few lessons suggested that we play for money, just for half a kopeck at a time, not with gain in mind, but simply to avoid playing for nothing – which, in his words, was the nastiest of habits. I agreed to this proposition too. Zurin ordered some rum punch and persuaded me to give it a try, saying once more that I had to get used to the service: what sort of service would it be without punch! I obeyed him. In the meantime we continued our game. Every sip from my glass made me bolder. I sent the balls flying over the edge every minute; all excited, I cursed the marker who was keeping the score in heaven knows what outlandish fashion; and I kept increasing the stake: in other words, I behaved like a young whelp who had broken loose for the first time. The hours passed imperceptibly.

Zurin looked at his watch, put down his cue, and declared that I had lost a hundred roubles. This embarrassed me a little because my money was in Savelich's hands. I started apologizing, but Zurin interrupted me:

"For pity's sake! Don't give it a thought. I can wait. And now let's go to Arinushka's."

What can I say? I concluded the day just as dissolutely as I had begun it. We ate supper at Arinushka's. Zurin kept filling my glass, repeating that I had to get used to the service. I could hardly stand on my feet when we got up from the table; it was midnight when Zurin drove me back to the inn.

Savelich was waiting for us on the porch. He groaned on seeing the unmistakable signs of my zeal for the service.

"What's happened to you, my dear sir?" he said in a pathetic tone. "Where did you get fuddled like that? My goodness gracious! I've never seen such mischief in all my life."

"Shut up, you old fool!" I replied, stammering. "You must be drunk, go to bed… and put me to bed."

The next morning I woke with a headache and could only dimly recall what had happened the day before. My reflections were interrupted by Savelich, who came in with a cup of tea.

"You're beginning early, Pyotr Andreich," he said, shaking his head. "You're beginning to play your pranks early. Who are you taking after? Neither your father nor your grandfather was a drunkard, I dare say; not to mention your dear mother, who's never touched anything but kvass* since the day she was born. And who's to blame for it all? That damned *m'sewer*, that's who. How many's the times, I remember, as he'd run to Antipyevna: '*Madame, jer voo pree vottka*!' Well, here's the result of *jer voo pree*! He set you a good example, didn't he, the son of a bitch! Did they really need to hire an infidel to look after the child, as if the master didn't have enough of his own folk!"

Ashamed of myself, I turned away from him and said, "Go away, Savelich. I don't want any tea."

But it was not easy to silence Savelich once he had started on a sermon.

"Now you can see, Pyotr Andreich, what it's like when you go on a spree. An aching head and no appetite. A drinking man's no good for nothing... Drink a glass of pickle juice with honey, or better yet, get over the night before with a little half-glass of vodka. What do you say?"

At this moment a boy came in with a note from I.I. Zurin. I opened it and read the following lines:

My dear Pyotr Andreyevich,

Be so good as to send me by my serving boy the hundred roubles I won from you yesterday. I need cash very urgently.

Ever at your service,

Ivan Zurin

There was no way out of it. Assuming an air of equanimity, I turned to Savelich – that "zealous guardian of all my cash and linen, indeed of all my business"* – and ordered him to hand the boy a hundred roubles.

"Why? What for?" asked the astonished Savelich.

"I owe it to the gentleman," I countered with the utmost coolness.

"Owe it?" asked Savelich, more and more amazed by the minute. "And when was it, sir, you found the time to get into this debt? Something's not right here. Say what you will, sir, I'm not paying a kopeck."

I thought that, if at this decisive moment I did not gain the upper hand over the obstinate old man, it would be difficult to free myself from his tutelage later on, and therefore I said, casting a haughty glance at him, "I am your master, you are my servant. The money is mine. I lost it at a game because that was my pleasure. As for you, I advise you not to try to be clever, but to do what you're told."

Savelich was so struck by my words that he just threw up his hands and stood rooted to the ground.

"What are you waiting for?" I bawled at him angrily.

He burst into tears. "Pyotr Andreich, young master," he uttered in a trembling voice, "don't break my heart. Light of my life, listen to me, an old man: write to this brigand that you were only joking and that we just don't have that kind of money. A hundred roubles! Gracious Lord! Tell him that your parents strictly forbade you to play for anything but nuts—"

"Enough of this nonsense," I interrupted sternly. "Bring the money here, or else I'll throw you out by the scruff of your neck."

Savelich looked at me in deep sorrow and went to fetch what I owed. I felt sorry for the poor old man, but I wanted to shake myself loose and prove that I was no longer a child. The money was delivered to Zurin. Savelich hurried to get me out of the accursed inn. He came to report that the horses were ready. I left Simbirsk with a troubled conscience and silent remorse, without saying goodbye to my instructor, nor imagining that I would ever see him again.

Chapter II

A Guide

Is this my land, this wretched land,
this land I do not know?
I did not come here of my own free will;
it was not my brave horse that brought me here.
What brought me here, a fine young lad and brave,
was recklessness, a youngster's boisterousness,
and a small sip of tavern liquor.

– An old song*

MY REFLECTIONS, as we rode along, were not very pleasant. I had lost, according to the value of money at that time, a considerable sum. Deep down I could not help recognizing that my behaviour at the Simbirsk inn had been foolish, and I also felt guilty about Savelich. All this was tormenting me. The old man sat on the box by the driver in a state of gloom, with his back to me, and kept silent except for clearing his throat occasionally. I was determined to make up with him, but did not know how to begin. At last I said:

"Listen, Savelich, that's enough. Let's make up. I'm sorry: I admit I was at fault. I misbehaved yesterday and unjustly offended you; I promise I'll be more sensible from now on and will listen to you. Don't be angry any more; let's make up."

"Oh, young master Pyotr Andreich," he answered, heaving a deep sigh, "it's with myself I'm angry; I'm to blame for everything. How could I leave you all by yourself at the inn! What's to be said? Sin it was led me astray: I took it into my head to drop in on the sexton's wife, have a gossip with my old friend. 'Tell a tale, end in jail' – that's what they say. Trouble, nought but trouble! How can I ever face the master and mistress? What'll they say when they hear that their child drinks and gambles?"

In order to reassure poor old Savelich, I gave him my word that from then on I would not dispose of one kopeck without his consent. He gradually calmed down, though he still muttered from time to time, shaking his head: "A hundred roubles! No trifle, is it?"

I was approaching my destination. A dreary wilderness, crosscut with ridges and ravines, extended all around me. All was covered with snow. The sun was setting. Our covered sleigh travelled along a narrow road or, to be exact, along a track cut by peasants' sledges. Suddenly the driver began casting frequent glances over to the side, until at last he turned to me, taking his hat off, and said, "Please, master, wouldn't it be better to turn back?"

"What for?"

"The weather's fickle: the wind's freshening up – see how it's blowing the snow."

"What does that matter?"

"But can't you see what's over there?" He pointed to the east with his whip.

"I don't see anything but white steppe and clear sky."

"But over there, there: that little cloud."

I did indeed see on the horizon a small white cloud, which I had at first mistaken for a distant hill. The driver explained that a small cloud like that betokened a blizzard.

I had heard of snowstorms in that region and knew that they could bury whole convoys. Savelich, in agreement with the driver, advised me to turn back. But the wind did not seem to me very strong; I hoped we could reach the next post station in good time, and I therefore gave orders to press forward as fast as possible.

The driver made the horses go at a gallop, but kept looking to the east. The animals moved along rapidly. The wind, however, was becoming stronger by the minute. The little cloud turned into a white cumulus, billowing upward, growing and gradually covering the whole sky. Snow began to fall, at first lightly, then suddenly in large flakes. The wind howled: we were in the middle of a snowstorm. In one minute the dark sky merged with the sea of snow. Everything was lost to sight.

"Well, master," shouted the driver, "we're in trouble: it's a blizzard."

I looked out of the sleigh: all I could see was darkness and whirling snow. The wind howled with such ferocity that it seemed alive; both Savelich and I were covered with snow; the horses could move only at a walk; they soon came to a standstill.

"Why aren't you going on?" I asked the driver impatiently.

"What's the good of going?" he answered, climbing off the box. "There's no telling as where we've got to, even now: there's no road, just darkness all around."

I started berating him, but Savelich took his part.

"Why didn't you listen to him?" he said crossly. "We could've returned to the wayside inn, filled up with tea and slept till the morning; the blizzard would've calmed down, and we could've gone on. Why the great haste? It'd be something else if you were hurrying to your wedding!"

Savelich was right. There was nothing we could do. The snow was falling thick and fast. It was piling up alongside the sleigh. The horses stood with their heads down and shuddered from time to time. The driver walked about, adjusting the harnesses for lack of anything better to do. Savelich grumbled; I looked in all directions, hoping to see some sign of human habitation or a roadway, but could not discern anything except the turbid whirl of the snowstorm... Suddenly I caught sight of something dark.

"Hey, driver," I called out, "what's that dark shape over there?"

The driver strained his eyes. "Heaven only knows, my lord," he said, climbing back into his seat. "Perhaps a cart, perhaps a tree; but it moves, I fancy: it must be either wolf or man."

I ordered him to drive towards the unknown object, which in its turn started moving towards us. In two minutes we met up with a man.

"Hello, my good man," the driver called to him. "Can you tell us where the road is?"

"The road's here all right: I'm standing on a firm strip of ground," the traveller answered, "but what's the use?"

"Listen, peasant friend," I said to him, "do you know this land? Will you guide me to a shelter for the night?"

"As for knowing this land," the traveller answered, "by the mercy of God I've travelled the length and breadth of it, on horseback and on foot, but you see what the weather's like: it doesn't take much to lose your way. It'll be best to stay here and wait; perhaps the blizzard will calm down, the sky will clear, and then we'll find the way by the stars."

His equanimity reassured me. I was already prepared, resigning myself to God's will, to spend the night in the middle of the steppe when suddenly the traveller climbed nimbly on the box and said to the driver, "Thank God, there's habitation nearby: turn to the right and go."

"Why should I turn right?" asked the driver with annoyance. "Where do you see the road? I know: 'another's steeds, another's gear; so drive them on, no need to fear!'"

It seemed to me the driver was right.

"Why actually *do* you think there's habitation nearby?" I asked the traveller.

"Because there was a gust of wind from over there," he answered, "and I smell smoke; so there's a village near."

His cleverness and his keen sense of smell amazed me. I told the driver to go forward. It was hard for the horses to trudge through the deep snow. The sleigh moved slowly, now gliding over a snowdrift, now falling into a gully and keeling over on this or that side. It was like the tossing of a ship on a stormy sea. Savelich groaned, constantly knocking into my side. I lowered the blind, wrapped myself in my fur coat and dozed off, lulled by the singing of the storm and quiet rocking motion.

I had a dream that I was never to forget, and that I still see as prophetic when I relate it to the events of my life. I hope the reader will forgive me, for he probably knows from experience how easy it is for people to fall into superstition, however great their contempt for unfounded beliefs may be.

I was in that state of mind and feeling in which reality yields to reveries and merges with them in the nebulous visions of deepening slumber. The blizzard, I fancied, was still raging, and we were still floundering in the snow-covered wilderness, but I suddenly beheld a gate and was driven into the courtyard of our manor house. My first thought was an apprehension that my father might be angry with me for this unintentional re-entrance under the paternal roof, construing it as deliberate disobedience. I jumped out of the sleigh with anxiety, and there was my mother waiting on the steps to meet me with an air of deep sorrow.

"Quiet," she said to me, "your father's on his deathbed and wants to bid farewell to you."

Struck by fear, I followed her into the bedroom. I saw a dimly lit chamber and people standing around the bed with sorrowful faces. I tiptoed up to the bed; Mother raised the bed curtain and said, "Andrei Petrovich, Petrusha has arrived: he heard about your illness and turned back; give him your blessing."

I got down on my knees and directed my eyes to the invalid. But what then? Instead of my father, there in the bed lay a peasant with a black beard, looking at me cheerfully. I turned to Mother in bewilderment, saying, "What's the meaning of this? This is not Father. And why should I ask a peasant for his blessing?"

"It's all the same, Petrusha," answered Mother; "it's he that'll stand in for Father for your wedding: kiss his dear hand and let him bless you."

I could not agree to that. The peasant jumped off the bed, drew an axe from behind his back, and started flourishing it in all directions. I wanted to run, but couldn't; the room was filling with dead bodies; I stumbled over the corpses and slipped in the pools of blood. The terrifying peasant called out to me kindly, "Don't be afraid, come to receive my blessing."

Horror and bewilderment overwhelmed me... And at that moment I woke up: the horses had stopped, and Savelich was nudging my arm, saying, "Get out, sir, we've arrived."

"Arrived where?" I asked, rubbing my eyes.

"At the wayside inn. With God's aid we drove straight into the fence. Quick, Your Honour, get out and warm yourself."

I stepped out of the sleigh. The blizzard was still blowing, though with less force by now. It was so dark you might be blind. The innkeeper came out to meet us at the gate, holding a lantern under the skirt of his coat. He led me into the front room, small but quite clean and lit by a torch. A rifle and a tall Cossack hat hung on the wall.

The innkeeper, a Yaik Cossack by origin,* seemed to be about sixty years old, still hale and hearty. Savelich brought in the chest with my tea service and asked that a fire be made for the tea, for which I thirsted more than I had ever done before. The innkeeper went to attend to the matter.

"And where is our guide?" I asked Savelich.

"Right here, Your Honour," answered a voice from above. Looking up at the bunks, I saw a black beard and two shining eyes.

"How are you doing, my good fellow? Are you all frozen?"

"I should think I am, in nothing but a thin jerkin. I had a sheepskin jacket, but, why deny it, I pawned it at a tavern last night: the frost didn't seem that fierce then."

At this moment the innkeeper brought in the boiling samovar, and I offered our guide a cup of tea; he climbed down from the bunks. His appearance struck me as rather remarkable: he was about forty, of medium height, lean and broad-shouldered. Some grey streaks were showing in his black beard, and his large lively eyes were wide awake. His face bore a rather pleasant though roguish expression. His hair was cropped close around the crown; he wore a ragged jerkin and Tatar trousers. When I handed him a cup of tea, he took a sip and made a wry face.

"Your Honour, be so kind, let them give me a glass of vodka: we Cossacks don't drink tea."

I readily fulfilled his wish. The innkeeper took a bottle and a glass from the cupboard and went up to him, looking in his face.

"Ah," he said, "so you're in these parts again, are you? Where have you sprung from?"

My guide winked at the innkeeper suggestively and answered with a proverb, "'I flew into the garden and pecked at the hemp; grandma threw a stone at me, but past me it went.' And how are your fellows doing?"

"Our fellows!" the innkeeper answered, keeping up the figurative talk. "They were about to ring the vesper bell, but the priest's wife stopped them: the priest's out visiting, there's devils in the churchyard."

"Hold your tongue, old man," retorted my vagabond. "Come a little rain, and there'll come some little mushrooms; and come some little mushrooms, there'll be a basket too. But now," he winked once more, "hide the axe behind your back: the ranger's on his rounds. Your Honour, here's to your good health!" With these words he took the glass, crossed himself, and drank the vodka down in one gulp. Then he bowed to me and returned to his bunk.

I could not understand any of this thieves' repartee at the time, but later gathered that they had been alluding to the affairs of the Yaik Host, which had only just been pacified after the revolt of 1772.* Savelich listened with an air of great disapproval. He kept glancing suspiciously now at the innkeeper, now at our guide. This wayside inn, or *umyot* as they call them in that region, was in a remote place in the middle of the steppe, far from any habitation, and seemed very like a robbers' den. But there was nothing we could do. It was unthinkable to continue the journey. Savelich's anxiety amused me a great deal. In the meantime, I prepared for the night and lay down on a bench. Savelich decided to climb up on the stove; the innkeeper stretched out on the floor. Soon the whole cabin was snoring; I fell asleep as though I'd been slain.

Waking rather late the next morning, I saw that the storm had passed. The sun was shining. The snow covered the boundless steppe like a dazzling blanket. The horses were harnessed. I settled accounts with the innkeeper, who charged such a modest sum that Savelich did not even argue with him or start his usual haggling, and quite forgot his suspicions of the night before. I called for our guide, thanked him for his help, and told Savelich to give him half a rouble for vodka. Savelich knitted his brows.

"Half a rouble for vodka!" he exclaimed. "And why? Because you kindly drove him to the inn? It's for you to say, sir, but we don't have any half-rouble pieces to spare. If you tip every man you meet, you'll soon go hungry yourself."

I could not argue with Savelich. I had promised that he would have full control of my money. It vexed me, however, that I was unable to reward the man who had saved me, if not from disaster, then at least from a very unpleasant situation.

"All right," I said with full composure, "if you don't want to give him half a rouble, pull something out from among my clothes. He is dressed too lightly. Give him my hare-skin coat."

"Have mercy on me, young master Pyotr Andreich!" said Savelich. "What does he need your hare-skin coat for? He'll sell it for drink, the dog, at the first tavern."

"It's not your headache, greybeard," my vagabond said, "whether I sell it for drink or not. His Honour's giving me a coat off his own shoulders: that's his pleasure as master. You keep your peace and obey: that's your duty as servant."

"Don't you fear the Lord, you brigand?" responded Savelich, raising his voice. "You can see the child's not yet savvy enough, so you're glad to rob him, making the most of his inexperience. What do you want the young master's little coat for? You can't even stretch it across your damned hulking shoulders."

"Don't try to be clever," I said to my attendant. "Bring the coat here right now."

"God Almighty!" groaned Savelich. "A hare-skin coat, as good as new! And to whom? Not to anyone deserving, but to a threadbare drunkard!"

But the hare-skin coat appeared. The peasant proceeded to try it on then and there. Sure enough the coat, which even I had outgrown, was on the tight side for him. But somehow or other he managed to put it on, ripping it at the seams. Savelich almost howled when he heard the stitches tearing. The vagabond was exceedingly happy with my present. He saw me to the sleigh and said with a low bow, "Thank you, Your Honour! May the Lord reward you for your charity! I'll never forget your kindness."

He went on his way, and I continued my journey, ignoring Savelich's vexation. I soon forgot about yesterday's blizzard, my guide and the hare-skin coat.

As soon as I arrived in Orenburg I presented myself to the general. The man I saw before me was of tall build, but already bent with old age. His long hair was entirely white. His old faded uniform reminded one of a warrior of the Empress Anna's times,* and he had a heavy German accent. I handed him my father's letter. As soon as he saw the name he cast a quick glance at me.

"Gottness gracious," he said. "It vass only ze ozer day Andrei Petrovich vass your age, and now hass he such a big lad! Ach, how time flies!" He broke the seal and started reading the letter under his breath, making comments as he read on. "'My Gracious Sir, Andrei Karlovich, I trust that Your Excellency—' Stands he on tseremonies! Iss he not ashamed? Ditsipline, of course, kommes first, but iss zis any vay to write to an old kamerad? 'Your Excellency has not forgotten—' Hmm, hmm... 'and when... by the late Field Marshal Mün... on campaign... and also Karolinka too—' Ach, bruder! Doess he still remember our old pranks! 'And now, turning to business... my rascal to your care—' hmm... 'hold him in hedgehog-skin gloves.' Vot are hedgehog-skin gloves? It musst be ein Russisch saying. Vot doess it mean 'hold him in hedgehog-skin gloves?'" he repeated, turning to me.

"It means," I answered with as innocent an air as I could put on, "to treat kindly, not too severely, to allow as much freedom as possible, in other words, to hold him in hedgehog-skin gloves."

"Hmm, I see... 'and not to allow him much freedom—' No, hedgehog-skin gloves means not vot you say... 'enclose his identity certificate—' Ver iss it? Ah, here... 'to notify the Semyonovsky—' Very goot, very goot, efrysing vill be done. 'You will allow me to put rank aside and embrace you as a comrade and friend'... At last hass he realissed... And so on, and so forth... Vell, young friend," he said to me, having finished the letter and put the certificate aside, "efrysing vill be done: you vill be transferred to ze —— Regiment as an officer, and in order not to vaste time, you vill set out tomorrow for Fort Belogorsk,* ver you vill serve under the command of Captain Mironov, a goot, honest man. Zere you vill experience real service and learn ditsipline. In Orenburg zere iss nossing for you to do: dissipation iss not goot for a young man. As for today, you're cordially infited to dine viz me."

"From bad to worse," thought I. "I was already a sergeant of the Guards in my mother's womb, but what good has that done me? Where has it taken me? To the —— Regiment and to a godforsaken fort on the edge of the Kyrgyz-Kazakh steppes!"* I dined with Andrei Karlovich, in company with his old adjutant. Strict German economy reigned at his table, and I suspect that his fear of occasionally having to share his bachelor repast with an extra guest was one of the reasons why he dispatched me to the garrison with so much haste. The next morning I said goodbye to the general and set out for the fort to which I had been assigned.

Chapter III

The Fort

In the fort we make our quarter,
eating bread and drinking water;
and if ever barbarous
foemen come to sup with us,
we'll see our prized guests well fed:
every gun we'll load with lead.
– A soldier song*

Old-fashioned people, my dear sir.
– *The Young Hopeful**

FORT BELOGORSK was situated forty versts* from Orenburg. The highway led along the steep bank of the Yaik. The river was not yet frozen over, and its leaden waters showed a dismal black between the monotonous banks blanketed in white snow. On the other side stretched the Kyrgyz steppes. I immersed myself in thoughts that were mostly melancholy. Life in a garrison held little attraction for me. I tried to picture to myself Captain Mironov, my future commanding officer, and the image that came to mind was of a stern, short-tempered old man, ignorant of everything except the service, and ready to put me under arrest on bread and water for the merest trifle. In the meantime it was beginning to get dark. We were riding along quite fast.

"Is it far to the fort?" I asked my driver.

"It isn't," he answered; "you can already see it there."

I looked in every direction, expecting to see fearsome bastions, towers and a rampart, but I could see nothing except a small village bounded by a palisade of logs. On one side of it there were three or four haystacks, half-buried in snow; on the other, a sagging windmill with idly drooping bast sails.

"Where is the fort?" I asked in amazement.

"Right here," answered the driver, pointing to the little village, and as he spoke we drove in.

By the gate I saw an old cast-iron cannon; the streets were narrow and winding, the cottages low, mostly with thatched roofs. I gave orders to drive to the commandant's, and in a minute the sleigh stopped in front of a small wooden house, built on high ground near a church also of wood.

Nobody came out to meet me. I went up to the porch and opened the door to the anteroom. A veteran of advanced years sat on a table, sewing a blue patch on the elbow of a green uniform coat. I told him to announce me.

"Just go in, Your Honour," replied the veteran; "the family's at home."

I entered a small room, very clean and furnished in the old style. In the corner there stood a cupboard with crockery; on the wall hung an officer's diploma, framed and glazed; next to it pride of place was held by popular prints depicting the taking of Küstrin and Ochakov,* the choice of a bride, and a cat's burial.* An old lady in a padded jacket and with a scarf over her head was seated by the window. She was winding a hank of yarn, which a one-eyed old man, wearing an officer's uniform, held stretched out on his hands.

"What can we do for you, young man?" she asked without interrupting her work.

I answered that I had arrived to serve in the fort and had come to report for duty to my captain; and with these words I was about to turn to the one-eyed little old man, taking him for the commandant, but the lady of the house interrupted my prepared speech.

"Ivan Kuzmich isn't at home," she said. "He's visiting Father Gerasim; but no matter, young man, I'm his wife. You're very welcome: make yourself at home. Do sit down."

She called her maid and told her to fetch the Cossack sergeant. The little old man looked me up and down inquisitively with his one eye.

"May I be so bold as to ask," he said, "in which regiment you've served?"

I satisfied his curiosity.

"May I also inquire," he continued, "why it was your pleasure to transfer from the Guards to a garrison?"

I answered that that was the wish of my superiors.

"For conduct unbecoming an officer of the Guards, I suppose," continued my untiring interrogator.

"That's enough of your nonsense," the captain's wife said to him. "You can see the young man's tired after his journey: he's in no mood to prattle with you... Hold your hands straight... As for you, my dear young man," she turned to me, "don't be disheartened that they've shovelled you off to us, at the back of beyond: you aren't the first, nor will you be the last. You'll like it when you get used to it. It's been near five years since Alexei Ivanych Shvabrin was transferred to us for manslaughter by murder. Heaven knows what got into him – it must've been the Devil's work – but he went, you see, outside the city with a certain lieutenant, and they took their swords with them, and what do you know, they started jabbing at each other until Alexei Ivanych cut down the lieutenant – in front of two witnesses, what's more! What can you say? Everyone goes astray sometimes."

At this moment the sergeant, a well-built young Cossack, came into the room.

"Maximych," said the captain's wife to him, "assign this officer to a lodging – a clean one, mind you."

"Yes, madam, Vasilisa Yegorovna," replied the sergeant. "Should we perhaps billet His Honour at Ivan Polezhayev's?"

"Nonsense, Maximych," said the captain's wife. "Polezhayev's house is crowded as it is; besides, Ivan's a pal of mine, and he always takes care to treat us with due respect. Take the officer... What's your name and patronymic, dear? Pyotr Andreich? Take Pyotr Andreich to Semyon Kuzov's. The scoundrel has let his horse into my vegetable garden. How are things otherwise, Maximych? Everything all right?"

"Everything's been peaceful, thank God," said the Cossack,

"except that in the bathhouse Corporal Prokhorov got into a scuffle with Ustinya Negulina over a tubful of hot water."

"Ivan Ignatich," the captain's wife turned to the one-eyed little old man, "please sort the business out between Prokhorov and Ustinya: who's right, who's to blame. Then punish them both. Well, Maximych, you may go now, and God be with you. Pyotr Andreich, Maximych will take you to your lodging."

I bowed and took my leave. The sergeant led me to a cottage on the high riverbank, at the very edge of the fort. One half of the cottage was occupied by Semyon Kuzov's family; the other half was given to me. This consisted of one room, tolerably neat, divided in two by a partition. Savelich started unpacking, and I looked out of the narrow window. The melancholy steppe stretched out before me. To one side I could see a few huts; some chickens were roaming about the street. An old woman was standing on her porch with a trough in her hands calling her pigs, which responded with friendly grunts. This was the place where I was condemned to spend my youth! I was overcome by dejection; I left the window and went to bed without supper, despite the exhortations of Savelich, who kept saying in deep distress, "God Almighty! Won't eat anything! What'll the mistress say if the child falls sick?"

The next morning I had only just begun to dress when the door opened and a young officer, not very tall, with a swarthy face that was strikingly unattractive but exceptionally lively, came into the room.

"Please forgive me," he said in French, "for coming to introduce myself without ceremony. I heard of your arrival yesterday: the urge to see a human face at last so overwhelmed me that I couldn't restrain myself. You'll understand what I mean when you've been here for some time."

I could guess that this was the officer discharged from the Guards for a duel. We proceeded to introduce ourselves. Shvabrin was by no means a stupid man. His conversation was witty and entertaining. He described to me with great mirth the commandant's family and social circle, and the region where fate had brought me. I was roaring with laughter when the same veteran who had been mending his uniform in the commandant's anteroom the day before came in to convey Vasilisa Yegorovna's invitation to lunch. Shvabrin volunteered to come with me.

As we approached the commandant's house, we saw in a small square some twenty ancient veterans wearing three-cornered hats over their long hair. They were lined up, standing at attention. Facing them stood the commandant, a tall, well-preserved old man, wearing a nightcap and a thick cotton dressing gown. He came up to us as soon as he saw us, said a few kind words to me, then went back to drilling his men. We would have stopped to watch the drill, but he told us to go on in to Vasilisa Yegorovna, promising to come right behind us.

"There's not much for you to see here," he added.

Vasilisa Yegorovna received us informally and cordially, treating me like an old friend of the family. The veteran and Palashka were laying the table.

"What's the matter with my Ivan Kuzmich today, that he can't stop that drilling?" said the captain's wife. "Palashka, go and call the master to dinner. And where's Masha?"

At that moment a girl of about eighteen, with round rosy cheeks and light brown hair combed smoothly behind her blushing ears, came into the room. At first glance she did not make a great impression on me. I looked at her with prejudice because Shvabrin had described Masha, the captain's daughter, as a perfect ninny. Marya Ivanovna sat down in the corner and started sewing. In the meantime the cabbage soup had been put on the table. Vasilisa Yegorovna, still not seeing her husband, sent Palashka for him a second time.

"Tell the master that the guests are waiting, the cabbage soup's getting cold: praise God, there'll be plenty more opportunity for drilling; he'll have no difficulty yelling himself hoarse."

The captain soon arrived, accompanied by the one-eyed little old man.

"What do you mean by this, my dear?" the captain's wife said to him. "The food's been served for ages, but you never come when you're called."

"Listen, Vasilisa Yegorovna," answered Ivan Kuzmich, "duty kept me: I was drilling my old soldiers."

"Don't tell me that," she retorted. "Great glory, drilling your soldiers, indeed; they'll never learn the routines, and you don't know the first thing about them either. It'd be far better if you sat at home and prayed to God. Dear guests, please come and be seated."

We sat down to lunch. Vasilisa Yegorovna did not keep quiet for a moment, showering me with her questions: who were my parents, were they still alive, where did they live, and what were their circumstances? Informed of my father's three hundred serfs, she said:

"Fancy that! There are some rich people in this world, aren't there? All we have, my dear, is the one Palashka, but thank God we manage to make ends meet. There's just one problem: Masha. She's of marriageable age, but what does she have for a dowry? A fine-tooth comb, a besom, and a three-kopeck piece (God forgive me) to go to the bathhouse with. All will be fine if a good man turns up; otherwise she'll stay unmarried, a lifelong spinster."

I glanced at Marya Ivanovna: her face had gone all red, and tears were even dropping onto her plate. I felt sorry for her and quickly changed the subject.

"I've heard," I said apropos of nothing, "that some Bashkirs* are planning to attack your fort."

"Who told you that, my dear fellow?" asked Ivan Kuzmich.

"I heard it in Orenburg," I replied.

"Nonsense!" said the commandant. "We haven't heard of any such thing for a long time. The Bashkirs are a frightened lot; and the Kyrgyz* have been taught a lesson too. Don't worry; they won't poke their noses in here, and if they do, I'll give them a rap that'll keep them quiet for ten years."

"Isn't it frightening for you," I continued, turning to the captain's wife, "to stay in a fort that's exposed to such dangers?"

"It's a matter of getting used to it, my dear young man," she answered. "Twenty years ago, when we were transferred here from the regiment, these unbaptized dogs scared me out of my wits. I'd only have to see their lynx-fur hats and hear their war cries, and my heart'd stop beating, can you believe it? But now I've got so used to them that I don't stir an inch when it's reported that the scoundrels are roving around the fort."

"Vasilisa Yegorovna is a stout-hearted lady," remarked Shvabrin, with an important air. "Ivan Kuzmich is a witness to that."

"You'd better believe it," said Ivan Kuzmich. "The woman's no sissy."

"And how about Marya Ivanovna?" I asked. "Is she just as brave as you?"

"Masha brave?" responded her mother. "No, she's a coward. To this day she can't hear a gunshot without palpitations. And a couple of years ago, when Ivan Kuzmich took it into his head to fire our cannon on my name day, Masha, my poor darling, almost quit this world with fright. We've stopped firing the accursed cannon since then."

We rose from the table. The captain and his wife retired to lie down. I went to Shvabrin's and spent the whole evening with him.

Chapter IV

A Duel

So take up your position, I request.
You'll see then how I'll spike you through the chest!
– Knyazhnin*

A FEW WEEKS went by, and my life in Fort Belogorsk became not only tolerable, but even pleasant. At the commandant's I was treated like a member of the family. The master of the house and his wife were highly respectable people. Ivan Kuzmich, a private's son who had risen from the ranks, was a simple, uneducated, but honest and kind-hearted man. He was under his wife's thumb, which suited his easygoing disposition. Vasilisa Yegorovna used to regard military affairs as household business and governed the fort just like her own home. As for Marya Ivanovna, it did not take her long to overcome her shyness with me. We got to know each other. I found her to be a sensible and sensitive young woman. I myself hardly noticed how attached I was growing to the good-hearted family, even to Ivan Ignatich, the one-eyed garrison lieutenant, whom Shvabrin made out to have had an illicit liaison with Vasilisa Yegorovna. (There was not a shade of truth in this, but it did not worry Shvabrin.)

I was made an officer. My duties were no great burden. It was God that protected our fort: there were no inspections, no exercises, no patrols. The commandant did drill his soldiers from time to time for his own amusement, but he had not yet succeeded in getting all of them to tell right from left, even though, in order to avoid mistakes, they usually crossed themselves before every about-turn. Shvabrin had a few books in French. I began reading, and developed a taste for literature. In the morning I usually read, polished my style through translations, and sometimes even wrote verses. For lunch I almost always went to the commandant's house and stayed on, as a rule, for the rest of the day; some evenings Father Gerasim would also drop in with his wife Akulina Pamfilovna – the foremost bearer of news in the whole district. I did, of course, see Shvabrin every day, too, but his conversation was becoming less and less agreeable to me. I strongly disliked his perpetual jokes about the commandant's family, and especially his caustic comments about Marya Ivanovna. There was no other society in the fort, and I wished for no other.

Despite predictions, the Bashkirs were not stirring. Tranquillity reigned around our fort. But the peace was disturbed by an unexpected quarrel.

As I have mentioned, I developed an interest in literary pursuits. My efforts, judging by the standards of the time, were tolerable: Alexandr Petrovich Sumarokov* was, some years later, to accord much praise to them. One day I succeeded in writing a little song that I thought was satisfactory. As is well known, authors will sometimes, on pretence of asking for advice, seek a well-disposed listener. I too, having made a clean copy of my song, took it to Shvabrin, the only person in the fort who could appreciate the efforts of a poet. After a brief introduction I drew my notebook out of my pocket and read the following verses aloud:*

Thoughts of love I try to smother
and forget my pretty one;
shunning Masha, I'll recover
the independence I've foregone!

But those eyes that once entrapped me
are still there for me to see;
they've churned up the soul within me,
shattered my tranquillity.

Masha, understand my anguish,
show the sympathy I crave;
see the pain in which I languish,
know that I am still your slave.

"What do you think of it?" I asked, expecting the praise that I thought was unquestionably due to me. But to my great disappointment Shvabrin, who had generally been indulgent, this time unhesitatingly declared that my song was no good.

"And why?" I asked, concealing my annoyance.

"Because," he replied, "such verses are worthy of my former teacher, Vasily Kirilych Tredyakovsky, and strongly remind me of his amatory couplets."*

He took my notebook and began mercilessly picking apart every line and every word, making fun of me in the most sarcastic manner. I could bear it no longer: I tore my notebook out of his hands and declared that I would never again show him my literary works. Shvabrin laughed at this threat.

"We'll see," he said, "whether you'll keep your word. A poet needs a listener as much as Ivan Kuzmich needs his glass of vodka before dinner. And who is that Masha to whom you confess your tender passion and amorous woes? Could it be Marya Ivanovna by any chance?"

"It's none of your business who that Masha might be," I answered, frowning. "I don't need either your opinion or your guesses."

"Oho! A vain poet and a discreet lover!" continued Shvabrin, irritating me more and more. "But take some friendly advice from me: if you want to succeed, make use of more than paltry songs."

"Just what do you mean, sir? Please be so kind as to explain yourself."

"With pleasure. What I mean is that if you want Masha Mironova to come visiting you at dusk, give her a pair of earrings instead of tender verses."

My blood began to boil.

"And why are you of such an opinion about her?" I asked, suppressing my indignation with difficulty.

"Because," he answered with an infernal grin, "I know her ways and habits from experience."

"You're lying, scoundrel!" I exclaimed in a rage. "You're lying in the most shameless manner."

Shvabrin changed colour.

"You are not going to get away with that," he said, seizing my arm. "You'll give me satisfaction."

"Just as you wish, any time," I answered with joy. At that moment I could have torn him to pieces.

I immediately went to Ivan Ignatich, whom I found with a needle in hand: he had been entrusted by the captain's wife with stringing some mushrooms to be dried for the winter.

"Ah, Pyotr Andreich," said he, as he saw me, "come right in. What good fortune brings you here? What's on your mind, if I may ask?"

I explained to him in a few terse words that I had quarrelled with Alexei Ivanych, and that I would like to ask him, Ivan Ignatich, to be my second. He listened to me attentively, with his one eye wide open.

"Is it your pleasure to say," he responded, "that you want to impale Alexei Ivanych and wish me to be present as a witness? Is that it, if I may ask?"

"Exactly so."

"Have mercy on us, Pyotr Andreich! What's the idea? You've quarrelled with Alexei Ivanych? Big deal! A quarrel's nothing to die for. If he swore at you, you curse him back; if he hit you in the mug, you bash him on the ear, and once more, and again; and then go your separate ways; we'll see to it that you make up. But skewering your neighbour – is that a decent thing to do, if I may ask? That's supposing that you do skewer him; so much the worse for him – I'm not so fond of Alexei Ivanych myself. But what if he punctures *your* hide? How'll that feel? Who'll look a fool then, if I may ask?"

The arguments of the prudent lieutenant had no effect on me: I remained firm in my resolve.

"Just as you wish," said Ivan Ignatich. "Do what you think is best. But why should I be a witness to it? What business is it of mine? Two people get into a scuffle: is that something to gape at, if I may ask? By God's will I fought against the Swedes and the Turks; I've seen enough."

I tried to explain the role of a second to him as best I could, but Ivan Ignatich was incapable of comprehending it.

"Say what you will," he declared, "if I'm to get mixed up in this business at all, it will be to go and report to Ivan Kuzmich, as a soldier's duty requires, that there is a conspiracy in the fort to commit a criminal act, inimical to the interests of the state, and to inquire if the commandant would deem it advisable to take appropriate measures..."

I was alarmed and besought Ivan Ignatich not to say anything to the commandant. I had great difficulty in dissuading him from doing so, but at last he gave me his word, whereupon I beat a quick retreat.

As usual, I spent the evening at the commandant's house. I tried to appear cheerful and nonchalant so as not to arouse any suspicions and not to invite importunate questions, but I must admit I did not possess the kind of composure that people in such a position almost always boast of. I was easily moved and inclined to tenderness that evening. I found Marya Ivanovna even more appealing than usual. The thought that this might be the last time I would ever see her lent a touching aspect to her presence. Shvabrin also came by. I took him aside and told him about my conversation with Ivan Ignatich.

"What do we need seconds for?" he asked dryly. "We'll do without them."

We agreed to fight behind the haystacks outside the fort towards seven o'clock the next morning. To all appearances we were chatting so amiably that Ivan Ignatich, delighted, let the cat out of the bag.

"This is how it should have been all along," he said to me with a look of satisfaction. "Better a lean peace than a fat quarrel; lose face, but save your skin."

"What was that you said, Ivan Ignatich?" asked the captain's wife, who was telling fortunes by cards in the corner. "I didn't quite catch it."

Ivan Ignatich, noticing displeasure on my face and remembering his promise, grew confused and did not know what to answer. Shvabrin was quick enough to come to his aid.

"Ivan Ignatich approves of our reconciliation," he said.

"And who was it, dear, you quarrelled with?"

"Pyotr Andreich and I nearly had a rather nasty argument."

"What about?"

"A mere trifle, Vasilisa Yegorovna, just a song."

"Could you find nothing else to quarrel about? A song! And how did it happen?"

"This is how: Pyotr Andreich started singing in my presence a song he had recently composed, while I struck up my own favourite one:

"O daughter of the commandant,
stay in all night, don't gallivant.*

"A disagreement arose between us. Pyotr Andreich was angry at first, but later decided that everyone's free to sing what they want. That was the end of the matter."

I almost exploded with rage over Shvabrin's shameless indelicacy, but no one except me understood his rude allusion: at least no one seemed to pay any attention to it. From songs the conversation turned to poets, with the commandant remarking that they were all inveterate drunkards and debauchers. He advised me as a friend to leave versifying well alone as a pursuit incompatible with army service and one that led to no good.

Shvabrin's presence was unbearable to me. I soon took my leave of the commandant and his family. When I got home, I inspected my sword, tested its point, and went to bed, ordering Savelich to wake me just after six.

Next morning at the appointed time I was behind the haystacks waiting for my adversary. He, too, appeared soon.

"They might catch us at it," he said. "We must hurry."

We took off our uniform jackets, stood there in nothing but our shirts and drew our swords. At this moment Ivan Ignatich and five or so veterans appeared from behind the haystack. He summoned us to the commandant. We obeyed grudgingly. Surrounded by the soldiers, we marched behind Ivan Ignatich, who led the way to the fort in triumph, striding along with remarkable self-importance.

We arrived at the commandant's house. Ivan Ignatich opened the door and announced triumphantly, "The prisoners!"

We were met by Vasilisa Yegorovna.

"How now, my good sirs! What's this I hear? Plotting murder in our fort? Ivan Kuzmich, lock them up at once! Pyotr Andreich, Alexei Ivanych, hand over your swords, hand them over this instant! Palashka, take these swords to the storeroom. Pyotr Andreich, I didn't expect this of you! Aren't you ashamed of yourself? Alexei Ivanych is of another sort: it was murder he was discharged from the Guards for, and he doesn't fear the Lord God; but what about you? Are you going the same way?"

Ivan Kuzmich, in complete agreement with his spouse, kept repeating: "Yes, d'you hear, Vasilisa Yegorovna's right. Military regulations explicitly prohibit duels."

Palashka meanwhile had taken our swords and carried them off to the storeroom. I could not help bursting into laughter. Shvabrin maintained a solemn air.

"With all due respect to you, madam," he said to the captain's wife coolly, "I cannot refrain from remarking that you put yourself to unnecessary trouble setting yourself up as a judge over us. I suggest that you leave the matter to Ivan Kuzmich, within whose authority it lies."

"Ah, my dear sir!" retorted the captain's wife. "Are not husband and wife one flesh and one soul? Ivan Kuzmich! Why d'you stand there gaping? Lock 'em up separately in different cubbyholes, and keep 'em on bread and water until they're cured of this folly. And let Father Gerasim impose a penance on them, so they'll pray to God for forgiveness and show themselves repentant before men."

Ivan Kuzmich did not know what to do. Marya Ivanovna was extremely pale. By and by the storm blew over: the captain's wife calmed down and made us kiss each other. Palashka brought our swords back. We left the commandant's house to all appearances perfectly reconciled. Ivan Ignatich accompanied us.

"Didn't you feel any shame in denouncing us to the commandant," I asked him angrily, "when you'd given your word that you wouldn't?"

"God is my witness, I said nothing to Ivan Kuzmich," he replied. "Vasilisa Yegorovna wormed the secret out of me. It was she who saw to it all without the commandant's knowledge. But it's all over now: thank God it's ended as it has." With these words he turned off towards his house, leaving Shvabrin and me by ourselves.

"We can't just leave it at that," I said to him.

"Of course not," replied Shvabrin. "You shall answer with your blood for your impertinence. But they're likely to keep an eye on us: for a few days we'd better put on a show. Goodbye!" And we parted as if nothing was the matter.

Returning to the commandant's house, I sat down next to Marya Ivanovna as usual. Ivan Kuzmich was out, and Vasilisa Yegorovna was busy with her chores. Marya and I talked in a low tone. She tenderly reproached me for the anxiety I had caused them all by my quarrel with Shvabrin.

"I almost fainted," she said, "when I was told that the two of you were going to fight with swords. How strange men are! For one word, which they would probably have forgotten in another week, they're ready to shed blood and to sacrifice not only their lives, but also their clear conscience and the happiness of those who... But I'm convinced it wasn't you who started the quarrel. Alexei Ivanovich was probably to blame."

"Why do you think so, Marya Ivanovna?"

"I just do... He always sneers at everything. I don't like Alexei Ivanych. I find him offensive; yet, strangely, I'd be really upset if I thought he disliked me as much as I dislike him. Such a thought would worry me dreadfully."

"And what do you think, Marya Ivanovna? Does he like you or not?"

Marya Ivanovna was taken aback; she blushed.

"It seems to me..." she said, "indeed I do think he likes me."

"Why do you think so?"

"Because he once asked for my hand."

"Asked for your hand? He asked for your hand? When?"

"Last year. About two months before your arrival."

"And you refused?"

"As you can see. Alexei Ivanych is, of course, an intelligent man, of good family and comfortable circumstances, but the mere thought of having to kiss him publicly at the wedding service… No, not for anything! Not for all the riches in the world!"

Marya Ivanovna's words opened my eyes and shed light on a great many things. Now I could understand Shvabrin's relentless campaign of vilification. He had no doubt noticed our mutual attraction and tried to set us against each other. The words that had led to my quarrel with him appeared to me even more despicable now, when I saw them as a deliberate slander rather than just a coarse and indecent joke. My desire to punish the insolent slanderer grew even stronger, and I waited for an opportunity with impatience.

I did not have to wait long. The next day, as I sat composing an elegy and biting my pen in the hope that a rhyme would come my way, Shvabrin knocked at my window. I put down my pen, picked up my sword, and went out to him.

"Why delay the matter?" said Shvabrin. "They're not watching us. Let's go down to the river. No one will disturb us there."

We set out in silence. Having descended by a steep path, we stopped at the very edge of the river and drew our swords. Shvabrin was more skilled, but I was stronger and bolder; and I also made good use of the few fencing lessons Monsieur Beaupré, a former soldier, had given me. Shvabrin had not expected to encounter such a dangerous adversary in me. For a long time we were unable to inflict any harm on each other. At length, noticing that Shvabrin was beginning to get tired, I advanced on him vigorously and almost drove him right into the river. Suddenly I heard someone shout my name. I glanced back and saw Savelich running down the steep path towards me. At that moment I felt a sharp stab in my chest just under the right shoulder; I fell down and lost consciousness.

Chapter V

Love

Ah, you maiden, pretty-looking maiden!
Don't get married, maiden, while you're young:
ask your father and your mother, maiden,
ask your father, mother and your kin;
win yourself some worldly wisdom, maiden,
worldly wisdom – and a dowry too.

– A folk song

Should you find a better one than me,
then you'll forget;
should you find one worse than me,
then you'll remember.

– Another folk song*

When I came round, I could not remember for a while where I was and what had happened to me. I was lying in bed in an unfamiliar room, feeling very weak. Savelich stood before me with a candle in his hand. Someone was gently unwinding the bandages that had been tightly wrapped around my chest and shoulder. Gradually I regained full consciousness. Remembering my duel, I guessed I must have been wounded. At that moment the door creaked.

"Well, how is he?" whispered a voice that sent a thrill through my frame.

"Still the same," Savelich answered with a sigh. "Still unconscious, and it's already the fifth day."

I wanted to turn on my side but could not.

"Where am I? Who's here?" I said with an effort. Marya Ivanovna came up to my bed and bent over me.

"Well, how do you feel?" she asked.

"Heaven be praised!" I replied in a weak voice. "Is that you, Marya Ivanovna? Tell me..." Not strong enough to continue, I fell silent.

Savelich cried out. His face beamed with joy.

"He's come round! He's come round!" he kept repeating. "Thanks be to Thee, O Lord! Well, young master Pyotr Andreich, how you've scared me! No trifle, is it? The fifth day already!"

Marya Ivanovna interrupted him. "Don't speak too much to him, Savelich," she said. "He's still weak."

She went out and gently closed the door behind her.

My thoughts were in turmoil. Evidently I was at the commandant's house; Marya Ivanovna had just been in to see me. I wanted to put some questions to Savelich, but the old man shook his head and covered his ears with his hands. I closed my eyes with annoyance and soon fell into a deep sleep.

Waking, I called Savelich, but instead of him I saw Marya Ivanovna before me; her angelic voice greeted me. I cannot express the joyous feeling that overwhelmed me at that moment. I seized her hand and pressed my face against it, bathing it in tears of emotion. Masha did not take it away... Suddenly her lips touched my cheek, and I felt a fresh, burning kiss. Fire shot through my veins.

"Dear, kind Marya Ivanovna," I said to her, "be my wife, consent to make me happy."

She recovered herself.

"For heaven's sake, calm yourself," she said, withdrawing her hand. "You're still not out of danger: your wound may reopen. Take care of yourself, if only for my sake."

With these words she went out, leaving me in raptures. Happiness was reviving me. She would be mine! She loved me! The thought filled my whole being.

From that time on, I got better by the hour. There being no other medical men in the fort, the regimental barber attended to my wound, and fortunately he did not try to be too clever. Youth and nature speeded my recovery. The commandant's whole family was nursing me. Marya Ivanovna hardly ever left my bedside. It goes without saying that as soon as another opportunity presented itself I resumed my interrupted declaration of love; this time Marya Ivanovna heard me out with more patience. She acknowledged her heartfelt attachment to me without any affectation and said that her parents would certainly be glad of her happiness.

"But consider carefully," she added, "won't your family raise objections?"

I pondered. I had no doubt about my mother's tender-heartedness; but, familiar with my father's nature and way of thinking, I suspected that my love would not move him much, and that he would view it as a young man's folly. I frankly admitted as much to Marya Ivanovna, and resolved to write to Father as eloquently as I possibly could, asking for his paternal blessing. I showed the letter to Marya Ivanovna, who found it so convincing and touching that she did not have the slightest doubt about its effect, and she abandoned herself to the feelings of her gentle heart with all the trustfulness of youth and love.

With Shvabrin I made matters up during the first days of my convalescence. Ivan Kuzmich, scolding me for the duel, had said, "Aye, Pyotr Andreich, I should really throw you in prison, but you've already been punished as it is. As for Alexei Ivanych, he's been shut in the granary under guard, and Vasilisa Yegorovna's locked his sword away. Let 'im reflect and repent at his leisure."

I was too happy to harbour resentment in my heart. I pleaded for Shvabrin, and the good-hearted commandant, with his wife's consent, set him free. Shvabrin came to see me: he expressed deep regret over what had happened between us; he admitted it had been his fault entirely, and begged me to forget all about it. Not being rancorous by nature, I sincerely forgave him, both for our quarrel and for the wound he had inflicted on me. Ascribing his slander to the chagrin of wounded pride and scorned love, I generously excused my luckless rival.

I soon recovered fully and was able to move back to my lodging. I waited impatiently for an answer to my letter, not daring to hope but trying to suppress dark forebodings. I had not yet spoken with Vasilisa Yegorovna and her husband, but I knew it would not come as a surprise to them. Certain of their consent before we ever asked for it, Marya Ivanovna and I did not try to conceal our feelings from them.

At last one evening Savelich came into my room holding a letter in his hand. I seized it with trembling fingers. The address was written in my father's hand. This indicated something important, since it was usually Mother who wrote to me, with Father adding only a few lines at the end. I could not bring myself to open the envelope for a long time: I just kept reading and rereading the formal superscription: "To my son Pyotr Andreyevich Grinyov, Fort Belogorsk, Orenburg Province." I tried to divine by the handwriting in what spirit the letter had been written. When I did break the seal at last, I could see at first glance that the whole business had gone to the devil. The contents of the letter were as follows:

My son Pyotr,

Your letter, in which you ask for our parental blessing and consent to your marriage to Mironov's daughter Marya Ivanovna, arrived on the 15th of this month. Not only do I not intend to give you my blessing or consent, but I have a mind to get hold of you and teach you a lesson in a way befitting a whelp, despite your rank as an officer: for you have demonstrated that you are as yet unworthy to carry the sword presented to you for the defence of the fatherland and not for duels with other scamps like yourself. I will immediately write to Andrei Karlovich asking him to transfer you as far away from Fort Belogorsk as possible, where you will be cured of this folly. Your dear mother, on hearing of your duel and wound, was taken ill with grief and is still in bed. What will become of you? I pray to God that you shall reform, although I hardly dare trust in such divine mercy.

Your father, A.G.

Reading this letter evoked several feelings in me. The harsh expressions that my father had so unsparingly indulged in offended me deeply. The disdain with which he had referred to Marya Ivanovna seemed to me both improper and unjust. The thought of being transferred from Fort Belogorsk terrified me. What distressed me most, however, was the news of my mother's illness. I was indignant with Savelich, for I did not doubt that my parents had learnt of my duel through him. After pacing up and down my narrow room for some time, I stopped before him and said with a menacing air:

"It clearly hasn't been enough for you that I was wounded because of you and teetered on the brink of the grave for a whole month: you also wish to destroy my mother."

Savelich was thunderstruck.

"Have mercy on me, sir," he said, almost sobbing. "What is this you're saying? That you were wounded because of me? God be my witness, I was a-running to throw my own breast between you and Alexei Ivanych's sword! It's just that my accursed old legs couldn't carry me fast enough. And what have I done to your dear mother?"

"What have you done?" I said "Who told you to write and inform on me? Or were you assigned to spy on me?"

"Me write and inform on you?" Savelich replied in tears. "God Almighty! Just read, if you please, what the master writes to me: you'll see if I've been informing on you."

He took a letter from his pocket and gave me the following to read:

You ought to be ashamed of yourself, old cur, that despite my strict orders you failed to report on my son Pyotr Andreyevich, and that strangers have had to inform me of his pranks. Is this how you carry out your duty and the will of your master? I will send you, old cur, into the fields to herd swine for concealing the truth and pandering to the youth. Immediately upon receipt of this letter I order you to give me an account of his health, which I am told has improved, and of where exactly he has been wounded and whether he has received proper treatment.

It was obvious that Savelich had a clear conscience and I had unjustly offended him with my reproaches and suspicions. I apologized to him, but the old man remained inconsolable.

"I never thought I'd live to see this," he repeated. "This is the reward I get from my masters. I'm an old cur and a swineherd, am I? And the cause of your wound? Nay, young master Pyotr Andreich! Not me, it's that accursed *m'sewer* who's to blame: 'twas him taught you how to poke others with iron skewers and stamp your foot, as if poking 'n' stamping could drive an evil man away! Much need there was to throw away money, hiring that *m'sewer*!"

But who then took it on himself to inform my father of my conduct? The general? He had not shown himself much troubled on my account; and in any case Ivan Kuzmich had not thought it necessary to report my duel to him. I was at a loss. Finally my suspicions fastened on Shvabrin. He alone could have profited by the denunciation, which could have led to my removal from the fort and my separation from the commandant's family. I went to report all this to Marya Ivanovna. She met me on the porch.

"What's happened to you?" she asked as soon as she saw me. "How pale you are!"

"It's all over!" I answered, handing her my father's letter. It was her turn to blanch. Having read the letter, she returned it to me with a trembling hand and said in a faltering voice:

"Evidently, fate has ordained otherwise... Your parents do not wish to receive me into their family. The Lord's will be done! God knows better than we do what is good for us. There's nothing to be done, Pyotr Andreich: I hope you at least will find happiness..."

"This is not to be!" I exclaimed, seizing her hand. "You love me: I am ready for anything. Let's go and throw ourselves at your parents' feet: they're simple people, not cold-hearted snobs. They will give us their blessing, we'll get married, and with time, I'm sure, we'll soften Father's heart. Mother will be on our side, and he'll forgive me."

"No, Pyotr Andreich," Masha replied. "I will not marry you without your parents' blessing. Without their blessing you'll never find happiness. Let us acquiesce in the Lord's will. If you find the one destined for you, if you give your heart to another – God be with you, Pyotr Andreich; for both of you I'll..."

She burst into tears and left me. I had an impulse to follow her into the house, but realizing that I would not be able to control myself, I went back to my lodging.

I was sitting deep in thought; suddenly Savelich interrupted my reflections.

"Here, sir," he said, handing me a piece of paper covered with writing, "see if I'm an informer against my master and if I try to set father and son against each other."

I took the paper from his hand: it was his answer to the letter he had received. Here it is, word for word:

Andrei Petrovich, Sir, Our Gracious Master,

I am in receipt of your gracious letter in which it pleases you to be angry with me, your serf, and in which you say that I ought to be ashamed of myself for not carrying out my master's orders; but I, not an old cur but your faithful servant, do obey my master's orders, and my hair has turned grey in your zealous service. I did not write to you about Pyotr Andreich's wound in order not to affright you unnecessarily; and I hear that, as it is, the mistress, Avdotya Vasilyevna, protectress of us all, has taken to bed with grief, and I will pray to God to restore her to health. And Pyotr Andreich was wounded under the right shoulder, in the chest just under the bone, the cut being a vershok *and a half deep,* and he lay in bed at the commandant's house, where we had brought him from the riverbank, and he was treated by the local barber Stepan Paramonov; and by now Pyotr Andreich, Heaven be thanked, has entirely recovered, and there is nothing but good to be written about him. The commandant, I hear, is satisfied with him, and Vasilisa Yegorovna treats him as if he were her own son. And if a little incident did befall him, that's nothing to a youngster's discredit; the horse has four legs, and yet he stumbles. And if it please you, as you wrote, to send me into the fields to herd swine, it is within your lordly power. Herewith I bow before you as a slave,*

Your faithful servant,

Arkhip Savelyev

I could not help smiling several times as I read the good-hearted old man's epistle. I was not in a condition to reply to my father; as for reassuring my mother, it seemed to me that Savelich's letter was sufficient.

From that time my situation changed. Marya Ivanovna hardly ever spoke to me and made every effort to avoid my company. The commandant's house became a disagreeable place for me. Gradually I got used to sitting at home by myself. Vasilisa Yegorovna reproached me for it at first, but, seeing my stubbornness, left me in peace. I saw Ivan Kuzmich only when duty required it. With Shvabrin I seldom came into contact, and then only reluctantly, all the more so since I noticed in him a veiled hostility towards me, which confirmed my suspicions. My life became unbearable. I fell into a despondent brooding, made worse by solitude and idleness. In my isolation my love for Marya blazed out of control and became more and more of a torment. I lost the taste for reading and literary pursuits. I lapsed into depression. I was afraid I would either lose my mind or throw myself into dissipation. But some unexpected developments, which were to have a profound effect on the whole of my life, suddenly gave my soul a powerful and salutary shock.

Chapter VI

The Pugachov Rebellion

Listen, young lads, to our tales,
to the ones we old gaffers will tell.
– A song*

BEFORE I RELATE the extraordinary events that I was to witness, I must say a few words about the conditions prevailing in Orenburg Province at the end of 1773.

This extensive and rich province was inhabited by a number of semi-barbarian peoples who had only recently accepted the Russian emperors' suzerainty. Because of their frequent revolts, their ways unaccustomed to law and civilized life, and their instability and cruelty, the government could keep them under control only by maintaining constant surveillance. Forts were built in convenient locations and settled mostly by Cossacks, who had for a long time held possession of the banks of the Yaik. But these Yaik Cossacks, whose duty it was to guard the peace and safety of the region, had themselves for some time been restless subjects, posing a threat to the government. In 1772 a revolt broke out in their main town. Its cause lay in the strict measures taken by Major-General Traubenberg to bring the Host to a proper state of obedience. As a result, Traubenberg was brutally murdered; the Cossacks took control of their own governance again; and finally their revolt was crushed by grapeshot and ruthless punishments.

All this had happened a short time before my arrival at Fort Belogorsk. By now everything was quiet, or at least seemed so; the authorities, however, had too easily put their trust in the wily rebels, who feigned repentance but who in fact harboured a secret resentment and were waiting for a suitable opportunity to renew their disturbances.

I return to my narrative.

One evening (this was at the beginning of October 1773) I was sitting at home by myself, listening to the howl of the autumn wind and gazing through my window at the clouds speeding past the moon, when a messenger came to call me to the commandant. I set out at once. Shvabrin, Ivan Ignatich, and the Cossack sergeant were with him. Neither Vasilisa Yegorovna nor Marya Ivanovna was in the room. The commandant greeted me with an anxious look. He locked the door, seated everyone except the sergeant, who remained standing by the door, and, taking a sheet of paper from his pocket, said to us, "Gentlemen, fellow officers, I have received important news. Listen to what the general writes."

He put on his glasses and read the following:

To Captain Mironov, Commandant of Fort Belogorsk:

Confidential.

Herewith I wish to inform you that the fugitive Don Cossack Yemelyan Pugachov, a schismatic, has with unpardonable insolence assumed the name of the late Emperor Peter III, has gathered a villainous horde, has incited mutiny in settlements along the Yaik and has already occupied and destroyed several forts, looting and murdering everywhere. For this reason you are commanded, Captain, immediately upon receipt of this letter to take all necessary measures to repulse, and if possible entirely destroy, the above-mentioned villain and impostor, should he march on the fort entrusted to your care.*

"Take all necessary measures indeed!" said the commandant, removing his glasses and folding the letter. "Easier said than done. The villain is evidently strong, and we have only a hundred and thirty men – not counting the Cossacks, who cannot be relied on – no discredit to you, Maximych." The sergeant grinned. "But we have no other choice, gentlemen: be meticulous in carrying out your duties, send out patrols and post guards at night; and in case of an attack lock the gates and assemble the men. You, Maximych, keep a sharp eye on your Cossacks. The cannon must be inspected and thoroughly cleaned. And first and foremost, keep all this a secret, so that nobody in the fort learns of it sooner than necessary."

Having given these orders, Ivan Kuzmich dismissed us. I went out with Shvabrin, turning over in my mind what I had just heard.

"What do you think?" I asked him. "How's this going to end?"

"God only knows," he replied. "Let's wait on events. For the time being I see nothing that should give us concern. Indeed, if..." On that word he fell to thinking and started distractedly whistling an aria from a French opera.

Despite all our precautions, the news of Pugachov's appearance on the scene spread through the fort. Although Ivan Kuzmich had great respect for his wife, he would not for anything have revealed to her an official secret entrusted to him. Having received the general's letter, he rather craftily got her out of the house by telling her that Father Gerasim had received some exciting news from Orenburg, which he was keeping in great secret. Vasilisa Yegorovna immediately felt like visiting the priest's wife and, on Ivan Kuzmich's advice, took Masha along, lest she should be bored left on her own.

Having taken sole possession of the house, Ivan Kuzmich immediately sent for us, locking Palashka meanwhile in the storeroom to prevent her from eavesdropping.

Vasilisa Yegorovna had no success in prising any secret out of the priest's wife, and when she returned home, she learnt that Ivan Kuzmich had called a meeting, locking Palashka up in her absence. She guessed that she had been duped by her husband, and she besieged him with questions. But Ivan Kuzmich was prepared for the assault. He betrayed no confusion and briskly answered his inquisitive helpmate, "You know, old girl, the women in the fort have taken up the habit of burning straw in the stoves, which might cause accidents, and so I gave strict orders that in the future they should burn not straw, but twigs and fallen branches."

"But why did you have to lock Palashka up?" asked the captain's wife. "Why did the poor wench have to sit in the storeroom until we came home?"

For this question Ivan Kuzmich was not prepared: he became confused and muttered something incomprehensible. Vasilisa Yegorovna realized that her husband was deceiving her, but knowing well that she could not get anything out of him she cut the interrogation short and switched to the topic of pickled cucumbers, for which Akulina Pamfilovna had a most unusual recipe. Vasilisa Yegorovna could not sleep all night for trying to guess what could be on her husband's mind that she was not allowed to know.

The next day, as she was returning from mass, she saw Ivan Ignatich picking out of the cannon rags, pebbles, bits of wood and bone, and other rubbish that the children had thrown in there.

"What could these military preparations mean?" pondered the captain's wife. "Could it be that a Kyrgyz raid is expected? But would Ivan Kuzmich conceal such trifles from me?" She called out to Ivan Ignatich, firmly resolved to worm out of him the secret that tormented her feminine curiosity.

At first she made some observations concerning household matters, like a magistrate who begins an interrogation with irrelevant questions in order to put the defendant off his guard. Then, after a pause, she heaved a deep sigh and said, shaking her head, "Oh, Lord God! What news! What'll come of all this?"

"Never fear, good madam," answered Ivan Ignatich. "The Lord is merciful: we have enough soldiers and plenty of powder, and I've cleaned out the cannon. With a little luck we'll drive Pugachov back. 'God won't give us up, and hog won't eat us up.'"

"And what kind of man is this Pugachov?" asked the captain's wife.

Ivan Ignatich now realized that he had let the cat out of the bag, and he bit his tongue. But it was too late. Vasilisa Yegorovna, giving her word not to pass the secret to anyone, made him reveal the whole thing.

She kept her promise, not breathing a word to anyone – except the priest's wife, and to her only because her cow was still grazing on the steppe and might be captured by the miscreants.

Soon the whole fort was buzzing with talk about Pugachov. There were several rumours. The commandant dispatched the sergeant to find out what he could from neighbouring settlements and forts. The sergeant came back two days later, reporting that about sixty versts from the fort he had seen a large number of campfires, and that according to the Bashkirs an immense force was approaching. But he could not say anything more positive, because he had not dared venture farther.

Unusual agitation could be observed among the Cossacks of the fort: they gathered in groups in every street and talked in a low tone, but dispersed as soon as they saw a dragoon or a garrison soldier. Spies were sent to mingle with them. The Kalmyk* Yulay, a Christian convert, brought important intelligence to the commandant. The sergeant's report, according to Yulay, was false: on his return, the shifty Cossack had told his comrades that he had in fact been to the rebels' camp and presented himself to their leader, who let him kiss his hand and had a long talk with him. The commandant immediately took the sergeant into custody and appointed Yulay in his place. The Cossacks took this new development with manifest displeasure. They grumbled loudly, so much so that Ivan Ignatich, who executed the commandant's order, actually heard them saying, "You'll live to regret that, you garrison rat!" The commandant was planning to interrogate his prisoner the same day, but he escaped, no doubt with the aid of accomplices.

Another development increased the commandant's anxiety. A Bashkir carrying copies of a seditious manifesto was captured. In view of this, the commandant wanted to convene his officers again, and again to get Vasilisa Yegorovna out of the house on some plausible pretext. But since he was a simple-hearted and straightforward man, he could think of no ruse except the one he had already employed.

"Listen, Vasilisa Yegorovna," he said clearing his throat, "Father Gerasim, I hear, has received from the city—"

"That's enough of your lies, Ivan Kuzmich," his wife interrupted him. "I can see you want to call a meeting and talk about Yemelyan Pugachov without me, but this time you're not going to trick me."

Ivan Kuzmich opened his eyes wide. "Well, old girl," he said, "stay if you already know all about it: we can just as well talk in your presence."

"That's more like it, there's a good man," she answered. "Cunning doesn't suit you. Just send for those officers."

We assembled once more. Ivan Kuzmich, in the presence of his wife, read aloud Pugachov's manifesto, written by some semi-literate Cossack. The impostor declared his intention to march on our fort immediately; he invited the Cossacks and soldiers to join his band and admonished the commanders not to offer any resistance on pain of death. The manifesto was written in a crude but forceful language that was bound to make a dangerous impression on the minds of simple people.

"What a scoundrel!" exclaimed the captain's wife. "How does he dare propose such things to us! To meet him outside the fort and lay our flags at his feet! Oh, the son of a bitch! Doesn't he realize that we've been in the service for forty years and have, by the mercy of God, seen a thing or two? Can there be commanders who've obeyed the impostor?"

"There shouldn't be, certainly," Ivan Kuzmich answered. "But I hear that the villain has already taken many forts."

"He does seem to be really strong," remarked Shvabrin.

"We will learn about his actual strength right now," said the commandant. "Vasilisa Yegorovna, give me the key to the barn. Ivan Ignatich, bring the Bashkir here and tell Yulay to fetch a whip."

"Wait a minute, Ivan Kuzmich," said the commandant's wife, getting up. "Let me take Masha somewhere out of the house: I don't want her to be terrified by the screams. And to tell you the truth, I haven't much of a taste for torture either. I wish you the best."

Torture was so deeply ingrained in judicial procedure in the old days that the noble decree by which it was eventually abolished remained without effect for a long time.* It was thought that the offender's own confession was indispensable if his guilt was to be fully established – an idea that not only lacks foundation, but is diametrically opposed to sound legal thinking; for if a denial by the accused is not accepted as proof of his innocence, then an admission by him should be even less of a proof of his guilt. Even today I sometimes hear old judges express regret over the abolition of this barbaric practice. In the days of my youth no one – neither the judges nor the accused – doubted that torture was necessary. Therefore the commandant's order neither surprised nor troubled any of us. Ivan Ignatich went to fetch the Bashkir, who was locked in Vasilisa Yegorovna's barn, and in a few minutes the captive was led into the anteroom. The commandant ordered him to be brought before him.

The Bashkir stepped across the threshold with difficulty (he was in irons) and, taking off his tall hat, remained standing by the door. I glanced at him and shuddered. I shall never forget this man. He appeared to be over seventy. His nose and ears were missing. His head was shaved; in place of a beard he had a few grey hairs sticking out; he was small, thin and bent; but fire still sparkled in his narrow slit eyes.

"Aha!" said the commandant, recognizing by the terrible marks one of the rebels punished in 1741. "So you're an old wolf who's been caught in our traps before. I can tell by your well-shorn nob, it's not the first time you've rioted. Come a little closer and tell me who sent you."

The old Bashkir remained silent and stared at the commandant with an air of total incomprehension.

"Why are you silent?" continued Ivan Kuzmich. "Or don't you understand Russian? Yulay, ask him in your tongue who's sent him into our fort?"

Yulay repeated Ivan Kuzmich's question in Tatar. But the Bashkir gazed back at him with the same expression and did not answer a word.

"*Yakshi*,"* said the commandant. "I'll make you speak up if that's what you want. Fellows, take this clownish striped gown off him and hemstitch his back. But mind, Yulay, don't spare him!"

Two veterans started undressing the Bashkir. He kept glancing about him like a little wild animal caught by children. One of the veterans grabbed the Bashkir's arms and, twining them around his own neck, lifted the old man on his shoulders; meanwhile Yulay picked up the whip and flourished it. At that point the Bashkir gave out a moan in a weak, imploring voice and, shaking his head, opened his mouth, in which there was a truncated stump instead of a tongue.

When I reflect that this happened in my own lifetime, and that since then I have lived to see Emperor Alexander's mild reign, I cannot help marvelling at the rapid progress of enlightenment and the spread of humane principles. Young man! If my memoirs fall into your hands, remember that the best and most enduring changes are those arising from an improvement of moral standards without violent upheavals of any kind.

We were all horror-stricken.

"Well," said the commandant, "we'll obviously not get any sense out of him. Yulay, take the Bashkir back to the barn. With you, gentlemen, I have a few more things to talk over."

We were just beginning to discuss our situation when Vasilisa Yegorovna burst into the room, breathless and beside herself with alarm.

"What's up with you?" asked the commandant in astonishment.

"My dear sirs, calamity's upon us!" Vasilisa Yegorovna answered. "Lower Ozyornaya was taken this morning.* Father Gerasim's hired man has just returned from there. He saw them take it. The commandant and all the officers have been hanged. All the soldiers have been taken prisoner. It won't be long before the villains are here."

This unexpected news was a great shock to me. I knew the commandant of Fort Lower Ozyornaya, a quiet and modest young man: only two months before he and his young wife had passed through our fort on their way from Orenburg and spent the night at Ivan Kuzmich's house. Lower Ozyornaya was about twenty-five versts from our fort. We could expect Pugachov's attack at any moment. I vividly imagined the fate awaiting Marya Ivanovna, and my heart sank.

"Listen, Ivan Kuzmich," I said to the commandant, "it is our duty to defend the fort to our last breath; that goes without saying. But we must think of the safety of the women. Please send them off to Orenburg, if the road is still open, or to a more secure fort somewhere far away, out of the brigand's reach."

Ivan Kuzmich turned to his wife and said, "Indeed, old girl, wouldn't it be better to send you to some place farther off while we take care of these rebels?"

"Nonsense!" replied the commander's wife. "Where's a fort that bullets can't reach? What's wrong with the safety of Belogorsk? Thank God, we've lived in it for close to twenty-two years. We've seen the Kyrgyz and the Bashkir: we'll sit out Pugachov's siege too."

"Well, old girl," rejoined Ivan Kuzmich, "stay, if you trust our fort; but what are we going to do with Masha? All well and good, if we sit out the siege or relief comes in time; but what if the villains take the fort?"

"Well, then..." Vasilisa Yegorovna stopped short, falling silent with an extremely anxious look.

"No, Vasilisa Yegorovna," continued the commandant, noticing that his words had made an impression, perhaps for the first time in his life. "It won't do to let Masha stay here. Let's send her to Orenburg, to her godmother: there they have enough troops and cannon, and the walls are of stone. And I'd advise you to go there too: old woman or not, just look at what might happen to you if they storm the fort."

"All right," she said, "let it be so: we'll send Masha off. As for me, don't even dream of asking me; I won't go. There's no earthly reason why I should part with you in my old age and seek a lonely grave in a strange place. Live together, die together."

"You may be right about that," said the commandant. "But we've no time to lose: go and get Masha ready for the journey. We'll send her off at daybreak tomorrow, and we'll provide her with a convoy, as well, though we hardly have men to spare. But where is she?"

"She's at Akulina Pamfilovna's," the commandant's wife replied. "She felt faint on hearing about the fall of Lower Ozyornaya: I hope she won't fall sick. God Almighty, what times we've lived to see!"

Vasilisa Yegorovna left to see to her daughter's departure. The discussions with the commandant were still going on, but I no longer took part in them or listened to what was being said. Marya Ivanovna came to supper, her face pale and her eyes red with weeping. We ate in silence and rose from the table earlier than usual. Wishing the whole family goodnight, we set off home. I had deliberately left my sword behind, however, and went back for it: I had a premonition that I would find Masha alone. Indeed she met me in the doorway and handed me my sword.

"Goodbye, Pyotr Andreich!" she said in tears. "They're sending me to Orenburg. Take care of yourself and be happy: perhaps the Lord will so ordain that we'll meet again; if not..." She burst into sobs. I embraced her.

"Farewell, my angel," I said. "Farewell, my darling, my beloved one! Whatever happens to me, you can be sure that my last thought and last prayer shall be for you!"

Masha sobbed, resting her head on my breast. I kissed her fervently and hurried from the room.

Chapter VII

The Assault

My head, my poor old head,
this head that's served so well!
My poor old head has served
these three and thirty years.
And what's it earned, this poor old head?
No profit for itself, no joy,
no word of kindness,
no high rank;
all this old head has earned
are two tall posts,
a maple crossbeam
and a silken noose.

– A folk song*

THAT NIGHT I did not sleep, nor did I undress. At daybreak I intended to go to the gate of the fort, through which Marya Ivanovna would be leaving, and say farewell to her for the last time. I felt a great change in myself: my agitated state of mind was much less oppressive than the dejection that had overwhelmed me of late. Vague but alluring dreams mingled in my thoughts with the sadness of separation; and I awaited danger impatiently, with a feeling of noble ambition. The night passed imperceptibly. I was just about to leave the house when my door opened and a corporal came in to report that our Cossacks had left the fort during the night, forcibly taking Yulay with them, and that strange men were reconnoitring the area around the fort. The thought that Marya Ivanovna would not be able to get away terrified me; I hastily gave some instructions to the corporal and rushed to the commandant's.

It was already getting light. As I sped along the street I heard someone call me. I stopped. "Where are you running?" asked Ivan Ignatich, catching up with me. "Ivan Kuzmich is on the rampart and has sent me to fetch you. Pugach has arrived."*

"Has Marya Ivanovna got away?" I asked with a fluttering heart.

"She couldn't," replied Ivan Ignatich. "The road to Orenburg is cut, and the fort is surrounded. Things are looking bad, Pyotr Andreich!"

We went to the rampart, which was a natural elevation reinforced by a palisade. All of the inhabitants of the fort were already crowding there. The garrison stood under arms. The cannon had been hauled here the night before. The commandant paced up and down before his little troop. The approach of danger inspired the old warrior with unusual vigour. Some twenty people were riding about on the steppe, not far from the fort. They appeared to be Cossacks, but there were also some Bashkirs among them, easily distinguishable by their lynx hats and quivers. The commandant inspected his troop, saying to the soldiers, "Well, my lads, we'll stand up today for our Mother the Empress and show the world we're courageous people, true to our oath."

The soldiers loudly voiced their zeal. Shvabrin stood next to me with his gaze fixed on the enemy. The people riding about on the steppe noticed some movement in the fort; they gathered in a group and began talking among themselves. The commandant ordered Ivan Ignatich to aim the cannon at the group, and he himself applied the fuse. The ball whizzed over their heads, causing no harm to anyone. The horsemen scattered and instantly galloped out of sight: the steppe became empty.

At this moment Vasilisa Yegorovna appeared on the rampart, accompanied by Masha, who did not want to be parted from her mother.

"Well," asked the commandant's wife, "how's the battle going? And where's the enemy?"

"The enemy isn't far off," Ivan Kuzmich replied. "With God's help we'll be all right. Well, Masha, are you frightened?"

"No, papa," answered Masha. "It's more frightening to be left alone at home."

She looked at me and made an effort to smile. I involuntarily grasped the hilt of my sword, remembering that I had received it from her hands the evening before as if for the defence of my beloved. My heart glowed. I imagined myself her knight-protector. I longed to prove that I was worthy of her trust and waited impatiently for the decisive moment.

At this point new throngs of horsemen appeared from behind a ridge half a *verst* from the fort, and soon the whole steppe was covered with multitudes, armed with lances and bows and arrows. Among them, on a white horse, rode a man in a red caftan, with his sabre drawn: this was Pugachov himself. He stopped; his men gathered around him; and, evidently at his command, four of them peeled off from the group and galloped right up to the fort at full speed. We recognized them as defectors from our own fort. One of them brought a sheet of paper under his hat; another held, stuck on the point of his lance, the head of Yulay, which he swung in a broad arc and hurled at us over the palisade. The poor Kalmyk's head fell at the commandant's feet. The traitors were shouting, "Don't shoot: come out of the fort to greet the Sovereign. The Sovereign is here!"

"I'll teach you who's here!" cried Ivan Kuzmich. "Ready, lads, fire!"

Our soldiers fired a volley. The Cossack holding the letter swayed in his saddle and fell off his horse; the others galloped back. I looked at Marya Ivanovna. Terror-stricken by the sight of Yulay's bloody head and deafened by the volley, she seemed bedazed. The commandant summoned the corporal and ordered him to take the sheet of paper from the dead Cossack's hand. The corporal went out into the field and came back leading the dead man's horse by the bridle. He handed the letter to the commandant. Ivan Kuzmich read it to himself and tore it to pieces. In the meantime the rebels were plainly preparing for action. Soon bullets came whizzing by our ears, and several arrows fell close to us, sticking in the ground or in the palisade.

"Vasilisa Yegorovna," said the commandant, "this is no place for women. Take Masha away: as you can see, the poor girl's more dead than alive."

Vasilisa Yegorovna, tamed by the bullets, glanced at the steppe, which was all astir, and turned to her husband, saying, "Ivan Kuzmich, life and death are in God's hands: give your blessing to Masha. Masha, go to your father."

Masha, pale and trembling, went up to Ivan Kuzmich, dropped to her knees and bowed to the ground before him. The old commandant made the sign of the cross over her three times, then raised her up and kissed her, saying in a voice of deep emotion:

"Well, Masha, be happy. Pray to God: he will not forsake you. If a good man should come along, God grant you peace and happiness. Live with him as I have lived with Vasilisa Yegorovna. And now, farewell, Masha. Vasilisa Yegorovna, do take her away, be quick!"

Masha threw her arms around his neck and burst into sobs.

"Let me kiss you, too," said the commandant's wife, weeping. "Farewell, my dear Ivan Kuzmich! Forgive me if I've ever vexed you in any way!"

"Farewell, farewell, old girl," said Ivan Kuzmich, embracing his old woman. "But that's enough, now. Go home, please do; and if there's time, dress Masha in a peasant smock."

The commandant's wife and daughter moved away. I followed Marya Ivanovna with my eyes; she glanced back and acknowledged me. Then Ivan Kuzmich turned back to us and concentrated all his attention on the enemy. The rebels gathered around their leader and all at once began dismounting.

"Steady now," said the commandant, "the assault is coming."

At that moment the rebels burst into terrifying shrieks and screams and rushed towards the fort. Our cannon was loaded with grapeshot. The commandant let the rebels come up close and suddenly fired again. The shot tore into the middle of the crowd. The rebels scattered right and left, and fell back. Their leader alone remained at the front... He brandished his sabre and appeared to be fervently exhorting the others... The shrieks and the screams, which had died down for a moment, instantly revived.

"Now, lads," said the commandant, "open the gate and beat the drum! Forward, lads! Charge! Follow me!"

The commandant, Ivan Ignatich and I were outside the rampart in no time, but the intimidated garrison did not budge. "What's up, lads, why are you standing there?" shouted Ivan Kuzmich. "We can die but once: it's a soldier's duty."

At that moment the rebels charged and burst into the fort. The drum fell silent; the garrison threw down their weapons; I was hurled to the ground, but I got up and entered the fort with the rebels. The commandant, wounded in the head, stood in the midst of a group of villains, who were demanding the keys from him. I was on the point of rushing to his aid, but some hefty Cossacks seized me and bound me with their belts, repeating, "You'll get your deserts, the lot of you, for disobeying His Majesty!" They dragged us through the streets; the inhabitants of the fort came out of their houses offering bread and salt.* The church bells rang. Suddenly a shout came from the throng that the Sovereign was in the square awaiting the prisoners and receiving oaths of allegiance. The crowd surged towards the square; we were hustled there too.

Pugachov sat in an armchair on the porch of the commandant's house. He was wearing a red Cossack caftan edged with braid. His tall sable hat with golden tassels was pulled right down to his flashing eyes. His face seemed familiar to me. He was surrounded by Cossack leaders. Father Gerasim, pale and trembling, stood by the porch with a cross in his hands and appeared to be silently imploring him to spare the lives of the victims who were to be brought before him. Gallows were being hastily erected in the square. The Bashkirs drove the crowd back as we approached, and we were brought before Pugachov. The bells stopped ringing; deep silence enveloped the scene.

"Which one is the commandant?" the pretender asked.

Our sergeant stepped forward and pointed at Ivan Kuzmich. Pugachov looked at the old man menacingly and asked him, "How dared you oppose me, your Sovereign?"

The commandant, languishing from his wound, gathered his last strength and replied in a firm voice, "You're no sovereign to me, you're a bandit and an impostor, d'you hear?"

Pugachov sullenly knitted his brows and waved a white handkerchief. Several Cossacks grabbed the old captain and dragged him to the gallows. We saw the mutilated Bashkir we had interrogated the day before astride the crossbeam. He held a rope in his hand,

and in another minute I saw poor Ivan Kuzmich hoisted into the air. Then Ivan Ignatich was led before Pugachov, who said to him, "Swear your allegiance to your Sovereign, Peter!"

"You're not our sovereign," replied Ivan Ignatich, repeating his captain's words. "You, fellow, are a bandit and an imposter!"

Pugachov waved his handkerchief once more, and the good lieutenant was soon hanging next to his old commander.

It was my turn. I was looking at Pugachov boldly, ready to repeat the answer my noble comrades had given him. At that moment, to my indescribable astonishment, I beheld among the rebel leaders Shvabrin, his hair cropped close around the crown after the Cossack fashion, and wearing a Cossack caftan. He approached Pugachov and whispered a few words in his ear.

"Hang him!" said Pugachov, not even looking at me. They threw the noose around my neck. I prayed silently, offering God sincere repentance for all my sins and imploring Him to save all those dear to my heart. I was dragged under the gallows.

"Don't be scared, don't be scared!" repeated my executioners, wishing, in all truth perhaps, to give me courage.

Suddenly I heard a shout:

"Stop, damn you! Hold it!"

The hangmen stopped. I glanced around: Savelich was prostrate at Pugachov's feet.

"Father to us all!" my poor old attendant was saying. "What good'll the death of the noble child do to you? Let 'im go; they'll pay you a ransom for 'im, they will; and for fear and example, if you want, have me, an old man, hanged."

Pugachov gave a signal; they immediately untied me and set me free.

"The Tsar Our Father has pardoned you," they told me.

I cannot say at that moment I was pleased to be spared; but neither can I say that I regretted it. My feelings were too confused. I was brought to the pretender once more and made to kneel before him. Pugachov held out his sinewy hand to me.

"Kiss his hand! Kiss his hand!" they were saying around me.

But I would have preferred the cruellest death to such a foul abasement.

"Pyotr Andreich, young master!" whispered Savelich, standing behind me and nudging me. "Don't be obstinate! What does it cost you? Don't give a damn, just kiss the scound— Argh! Kiss that hand of his."

I did not stir. Pugachov let his hand fall and said mockingly, "His Honour, I see, is dazed with joy. Raise him up!"

They lifted me up and released me. I watched the rest of the horrifying comedy.

The inhabitants of the fort came up to take the oath. One by one they approached, kissed the crucifix and then bowed to the pretender. The garrison soldiers also stood there. The tailor of the platoon, armed with his blunt scissors, was snipping off their locks.* They shook their clipped hair off and went up to kiss the hand of Pugachov, who pronounced them pardoned, and accepted them into his band. All this lasted for about three hours. At last Pugachov rose from the armchair and came down from the porch, accompanied by his chiefs. His white horse with richly ornamented harness was brought to him. Two Cossacks grasped him by the elbows and lifted him into the saddle. He announced to Father Gerasim that he would dine at his house. At this moment a woman's scream was heard. Several brigands had just dragged Vasilisa Yegorovna, dishevelled and stripped naked, out on the porch. One of them had already decked himself out in her padded jacket. Others were lugging feather beds, chests, a tea service, linen and all manner of spoils.

"Please, my dear fellows," shouted the poor old woman, "let me be. Dear sirs, take me to Ivan Kuzmich." Suddenly she glanced at the gallows and recognized her husband. "Blackguards!" she screamed in a frenzy. "What have you done to him? Ivan Kuzmich, light of my life, poor, brave old soldier! No Prussian bayonets, no Turkish bullets harmed you; it wasn't in honest battle you laid down your life; you've been slain by a runaway jailbird!"

"Make the old witch shut up!" said Pugachov.

A young Cossack struck her on the head with his sabre, and she fell dead on the steps of the porch. Pugachov rode away; the crowd surged after him.

Chapter VIII

The Uninvited Guest

An uninvited guest is worse than a Tatar.
– A popular saying

THE SQUARE WAS DESERTED. I remained standing in the same place and could not gather my thoughts, thrown into disarray by all these horrifying experiences.

Uncertainty about the fate of Marya Ivanovna troubled me most. Where was she? What had happened to her? Had she managed to hide? Was her hiding place safe? My head full of alarming thoughts, I went into the commandant's house. It had been completely stripped: chairs, tables and chests were broken; crockery smashed; everything ransacked. I ran up the narrow staircase leading to the bedchambers, and for the first time ever entered Marya Ivanovna's room. Her bed had been turned upside down; her wardrobe was broken and plundered; a sanctuary lamp was still burning in front of the empty icon-holder. A mirror on the wall between the windows had also escaped destruction. Where was the inhabitant of this humble virginal cell? A terrible thought passed through my mind: I imagined her in the hands of the marauders. My heart sank. I burst into bitter, bitter tears and loudly called out the name of my beloved. At that moment I heard a slight noise: Palasha, pale and trembling, came out from behind the wardrobe.

"Oh, Pyotr Andreich!" she said, clasping her hands. "What a day! What horrors!"

"And Marya Ivanovna?" I asked impatiently. "What's happened to Marya Ivanovna?"

"The young mistress is alive," replied Palasha. "She's hiding at Akulina Pamfilovna's."

"With the priest's wife?" I exclaimed in horror. "My God! But Pugachov is there!"

I rushed out of the room, was on the street in a flash, and ran headlong to the priest's house, oblivious to everything around. From inside the house shouts, laughter and songs could be heard: Pugachov was feasting with his comrades. Palasha ran up behind me. I sent her in to call Akulina Pamfilovna out without attracting attention. In a minute the priest's wife came out to the anteroom with an empty decanter in her hand.

"For heaven's sake, where is Marya Ivanovna?" I asked her with inexpressible agitation.

"She's lying on the bed, is my little dove, right there behind the partition," answered the priest's wife. "We almost had a mishap, Pyotr Andreich, but thank God it's turned out all right. The villain had just sat down to dinner when my poor darling came to, and gave out a groan! My heart stood still: he heard it! 'And who's groaning back there, grandma?' I doubled over before the impostor: 'That's my niece, Your Majesty: she's very poorly; she's been lying in bed these two weeks.' 'And is your niece young?' 'She is, Your Majesty.' 'Let me see her, grandma, this niece of yours.' My heart leapt into my throat, but there was nothing I could do. 'Just as you wish, Your Majesty: only the poor girl can't get up and come to Your Highness.' 'That's all right, grandma, I'll go and take a look at her myself.' And that's just what he did, damnation on him: he went behind the partition and, just imagine, pulling the curtain aside, laid his hawk-eyes on her! But the Lord saved us; nothing happened. Father and I, can you believe it, were already preparing for martyrdom, but fortunately Masha, my little dove, didn't recognize him. God Almighty, what days we've lived to see! Unspeakable! Poor Ivan Kuzmich! Who would have thought? And Vasilisa Yegorovna! And Ivan Ignatich! Why him, too? But how come they spared you? And what do you think of Shvabrin, Alexei Ivanych? Do you know he's had his hair cut like a Cossack and is sitting right in there with them, feasting? Nimble, ain't he? And when I said that about my sick niece, he looked at me, can you imagine, as if piercing me through with a knife, but he didn't give us away, for which, at least, we should be grateful to him."

At this time we heard the guests' drunken shouts and Father Gerasim's voice. The guests were demanding more liquor, and the host was calling his spouse. She fell into a flutter.

"Go home now, Pyotr Andreich," she said; "I've no time for you: the brigands are on a binge. If you don't watch it, you'll fall into some drunkard's hands. Goodbye, Pyotr Andreich! What's to be, will be: maybe God won't desert us."

The priest's wife left me. Somewhat reassured, I went back to my lodging. As I passed by the square I saw a number of Bashkirs crowding around the gallows and pulling the boots off the hanged men's feet: I could hardly restrain my indignation, but I knew it would be useless to try to interfere. Plunderers were roaming the fort, robbing the officers' houses. The place resounded with shouts of drunken rebels. I reached home. Savelich met me on the threshold.

"Thank God!" he exclaimed when he saw me. "I was afeared the brigands had laid hands on you again. Well, young master Pyotr Andreich! Can you believe it? They've robbed us clean, the scoundrels: clothes, linen, crockery, everything – they've left nothing. But never mind! Thank God they've let you off in one piece. By the way, sir, you recognized the chieftain, didn't you?"

"No, I didn't. Who is he?"

"You didn't, young master? Have you forgotten the drunkard who swindled you out of your jacket at the wayside inn? That little hare-skin jacket was still quite new, but the bastard ripped it apart, struggling into it."

I was astounded. Indeed, the similarity between Pugachov and my guide was striking. I came to realize that the two were one and the same person, which explained why I had been spared. I could not help marvelling at such a strange chain of circumstances: my childhood jacket, given as a present to a vagabond, saved me from the noose, and the drunkard who had been loafing around wayside inns was now setting siege to forts and shaking an empire to its foundations!

"Would you like to have something to eat?" asked Savelich, unswerving in his habits. "There's nothing at home, but I can hunt up something and cook it for you."

Left alone, I sank into reflections. What was I to do? To remain in a fort occupied by the brigand or to join his band – both were unbecoming to an officer. My duty demanded that I present myself where my service could still be useful to the fatherland in the present critical circumstances... But love eloquently counselled me to stay close to Marya Ivanovna, to be her defender and protector. Although I anticipated that the course of affairs could not fail to change soon, I could still not help trembling when I thought of the dangers of her present situation.

My reflections were interrupted by the arrival of one of the fort's Cossacks with the announcement that "His Imperial Highness demands your presence" .

"Where is he?" I asked, getting ready to obey the command.

"At the commandant's house," answered the Cossack. "After dinner the Tsar Our Father went to the bathhouse, and now he's resting. Well, Your Honour, everything shows that he's a person of distinction: at dinner he was pleased to eat two roast suckling pigs, and he had his steam bath so hot that even Taras Kurochkin couldn't bear it – he had to hand the birch twigs to Fomka Bikbayev and could just barely revive himself with cold water. All his ways are majestic, there's no denying... In the bathhouse, they say, he was showing off the marks of tsarship on his chest: a two-headed eagle the size of a five-kopeck piece on one side, and his own image on the other."

I did not think it necessary to dispute the Cossack's opinions, and proceeded with him to the commandant's house, trying to anticipate what my meeting with Pugachov would be like and to guess how it would end. As the reader can imagine, I was not altogether composed.

It was beginning to get dark when I arrived at the commandant's house. The gallows with its victims loomed dark and terrifying. The body of the commandant's poor wife still lay at the foot of the steps, where two Cossack sentries were standing on guard. The Cossack who accompanied me went to announce me and, returning immediately, led me into the room where I had taken such a tender farewell of Marya Ivanovna the evening before.

An extraordinary picture greeted my eyes: at the table, covered with a cloth and laden with bottles and glasses, sat Pugachov and about ten Cossack chiefs, with their hats on, in colourful shirts, their cheeks flushed with liquor and their eyes sparkling. Neither Shvabrin nor our sergeant – treachery's newest recruits – was there among them.

"Ah, Your Honour!" said Pugachov on seeing me. "Welcome. Please be seated."

His companions moved over to make room for me. I sat down silently at the end of the table. My immediate neighbour, a well-built, handsome young Cossack, poured a glass of ordinary vodka for me, which I did not touch. I surveyed the gathering with curiosity. Pugachov sat in the place of honour, with his elbow on the table, resting his black beard on his broad fist. His features, regular and rather pleasant, had nothing ferocious about them. He often turned to a man of about fifty, calling him Count* or Timofeich, and sometimes honouring him with the title of uncle. All present treated one another as comrades, showing no particular deference to their leader. They talked about that morning's assault, the success of the uprising, and their future operations. Each one bragged, proffered his opinions and freely disputed those of Pugachov. It was at this strange military council that they decided to march on Orenburg – a bold decision, but one that was almost to be crowned with calamitous success. It was declared that the campaign would begin the next morning.

"Well, brothers," said Pugachov, "let's sing my favourite song before we break up for the night. Chumakov,* you start!"

My neighbour struck up a doleful barge-hauler's song* in a high-pitched voice, and the others joined him in chorus:

> Stop rustling your leaves, you green oak wood, dear mother;
> just let this good lad think his thoughts undisturbed.
> For tomorrow this good lad will have to give answer
> before a stern judge, yes, our great Tsar himself.

And my sovereign the Tsar will enquire of me thus:
"Just tell me, you sturdy young peasant boy, tell me,
who joined you in thieving, who joined you in raiding?
Were there many brave comrades that rode with you out?"
"I'll tell you, Our Hope, our great Tsar, true believer,
I'll tell you the truth, all the truth, nothing less:
the comrades I've had, Sovereign-Tsar, are a foursome:
the first of my comrades is night, the dark night;
the second, my knife, forged of damascene steel;
third comrade of mine is my mettlesome horse;
and fourth of my comrades, my tautly strung bow.
I have messengers too, my sharp arrows, well hardened."
Then Our Hope, our great Tsar, true believer, will speak:
"Good for you, sturdy lad, peasant boy, good for you!
You've learnt well how to thieve, you've learnt well how to answer,
and I'll grant you for that, sturdy boy, due reward:
yes, a tall, spacious home in the country I'll grant you,
yes, a home with two posts and a crossbeam to fit.

I cannot describe what effect this folk song about the gallows, sung by people destined for the gallows, had on me. Their fearsome faces, their harmonious voices and the doleful intonation they gave to the song's already expressive words – all this stirred me with a kind of poetic dread.

The guests drank one more glass, rose from the table and wished Pugachov goodnight. I wanted to leave with them, but Pugachov said to me, "Don't go: I want to have a talk with you."

We remained face to face.

For some minutes both of us sat silent. Pugachov fixed his gaze on me, occasionally screwing up his left eye with a wonderfully roguish and mocking expression. At last he burst into laughter with such unaffected merriment that, looking at him, I started laughing myself, not knowing why.

"Well, Your Honour?" he said to me. "You got scared, didn't you, when my lads threw the rope around your neck? Frightened out of your wits, weren't you? And I vow you would've dangled from the crossbeam if it hadn't been for your servant. I recognized the old devil immediately. Well, Your Honour, did you think that the man who guided you to the wayside inn was your Sovereign Majesty?" He assumed a solemn and mysterious air. "You'd committed a serious offence against me," he continued, "but I pardoned you for your charity, for doing me a favour at a time when I was forced to hide from my enemies. But that is just the beginning. You'll see how I reward you when I regain my empire! Do you promise to serve me with zeal?"

The rogue's question and boldness seemed so amusing to me that I couldn't restrain a smile.

"What are you smiling at?" he asked, frowning. "Or don't you believe that I am your Sovereign Majesty? Give me a straight answer."

I was perplexed. I could not acknowledge a vagabond as my sovereign – that would have seemed inexcusable cowardice to me – but to call him an impostor to his face was to invite my own ruin. It seemed to me that to make the gesture now that I had been ready to make under the gallows, in front of the whole crowd, in the first heat of indignation, would be useless braggadocio. I wavered. Pugachov was sullenly waiting for my reply. At length (and to this day I remember the moment with pride) my sense of duty triumphed over my human frailty. I replied to Pugachov:

"Listen, let me tell you the honest truth. Think of it yourself, can I acknowledge you as my sovereign? You're a sharp-witted person: you'd be the first to realize that I was lying."

"And who am I then, in your opinion?"

"God only knows; but whoever you may be, you're playing a dangerous game."

Pugachov cast a quick glance at me.

"So you don't believe," he said, "that I am your sovereign Peter III? All right. But surely victory's for the venturesome? Didn't Grishka Otrepyev become tsar long ago? * Take me for what you wish, but don't play me false. Why should you worry whether I'm this person or that? Whoever's priest, they call him 'Father'. Serve me with conviction and truth, and I'll make you field marshal and prince. What do you say?"

"No," I replied firmly. "I'm a nobleman by birth; I have sworn allegiance to Her Majesty the Empress; I cannot serve you. If you really wish me well, let me go to Orenburg."

Pugachov thought for a while.

"But if I let you go," he asked, "will you promise at least not to fight against me?"

"How could I promise such a thing?" I answered. "You know yourself it doesn't depend on my own wishes: if I'm commanded to go against you, I'll go, there's nothing else I can do. You're a leader now; you demand obedience from your men. Indeed what would it look like if I refused to serve when my services were needed? My life is in your hands: if you let me go, I'll be grateful; if you execute me, God shall be your judge; in any case, I've told you the truth."

My sincerity impressed Pugachov.

"So be it," he said, slapping me on the shoulder. "If you're hanging a man, hang him; if you're pardoning a man, pardon him. Go wherever you want and do what you like. Come and say goodbye tomorrow; and now go to bed: I'm beginning to feel sleepy myself."

I left Pugachov and went out onto the street. The night was still and frosty. The moon and the stars shone brightly, illuminating the square and the gallows. In the fort everything was quiet and dark. Only in the tavern a light still shone and the sound of late drunkards could be heard. I looked at the priest's house. Shutters and gate were closed. Everything seemed to be quiet inside.

Arriving at my lodging, I found Savelich worrying over my absence. He was overjoyed when he heard I was allowed to go free.

"Thank gracious Heaven!" he said, crossing himself. "We'll leave the fort at crack of dawn tomorrow and go where our eyes look. I've prepared a little something for you: eat, young master, and sleep as in Christ's bosom till morning."

Following his advice, I ate my supper with good appetite and, worn out in body and mind, fell asleep on the bare floor.

Chapter IX

Separation

Sweet it's been to be united,
I with you, my lovely heart;
sad, oh sad, to be divided,
sad as from my soul to part.
– Kheraskov*

EARLY NEXT MORNING I was awakened by the beating of a drum. I went to the assembly point. Pugachov's hordes were already lined up next to the gallows, where the victims of the previous day were still hanging. The Cossacks sat on horseback, the soldiers stood under arms. Banners were flying. Several cannon, among which I recognized ours, were placed on gun carriages. All the inhabitants of the fort were here, too, waiting for the pretender. In front of the porch of the commandant's house a Cossack was holding a beautiful white Kyrgyz horse by the bridle. I looked about for the corpse of the commandant's wife. It had been pushed somewhat to the side and covered with a piece of matting. At last Pugachov appeared in the doorway. All the people bared their heads. Pugachov stopped on the porch and exchanged greetings with everyone. One of his chiefs gave him a bag filled with copper coins, which he proceeded to scatter about by the handful. People threw themselves on the coins with shouts: the transaction did not pass without some bodily injury. Pugachov was surrounded by his chief followers, including Shvabrin. Our eyes met: the contempt he could read in mine made him turn away with an expression of genuine spite and affected scorn. Seeing me in the crowd, Pugachov nodded to me and called me to him.

"Listen," he said to me, "set out for Orenburg at once, and tell the governor and all the generals to expect me in a week. Advise them to meet me with filial love and submission: otherwise they won't escape merciless execution. Have a pleasant journey, Your Honour!" Then he turned to the people and said, pointing to Shvabrin, "Here, my children, is your new commander: follow his orders in everything; he's answerable to me for you and the fort."

I heard these words with horror: Shvabrin was to be commander of the fort, and Marya Ivanovna to remain under his power! Lord, what was to become of her! Pugachov came down from the porch. His horse was brought to him. He deftly leapt into the saddle, not waiting for his Cossacks to help him.

At this moment I saw Savelich step out of the crowd, go up to Pugachov, and hand him a sheet of paper. I could not imagine what would come of this.

"What is this?" asked Pugachov severely.

"Read, if you please, and you will see," answered Savelich.

Pugachov took the paper and scrutinized it for a long time with an air of importance.

"What difficult handwriting," he said at last. "Our illustrious eyes cannot make out any of it. Where's my chief secretary?"

A young fellow in a corporal's uniform ran swiftly up to Pugachov.

"Read it aloud," said the pretender, handing him the paper.

I was extremely curious to learn what my attendant could possibly have written to Pugachov. The chief secretary began to read the following in a thunderous voice, drawing out each word syllable by syllable:

"Two dressing gowns, one of calico and one of striped silk, worth six roubles."

"What does this mean?" asked Pugachov, frowning.

"Just tell 'im to read further," Savelich calmly replied.

The chief secretary continued:

"A uniform coat made of fine green cloth, seven roubles.

"A pair of white broadcloth pantaloons, five roubles.

"Twelve Dutch linen shirts with ruffles, ten roubles.

"A hamper with a tea service, two and a half roubles."

"What nonsense is all this?" interrupted Pugachov. "What business of mine are hampers and pantaloons with ruffles?"

Savelich cleared his throat and began to explain.

"This, so please Your Honour, is an inventory of my master's goods that the scoundrels made off with."

"What scoundrels?" Pugachov asked menacingly.

"I crave pardon: my tongue slipped," Savelich answered. "Scoundrels or no scoundrels, but it was your lads as went ransacking and plundering. Don't be angry: even a horse with four legs stumbles. But tell 'im to finish the list."

"Read on," said Pugachov.

The secretary continued:

"A chintz coverlet, and another one of taffeta quilted with cotton wool, four roubles.

"A fox-fur coat, lined with woollen cloth, forty roubles.

"And finally a hare-skin coat, given to Your Grace at the wayside inn, fifteen roubles."*

"And what else!" exclaimed Pugachov, his eyes flashing.

I must confess I felt extremely alarmed for my poor attendant. He was about to launch into further explanations, but Pugachov cut him short.

"How dare you pester me with such trifles?" he cried, tearing the paper from the secretary's hand and flinging it in Savelich's face. "Stupid old idiot! They've been robbed: so what? You should pray for me and my men for the rest of your life, old sod: you and your dear master could both be hanging here among the others who've disobeyed me... Hare-skin coat! I'll give you a hare-skin coat! Before you know it, I'll have you flayed alive and a coat made of your skin!"

"Do as you please," replied Savelich, "but I'm a man in bondage, responsible for my master's chattels."

Pugachov was evidently in a fit of magnanimity.

He turned away and rode off without saying another word. Shvabrin and the chiefs followed him. The band marched out of the fort in an orderly fashion. The crowd went to see Pugachov off. I remained alone with Savelich in the square. My attendant held the inventory in his hands, reading it over and over with a look of deep regret.

Seeing my good relations with Pugachov he had hit on the idea of putting this to good use, but his artful stratagem had not worked. I thought of scolding him for his inappropriate zeal, but I could not refrain from laughing.

"Aye, you can laugh, sir," he responded, "you can laugh, but when it comes to having to buy all of 'em things anew, you won't find it funny."

I hurried to the priest's house to see Marya Ivanovna. The priest's wife met me with sad news: during the night Marya Ivanovna had developed a high fever. She was lying unconscious, in a delirium. The priest's wife led me into the girl's room. I tiptoed up to her bed. I was struck by the change in her face. She did not recognize me. I stood for a long time in her presence, deaf to Father Gerasim and his good wife, who, I think, were trying to console me. Gloomy thoughts troubled my mind. The plight of the poor defenceless orphan, left amongst the vicious rebels, and my own inability to help her filled me with horror. Shvabrin: it was above all Shvabrin who preyed on my thoughts. Invested with authority by the pretender, put in charge of the fort where the unfortunate girl – an innocent target of his hatred – remained, he might resolve to do anything. But what could I do? How could I help her? How could I free her from the villain's hands? There was only one means left to me: I decided to set out for Orenburg immediately in order to hasten the deliverance of Belogorsk and, if possible, to assist in it. I said farewell to the priest and Akulina Pamfilovna, fervently entreating the good woman to take care of the one whom I already regarded as my wife. I took the poor girl's hand and kissed it, bathing it in tears.

"Farewell," said the priest's wife as she saw me off. "Farewell, Pyotr Andreich. Perhaps with God's help we'll meet in better times. Don't forget us and write to us as often as you can. Poor Marya Ivanovna has no one but you now to comfort and protect her."

When I reached the square, I stopped for a moment, looked at the gallows and bowed to it. Then I left the fort, setting out along the Orenburg highway, accompanied by Savelich, who never lagged far behind.

I was walking on, immersed in my thoughts, when I suddenly heard the clatter of horses' hooves behind me. As I looked around I saw a Cossack galloping from the fort, pulling along a Bashkir horse by the reins and making signs to me from afar. I stopped and soon recognized our sergeant. When he reached us, he got off his horse and said, handing me the reins of the other one, "Your Honour, the Tsar Our Father is sending you as a present this horse and a fur coat off his own back." (There was a sheepskin coat tied to the saddle.) "And," the sergeant added with a stammer, "he's also made a present of half a rouble to you… but I seem to have lost it along the way: please be generous and forgive me."

Savelich eyed him askance and growled, "Lost it along the way indeed! And what's jingling under your shirt? Don't you have no shame?"

"Jingling under my shirt?" rejoined the sergeant without the slightest embarrassment. "God bless you, old man. It's the bridle jingling, not coins."

"All right," I said, putting an end to the dispute. "Please give my thanks to him who sent you; as for the half-rouble you've lost, try to find it on your way back and keep it for vodka."

"Most grateful to Your Honour," he replied, turning his horse around. "I will for ever be praying for you."

With these words he galloped off, holding his shirt against his chest with one hand. In a minute he disappeared from our sight.

I put the fur coat on and got on the horse, seating Savelich behind me.

"D'you see now, sir," said the old man, "I didn't petition the rascal for nothing: the impostor felt ashamed of himself, though I will say that a lanky Bashkir jade and a sheepskin coat ain't worth half what the rascals stole from us and what you yourself were kind enough to give 'im. But they'll come in useful: even a scruffy dog gives a scrap of fur."

Chapter X

Town under Siege

> *... seized fields and hills, and from a summit*
> *looked down upon the city like an eagle.*
> *He gave command: "Within the camp prepare*
> *our thunder-power; keep it hidden there,*
> *and bring it near the city once it's night."*
> – Kheraskov*

As we approached Orenburg we saw a group of convicts, their heads shaved and their faces disfigured by the torturer's tongs. They were working around the fortifications under the supervision of veterans from the garrison. Some were carting away the rubbish that had accumulated in the trench; others were digging with spades; on the ramparts masons were carrying bricks and repairing the city walls. At the gate the sentries stopped us and demanded our identity papers. As soon as the sergeant heard that I was coming from Belogorsk, he took me straight to the general's house.

I found him in his garden. He was inspecting some apple trees, already stripped bare by the breath of autumn, and with the aid of an old gardener was carefully wrapping them in warm straw. His face wore an expression of calm, good health and benevolence. He was glad to see me and questioned me about the horrible events I had witnessed. I told him everything. He listened to me attentively, though he continued to cut back dead branches all the while.

"Poor Mironov!" he said when I had finished my sad story. "I am sorry about him: he was a good officer. And Madame Mironov was a good-hearted lady, and what an expert at pickling mushrooms! But what happened to Masha, the captain's daughter?"

I replied that she had remained at the fort, in the care of the priest's wife.

"Oh, that's bad," remarked the general, "that's very bad. You cannot count on any discipline among the brigands. What'll become of the poor girl?"

I answered that Fort Belogorsk was not far off, and that His Excellency would presumably not wait long before dispatching troops to liberate its poor inhabitants. The general shook his head doubtfully.

"We'll see, we'll see," he said. "We'll have a chance to talk more about that. Come over for a cup of tea: a council of war is to be held at my house today. You can give us reliable information about this rascal Pugachov and his army. In the meanwhile go and take a rest."

I retired to the lodging assigned to me, where Savelich had already set up house. I waited impatiently for the appointed time. As the reader can imagine, I did not fail to appear at the council that was to have such great influence on my fate. I was at the general's before the appointed hour.

I found one of the city officials with him – the director of the custom house if I rightly remember – a rotund, high-coloured little old man wearing a brocade caftan. He asked me many questions about the fate of Ivan Kuzmich, who, he said, had been the godfather of one of his children. He often interrupted me with additional questions and moral observations, which revealed him as a man, if not well versed in the military arts, at least endowed with shrewdness and native wit. Meanwhile the other people who had been invited to the council arrived. Except for the general himself, there was not one military man among the members of the council. When everybody was seated and tea had been served, the general gave a very clear and detailed account of the situation.

"And now, gentlemen," he continued, "we must decide in what way to operate against the rebels: offensively or defensively? Each of the two methods has its advantages and disadvantages. Offensive action offers more hope for a speedy annihilation of the enemy, whereas defensive action is safer and more reliable. Well, let us put the question to the vote according to the established rules of order, that is, beginning with those holding the lowest ranks. Ensign," he continued, turning to me, "be so good as to give us your opinion."

Rising, I first described Pugachov and his band in a few words, then resolutely declared that the pretender could in no way stand up to a regular army.

The officials listened to my opinion with obvious disapproval. They regarded it as evidence of a young man's impetuosity and daring. There arose a murmur, and I could distinctly hear somebody pronouncing under his breath the word "greenhorn." The general turned to me and said with a smile:

"Ensign, at councils of war the first votes are usually cast in favour of offensive operations: this is in the order of things. Let us now continue with the polling of opinions. Mr Collegiate Councillor, would you tell us what you think?"

The little old man in the brocade caftan quickly downed his third cup of tea, much diluted with rum, and gave the general the following answer:

"I think, Your Excellency, that our action should be neither offensive nor defensive."

"How now, Mr Collegiate Councillor," rejoined the surprised general. "The science of tactics knows no other way: you take either offensive or defensive measures."

"Your Excellency, take bribing measures."

"Oho-ho! Your idea is quite sensible. Bribing is allowed in tactics, and we will take your advice. We can offer a reward of, say, seventy, or perhaps even a hundred roubles for the rascal's head, from the secret funds."

"For that reward," interrupted the director of the custom house, "the brigands will surrender their chieftain, his hands and feet clapped in irons, or I'll be a Kyrgyz ram, not a collegiate councillor."

"We will think about this and discuss it some more," answered the general. "But to be on the safe side, we must also take military measures. Gentlemen, cast your votes according to the rules of order."

All opinions turned out to be contrary to mine. All the officials spoke about the unreliability of our troops, the uncertainty of success, the need for caution and the like. All thought it more prudent to stay under the protection of the cannon, behind sturdy stone walls, than to test our luck at arms in the open field. At last the general, having listened to all the opinions, shook the ashes out of his pipe and made the following speech:

"My dear sirs, I must declare on my part that I am in full agreement with the ensign, for his opinion is based on the rules of sound tactics, which almost always prescribe offensive rather than defensive action."

He stopped to fill his pipe. My vanity received a boost. I cast a proud glance at the officials, who were whispering among themselves with a look of disappointment and alarm.

"But, my dear sirs," he continued, emitting a thick puff of tobacco smoke as well as a deep sigh, "I dare not take such a great responsibility on myself when the stake is the safety of the provinces entrusted to me by Our Most Gracious Sovereign, Her Imperial Majesty. Therefore I cast my vote with the majority, which has resolved that it is most prudent and least dangerous to await the siege inside the city, and to repulse the attack of the enemy by the force of artillery and, if possible, by sorties."

It was the officials' turn to look at me derisively. The council dispersed. I could not help deploring the weakness of the venerable warrior, who was, against his own conviction, following the advice of untrained and inexperienced people.

A few days after this memorable meeting of the council, we learnt that Pugachov was approaching Orenburg just as he had promised. I could see the rebel army from the top of the city walls. It seemed to me that it had increased tenfold since the time of the assault I had witnessed. The rebels also had artillery, taken from the small forts they had conquered. Remembering the council's decision, I could foresee a long confinement within the walls of Orenburg,* and almost wept with resentment.

I will not describe the siege of Orenburg, which belongs to history rather than to a family chronicle. I will only say briefly that this siege, due to the carelessness of the local authorities, was calamitous for the citizens, who suffered from hunger and all kinds of other deprivations. It can readily be imagined that life in Orenburg was well-nigh intolerable. All were waiting for their destiny in a state of despondency; all bemoaned the high prices, which were terrible indeed. The citizens grew accustomed to cannon balls landing in their yards; even Pugachov's attacks did not arouse interest any more. I was dying of ennui. Time wore on. No letters came from Belogorsk. All the roads were cut. Separation from Marya Ivanovna was becoming unbearable to me. I was tormented by uncertainty about her fate. Sorties were my only diversion. By the kindness of Pugachov, I had a good horse, with which I shared my meagre rations and on which I rode out daily to exchange shots with Pugachov's mounted units. In these skirmishes the advantage was usually on the side of the villains, well provided as they were with food, drink and good horses. The garrison's emaciated cavalry could not cope with them. At times our starving infantry also sallied out into the field, but the deep snow prevented it from operating successfully against the mounted units, which were scattered far and wide. The artillery thundered in vain from the high walls, and if taken into the field, the guns sank into the snow and could not be moved by the exhausted horses. Such was the nature of our military operations. This was what the officials of Orenburg called caution and prudence.

One day, when we had somehow succeeded in scattering and putting to flight quite a dense throng, I rode up against a Cossack who had fallen behind his comrades; I was about to strike him with my Turkish sabre when he took his hat off and cried, "Good day to you, Pyotr Andreich! How do you do?"

Looking at him, I recognized our sergeant. I was overjoyed to see him.

"Good day to you, Maximych," I said to him. "How long ago did you leave Belogorsk?"

"Not long, Your Honour, Pyotr Andreich; I came back only yesterday. I've brought along a little letter for you."

"Where is it?" I cried, suddenly all flushed.

"It's right here on me," replied Maximych, thrusting his hand under his shirt. "I promised Palasha I'd get it to you somehow."

With these words he handed me a folded piece of paper and

galloped off immediately. I unfolded it and, trembling, read the following lines:

> *It was God's will that I should be deprived of both my father and mother at once; I have not one relation or protector in the whole world. I am turning to you, knowing that you have always wished me well, and that you are ever ready to help others. I pray to God that this letter may somehow reach you! Maximych has promised to deliver it to you. Palasha has heard from him that he often sees you from a distance in sallies, and that you do not take the least care of yourself, forgetting those who pray to God with tears in their eyes for you. I was ill for a long time, and when I recovered, Alexei Ivanovich, who is the fort's commandant in place of my dear late father, forced Father Gerasim, for fear of Pugachov, to hand me over to him. I live in our house under guard. Alexei Ivanovich is trying to compel me to marry him. He says he saved my life by not exposing Akulina Pamfilovna's hoax, when she told the villains that I was her niece. But I would sooner die than marry a man like Alexei Ivanovich. He treats me very cruelly and threatens that if I don't change my mind and consent to his proposal, he will bring me to the villain's camp, and there "you'll meet the fate of Lizaveta Kharlova."* I have asked Alexei Ivanovich to let me think it over. He has agreed to wait another three days; but if I am still not willing to marry him then, there will be no mercy. Pyotr Andreich, dear friend, you are my only protector: please help a poor girl! Please implore the general and all the commanders to send a relief force to us as soon as possible, and come yourself if you can. I remain your poor humble orphan,*
>
> *Marya Mironova*

I almost went out of my mind when I read this letter. I galloped towards the city, unmercifully spurring my poor horse. On the way I turned over in my mind several schemes for rescuing the poor girl, but could not think of anything practicable. Reaching the city, I went straight to the general's and burst into his quarters.

He was pacing up and down his room, smoking his meerschaum pipe. On seeing me, he stopped. He must have been struck by the expression on my face, for he anxiously inquired after the reason for my precipitate visit.

"Your Excellency," I said to him, "I am turning to you as I would to my own father; for the love of God, please do not refuse my request: the happiness of my whole life is at stake."

"What's the matter, my dear fellow?" asked the old man, astonished. "What can I do for you? Speak your mind."

"Your Excellency, would you give me permission to take a platoon of garrison soldiers and about fifty Cossacks to liberate Fort Belogorsk?"

The general stared at me, obviously assuming that I had lost my mind (in which he was not far wrong).

"How now? To liberate Fort Belogorsk?" he asked at last.

"I'll vouch for our success," I answered fervently. "Just let me go, please!"

"No, young man," he said, shaking his head. "Over such a long distance the enemy could easily cut you off from communication with your headquarters and achieve a decisive victory over you. When lines of communication are broken—"

I was alarmed to see him getting involved in tactical considerations, and I hastened to interrupt him.

"Captain Mironov's daughter," I told him, "has sent me a letter asking for help: Shvabrin is trying to force her to marry him."

"Is he indeed? Oh, that Shvabrin is an inordinate *Schelm*,* and if he ever falls into my hands, I'll have him tried within twenty-four hours, and we'll shoot him on the parapet of the fortress! But for the time being we must be patient—"

"Be patient!" I cried, completely beside myself. "And in the meanwhile have him marry Marya Ivanovna!"

"Oh, that's no great tragedy," retorted the general. "It's better for her to be Shvabrin's wife for the time being, since he can protect her under the present circumstances; and, after we've shot him, God will provide other suitors for her. Nice little widows don't stay old maids for long; that is, I meant to say, a young widow will find herself a husband quicker than a maiden will."

"I'd sooner die," I cried in a fury, "than yield her to Shvabrin!"

"Oho-ho!" said the old man. "Now I understand: evidently you're in love with Marya Ivanovna. Oh, that's a different matter. My poor lad! But even so I cannot give you a platoon of soldiers and fifty Cossacks. Such an expedition would not be prudent, and I cannot take the responsibility for it."

I lowered my head; despair overcame me. Suddenly an idea flashed through my mind. What it entailed, the reader will see in the next chapter – as old-fashioned novelists say.

Chapter XI

The Rebel Encampment

The lion, though by nature fierce, had eaten well.
"You've kindly visited my lair. But why? Please tell,"
he asked engagingly.

– A. Sumarokov*

I LEFT THE GENERAL and hurried back to my lodging. Savelich met me with his usual remonstrances.

"Why are you so keen, sir, to keep picking fights with drunken brigands? Is that worthy of a gentleman? These ain't normal times: you'll be a gonner, and for no purpose. It'd be something else if you were marching against them Turks or Swedes, but one's ashamed even to name the one you're sallying out against."

I interrupted his discourse with a question: how much money did I have, all told?

"There'll be enough," he answered with a look of satisfaction. "Much as the rascals rummaged, I managed to hide some."

With these words he drew from his pocket a long knitted purse full of silver.

"Well, Savelich," I said to him, "give me half now and keep the other half for yourself. I am going to Fort Belogorsk."

"Pyotr Andreich, young master!" said my good-natured attendant in a trembling voice. "Don't tempt the Lord! How could you set out now, when all the roads are cut off by the brigands? Pity your parents at least, if you don't pity yourself. Where are you riding off to? What for? Wait a spell: troops'll be coming a-catching the rascals, and then you can go off north, south, east or west."

But I was firm in my resolve.

"It's too late to discuss it," I said to the old man. "I must go: I can't do otherwise. Don't be upset, Savelich: God is merciful, perhaps we'll meet again. But listen, don't have scruples now, don't be sparing. Buy yourself what you need, even if the price is three times what it should be. I'm giving you the money. In case I don't return in three days—"

"What's that you're saying, sir?" Savelich interrupted me. "That I should let you go by yourself? Don't even dream of it! If you're so set on going, I'll follow after you on foot if need be, but I won't desert you. That I should sit here, behind them stone walls without you! I haven't yet gone off my head, have I? Say what you will, sir, I'm not budging from your side."

Knowing well that I could not out-argue Savelich, I let him get ready for the journey. In half an hour I mounted my good horse, while Savelich got on an emaciated, lame jade, which a citizen had given him free, having nothing to feed it with. We rode to the city gates; the sentries let us through; we left Orenburg behind.

It was beginning to get dark. We had to pass by the settlement of Berda,* Pugachov's den. The road there was buried under snow, but one could see tracks made by horses, renewed daily, all across the steppe. I rode at a full trot. Savelich could barely follow me at a distance, and kept shouting after me every minute, "Easy, sir, for God's sake, easy! My damned nag can't keep up with your long-legged devil. Where you hurrying to? It'd be something else if we were rushing to a feast, but it's the executioner's axe that's waiting for us, you'll see… Pyotr Andreich! Young master, Pyotr Andreich! Don't ruin us!… God Almighty, the noble child's going to perish!"

We could soon see the lights of Berda twinkling. We approached the ravines – the settlement's natural defences. Savelich would not be left behind and did not cease his plaintive entreaties. I had hoped to skirt the settlement unnoticed, but suddenly I beheld, right in front of me in the dusk, five or so peasants armed with cudgels: these were sentries at the outer edge of Pugachov's camp. They challenged us. Not knowing the password, I wanted to ride by them in silence, but they immediately surrounded me, and one of them caught my horse by the bridle. I drew my sabre and struck the peasant on the head: his hat saved his life, but he staggered and let go of the bridle. The others fell back in confusion: I took advantage of this moment and galloped off spurring my horse.

The darkness of the descending night might have saved me from any further danger, but looking back I suddenly noticed that Savelich was not following me. On his lame horse the poor old man had not been able to get away from the brigands. What was I to do? Having waited a few minutes and satisfied myself that he had been detained, I turned my horse around and set off to rescue him.

As I approached the ravine, I could hear in the distance noise, shouts and the voice of my Savelich. I rode on faster and soon found myself in the midst of the peasant sentries who had stopped me a few minutes before. They had Savelich with them. They had dragged the old man off his jade and were getting ready to tie him up. My arrival greatly pleased them. They threw themselves on me with shouts and pulled me off my horse in no time. One of them, evidently their leader, declared that he would take us directly to the Sovereign.

"It's up to Our Father the Tsar," he added, "whether he'll order you to be hanged now or wait for God's daylight."

I did not resist; Savelich followed my example; and the sentries led us away in triumph.

We crossed the ravine and entered the settlement. There were lights in every cottage. Noise and shouts could be heard everywhere. We came across many people on the streets, but in the dark nobody paid any attention to us, and nobody realized I was an officer from Orenburg. We were led straight to a cottage that stood at the crossroads. There were several barrels of liquor and two cannon by the gate.

"Here's the palace," said one of the peasants. "We'll announce you at once."

He went inside. I glanced at Savelich: the old man was crossing himself and muttering a prayer. We waited for a long time; at last the peasant returned and said to me, "Follow me: Our Father has said to let the officer in."

I entered the cottage – or palace, as the peasants called it. It was lit by two tallow candles, and its walls were hung with gold paper; otherwise, the benches, the table, the wash basin hanging on a rope, the towel on a nail, the oven-fork in the corner, and the broad hearth covered with pots – everything was just as it would be in an ordinary cottage. Pugachov, dressed in a red caftan and a tall hat, sat under the icons, with his arms akimbo in a self-important manner. Some of his chief associates stood by him with a feigned look of servility. It was evident that the news of the arrival of an officer from Orenburg had aroused great curiosity in the rebels, and they had prepared to receive me with pomp. Pugachov recognized me at first glance. His assumed self-importance disappeared immediately.

"Ah, Your Honour," he said to me gaily, "how do you do? What brought you to these parts?"

I replied that I had been travelling on my own business but his men had stopped me.

"And what business is that?" he asked me.

I did not know what to reply. Assuming that I did not want to enter into explanations before witnesses, Pugachov turned to his comrades, telling them to leave. All of them obeyed except for two, who did not stir from their places.

"You can safely talk in their presence," Pugachov told me; "I hide nothing from them."

I threw a sidelong glance at the pretender's confidants. One of them, a frail, hunched little old man with a thin grey beard, had nothing noteworthy about him except for a blue ribbon draped across his shoulder,* over his grey tunic. But I shall never forget his companion. He was tall, burly and broad-shouldered, and appeared to be about forty-five years of age. His thick red beard, his gleaming grey eyes, his nose without nostrils, and reddish patches on his forehead and cheeks lent an indescribable expression to his broad pockmarked face. He wore a red shirt, a Kyrgyz robe and Cossack trousers. The former (as I was to learn) was the runaway corporal Beloborodov, and the latter Afanasy Sokolov (nicknamed Khlopusha), a criminal sentenced to penal servitude who had escaped from Siberian mines three times.

Despite the worries that had been absorbing all my attention, the company in which I unexpectedly found myself profoundly stirred my imagination. But Pugachov soon roused me with a question: "Tell us then: what business brought you out of Orenburg?"

A strange thought entered my mind: it seemed to me that providence, bringing me face to face with Pugachov for the second time, was presenting me with an opportunity to execute my plans. I resolved to take advantage of it, and, with no time to reflect on what I was getting into, replied to Pugachov, "I was going to Fort Belogorsk to rescue a mistreated orphan girl."

Pugachov's eyes flashed.

"Who among my men dares mistreat an orphan?" he cried. "Be his head stuffed with brains fit to burst, he won't escape my judgment! Speak: who's the culprit?"

"Shvabrin is the culprit," was my answer. "He's keeping as his prisoner the girl you saw lying ill at the priest's house. He wants to force her to marry him."

"I'll teach Shvabrin a lesson or two," Pugachov said menacingly. "He'll learn what it costs under my rule to take the law into his own hands and mistreat folk. I'll hang him."

"Allow me to put in a word," Khlopusha said in a hoarse voice. "You were in a hurry to appoint Shvabrin fort commander; now you're in a hurry to hang him. You already offended the Cossacks when you put a nobleman over them; now you want to frighten the nobles by executing them at the first accusation."

"No need either to pity or to favour them!" said the little old man with the blue ribbon. "There'll be no harm in hanging Shvabrin; but it wouldn't be amiss, either, to interrogate this officer thoroughly – about why he's honoured us with a visit. If he doesn't recognize you as his sovereign, why's he seeking justice from you, and if he does recognize you, what's he been doing sitting in Orenburg with your foes till the present day? Won't you give orders for him to be taken down to the chancery and for a good fire to be lit in the furnace? His Grace, I suspect, has been sent by the commanders of Orenburg to spy on us."

The old villain's logic seemed quite convincing to me. A shiver ran down my spine when I reflected in whose hands I was. Pugachov noticed my confusion.

"How about that, Your Honour?" he asked, winking at me. "My field marshal seems to be talking sense. What do you think?"

Pugachov's jocularity restored my courage. I answered calmly that I was in his power and he was free to deal with me in whatever way he thought fit.

"All right," said Pugachov. "Now tell us, in what condition is your town?"

"Thank God," I answered, "all is well."

"All is well!" repeated Pugachov. "And what about the people dying of hunger?"

The pretender spoke the truth, but I felt duty-bound to assert that all that was empty rumour, and that in fact there was enough of all kinds of supplies in Orenburg.

"You can see," the little old man chimed in, "that he's lying right to your face. All the fugitives have consistently reported that there is famine and disease in Orenburg, that they're feeding on carrion, thinking themselves lucky for it, yet His Grace asserts that there's enough of everything. If you want to hang Shvabrin, hang this young adventurer, too, on the same gallows, so that neither of them need feel jealous of the other."

The words of the accursed old man seemed to be swaying Pugachov. Fortunately, Khlopusha started contradicting his companion.

"That's enough, Naumych," he said. "All you ever want is to strangle and slaughter. Great hero, aren't you? Take a look: body and soul are scarcely held together. You're staring into the grave yourself, but you still want to exterminate other folk. Haven't you already got enough blood on your conscience?"

"And since when have you become a saint?" retorted Beloborodov. "Whence this sudden compassion?"

"Of course," answered Khlopusha, "I'm also a sinner. This hand," here he clenched his bony fist and, rolling up his sleeve, bared his hairy arm, "this hand, too, is guilty of shedding Christian blood. But I've slain foes, not guests; at the crossroads and in the dark forest, not at home sitting by the stove; with bludgeon and axe, not with an old woman's jabbering."

The old man turned away and muttered the words, "rip-nose!"

"What are you whispering there, old devil?" yelled Khlopusha. "I'll give you 'rip-nose'; just wait, your time's coming too. God will grant you too a sniff of the torturer's tongs… And in the meantime mind I don't pull your scraggy beard out!"

"Generals!" exclaimed Pugachov solemnly. "That's enough of your quarrels. There'd be no harm in it if those Orenburg dogs were all twitching their legs below the same crossbeam, but we'll come to a bad end if our own hounds start snapping and snarling at one another. Please make up."

Khlopusha and Beloborodov did not say a word, just glared at each other sullenly. I felt the necessity of changing the topic of the conversation, which could have ended in a way very unfavourable to me, and I turned to Pugachov, saying with a cheerful expression, "Oh, I almost forgot to thank you for the horse and the coat. Without your help I would've never reached the city and would've frozen on the highway."

My ruse worked. Pugachov cheered up.

"One good turn deserves another," he said with a wink and a twinkle in his eyes. "Tell me now, why are you so concerned about the girl Shvabrin is mistreating? Has she kindled a flame in your young heart? Has she?"

"She's my fiancée," I answered Pugachov, seeing a favourable change in the weather and having no reason to conceal the truth.

"Your fiancée!" cried Pugachov. "Why didn't you tell me before? We'll have you married and feast at your wedding!" Then he turned to Beloborodov: "Listen, field marshal, His Honour and I are old friends: let's sit down to supper and then sleep on the matter. We'll see in the morning what we should do with him."

I would have been glad to decline the honour, but there was no way out of it. Two young Cossack girls, daughters of the owner of the cottage, laid the table with a white cloth, bringing in some bread, fish soup and several bottles of vodka and beer: once more I found myself sharing a table with Pugachov and his terrifying comrades.

The orgy to which I became an involuntary witness lasted well into the night. At length intoxication began to get the better of the party. Pugachov fell asleep in his chair; his comrades rose and signalled to me to leave him. I went out with them. By Khlopusha's order the sentry led me to the chancery cottage, where I found Savelich and where they locked us in. My attendant was so confounded by all that had happened that he did not even ask me any questions. He lay down in the dark, sighing and moaning for a long time; at last he started snoring, while I gave myself over to musings, which did not allow me a wink of sleep all night.

The next morning Pugachov sent for me. As I approached his quarters, I saw at the gate a covered sleigh, with a troika of Tatar horses harnessed to it. There was a crowd in the street. I met Pugachov at the entrance: he was dressed for the road, in a fur coat and a Kyrgyz hat. His companions of the night before surrounded him, assuming an air of submission that was in sharp contrast to all I had witnessed the previous evening. Pugachov greeted me merrily and ordered me to get into the sleigh with him.

We took our seats.

"To Fort Belogorsk!" said Pugachov to the broad-shouldered Tatar driver, who was controlling the three horses from a standing position. My heart pounded. The horses hurtled forward, the bells jingled, the sleigh dashed forth...

"Stop! Stop!" I heard an all-too-familiar voice, and I caught sight of Savelich running towards us in the street. Pugachov gave orders to stop.

"Pyotr Andreich, young master!" cried my attendant. "Don't forget me in my old age among these scoundr—"

"Oh, you old gaffer!" said Pugachov. "Fate's brought us together again. All right, sit on the box."

"Thank you, my Sovereign, thank you, Father," said Savelich taking his seat. "May the Lord keep you in good health for a hundred years for taking pity on an old man and comforting him. I'll pray for you all my life, and I'll never even mention the hare-skin coat again."

That hare-skin coat might finally have made Pugachov angry in earnest. But happily he either did not hear the unfortunate allusion or chose to ignore it. The horses set off at a gallop; the people in the street stopped and bowed from the waist. Pugachov nodded to them right and left. In another minute we left the settlement behind and went whizzing over the smooth surface of the highway.

The reader can easily imagine what I felt at that moment. In a few hours I was to see the girl whom I had already considered lost to me for ever. I imagined the moment of our reunion… I also thought about the man in whose hands my fate rested and with whom, by a series of strange coincidences, I was mysteriously linked. I remembered the wanton cruelty and bloodthirsty ways of this same man, who was now volunteering to be the deliverer of my loved one! Pugachov did not know that she was the daughter of Captain Mironov; an exasperated Shvabrin could reveal it all to him; or he might find out the truth in some other way… What would then become of Marya Ivanovna? A shiver ran down my spine, and my hair stood on end at the very thought…

Suddenly Pugachov interrupted my thoughts, turning to me to ask, "What is Your Honour brooding over?"

"How could I not be brooding?" I answered. "I am an officer and a nobleman; only yesterday I was fighting against you; yet today I'm riding in the same sleigh with you, and the happiness of my whole life depends on you."

"And what about it?" asked Pugachov. "Are you scared?"

I answered that having already been spared by him once, I was hoping not only for his mercy but even for his help.

"And you're right, by God, you're right!" said the pretender. "You saw how my fellows scowled at you; even this morning the old man insisted that you were a spy and should be tortured and hanged; but I wouldn't consent," he added, lowering his voice so that Savelich and the Tatar would not be able to hear, "because I remembered your glass of vodka and hare-skin coat. You can see I'm not as bloodthirsty as your people claim."

I remembered the taking of Fort Belogorsk, but I did not think it necessary to contradict him, and made no answer.

"What do they say about me in Orenburg?" asked Pugachov, after a pause.

"Well, they say that coping with you is no easy matter; you've certainly made your mark."

The pretender's face showed that his vanity was gratified.

"Yes!" he said with a cheerful expression. "I fight with skill, don't I? Have your people in Orenburg heard about the battle at Yuzeyeva?* Forty generals killed, four armies taken captive. What do you think: could the Prussian King stand up to me?"

The impostor's bragging amused me.

"What do you think yourself?" I said. "Could you get the better of Frederick?"

"Of Fyodor Fyodorovich?* And why not? After all, I'm getting the better of your generals, and they've beaten him more than once. Fortune has favoured my arms so far; but it's been nothing yet: just wait and see how I'll march on Moscow."

"So you're proposing to march on Moscow?"

The pretender pondered a little and said in an undertone, "Heaven only knows. My street's a narrow one: I've little freedom. My fellows are always trying to be clever. They're crooks. I've got to keep my ears pricked: at the first sign of failure they'll try to save their necks in exchange for my head."

"Exactly so!" I told him. "Wouldn't it be better if you yourself left them before it was too late, and threw yourself on the Empress's mercy?"

Pugachov's face broke into a bitter smile.

"No," he answered. "It's too late for me to repent. There'll be no mercy for me. I'm going to continue as I began. You can never be sure: perhaps I'll succeed! After all, Grishka Otrepyev reigned over Moscow, didn't he?"

"And do you know how he ended up? He was thrown out of a window, butchered and burnt, and his ashes were loaded in a cannon and fired!"

"Listen," said Pugachov with frenzied inspiration. "I'll tell you a tale that I heard from an old Kalmyk woman when I was a child. Once the eagle asked the raven, 'Tell me, raven-bird, why is it that you live three hundred years in this bright world, and I am allotted only three and thirty?' 'The reason is, my friend,' answered the raven, 'that you drink live blood while I feed on carrion.' The eagle thought, 'Why don't we try the same food?' Very well. Off flew the eagle and the raven. Suddenly they saw a fallen horse; they came down and settled on it. The raven started tearing at it, praising it. The eagle pecked at it once, pecked at it twice, then flapped its wings and said to the raven, 'No, friend raven: rather than live on carrion for three hundred years, I'll choose one drink of living blood, then take what God brings.' How do you like this Kalmyk tale?"*

"Clever," I replied. "But in my opinion, to live by murder and plunder is the same as pecking carrion."

Pugachov looked at me with surprise and did not answer. We both fell silent, each engrossed in his thoughts. The Tatar struck up a melancholy tune; Savelich swayed from side to side on the box, asleep. The sleigh dashed along the smooth, snow-covered highway... Then I caught sight of a little village on the steep bank of the Yaik, with its palisade and bell tower – and in another quarter of an hour we rode into Fort Belogorsk.

Chapter XII

The Orphan

As our little apple sapling
has no leafy crown nor spreading branches,
even so our little princess
has no father nor a mother.
To prepare her trousseau she'll have no one;
to pronounce a blessing she'll have no one.
– A wedding song*

THE SLEIGH drew up to the porch of the commandant's house. The people recognized Pugachov's bell and ran crowding after us. Shvabrin met the pretender on the porch. He was dressed like a Cossack and had grown a beard. The traitor helped Pugachov out of the sleigh, voicing his joy and zeal in obsequious terms. When he saw me he became confused, but he soon recovered himself and offered his hand, saying, "So you, too, are on our side? High time!"

I turned away and gave no answer.

My heart ached when we entered the long-familiar room, where the late commandant's commission still hung on the wall as a melancholy epitaph upon the past. Pugachov sat down on the same sofa on which Ivan Kuzmich used to be lulled to sleep by the grumbling of his spouse. Shvabrin himself brought in some vodka to offer to the pretender. Pugachov emptied his glass and said to him, pointing at me, "Offer some to His Honour, too."

Shvabrin came up to me with his tray, but I turned away from him once more. He seemed to be extremely ill at ease. With his usual perceptiveness he could, of course, guess that Pugachov was dissatisfied with him. He was cringing with fear before the pretender and kept glancing at me with suspicion. Pugachov asked him how things were at the fort, what he had heard about enemy troops and so forth, and then suddenly turned on him with a question: "Tell me, brother, what girl is this you're keeping here locked up? Show her to me."

Shvabrin turned pale as a corpse.

"Your Majesty," he said in a trembling voice, "Your Majesty, she's not locked up... She's sick... She's in bed in her room."

"Take me to her, then," said the pretender, rising from his seat.

There was no way to refuse him. Shvabrin went forward to lead Pugachov to Marya Ivanovna's room. I followed behind.

Shvabrin stopped on the stairs.

"Your Majesty," he said, "you're free to demand of me whatever you wish, but do not order me to let a stranger into my wife's bedroom."

I shuddered.

"So you're married!" I said to him, ready to tear him into pieces.

"Quiet!" Pugachov interrupted me. "This is my business. And you," he continued, turning to Shvabrin, "stop making excuses and raising difficulties: whether she's your wife or not, I will bring in whomever I please. Follow me, Your Honour."

Shvabrin stopped once more at the door of the bedroom and said in a faltering voice, "Your Majesty, I must warn you that she's in a delirium and has been raving incessantly for the last three days."

"Open the door!" said Pugachov.

Shvabrin searched his pockets and declared that he had not brought the key with him. Pugachov kicked the door; the lock flew off, the door swung open, and we entered.

I took one look and froze with fright. Marya Ivanovna, in a tattered peasant dress, pale and thin, with her hair dishevelled, sat on the floor. A jug of water covered with a chunk of bread stood before her. Seeing me, she shuddered and cried out. What I felt at that moment I cannot describe.

Pugachov looked at Shvabrin and said with a sarcastic smile, "Nice sick ward you have!" Then, approaching Marya Ivanovna: "Tell me, dear heart, what's your husband punishing you for? What have you done to offend him so?"

"My husband!" she repeated. "He's not my husband. I'll never be his wife! I've resolved I'd sooner die, and I will die if I'm not set free."

Pugachov looked at Shvabrin menacingly.

"How dare you deceive me?" he asked him. "Do you know, rascal, what you deserve for this?"

Shvabrin fell on his knees... At that moment my contempt for him muffled all the hatred and anger I bore him. I was disgusted to see a nobleman grovelling at the feet of a fugitive Cossack. Pugachov relented.

"I'll pardon you this time," he said to Shvabrin, "but bear in mind that one more offence, and this one will also be remembered." Then he turned to Marya Ivanovna, saying to her kindly, "Go free, pretty maiden: I grant you freedom. I am your Sovereign."

Marya Ivanovna cast a quick glance at him and guessed that the murderer of her parents was standing before her. She covered her face with both hands and fainted away. I rushed to her side; but at this moment my old acquaintance Palasha pushed her way boldly into the room and took over the care of her young mistress. Pugachov left the bedroom, and the three of us went to the parlour.

"Well, Your Honour," said Pugachov, laughing, "we've rescued the pretty maiden! What do you think, should we send for the priest and make him marry his niece to you? I'll be father by proxy, if you like, and Shvabrin can be your best man: we'll feast and drink and banish sorrow!"

What I had feared now happened. Hearing Pugachov's suggestion, Shvabrin flew into a passion.

"Your Majesty!" he shouted, beside himself. "I'm guilty, I lied to you, but Grinyov is also deceiving you. This girl is not the niece of the Belogorsk priest: she's the daughter of Ivan Mironov, who was executed when the fort was taken."

Pugachov fixed his fiery eyes on me.

"What's this now?" he asked me, bewildered.

"Shvabrin is telling the truth," I answered firmly.

"You didn't mention this to me," Pugachov remarked, and a cloud came over his features.

"Just consider," I replied, "could I have declared in front of your men that Mironov's daughter was alive? They would've torn her to pieces. Nothing could've saved her!"

"That's true enough," laughed Pugachov. "My drunkards wouldn't have spared the poor girl. That old dear, the priest's wife, did right to deceive them."

"Listen," I continued, seeing his favourable mood, "I don't know what to call you, and I don't wish to know... But God is my witness, I'd be glad to repay you with my life for what you've done for me. Only don't demand of me anything that is against my honour and Christian conscience. You are my benefactor. Please conclude the matter as you began it: let me and the poor orphan go free, wherever God will guide us. And wherever you may be, whatever may happen to you, we will pray to God every day to save your sinful soul..."

Pugachov's hardened soul, it seemed, was touched.

"Oh, well, let it be as you say," he said. "Hang him or spare him: don't do things by halves. That is my principle. Take your beautiful one, go with her where you want, and may God grant you love and wisdom!"

Then he turned to Shvabrin and ordered him to issue me a pass for all the outposts and forts that were under his control. Shvabrin, entirely crushed, stood rooted to the ground. Pugachov went to inspect the fort. Shvabrin followed him, while I stayed under the pretext of making preparations for our departure.

I ran to the bedroom. The door was locked. I knocked.

"Who's there?" asked Palasha.

I called out my name. Marya Ivanovna's sweet voice answered from behind the door. "Wait a moment, Pyotr Andreich. I'm changing. Go to Akulina Pamfilovna's: I'll be there in a minute."

I obeyed and went to Father Gerasim's house. Both he and his wife ran out to greet me. Savelich had already spoken to them.

"Welcome, Pyotr Andreich," said the priest's wife. "It was God's will that we should meet again. How are you? We've been talking about you every day. And Marya Ivanovna, my little lamb, what has she gone through without you! But tell me, dear, how come you get on so well with Pugachov? How is it that he didn't dispatch you to kingdom come? For that at least we should be grateful to the villain."

"That'll do, old woman," Father Gerasim interrupted her. "There's no need to blurt out everything that's in your head. In multitude of words there's no salvation. Pyotr Andreich, sir! Welcome, step right in. It's been a long, long time since we saw you last."

The priest's wife invited me to partake of whatever food there was in the house, and talked incessantly. She told me how Shvabrin had forced them to surrender Marya Ivanovna to him; how Marya Ivanovna had wept, unwilling to part with them; how she had managed to keep in touch with them through Palashka (a quick-witted lass, who had made even the sergeant dance to her tune); how she had advised Marya Ivanovna to write a letter to me, and so forth. I told her my own story briefly. The priest and his wife both crossed themselves when they heard that Pugachov had found out about their deception.

"The power of the cross protect us!" said Akulina Pamfilovna. "May God make the storm pass over! Oh, but that Alexei Ivanych: a nasty bit of work, I'll vow!"

At that moment the door opened, and Marya Ivanovna came in with a smile on her pale face. She had shed her peasant costume and was dressed as always before, simply and attractively.

I seized her hand and for a long time could not utter a single word. We both kept silent from fullness of heart. Our host and hostess, feeling their presence superfluous, both left the room. We remained all alone. The whole world was forgotten. We talked and talked, and could not talk enough. Marya Ivanovna related to me everything that had happened to her since the taking of the fort; she described the full horror of her situation and all the torments she had experienced at the hands of the detestable Shvabrin. We recalled the earlier happy days too... We both wept... At length I started outlining my plans to her. She could certainly not stay in the fort, under Pugachov's authority and Shvabrin's command. It would also have been senseless to go to Orenburg, subjected as it was to all the vicissitudes of a siege. Nor had she a single relation in the whole world. I suggested to her that she go to my parents at their country estate. At first she hesitated: she knew my father's unfriendly feelings towards her and this frightened her. I reassured her. I knew that my father would consider it a blessing and an obligation to shelter the daughter of an honoured warrior who had given his life for the fatherland.

"My dear Marya Ivanovna!" I said at last. "I regard you as my wife. Extraordinary circumstances have united us inseparably: nothing in the world can part us."

She listened to me simply, without affected bashfulness or coy reluctance. She felt that her fate was linked with mine. But she repeated that she would be my wife only if my parents gave their consent. I did not contradict her. We kissed fervently, devotedly – and thus everything was settled between us.

After an hour the sergeant brought along my pass, with the pretender's signature scrawled on it, and told me that Pugachov wished to see me. I found him ready to leave. I cannot describe what I felt as I said farewell to this terrifying man, a monster and a blackguard to everyone except me. Why not confess the truth? At that moment I was drawn to him by a strong sense of sympathy. I ardently wished to extricate him from the company of the villains whose leader he was, and to save his head before it was too late. Shvabrin and the people crowding around us prevented me from expressing to him all the feelings that filled my heart.

We parted as friends. Seeing Akulina Pamfilovna in the crowd, Pugachov shook his finger at her and winked at her significantly; then he climbed into his covered sleigh, giving orders to drive to Berda, and as the horses started off, he leant out once more, shouting to me, "Farewell, Your Honour! Perhaps we'll see each other again!"

I was indeed to see him again, but in what circumstances!

Pugachov was gone. For a long time I gazed at the white steppe as his troika rapidly crossed it. The people dispersed. Shvabrin disappeared. I returned to the priest's house. Everything was ready for our departure, and I did not want to delay it any longer. Our belongings were all placed in the commandant's old carriage. The drivers harnessed the horses in no time. Marya Ivanovna went to pay a farewell visit to her parents' grave in the churchyard. I wanted to accompany her, but she asked me to let her go by herself. She returned after a few minutes, shedding silent tears. The carriage drew up. Father Gerasim and his wife came out on the porch. Three of us – Marya Ivanovna, Palasha and I – took our seats inside the carriage, while Savelich climbed up on the box.

"Farewell, Marya Ivanovna, my little dove! Farewell, Pyotr Andreich, our bright falcon!" said the good-hearted Akulina Pamfilovna. "Have a safe journey, and may God grant happiness to you both!"

We set off. I caught sight of Shvabrin standing at the window in the commandant's house. His face wore a surly expression of spite. I did not wish to appear to be triumphing over an annihilated enemy and turned my eyes the other way. At last we passed through the gate and left Fort Belogorsk for ever.

Chapter XIII

Arrest

"Please don't be angry, sir: my duties now entail
that I this very hour must send you off to jail."
"All right, then: I'm prepared; but it's my expectation
that you'll allow me first to give an explanation."
– Knyazhnin*

I COULD HARDLY BELIEVE my good fortune at being so unexpectedly reunited with the dear girl whose fate had so terribly worried me even that morning: all that had happened to me seemed like an empty dream. Marya Ivanovna gazed pensively now at me, now at the highway; she had evidently not had enough time to come to her senses and recover her old self. Drained of emotions, we were both silent. In a couple of hours, which had gone by almost unnoticed, we were at the next fort, also under Pugachov's rule. Here we changed horses. The speed with which they were harnessed and the eagerness with which the bearded Cossack, appointed commandant by Pugachov, tried to oblige us seemed to indicate that, thanks to the loquacity of our driver, I was being taken for a court favourite of the pretender.

We continued our journey. It was beginning to get dark. We approached a small town, which the bearded commandant had reported to be occupied by a strong detachment on its way to join forces with the pretender. We were stopped by the sentries. To the challenge, "Who goes there?" our driver replied in a thunderous voice, "The Sovereign's trusty friend with his bride." Suddenly a throng of hussars surrounded us, swearing frightfully.

"Get out of there, devil's trusty friend!" the bewhiskered sergeant said to me. "A nice hot bath is waiting for you, and for your bride."

I got out of the carriage and demanded to be taken to their commander. Seeing an officer, the soldiers stopped swearing. The sergeant led me off to the major. Savelich followed right behind me, muttering to himself, "So much for the Sovereign's trusty friend! Out of the frying pan into the fire! God Almighty! How's all this going to end?" The carriage followed us at a walking pace.

In five minutes we reached a brightly lit little house. The sergeant left me guarded by the sentries and went in to announce me. He returned immediately, declaring that His High Honour had no time to receive me, and had ordered him to take me off to prison and to bring my bride to him.

"What does this mean?" I shouted in a rage. "Has he lost his mind?"

"That I daren't judge, Your Honour," answered the sergeant, "but His High Honour's given orders that Your Honour should be taken off to prison and Her Honour should be brought before His High Honour, Your Honour."

I sprang onto the porch. The sentries did not attempt to stop me, and I dashed straight into the room where the hussar officers, some six of them, were playing cards. The major was dealing. How great was my surprise when at the first glance I recognized Ivan Ivanovich Zurin, who had at one time fleeced me in the Simbirsk tavern!

"Is it possible?" I cried. "Ivan Ivanych! Is it you?"

"Good grief! Pyotr Andreich! What brings you here? Where've you come from? Welcome, brother. Would you like a card?"

"Thank you kindly. I'd rather you assigned me to a lodging."

"What lodging? Stay with me."

"I can't: I'm not by myself."

"Well, bring your comrade, too."

"I'm not with a comrade. I'm… with a lady."

"With a lady? Where did you get your hands on her? Oho, brother!" Here Zurin whistled so expressively that everybody burst into laughter, and I was thoroughly embarrassed.

"Well," continued Zurin, "be it as you wish. You'll have lodgings. It's a pity, though… We could've had a good time, as of old… But hey, boy! Why aren't they bringing in Pugachov's little lady friend? Or is she balking? Tell her not to be afraid: the gentleman is handsome and will do her no harm; give her a slap, and be smart about it."

"What do you mean?" I said to Zurin. "What little lady friend of Pugachov's? It's the daughter of the late Captain Mironov. I rescued her from captivity, and I'm now taking her to my father's estate, where I intend to leave her."

"How? Is it you then whose arrival they just announced? For pity's sake, what does all this mean?"

"I'll tell you about it later. But now, for heaven's sake, reassure the poor girl, whom your hussars have frightened so."

Zurin immediately proceeded to make the necessary arrangements. He himself came out in the street to apologize to Marya Ivanovna for the accidental misunderstanding and ordered the sergeant to assign to her the best apartment in town. I myself stayed to spend the night with him.

We had supper, and when we were left alone, I related my adventures to him. He listened to me attentively. When I finished, he shook his head, saying:

"All this is fine, brother, except for one thing: what the devil do you want to get married for? Honest officer that I am, I don't want to leave you under any misapprehension: believe you me, marriage is folly. Why would you want to trifle with a wife and waste your time looking after babies? Ugh! Take my advice: shake off this captain's daughter. I've cleared the highway to Simbirsk: it's safe now. Send her off to your parents by herself tomorrow, and stay with my detachment. There's no point in trying to return to Orenburg. If you fall into the rebels' hands again, you'll hardly be able to extricate yourself one more time. That way this amorous folly will pass of itself, and all will be fine."

Although I did not quite agree with him, I nevertheless recognized that duty and honour demanded my presence in the Empress's army. I decided to follow Zurin's advice and send Marya Ivanovna to my parents' estate while I stayed with his detachment.

Savelich came in to help me undress: I told him to be ready to set out for the journey with Marya Ivanovna the next morning. At first he balked at the idea.

"What d'you mean, sir? That I should forsake you? Who'd be looking after you? What'll your parents say?"

Knowing my attendant's stubborn nature, I resolved to get round him by soft words and candour.

"Arkhip Savelich, my friend," I said to him, "don't refuse me your favour, be my benefactor: I don't need any servants here, and I'd be worried if Marya Ivanovna were to set out on the road without you. Serving her, you'll be serving me, for I've firmly resolved to marry her as soon as circumstances permit."

Savelich clasped his hands with a look of indescribable astonishment.

"To marry!" he repeated. "The child wants to marry! And what'll your dear father say? And your dear mother, what'll she think?"

"They'll consent," I answered; "they'll be sure to consent when they get to know Marya Ivanovna. I'm placing my hopes in you, too. Father and Mother trust you: you'll plead for us, won't you?"

The old man was touched.

"Oh, dear master, Pyotr Andreich," he replied, "early though you've taken it into your head to marry, it's true that Marya Ivanovna is such a good-hearted young lady that it'd be a crime to miss the opportunity. Be it as you wish then! I'll accompany her, God's little angel, and will humbly tell your parents that such a bride doesn't even need a dowry."

I thanked Savelich and went to bed, sharing Zurin's room. All wrought up and excited, I chattered away. At first Zurin conversed with me willingly, but gradually his answers grew less and less frequent and coherent, until at last he answered one of my questions with a snore and a whistle. I stopped talking and soon followed his example.

I went to see Marya Ivanovna the next morning. I told her about my intentions. She acknowledged them to be prudent and immediately consented. Zurin's detachment was to leave the town that same day. There was no reason to delay matters. I parted with Marya Ivanovna there and then, entrusting her to Savelich's care and furnishing her with a letter to my parents. She burst into tears.

"Farewell, Pyotr Andreich," she said in a soft voice. "God only knows if we'll see each other again, but I will never forget you: till my dying day you alone shall live in my heart."

I was unable to reply. There were people around us, and in their presence I did not wish to give full rein to the emotions stirring within me. At last she left. I returned to Zurin sad and silent. He wanted to cheer me up, and I myself was seeking distraction: we spent the day wildly and noisily. In the evening we set out on our march.

This was at the end of February. Winter, which had hindered military operations, was drawing to its close, and our generals were preparing for concerted action. Pugachov was still encamped close to Orenburg. In the meantime government troops were closing in around him and converging on the robbers' den. The rebel villages submitted to legal authority at the first sight of our troops; the bands of brigands were fleeing from us everywhere; and all signs pointed to an early and happy conclusion of the affair.

Prince Golitsyn soon defeated Pugachov at Fort Tatishcheva, scattering his hordes and lifting the siege of Orenburg.* The rebellion, it appeared, had been dealt the last, decisive blow. At this time Zurin's detachment was ordered out against a band of Bashkirs, who scattered before we could set eyes on them. Spring caught us in a Tatar hamlet. The rivers overflowed, and the roads became impassable. Our only comfort in our idleness was the thought that this tedious and petty war against brigands and savages would soon be over.

But Pugachov had not been captured. He re-emerged in the area around the Siberian metal works, gathered new bands there and recommenced his villainous acts.* Reports about his success were making the rounds again. We learnt that he had destroyed several Siberian forts. Soon after, rumours of the taking of Kazan and of the pretender's advance on Moscow* alarmed the army commanders, who had been negligently idle, believing optimistically in the despised rebel's impotence. Zurin received orders to cross the Volga.*

I will not go into the details of our campaign and of the end of the war. I will only say that the disaster reached extreme proportions. We passed through villages ravaged by the rebels and had no alternative but to requisition from the poor villagers whatever they had managed to salvage. Law and order had broken down everywhere; landowners were hiding in the forests. Bands of brigands were committing atrocities on every side; the commanding officers of various government detachments arbitrarily dealt out punishment or mercy; conditions were terrible in the whole vast region engulfed in the conflagration... May the Lord save us from another such senseless and merciless Russian rebellion!

Pugachov fled, pursued by Johann von Michelsohn. Soon afterwards we learnt of his total defeat. Finally Zurin received news of the pretender's capture,* and at the same time orders to proceed no farther. The war was over. I could at last return to my parents! I went into raptures at the thought of embracing them and seeing Marya Ivanovna, of whom I had not had any news. I leapt with joy like a child. Zurin laughed and said, shrugging his shoulders, "Mark my word, you'll come to a bad end! You'll marry – and that'll be the end of you, all for nothing!"

At the same time, however, a strange emotion poisoned my joy: I could not help feeling disturbed whenever I thought of the villain, bespattered by the blood of so many innocent victims, and of the execution awaiting him. "Yemelya, Yemelya,"* I said to myself with vexation, "why didn't you get spiked on a bayonet or come in the way of grapeshot! That would have been the best idea for you." How could I feel otherwise? His image was joined in my mind with a recollection of the mercy he had shown me at one of the most gruesome moments of his career and with the memory of my fiancée's deliverance from the hands of the detestable Shvabrin.

Zurin granted me a furlough. In a few days I was to be in the bosom of my family and to see my Marya Ivanovna again... But suddenly an unexpected storm burst on me.

On the appointed day of my departure, at the very moment I was about to leave, Zurin came into my hut holding a piece of paper in his hand and wearing an extremely serious look. A pang shot through my heart. I felt alarmed, though I did not know why. He sent my orderly out and declared that he had to talk to me about an official matter.

"What is it?" I asked anxiously.

"A slight unpleasantness," he answered, handing me the piece of paper. "Read what I've just received."

I began to read it: it was a secret order to the commanders of all army units to arrest me wherever I might be caught and to convey me immediately under guard to Kazan, to appear before the Secret Commission established to investigate Pugachov's case.

The paper almost fell out of my hands.

"There's nothing for it," said Zurin. "It's my duty to obey the order. Evidently, rumours of your friendly travels with Pugachov have somehow reached the government. I hope the matter will have no serious consequences and you will be able to justify yourself before the Commission. Don't be downhearted; set off at once."

My conscience was clear, and I did not fear the trial, but the thought that my cherished reunion with my beloved would have to be postponed, perhaps for several more months, appalled me. The wagon was ready. Zurin bade me a friendly farewell. I took my seat in the wagon. Two hussars with their swords drawn sat beside me, and we set out along the main highway.

Chapter XIV

Trial

The tales folk tell
are like the sea swell.
– A proverb*

I WAS SURE that the cause of the whole affair was my unauthorized departure from Orenburg. I could easily justify myself, for not only had sorties never been forbidden, they had been fully encouraged. I could be accused of unwise impetuosity, but not of disobedience. On the other hand, my friendly relations with Pugachov might have been reported by a number of witnesses and might have seemed, to say the least, highly suspicious. All during the journey I thought about the investigation awaiting me, turned over in my mind the answers I would give, and resolved to tell the plain truth before the tribunal, feeling certain that this was the simplest and, at the same time, the most reliable way to justify myself.

I arrived in Kazan, laid waste and ravaged by fire. Piles of cinders lined the streets instead of houses; blackened walls stuck out here and there, without roofs or windows. Such were the traces Pugachov had left behind. I was brought to the fortress, which had remained intact in the midst of the burnt-out city. The hussars delivered me over to the officer of the guard. He sent for a blacksmith. Fetters were put around my ankles and hammered tight. Then I was taken to the prison and left alone in a narrow, dark, kennel-like cell, with bare walls and a tiny window criss-crossed with iron bars.

Such a beginning was not a good omen. But I did not lose either courage or hope. I resorted to the consolation of all those in distress, experiencing for the first time the comfort derived from prayer that pours forth from a pure but lacerated heart. I went to sleep calmly, not worrying about what the future would bring.

The next morning the prison guard woke me with a summons from the Commission. Two soldiers conducted me across the yard to the commandant's house; they stayed in the entrance hall and let me proceed into the inner rooms by myself.

I entered a good-sized chamber. Two men were seated behind a table covered with papers: a general of advanced years, who looked stern and cold, and a young captain of the Guards, aged about twenty-eight, who had a pleasant appearance and smooth, easy manners. Behind a separate desk by the window sat the secretary, with a quill stuck behind his ear, bending over his paper, ready to take down my deposition. The interrogation began. I was asked my name and title. The general inquired if I was the son of Andrei Petrovich Grinyov, and when he heard my answer, he sternly rejoined, "A pity that such an honourable man should have such an unworthy son!"

I calmly replied that whatever the accusations hanging over me, I hoped to refute them by an honest account of the truth. He did not like my self-assurance.

"You're a sharp fellow," he said, frowning, "but we've dealt with sharper ones before now."

Then the young man asked me when and under what circumstances I had entered Pugachov's service, and what commissions I had carried out for him.

I answered with indignation that as an officer and a nobleman I could not have entered Pugachov's service and could not have accepted any commissions from him.

"How did it happen, then," rejoined my interrogator, "that this nobleman and officer was spared by the pretender while all his fellow officers were bestially murdered? How did it happen that this same officer and nobleman feasted with the rebels as their friend and accepted presents, such as a fur coat, a horse and half a rouble, from the chief villain? What gave rise to this strange friendship, and what were its foundations if not treason or at least despicable and inexcusable cowardice?"

I was deeply offended by the words of the Guards officer and heatedly began my justification. I related how my acquaintance with Pugachov had begun on the steppe during a blizzard, and how he had recognized and spared me after the taking of Fort Belogorsk. I said that I had indeed not scrupled to accept the sheepskin coat and horse from the pretender, but I had defended Fort Belogorsk against him to the last extremity. Finally I made reference to my general, who could testify to my zeal during the calamitous Orenburg siege.

The stern old man picked up an opened letter from the table and read aloud the following:

In answer to Your Excellency's letter of inquiry with regard to Ensign Grinyov, who is alleged to have involved himself in the recent uprising and to have entered into such dealings with the villain as constitute a breach of duty and a breaking of his oath of allegiance, I have the honour to report that the above-named Ensign Grinyov served in Orenburg from the beginning of October 1773 till 24th February of the current year, on which date he departed from the city, never again reporting for duty under my command. Further, it has been reported by fugitives that he visited Pugachov in his encampment and rode together with him to Fort Belogorsk, where he had earlier been stationed; as for his conduct, I can—

Here the old man interrupted his reading and said to me grimly, "What can you say in your defence now?"

I was going to continue as I had begun, explaining my relations with Marya Ivanovna just as frankly as I had explained everything else, but suddenly I was overcome by an uncontrollable feeling of disgust. It occurred to me that if I named her, the Commission would summon her to testify: the thought of getting her name entangled with the vile denunciations of scoundrels, and of bringing her here for a confrontation with them, struck me as so horrible that I started to stammer in confusion.

My judges, who seemed to have begun listening to my answers with a little more benevolence, grew prejudiced against me once more as they saw my confusion. The Guards officer requested that I be confronted with the principal witness who had denounced me. The general ordered "yesterday's scoundrel" brought in. I turned towards the door with great interest, awaiting the appearance of my accuser. In a few minutes there was a clanking of chains, the door opened, and Shvabrin entered. I was astonished to see how much he had changed. He was terribly thin and pale. His hair, jet-black only a short while before, had turned entirely grey, and his long beard was dishevelled. He repeated his accusations in a weak but defiant voice. According to his testimony, I had been sent to Orenburg by Pugachov as a spy; had sallied out daily in order to pass written reports to the rebels about conditions in the city; and in the end had openly gone over to the pretender's side, travelling with him from fort to fort and doing everything in my power to cause harm to my fellow traitors so as to occupy their places and gain more favours from the pretender. I listened to him silently and was satisfied on one score: the vile scoundrel had not pronounced the name of Marya Ivanovna. I do not know whether his vanity forbade any thought of the girl who had rejected him with contempt, or whether he harboured in his heart a spark of the same feeling that made me silent – in any case, the name of the Belogorsk commandant's daughter was not mentioned before the Commission. I grew even more firm in my resolve, and when the judges asked me what I had to say in refutation of Shvabrin's testimony, I replied that I wished to stand by my previous statement and had nothing else to add in self-justification. The general ordered us to be conducted from the room. We went out together. I looked at Shvabrin calmly and did not say a single word to him. He broke into a spiteful grin, lifted his shackles and hurried past me. I was led back to prison and was not summoned for further interrogation.

I was not a witness to everything that I still have to relate to the reader, but I have heard it told so many times that even the minutest details have been engraved on my memory, as if I myself had been invisibly present at the events.

My parents received Marya Ivanovna with the sincere cordiality characteristic of people in the olden times. They regarded the opportunity to shelter and comfort the poor orphan as God's blessing. They soon grew genuinely fond of her, for it was impossible not to love her once you came to know her. My father no longer regarded my love as mere folly, and my mother could not wait to see her Petrushka married to the captain's charming daughter.

The whole family was thunderstruck by the news of my arrest. Marya Ivanovna had related my strange acquaintance with Pugachov so innocently that it not only did not worry my parents, but even made them laugh heartily. My father was loath to think that I could possibly have been involved in a vile rebellion aimed at overthrowing the monarchy and exterminating the nobility. He closely interrogated Savelich. My attendant did not conceal that his master had received hospitality from Pugachov, and that the villain had indeed shown him favour, but he swore that there had never been even a suspicion of treason. My old ones felt reassured and waited impatiently for more favourable tidings. Marya Ivanovna was extremely worried, but being endowed with modesty and caution to the highest degree, she kept silent.

A few weeks passed... Then, unexpectedly, my father received a letter from St Petersburg, from our relation Prince B——. The Prince was writing about me. After the usual introductory remarks, he informed my father that the suspicions concerning my participation in the rebels' evil designs had unfortunately proved to be all too well-founded, and that I ought to have been subject to exemplary execution; but the Empress, in consideration of the father's services and advanced years, had pardoned the guilty son, exempting him from shameful execution but ordering him exiled to a distant part of Siberia for permanent settlement.

This unexpected blow almost killed my father. He lost his usual firmness of character, and his sorrow (which he would normally have borne in silence) poured forth in bitter lamentations.

"What!" he would repeat, working himself into a rage. "My son was a party to Pugachov's evil designs! Merciful God, what have I lived to see! The Empress is exempting him from execution! Will that make me feel any easier? It's not the execution that's horrible: one of my forebears was publicly beheaded in Moscow defending his sacred convictions; and my father suffered along with Volynsky and Khrushchov.* But that a nobleman should break his oath and ally himself with brigands, murderers and runaway serfs!… It's a shame and disgrace to our family!"

Alarmed by his despair, my dear mother did not dare weep in his presence and tried to console him by talking about the unreliability of rumours and the fickleness of the world's opinions. But my father was inconsolable.

The person who suffered most, however, was Marya Ivanovna. Convinced that I could have vindicated myself if I had wanted to, she guessed the truth and blamed herself for my misfortune. She concealed her tears and torments from everybody, but incessantly brooded over what means she could employ to rescue me.

One evening my father was sitting on the sofa leafing through the pages of the Court Almanac. His thoughts, however, were far away, and the reading did not produce the usual effect on him. From time to time he would whistle an old military march. My mother was knitting a woollen jersey in silence, occasionally dropping a tear on her work. Suddenly Marya Ivanovna, who was also sitting over her work, declared that her affairs required her to travel to St Petersburg, and asked if they could provide her with the means to undertake the journey. It saddened my mother very much.

"Why do you need to go to St Petersburg?" she asked. "Do you too want to forsake us?"

Marya Ivanovna answered that her whole future depended on this trip, and that she was going to seek protection and help from the powers that be, as the daughter of a man who had suffered for his faithful service.

My father lowered his head: every word that reminded him of his son's presumed crime pained him and sounded like a bitter reproach to him.

"Go, my dear, go," he said with a sigh. "We wouldn't want to stand in the way of your happiness. God grant you a good man, not a publicly dishonoured traitor, for a husband."

He rose and went out of the room.

Left alone with my mother, Marya Ivanovna explained something of her plans to her. Mother embraced her with tears in her eyes and prayed to God for the success of her undertaking. They equipped Marya Ivanovna for the journey, and in a few days she set out, accompanied by her faithful Palasha and by the equally faithful Savelich, who, forcibly separated from me, was comforted by the thought that he was at least serving my betrothed.

Marya Ivanovna arrived safely in Sofiya,* and hearing at the post station that the court currently resided at Tsarskoye Selo, she stopped there. A small space was screened off for her behind a partition. The stationmaster's wife immediately entered into a conversation with her, informing her that she was a niece of the court stoker, and initiating her into all the mysteries of court life. She told her what time the Empress usually woke up, drank her coffee, and went out walking; which dignitaries were currently surrounding her; what she had graciously said over the table the day before; and whom she had received in the evening – to put it briefly, Anna Vlasyevna's conversation was worth several pages of historical memoirs and, if preserved, would have been a precious gift to posterity.

Marya Ivanovna listened to her attentively. They walked out into the park. Anna Vlasyevna related the history of every avenue and every little bridge. Having walked to their hearts' content, they returned to the post station highly satisfied with each other.

The next morning Marya Ivanovna woke early, got dressed and stole out into the park. It was a beautiful morning; the rays of the sun fell on the tops of the lime trees, whose leaves had already turned yellow under autumn's fresh breath. The wide lake glittered motionless. The swans, just awakened, swam out majestically from behind the bushes that overhung the banks. Marya Ivanovna walked round the lovely meadow where a monument commemorating Count Pyotr Alexandrovich Rumyantsev's recent victories had just been erected.* Suddenly a little white dog of English breed ran barking towards her. Frightened, Marya Ivanovna stopped. At the same moment she heard a pleasant feminine voice say, "Don't be afraid; she won't bite you."

Marya Ivanovna caught sight of a lady seated on a bench opposite the monument. She sat down on the other end of the bench. The lady looked at her intently, and on her part Marya

Ivanovna, casting a few oblique glances at her, also managed to size up the lady from head to foot. She wore a white morning dress, a nightcap, and a padded sleeveless jacket. She seemed to be about forty. Her round, rosy cheeks expressed dignity and calm; and her blue eyes, together with the shadow of a smile playing on her lips, were inexpressibly charming. The lady was the first to break the silence.

"You do not live around here, I take it," she said.

"No, ma'am. I arrived from the country only yesterday."

"Did you come with your parents?"

"No, ma'am, I came by myself."

"By yourself! But you're so young!"

"I have neither father nor mother."

"You must have come on some business, of course?"

"Yes, ma'am. I have come to present a petition to the Empress."

"As an orphan, you're probably complaining against injustice and maltreatment?"

"No, ma'am. I have come to ask for mercy, not for justice."

"Allow me to ask, who are you?"

"I am the daughter of Captain Mironov."

"Captain Mironov! The same who was commandant of one of the forts in the Orenburg region?"

"Yes, ma'am."

The lady appeared to be moved.

"Forgive me," she said in an even kinder voice, "if I'm meddling in your affairs, but I'm frequently at court: do tell me what it is you're petitioning for, and perhaps I'll be able to help."

Marya Ivanovna rose to her feet and thanked her respectfully. She was instinctively drawn to this unknown lady, whose every gesture inspired confidence. Marya Ivanovna drew from her pocket a folded piece of paper and handed it to her unknown benefactress, who proceeded to read it to herself.

She began reading with an attentive and benevolent air, but suddenly her countenance changed, and Marya Ivanovna, who had been watching her every movement, was alarmed to see a stern expression come over her features, which had been so pleasant and serene only a moment before.

"So you're interceding for Grinyov?" she asked coldly. "The Empress cannot pardon him. He went over to the pretender, not out of ignorance or gullibility, but as an immoral and dangerous scoundrel."

"Oh, that's not true!" cried Marya Ivanovna.

"What do you mean, 'not true'?" rejoined the lady, colouring.

"It isn't true, God is my witness, it isn't! I know all about it, I'll relate it all to you. Only for my sake did he expose himself to the misfortunes that befell him. And if he didn't vindicate himself before the court, it was only because he didn't want to involve me."

She then ardently related everything that is already known to the reader.

The lady listened to her with attention. Then she asked, "Where are you staying?" When she heard that Marya had put up at Anna Vlasyevna's, she added with a smile, "Oh, yes, I know. Goodbye, and don't tell anyone about our meeting. I hope you won't have to wait long before you receive an answer to your letter."

With these words, she rose and proceeded on through an arbour, while Marya Ivanovna, filled with joyous hope, returned to Anna Vlasyevna's.

Her hostess scolded her for taking an early morning walk in autumn, claiming that it was bad for a young girl's health. She brought in the samovar and was about to embark, over a cup of tea, on her interminable stories about the court when a carriage from the palace drove up to the porch, and the Empress's chamberlain came in to announce that Her Majesty graciously summoned the maiden Mironova to her presence.

Anna Vlasyevna was astonished and fell into a flutter.

"Bless me!" she cried. "Her Majesty is summoning you to court! How did she learn about you? And how can you, my dear child, present yourself before her? I'll warrant you don't even know how to carry yourself at court... Hadn't I better accompany you? I could at least give you a few hints. And how can you go in your travelling robe? Hadn't we better send to the midwife for her yellow dress that's got a hoop skirt?"

The chamberlain declared that it was the Empress's wish that Marya Ivanovna come by herself and in whatever she happened to be wearing. There was no helping it: Marya Ivanovna got into the carriage and set out for the palace, accompanied by Anna Vlasyevna's advice and blessings.

Marya Ivanovna had a presentiment that our fate was about to be decided: her heart throbbed violently and irregularly. In a few minutes the carriage stopped in front of the palace. Marya Ivanovna mounted the stairs with trepidation. The doors opened wide before her. She passed through a long row of magnificent rooms with no one present; the chamberlain showed her the way. At length, when they came to a closed door, he said he would announce her and left her alone.

The thought of finding herself face to face with the Empress frightened her so much that she could hardly stand on her feet. After a moment the door opened, and she was admitted into the Empress's boudoir.

The Empress was sitting at her dressing table. She was surrounded by several courtiers, who respectfully made way for Marya Ivanovna. The Empress turned towards her with a kindly expression, and Marya Ivanovna recognized the lady to whom she had so candidly told her story only a little while before. The Empress bade her come closer and said with a smile:

"I am glad I have been able to keep my word and grant your request. The matter has been seen to. I am convinced of the innocence of your fiancé. Here is a letter; I would be grateful if you would personally deliver it to your future father-in-law."

Marya Ivanovna took the letter with a trembling hand, burst into tears, and fell at the Empress's feet. The latter lifted her up and kissed her. She entered into a conversation with her.

"I know you are not rich," she said, "but you should not worry about the future, for I feel indebted to the daughter of Captain Mironov. I will undertake to see to your welfare."

After making a fuss of the poor orphan, the Empress let her go. Marya Ivanovna left in the same palace carriage she came in. Anna Vlasyevna, who had been waiting for her return with impatience, smothered her with questions but received only inattentive answers. She was dissatisfied with the young woman's inability to recollect details, but she attributed it to her provincial shyness and generously forgave her. Marya Ivanovna set out to return to the country the same day, without so much as taking one curious look at St Petersburg...

* * * * * * *

With this the memoirs of Pyotr Andreyevich Grinyov come to an end. Family tradition has it that he was released from confinement at the end of 1774 on the Sovereign's personal order; and that he was present at the execution of Pugachov, who recognized him in the crowd and acknowledged him with a nod of his head, which in another minute was displayed to the people lifeless and bloodied. Soon afterwards Pyotr Andreyevich married Marya Ivanovna. Their progeny thrives to this day in Simbirsk Province. Thirty versts from —— there is a village that now belongs to ten proprietors.* In one wing of the manor house a letter from Catherine II, written in her own hand, is displayed, framed and glazed. Addressed to Pyotr Andreyevich's father, it vindicates his son and praises the heart and mind of Captain Mironov's daughter. Pyotr Andreyevich Grinyov's manuscript was given to me by one of his grandsons, who had heard that I was engaged in a historical study of the times described by his grandfather. I have decided, with the family's permission, to issue Grinyov's manuscript as a separate publication, choosing an appropriate epigraph for each chapter and taking the liberty of changing some of the proper names.

– The Editor
19th October 1836*

Notes to
The Captain's Daughter

p. 25, *He could be... his father*: From Act III, Sc. 6, of *Khvastun* (*The Braggart*, 1784–85), a comedy by Yakov Borisovich Knyazhnin (1742–91). The first line is spoken by Verkholyot in reference to his rival in love, Zamir. Pretending to be a rich, influential count, Verkholyot claims he could make Zamir a captain of the Guards. The person answering is Cheston, the wise old man of the comedy; what he implies is that serving in the active army would be better for a young man's character. Verkholyot, who does not know that Cheston is Zamir's father, misunderstands Cheston's words and imagines that the old man is siding with him against Zamir.

p. 25, *Count Münnich*: Burkhard Christoph Münnich (1683–1767), a German by birth, came to Russia during the reign of Peter I and was appointed president of the War College by the Empress Anna. He was exiled to Siberia by her successor Elizabeth, but rehabilitated by Peter III. After the palace revolution of 1762, in which Catherine II ousted her husband Peter III, Münnich, having remained loyal to the deposed Tsar, once more lost influence at court.

p. 25, *in 17—*: In the manuscript Pushkin indicated the date of the elder Grinyov's retirement as 1762. That date might have simply referred to Peter III's February 1762 edict exempting the nobility from obligatory state service. But if considered along with the elder Grinyov's association with Münnich, the date 1762 would have suggested that he, too, had adhered to his oath of allegiance to Peter III, which would have explained his reluctance to let his son go to St Petersburg to serve under the "usurper" Catherine II and lent greater poignancy to his son's friendly relations with Pugachov, who claimed to be Peter III. (Peter had actually been killed shortly after the palace coup in 1762, but rumours circulated that he was in hiding, and several impostors appeared, claiming to be the Tsar.)

The reason Pushkin removed the last two digits of the date 1762 from the final version was (as an extant fragment containing his calculation of the young Grinyov's age shows) that if his father had not married until after he retired in 1762, the young Pyotr could not have been sixteen before the Pugachov Rebellion broke out in 1773.

p. 25, *Simbirsk Province*: Simbirsk, now renamed Ulyanovsk after Lenin (born Vladimir Ulyanov), who was born there, is a city on the right bank of the middle Volga, nearly one thousand kilometres east of Moscow.

p. 25, *they registered me as a sergeant in the Semyonovsky Regiment*: Such early registration was advantageous because, for purposes of advancement in rank, years of service were counted from the date of registration. In this way pre-registered sons of noblemen could enter the Guards as officers, without first having to serve in the ranks. The Semyonovsky Regiment, established by Peter I in 1683 in the village of Semyonovskoye, was one of the elite regiments of the Guards.

p. 26, *French, German, and all the sciences*: An ironic allusion to the comedy *Nedorosl* (*The Young Hopeful*, 1782) by Denis Ivanovich Fonvizin (1745–92). In Act I, Sc. 6, the local squire's wife boasts that a German tutor (who had actually been a coachman at home) is teaching her adolescent son "French and all the sciences".

p. 27, *both Russian crosses*: The crosses of St Andrew and St Alexander Nevsky, instituted in 1698 and 1725 respectively.

p. 29, *Orenburg*: A provincial capital and fortress in the southern Urals, on the middle Yaik (now Ural) River. From the Grinyovs' home near Simbirsk it was in the diametrically opposite direction from St Petersburg.

p. 29, *the sovereign to whom you swear allegiance*: Grinyov senior does not mention the current sovereign, Catherine II, by name, perhaps because, remaining privately loyal to her murdered husband Peter III, he continues to regard her as a usurper.

p. 30, *to receive new recruits*: Each landowner was required periodically to surrender a specified number of serfs to the state for military service. These recruits were brought from neighbouring estates to regional centres, where their future commanding officers received them into their units.

p. 31, *kvass*: A lightly alcoholic traditional Russian drink, made from fermented rye flour or bread.

p. 32, *zealous guardian… all my business*: A quotation from the verse epistle 'A Letter to My Servants Shumilov, Vanka and Petrushka' (1769) by Fonvizin (see note to page 26). Fonvizin addressed these words to Mikhail Shumilov, his "dear tutor, instructor and teacher".

p. 34, *Is this my land… tavern liquor*: Adapted from a song first published in a collection by Mikhail Dmitriyevich Chulkov (1743–93) in 1773 and later republished in an enlarged collection by Nikolai Ivanovich Novikov (1744–1818) in 1780. It is probable that Pushkin used Novikov's edition as the source of his song quotations.

p. 39, *a Yaik Cossack by origin*: A Cossack from the region of the Yaik River, which was renamed Ural subsequent to the Pugachov Rebellion. It rises in the Ural mountains and flows south-westwards into the Caspian.

p. 40, *pacified after the revolt of 1772*: The revolt lasted from January 1772 to the summer of the same year. For further details see Chapter I of *A History of Pugachov*.

p. 41, *the Empress Anna's times*: The Empress Anna, daughter of Tsar Ivan V and a niece of Peter the Great, reigned from 1730 to 1740. It was a time when the court and army were dominated by a group of the Empress's German favourites, including Field Marshal Münnich (see note to page 25). General Andrei Karlovich R—— is modelled on Ivan Andreyevich Reinsdorp (1730–1781), military governor of Orenburg Province from 1763 to 1782 (described in detail in *A History of Pugachov*), but in *The Captain's Daughter* Pushkin makes the governor considerably older than Reinsdorp was. In fact, Reinsdorp had joined the Russian army only in 1746, and therefore could not have worn a uniform dating back to the reign of the Empress Anna, nor could he have participated in Münnich's Prussian campaign (1733), to which the elder Grinyov's letter, quoted in the next paragraphs, refers.

p. 42, *Fort Belogorsk*: A fictional location.

p. 42, *Kyrgyz-Kazakh steppes*: An area to the north of the Caspian and to the east of the Yaik River, in what is now Kazakhstan.

p. 44, *In the fort… with lead*: Probably Pushkin's own composition in imitation of soldier songs.

p. 44, *Old-fashioned people, my dear sir*: From Act III, Sc. 5, of Fonvizin's comedy (see note to page 26).

p. 44, *versts*: A verst is an old Russian measurement of distance, equivalent to about 1.06 kilometres or two-thirds of a mile.

p. 45, *Küstrin and Ochakov*: The Prussian fort of Küstrin on the Oder was besieged by the Russian army in 1758; Ochakov, on the Black Sea, was wrested from the Turks by Münnich in 1737, although it was handed back soon afterwards.

p. 45, *a cat's burial*: *The Cat's Burial* was a popular satirical print about Peter the Great. Peter was seen as the cat, being buried by mice representing his opponents. Pugachov claimed to be a successor and namesake of Peter's. Interpreted in this way all of the tawdry pictures on the Mironovs' wall foreshadow events in the novel.

p. 49, *Bashkirs*: A Muslim Turkic people, whose heartlands were in the southern Urals and thereabouts. They were nominally subjects of the Russian empire, but often in revolt.

p. 49, *Kyrgyz:* A nation of Muslim Turkic nomads who roamed the steppe to the southeast of the Urals.

p. 51, *So take up your... the chest!*: An inexact quotation from Act IV, Sc. 12, of the comedy *Chudaki* (*Eccentrics*) (1790) by Knyazhnin (see note to page 25). The scene cited is a comic duel between two servants.

p. 52, *Sumarokov*: Alexandr Petrovich Sumarokov (1717–77) was a prolific poet, popular in his day, but by the end of the eighteenth century considered the epitome of old-fashioned versifying; so his praise for Grinyov's poetry is of dubious value.

p. 52, *the following verses*: These verses ascribed to Grinyov actually come from a collection of songs compiled by Chulkov and published in 1770.

p. 53, *Tredyakovsky*: Vasily Kirillovich Tredyakovsky (1703–68) was both a teacher and a poet. As a poet he was notorious for a heavy and archaic style, so Shvabrin's comment was patently uncomplimentary.

p. 56, *O daughter... gallivant*: From a song, set to music by Ivan Prach, in a collection of Russian folk songs compiled by the poet and polymath Nikolai Alexandrovich Lvov (1753–1803) and published in 1792.

p. 60, *Ah, you maiden... you'll remember*: The two epigraphs both come from folk songs in the collection published by Chulkov in 1770.

p. 66, *a vershok and a half deep*: A *vershok* is an old Russian measure of length equivalent to 4.4 centimetres.

p. 68, *Listen, young lads… will tell*: From a song about the taking of Kazan by Ivan the Terrible that appeared in the collection published by Chulkov in 1770.

p. 69, *schismatic*: That is, a member of the Old Believers, a sect that broke away from the Russian Orthodox Church in the seventeenth century in protest against liturgical reforms introduced under the patriarchate of Nikon (1652–66).

p. 72, *Kalmyk*: The Kalmyks were a race of Buddhist Mongolian nomads, originally from Central Asia, who occupied an area around the lower Volga to the north of the Caspian Sea.

p. 73, *the noble decree… for a long time*: Catherine II was against the use of torture. She abolished it by an unpublished order in 1774, confirmed by a decree of 1782. Her grandson Alexander I reconfirmed the abolition of torture in a decree of 1801, but it continued in use for some time thereafter.

p. 74, *Yakshi*: Bashkir for "very well".

p. 75, *Lower Ozyornaya was taken this morning:* The capture of Lower Ozyornaya, a historical event, is described in Chapter 2 of *A History of Pugachov*.

p. 78, *My head, my poor old head… noose*: From a song about the execution of a leader of the *streltsy* ("musketeers"), a permanent garrison of hereditary infantrymen who guarded the Kremlin and policed Moscow, until they were suppressed by Tsar Peter I at the end of the seventeenth century. The song appeared in Chulkov's collection. The epigraph gains irony from the fact that Pugachov claimed to be Peter's namesake and successor.

p. 79, *Pugach has arrived*: "Pugach" was Pugachov's nickname, bearing an association with the common noun *pugach* – meaning either "toy pistol" or "screech owl" – derived from the verb *pugat* ("to frighten").

p. 82, *offering bread and salt*: A traditional Russian ritual of welcome.

p. 84, *snipping off their locks*: Russian soldiers at this time wore their hair long. They were made to have their hair cut, Cossack-fashion, as a sign that they had joined the rebels.

p. 89, *Count*: Following Pugachov's example of impersonating Tsar Peter III, some of his closest associates took on the titles of aristocrats at the St Petersburg court.

p. 89, *Chumakov:* Fyodor Fedotovich Chumakov was one of Pugachov's aides and his chief of artillery. After Pugachov's final defeat, he captured Pugachov and handed him over to the tsarist authorities, earning a pardon in return.

p. 89, *barge-hauler's song*: A popular folk song that was published in Novikov's collection in 1780.

p. 91, *Grishka Otrepyev... long ago*: The young runaway monk Grishka Otrepyev invaded Russia from Poland in the reign of Boris Godunov (*r.* 1598–1605) claiming to be Crown Prince Dimitry, rightful heir to the Russian throne. This "False Dimitry" gained recognition as tsar after Boris's death, seized Moscow and reigned there for nearly a year before being murdered.

p. 93, *Sweet it's been... part*: From the lyric 'Separation' by the poet and writer Mikhail Matveyevich Kheraskov (1733–1807).

p. 95, *Two dressing gowns... fifteen roubles*: Except for the last item, Savelich's list originates from an actual document Pushkin had come across: a petition that a certain Court Councillor Butkevich had submitted to the government in the hope of receiving compensation for the losses he had suffered during the rebellion.

p. 98, *seized fields... night*: From Canto XI of *Rossiada* (1778), an epic poem by Kheraskov (see note to page 93) about Ivan the Terrible's seizure of Kazan from the Tatars in 1552. Pushkin begins the quotation in the middle of a line, omitting the subject of the sentence – "the Russian Tsar" – because the identification of Pugachov with an actual tsar would have been offensive to the censors, but his readers, brought up on *Rossiada*, would immediately have grasped the reference.

p. 101, *a long confinement within the walls of Orenburg*: The siege of Orenburg lasted from October 1773 to March 1774. It is described in Chapters 3–5 of *A History of Pugachov*.

p. 103, *the fate of Lizaveta Kharlova*: Lizaveta Kharlova was the young and attractive wife of the commandant of Lower Ozyornaya, executed early on in the rebellion by Pugachov. His wife was also subsequently captured by the rebels and forced to become Pugachov's concubine. She was later murdered by Pugachov's associates. For details, see Chapters 2 and 3 of *A History of Pugachov*.

p. 104, *Schelm*: "Rascal" (German).

p. 106, *The lion... engagingly*: These lines, in the style of a Sumarokov fable (see note to page 52), seem to have been written by Pushkin himself.

p. 107, *Berda*: Berda, which Pugachov made his headquarters during the siege of Orenburg, was about seven and a half kilometres from the town.

p. 109, *a blue ribbon draped across his shoulder*: A broad blue ribbon worn across the shoulder was part of the insignia of the Order of St Andrew, the highest Russian imperial decoration, normally awarded to those in the topmost ranks of the nobility.

p. 115, *battle at Yuzeyeva*: Yuzeyeva was a village, about thirty kilometres from Orenburg, where General Vasily Kar, sent by the government to relieve the town, encountered Pugachov. The battle, which took place on 8th November 1773, resulted in the government forces being forced to retreat with heavy losses (greatly exaggerated here, however, by Pugachov). For a description of the battle, see Chapter 3 of *A History of Pugachov*.

p. 115, *Frederick... Fyodorovich*: The reference is to the Prussian King Frederick II "the Great" (*r.* 1740–86). The Russian army was instrumental in defeating him at Kunersdorf (now Polish Kunowice) in 1759. However, later in life Frederick came to be regarded as a military genius, so that Pugachov's demeaning Russification of his name and claim to be able to get the better of him sound particularly arrogant.

p. 116, *this Kalmyk tale*: The tale has not been traced to folklore sources; possibly Pushkin picked it up himself during his visit to the Volga and Ural regions in 1833 to research his *A History of Pugachov*.

p. 117, *As our little... she'll have no one*: A version of a folk song heard and noted down by Pushkin.

p. 124, *Please don't be angry... explanation*: For Knyazhnin, see note to page 25. There is only a distant resemblance between these lines and a couplet in Knyazhnin's comedy *Khvastun*. In reality Pushkin seems to have made up this epigraph in Knyazhnin's style.

p. 128, *Prince Golitsyn... Orenburg*: Prince Pyotr Mikhaylovich Golitsyn (1738–75) defeated Pugachov's forces at Tatishcheva on 22nd March 1774. For an account of this operation and the relief of Orenburg, see Chapter 5 of *A History of Pugachov*.

p. 128, *He re-emerged... villainous acts*: For these events, see Chapters 6–8 of *A History of Pugachov*.

p. 128, *the taking of Kazan... Moscow*: Pugachov seized Kazan on 12th July 1774 and crossed the Volga, apparently to march on Moscow, six days later. The remaining events of the war took place to the west of the Volga.

p. 128, *Zurin received orders to cross the Volga*: The "Omitted Chapter" followed this paragraph in the draft of the novel. See Appendix I.

p. 129, *total defeat... capture*: General Johann von Michelsohn (also, Ivan Ivanovich Mikhelson) (1740–1807) finally crushed the rebels on 25th August 1774 about 110 kilometres from Tsaritsyn (modern Volgograd). The following month Pugachov was betrayed by his associates, handed over to the government and sent to Moscow under strong guard.

p. 129, *Yemelya*: A familiar form of Pugachov's Christian name Yemelyan.

p. 131, *A proverb*: Occurs in *Polnoye sobraniye russkikh poslovits i pogovorok* (*Complete Collection of Russian Proverbs and Sayings*), an 1822 publication of which Pushkin owned a copy.

p. 136, *Volynsky and Khrushchov*: Artemy Petrovich Volynsky (1689–1740) and Andrei Fyodorovich Khrushchov (1691–1740) were both executed in 1740 for opposing the Empress Anna's German favourite, Ernst Johann Biren (1690–1772).

p. 137, *Sofiya*: A township founded by Catherine II in 1780 adjacent to the tsars' summer palace and park south of St Petersburg; it was later amalgamated with a neighbouring settlement as Tsarskoye Selo (now renamed Pushkin). Its mention here is slightly anachronistic.

p. 137, *a monument... erected*: The reference is to the Kagul Obelisk, designed by Antonio Rinaldi (1710–94) and erected in 1771 to commemorate General Pyotr Alexandrovich Rumyantsev's (1725–96) campaign against Turkey in the summer of 1770, which culminated in a Russian victory by the river Kagul in Moldavia.

p. 141, *a village that now belongs to ten proprietors*: This reflects Russian law under the tsars, under which gentry estates were normally divided among all the heirs. Pushkin commented in several writings that ancient families would not have fallen into decline if the law had made the eldest child the only heir (as in Great Britain).

p. 141, *19th October 1836*: A manuscript copy bears the date of 23rd July rather than 19th October. The date given in the publication, however, was the twenty-fifth anniversary of the opening of the Imperial Lycée at Tsarskoye Selo, which Pushkin had entered among the first intake in 1811. He is known to have held fond memories of his time there, and so the date here should probably be interpreted not as the date on which Pushkin finished writing the novel but as a kind of dedication.

Part Two

A History of Pugachov

Introduction

From 1773 to 1775 Russia was beset by a huge revolt that shook the imperial establishment to its very foundations. Led by Yemelyan Pugachov, a Don Cossack pretending to be the deceased husband and predecessor of Catherine II, Peter III, the revolt began among the Cossacks of the Yaik, spread to the peoples of the Urals and then threatened to raise the peasants of the Volga. Regular units of the army had to be called in to suppress it. Later, Pugachov and the movement associated with him (*pugachovshchina*) became bywords for popular discontent, and aroused great fear on several occasions, not least in the early 1830s, when revolutions occurred throughout Europe. This dangerous situation appears to have been an important source of Pushkin's inspiration for the first serious study of the Pugachov Rebellion.

In preparation for this work, Pushkin noted that he read everything printed about the subject that he could find, as well as eighteen large folio volumes of various manuscripts, decrees, reports and so on. He visited the places where the events described by him took place, "checking dead documents against the words of eyewitnesses still alive, if very old, and again checking their fallible memory with historical criticism." In August and September 1833, he took a journey to the Volga and the Orenburg region beyond it, meeting former participants in the revolt and being struck by the "unadorned, simple truth" of what they had to say to him, in contrast to some of the contents of official documents. Their stories, traditions and songs greatly illumined for him episodes in the revolt and the personality of Pugachov. However, these sources were difficult for him to use: valuable and irreplaceable though he found them to be, he also understood the necessity of subjecting them to the strictest verification and circumspection. They were of less restricted use to him in his fictional recreation of the rebellion in *The Captain's Daughter*.

Some of the most important documents, especially the investigation and trial of Pugachov and his principal adherents, were kept inaccessible in the state archive. Moreover, in order to forestall the tsarist censorship, Pushkin restrained himself from comment on some of the critical questions concerning the revolt, such as the reasons for the mass insurgence of the peasantry. Nevertheless, *A History of Pugachov* deserves careful reading as not only the first, but also as a perceptive, study of one of the most significant aspects of the reign of Catherine II.

Andrei Grigoryevich Tartakovsky (*Otechestvennaya Istoriya*, 1, 2, 1999) suggests that Pushkin's study of the Pugachov Rebellion could well have been part of his concern with the eighteenth century as a whole. Moreover, in a draft of the preface to this study, Pushkin did indeed refer to the revolt as "one of the most curious episodes of the reign of Catherine II". And he began the actual Preface, dated 2 November 1833, with the observation that "This historical fragment was to form part of a work that I have now abandoned." A month before that, on 3rd October, one of Pushkin's hosts on a visit to an estate in Simbirsk, Nikolai Mikhaylovich Yazykov, wrote to the historian Mikhail Petrovich Pogodin of his famous guest: "He is breaking into the province of history [...] he intends [...] to write the history of Peter, of Catherine I and further right up to Paul I."

Therefore, Natan Yakovlevich Eidelman hit the nail on the head when he commented that in the early 1830s, when Pushkin was beginning to approach the eighteenth century, first *Pugachov* and *The Bronze Horseman*, then all the previous century became the object of his intense attention: "the tragedy of popular uprising, of [palace] revolts, of [supreme] power, of imposture, of the little man – all this became included in the range of ideas of the poet-historian." And so, to reiterate and emphasize the point made by Tartakovsky and supported by the earlier authority of Georgy Pantaleymonovich Makogonenko, *A History of Pugachov* was conceived as part of a larger work in the autumn of 1833. Moreover, he was now more prepared than ten years previously to give Catherine II a more positive appraisal as a continuer of the work of Peter I, praising her for her civilizing influence and for placing Russia on the threshold of Europe. In such a manner, Tartakovsky argues, Pushkin and other members of his circle were attempting with the most active strata of the nobility to incline the government towards more reforms, to place before it models of an "enlightened", monarchical state which could change the outlook of Nicholas I and his regime. The aggravation of the peasant question, even the threat of a new *pugachovshchina* against the background of the European revolutions of 1830–31, occupied Pushkin's mind to a considerable extent as he considered the original Pugachov Revolt.

What of the Emperor himself? On 6th December 1833, Pushkin made the request via the police chief, General Benckendorff, for the scrutiny of his work at the highest level. "I do not know if it will be possible for me to publish it," he wrote, "but I dare to hope that this historical fragment will be of interest to His Majesty, particularly in relation to the military actions of that time which have been hitherto poorly known." Early in the new year, at a court ball, Nicholas himself talked to Pushkin about the work, of which he had read the first volume, that is Chapters I to V. On 28th February 1834, Pushkin noted that the Sovereign had returned his manuscript with "businesslike" comments. About a third of them are stylistic or factual, and the overall intention could be characterized as to give the work a dry, straightforward aspect, removing all traces of an emotional evaluation of the revolt, especially of any sympathy for Pugachov himself or for his seventeenth-century predecessor Stenka Razin. Other deletions concern some of the difficulties experienced by the detachments of the army sent to suppress the revolt. A description of a church desecrated by the insurgents was also removed to protect the sensitivities of the spiritual authorities. Nicholas I added the imperial title to a mention of his brother Alexander I, and changed the word 'promoted' to 'appointed' to describe the unofficial elevation to rank of colonel of one of Pugachov's henchmen. These last two changes were in line with the Tsar's later order to change the title of the work from *A History of Pugachov* to *A History of the Pugachov Rebellion* with the observation that "a criminal such as Pugachov has no history". Generally speaking, however, his emendations of the manuscript of Pushkin's work concerned specific details rather than the general line, lending support to the observation of Tatyana Grigoryevna Zenger-Tsyavlovskaya, made in 1934, that the Tsar had acted less as censor and more as editor.

A hundred years before, at the end of 1834, *A History of the Pugachov Rebellion* was produced by the state printer and published "with the permission of the government". But many members of the Tsar's entourage were far from happy with the book's appearance. In late February 1835 Pushkin wrote in his diary that it was subject to much abuse. In particular, he observed, "Uvarov is a great scoundrel. He rails against my book as a subversive work". Now if Count Sergei Semyonovich Uvarov, minister of education from 1833 to 1849, and deviser of Russian nationalism's slogan "Orthodoxy, autocracy, nationality", adopted such a negative attitude to *A History of Pugachov*, this suggests a gulf on the subject between Nicholas I and his entourage. In other words, there was some justification for the observation of the early doyen of Soviet history, Mikhail Nikolayevich Pokrovsky: "Pugachov played a well-defined part on the chessboard of Nicholas, to frighten the landlords who did not want to yield any of their rights to the serfs." How ironic that Pokrovsky should take a more liberal view of Nicholas I than the post-Soviet Tartakovsky, whose analysis we have already considered, or the contemporary American academic Svetlana Evdokimova whose analysis we are about to consider.

Inevitably, *A History of Pugachov* and *The Captain's Daughter* demand comparison. On this point, Evdokimova reminds us in her book *Pushkin's Historical Imagination* (Yale UP, 1999) that the question of the relationship between history and fiction goes back as least as far as Aristotle, but has a peculiar relevance in the Russian context. As far as the early nineteenth century is concerned, the characteristics of European Romantic historiography – "a desire to supplement the traditional skills of the neoclassical historian, such as erudition and critical judgement, with creative myth-making and poetic insight" – were deeply rooted in Russian cultural tradition. In particular, the figure of the poet-historian, which it advanced, was especially appropriate for Pushkin, who was particularly interested in the relationship between history and imagination. While taking due cognizance of the postmodernist update of the argument that "there can be no objective historiography, and, therefore, a mythic or poetic consciousness lies behind all representations of reality", Evdokimova bases her approach on an analogy with physics, in particular with the concept of complementarity in quantum theory. While the picture of a particle, substance confined to a very small volume, and that of a wave, a field spread out over a larger space, are mutually exclusive, to quote Heisenberg, "going from one picture to the other and back again, we finally get the right impression of the strange kind of reality behind our atomic experiments". As with the dualism of particles and waves, so with the dualism between two different descriptions of the same reality in history and fiction.

Pushkin, Evdokimova claims, "did not believe in Truth, but in truths". Rejecting the views that *A History of Pugachov* and *The Captain's Daughter* should be read in tandem, and that the different approaches in the two works are the consequence of the aim of history to seek knowledge and the aim of fiction to achieve reconciliation, she argues that the "idealization" of Pugachov in the novel is the consequence of the fact that the impostor is seen through the eyes of the fictitious narrator, Pyotr Grinyov. Pushkin's characterization follows a pattern established by Walter Scott in his historical novels, which often depict "the middle of the road hero's spilt loyalties and his mediating role in the struggle between the two antagonistic camps" but also provide "a sub-plot that could be characterized as a duel of honour". Moreover, in Evdokimova's view, "the softening of the rebel's portrayal could be dictated by aesthetic considerations, and one should remember that in the novel, Pugachov appears both as a private and historical personage." In other words, "imagination" was at work in *The Captain's Daughter* while "history" ruled over *A History of Pugachov*.

For Evdokimova, "Pushkin does not privilege one kind of writing over the other, the trap that most theoreticians of both history and fiction rarely manage to avoid. Neither poet nor historian, according to Pushkin, can portray the way things really happened." She goes on to assert that "each genre, therefore, established the limits of context." However, like Tartakovsky, Evdokimova also seeks to place Pushkin's work in a social context. She quotes the French historian Augustin Thierry: "Bourgeois historiography is truth, not ideology, and it is so because the triumph of the bourgeoisie is the fulfilment of reason, of the universal, in history." But Thierry also celebrated the importance of Walter Scott as a master of historical divination, or insight, maintaining that "there is more true history in his novels of England and Scotland than in many compilations that still go by the name of histories." Pushkin agreed with Thierry about Scott, but could not emulate him and his colleagues in giving a central role in history to the French Revolution and the later development of liberal institutions through the agency of the middle class. "Instead," Evdokimova says, "he turned to the Russian past, in search of another 'formula' of Russian history, to the Russian *dvoryanstvo* [nobility] as a leading force in its historical development, and to the Russian revolution – that of Peter the Great." In Pushkin's view, only the nobility could limit the absolutism of the tsars. Here again, Evdokimova agrees with Tartakovsky. But she goes on to note that, because of the undeveloped nature of Russian society, the role of the individual and therefore of chance played a greater role for Pushkin in Russian history that in the history of other European countries.

Chance plays an important part in *The Captain's Daughter*. Yet Pushkin's invention of Grinyov as a narrator emphasizes the separate nature of fiction. On the other hand, in search for the character and motivation of the pretender, the passage in the novel where the pretender says that it is already too late for repentance is persuasive:

> "Listen," said Pugachov with frenzied inspiration. "I'll tell you a tale that I heard from an old Kalmyk woman when I was a child. Once the eagle asked the raven, 'Tell me, raven-bird, why is it that you live three hundred years in this bright world, and I am allotted only three and thirty?' 'The reason is, my friend,' answered the raven, 'that you drink live blood while I feed on carrion.' The eagle thought, 'Why don't we try the same food?' Very well. Off flew the eagle and the raven. Suddenly they saw a

fallen horse; they came down and settled on it. The raven started tearing at it, praising it. The eagle pecked at it once, pecked at it twice, then flapped its wings and said to the raven, 'No, friend raven: rather than live on carrion for three hundred years, I'll choose one drink of living blood, then take what God brings.' "

It might seem strange to follow the observation that the novel itself cannot help us in our search for the historical Pugachov with the suggestion that we might find inspiration in the words of the eagle as reported by the old Kalmyk woman to the fictional pretender, who relays them to the fictional hero of the novel. But one has to recall the epigraph of *A History of Pugachov*. Archimandrite Platon Lyubarsky was surely justified in his observation that not only historians but also Pugachov himself would not be able to achieve an adequate description of the man and the movement associated with him. In the face of such an impossibility, to dispense with the imagination of the poet-historian might be ill-advised.

The Kalmyk story was almost certainly one of the items collected by Pushkin in his research trip of August and September 1833, and among the material which he could not use in his historical account. Had he been less aware of the restrictions placed on the historian by rules of evidence, or on any writer by the tsarist censorship, Pushkin's work on the revolt of 1773–75 might have been published in a different form. But what we have remains as the most complete exercise of the great man in a genre to which he might have turned increasingly, had his life not been brought to its untimely end. *A History of Pugachov* is of abiding interest, not only for its place in the overall oeuvre but also for its own intrinsic value.

– Professor Paul Dukes

A HISTORY OF PUGACHOV

(1834)

Preface

This historical fragment was to form part of a work that I have now abandoned. In it I have brought together everything about Pugachov that the government has made public and everything that I have found trustworthy in the foreign authors writing about him. I have also had the opportunity to make use of some manuscripts, oral traditions, and accounts of eyewitnesses still alive.

The Pugachov file, still sealed as of now, used to be kept at the State Archives in St Petersburg, among other important documents that were at one time secret government papers but have subsequently become source materials for the historian. On ascending the throne, His Imperial Majesty issued a decree to have these documents put in order. These treasures were then brought out from the cellars, where they had been flooded several times and nearly destroyed.

The future historian who has permission to unseal the Pugachov file will easily correct and augment my work* – which is of necessity imperfect, though conscientious. A page of history on which one encounters the names of Catherine, Rumyantsev, the two Panins, Suvorov, Bibikov, Michelsohn, Voltaire, and Derzhavin must not be lost for posterity.

– A. Pushkin
2nd November 1833, Village of Boldino

To render a proper account of all the schemes and adventures of this bandit would, it seems to me, be almost impossible, not only for an average historian, but even for a superlative one. He is a man whose undertakings depended, not on rational considerations or military planning, but on daring, chance and good fortune. For this reason (I believe) Pugachov himself would not be in a position to recount the details of these undertakings, or even to recall a significant portion of them, since they were initiated, not just by him directly, but by his many undisciplined and foolhardy accomplices in several locations at once.

– Archimandrite Platon Lyubarsky*

Chapter I

THE ORIGIN OF THE YAIK COSSACKS – A POETIC LEGEND – THE TSAR'S CHARTER – PIRACY ON THE CASPIAN SEA – STENKA RAZIN – NECHAY AND SHAMAY – PETER THE GREAT'S INTENTIONS – INTERNAL DISTURBANCES – THE FLIGHT OF A NOMADIC PEOPLE – THE YAIK COSSACKS' MUTINY – THEIR SUPPRESSION

THE YAIK RIVER, renamed the Ural by decree of Catherine II, issues from the mountains that have given it its present name. It flows southward along the mountain range to the place where Orenburg was originally founded and where Fort Orsk is now located. Here it turns to the west, cutting through the rocky mountain ridge, and follows a course of more than 2,600 kilometres to the Caspian Sea. It irrigates part of Bashkiria; it serves as the south-eastern boundary of almost all of Orenburg Province; the trans-Volga steppes stretch up to its right bank; and from the left bank extends the gloomy wilderness where untamed tribes known to us as the Kyrgyz-Kazakhs lead their nomadic existence. Its current is swift; its murky waters abound in fish of all kinds; its banks are mostly of clay or sand, unforested, but, in the flood plains, suitable for cattle-raising. Near its delta it is overgrown with tall reeds – a hiding place for boars and tigers.

On this river in the fifteenth century there appeared Cossacks from the Don, who had been ranging over the Khvalynian Sea.*[1] They spent the winters on its banks, at that time still wooded and safe in their remoteness. They put out to sea again in the spring, plundered until late autumn and returned to the Yaik with the onset of winter. Moving farther and farther upstream from one place to the next, they at last chose for permanent settlement the strongpoint of Kolovratnoye, just over sixty kilometres from today's Uralsk.

In the neighbourhood of the new settlers some Tatar families were roaming. They had detached themselves from the nomad camps of the Golden Horde and were seeking free pastures on the banks of the same Yaik. At first the two races were at enmity, but with the passage of time they entered into friendly dealings: the Cossacks began to take wives from the Tatar camps. According to a poetic legend, the Cossacks, passionately attached as they were to unmarried life, resolved among themselves that each time they embarked on a new campaign they would kill all the newborn infants and abandon their wives. One of their hetmen, by the name of Gugnya, was the first to take pity on his young wife and break this cruel resolution; the rest of the Cossacks, following his example, submitted to the yoke of family life. To this day the people living on the banks of the Ural, by now civilized and hospitable, drink to the health of Grandmother Gugnikha at their feasts.[2]

Living by plunder and surrounded by hostile tribes, the Cossacks felt the need for a powerful protector, and during the reign of Tsar Mikhail they sent an envoy to Moscow with the request that the Sovereign take them under his sublime protection. Settling the Cossacks on the unclaimed lands along the Yaik could be seen as a territorial conquest of conspicuous importance. The Tsar received his new subjects kindly and presented them with a charter[3] for the Yaik River, granting it to them from its upper reaches to its delta, and permitting them to "make their living as free people".

The Yaik Cossacks grew rapidly in number. They continued to range across the Caspian Sea, joining up with the Don Cossacks to raid Persian merchant ships and plunder coastal settlements. The Shah complained to the Tsar. Letters of admonition were sent from Moscow to both the Don and the Yaik.

The Cossacks set off up the Volga to Nizhny Novgorod in boats still loaded with loot. From there they proceeded to Moscow and presented themselves at court, pleading guilty and each carrying an axe with an executioner's block. They were sent to Poland and to Riga in order to earn pardon for their misdeeds. Some *streltsy*[*] were dispatched to the Yaik, where they later merged into a single tribe with the Cossacks.

Stenka Razin* visited the settlements along the Yaik. According to the testimony of the chronicles, the Cossacks received him as an enemy. Their town was taken by this daring rebel, and the *streltsy* stationed there were either slain or drowned.[4]

According to tradition, confirmed by a Tatar chronicler, the campaigns of two Yaik hetmen, Nechay and Shamay,[5] took place in this same period. The first, having collected a band of volunteers, went to Khiva* in the hope of rich loot. Luck was on his side. After a difficult journey the Cossacks reached Khiva. The Khan with his army was away at war just then. Nechay occupied the city, meeting no resistance; but he overstayed and set out for the return march too late. Loaded down with loot, the Cossacks were overtaken by the Khan who had returned home; they were defeated and annihilated on the bank of the Syr Darya. No more than three returned to the Yaik with the news that the brave Nechay had perished. A few years later another hetman, named Shamay, set out in the tracks of the first. But he was taken captive by the Kalmyks of the steppe. Meanwhile, his Cossacks proceeded farther, lost their way, and never reached Khiva, arriving instead at the Aral Sea, on whose shore they were forced to spend the winter. Hunger overtook them. The luckless adventurers killed and ate one another. The majority perished. The survivors at last sent a message to the Khan of Khiva, asking him to receive them and save them from starvation. The Khivans came out for them, captured them all, and took them back as slaves to their city, where they disappeared. As for Shamay, the Kalmyks brought him back to the Yaik Host a few years later, probably for a ransom. After this, the Cossacks lost their taste for far-flung campaigns. They gradually grew accustomed to civic and family life.

The Yaik Cossacks obediently carried out military service according to the instructions they had received from Moscow, but at home they preserved their original mode of government. Complete equality of rights; hetmen and elders elected by the community as executors of communal resolutions during their period of office; circles, or meetings, at which each Cossack had a free voice and where all public issues were decided by majority vote; no written resolutions; "into sack and water" for treason, cowardice, murder and theft – these were the main features of their polity.[6] To the simple, crude laws brought along from the Don the Yaik Cossacks added others of local importance relating to fishing, which was the main source of their revenue, and to the procedure for enlisting the necessary number of Cossacks for military service – extremely complex arrangements, which were defined with the greatest attention to detail.[7]

Peter the Great introduced the first measures for integrating the Yaik Cossacks into the general system of government by the state. In 1720 the Yaik Host was put under the authority of the War College. The Cossacks rioted and burnt their town with the intention of fleeing into the Kyrgyz steppes, but were brutally brought to heel by Colonel Zakharov. A census was taken, services were defined, and wages were set. The Sovereign appointed the hetman of the Host himself.

Under the reigns of the Empresses Anna and Elizabeth, the government's policy was to complete the measures initiated by Peter. This was facilitated by the discord that had arisen between the Host's hetman Merkuryev and its elder Loginov, dividing the Cossacks into two factions: the hetman's on the one hand and Loginov's, or the people's, on the other. In 1740 it was decided that the Yaik Host's internal administration should be reorganized, and Neplyuyev, the governor of Orenburg at the time, submitted new arrangements in draft to the War College. For the most part, however, the plans and directives were not carried out until the accession to the throne of the Empress Catherine II.

As early as 1762 the Yaik Cossacks of the Loginov faction began complaining about oppressive measures taken by the chancery officials whom the government had imposed on the Host: they complained about the withholding of prescribed wages, about arbitrary taxes, and about infringements of ancient fishing rights and customs. The civil servants sent to investigate their complaints were either unable or unwilling to placate them. The Cossacks rose in revolt several times, and Major-Generals Potapov and Cherepov (the first in 1766, the second in 1767) were obliged to resort to force of arms and to the terror of executions. An investigating commission was set up in Yaitsk Township. Among its members were Major-Generals Potapov, Cherepov, Brümfeld and Davydov, and Captain of the Guards Chebyshov. The Host's hetman, Andrei Borodin, was dismissed; Pyotr Tambovtsev was elected in his place; and the chancery officials were enjoined to pay the Host, over and above the sums withheld, a considerable sum of compensation. The officials, however, managed to evade obeying this injunction. The Cossacks did not lose heart: they attempted to bring their legitimate complaints to the attention of the Empress herself. But the men they sent on this secret mission were arrested in St Petersburg on the orders of Count Chernyshov, president of the War College; they were put in fetters and punished as mutineers. Meanwhile, an order was issued to detail several hundred Cossacks for service in Kizlyar.* The local authorities used this opportunity to take new oppressive measures against the people in revenge for their resistance. It became known that the government intended to form the Cossacks into cavalry squadrons, and that orders had already been given to have their beards shaved. Major-General Traubenberg, who had been sent to Yaitsk for this purpose, found himself the target of popular indignation. The Cossacks were in a state of turmoil. At last, in 1771, mutiny burst out with full force.

What set it off was an event of importance in its own right. Peaceful Kalmyks, who had come from the borders of China at the beginning of the eighteenth century to live under the white Tsar's protection, were roaming over the immense steppes of Astrakhan and Saratov, in the region between the Volga and the Yaik. Ever since their arrival they had served Russia faithfully, guarding her southern borders. Russian police officials, taking advantage of their lack of sophistication and their remoteness from the central institutions of government, began to oppress them. The complaints of these peaceable and well-meaning people did not reach the higher administration. At last, having lost their patience, they decided to leave Russia and entered into secret contacts with the Chinese government. It was easy for them to move right up to the bank of the Yaik without arousing suspicion. Then, suddenly, thirty thousand wagonloads of them forded the river and set out across the Kyrgyz steppes towards the boundaries of their former homeland.[8] The government took hasty measures to stop the unexpected flight. The Yaik Host was ordered to pursue the fugitives, but the Cossacks (with very few exceptions) failed to obey and openly refused to perform any military service.

The local authorities resorted to the strictest measures to end the mutiny, but by now no punishment could subdue the embittered Cossacks. On 13th January 1771 they gathered in the town square, took the icons from the church, and went, under the leadership of the Cossack Kirpichnikov, to the house of Captain of the Guards Durnovo, who was in Yaitsk at the time in connection with the business of the investigating commission. They demanded the dismissal of the chancery officials and the payment of withheld wages. Major-General Traubenberg confronted them with troops and cannon, and ordered them to disperse, but neither his commands nor the remonstrances of the hetman had any effect. Traubenberg gave orders to open fire; the Cossacks rushed the cannon. A battle ensued; the mutineers gained the upper hand. Traubenberg tried to flee but was killed at the gate of his house; Durnovo was covered with wounds, Tambovtsev hanged, the chancery officials put under arrest, and new officials appointed in their place.

The mutineers were triumphant. They sent elected representatives to St Petersburg to explain and justify the bloody incident. Meanwhile, Major-General von Freymann had been dispatched from Moscow with a company of grenadiers and artillery to subdue them. Freymann arrived in Orenburg in the spring, waited there until the rivers subsided, and then, taking two light field detachments and a few Cossacks with him, went on to Yaitsk.[9] The mutineers, numbering 3,000, came out to face him: the two sides met at a point some seventy-five kilometres from the town. Fierce battles took place on 3rd and 4th June. Freymann cleared his path with grapeshot. The mutineers galloped home, collected their wives and children, and started crossing the Chagan River with the intention of escaping to the Caspian Sea. Freymann, who entered the town right on their heels, managed to keep the populace in by threats and remonstrances. Those who had already left were pursued and captured almost to a man. An investigating commission was set up in Orenburg under the chairmanship of Colonel Neronov. A good many of the mutineers were taken there. Since the prisons were overflowing, some were kept in booths in the cash and exchange markets. The earlier Cossack administration was liquidated. Authority was placed in the hands of the Yaik commandant, Lieutenant Colonel Simonov. The Host elder Martemyan Borodin and the other (civil) elder, Mostovshchikov, were ordered to attend his office. The ringleaders of the riot were whipped; about 140 people were exiled to Siberia; others were conscripted (NB: all of them deserted); the rest were pardoned and made to take a second oath of allegiance. Outwardly these strict and necessary measures restored order, but the peace was fragile. "Just watch out," the pardoned mutineers kept saying, "see what a shock we'll give Moscow." The Cossacks were still divided into two factions: the acquiescent and the dissident (or, as the War College aptly translated these terms, the obedient and the disobedient). Secret conferences took place at wayside *umyots*[10] and remote farmsteads across the steppe. Everything portended a new mutiny. Only a leader was missing. A leader was found.

Chapter II

PUGACHOV'S ARRIVAL ON THE SCENE – HIS ESCAPE FROM KAZAN – KOZHEVNIKOV'S TESTIMONY – THE PRETENDER'S FIRST SUCCESSFUL STEPS – THE ILEK COSSACKS' TREASON – THE TAKING OF FORT RASSYPNAYA – NUR-ALI KHAN – MEASURES TAKEN BY REINSDORP – THE TAKING OF LOWER OZYORNAYA – THE TAKING OF TATISHCHEVA – THE COUNCIL IN ORENBURG – THE TAKING OF CHERNORECHENSKAYA – PUGACHOV IN SAKMARSK

At this uneasy time an unknown vagrant was roaming from one Cossack homestead to another, taking jobs now with this, now with that master, and putting his hand to all manner of trades.[1] Having witnessed the suppression of the mutiny and the chastisement of its ringleaders, he went to a schismatic community on the Irgiz for a while. This community sent him at the end of 1772 to buy a supply of fish in Yaitsk, where he stayed at the house of the Cossack Denis Pyanov. He was noted for the boldness of his utterances – for heaping abuse on the authorities and inciting the Cossacks to flee to the lands of the Turkish Sultan. He claimed that the Don Cossacks would not take long to follow them, that at the border he had 200,000 roubles in cash and 70,000 roubles' worth of goods in readiness, and that some pasha or other was to supply the Cossacks with 5,000,000 after their arrival, until which time he had promised to pay each of them a monthly wage of twelve roubles. Further, the vagrant claimed that two regiments had set out from Moscow against the Yaik Cossacks, and that an uprising around Christmas or Epiphany was inevitable. Some of the "obedient" Cossacks wanted to arrest him and hand him over as a rabble-rouser to the commandant's chancery, but he vanished, along with Denis Pyanov, and was caught only later in the village of Malykovka (today's Volgsk),* on the information of a peasant with whom he had travelled the same road.[2] This vagrant was Yemelyan Pugachov, a Don Cossack and schismatic who had come from Poland with false documents, intending to settle among the schismatics living on the Irgiz River. Taken into custody, he was conveyed first to Simbirsk and then to Kazan; and since anything concerning the affairs of the Yaik Host could appear significant in the circumstances of the time, the governor of Orenburg deemed it necessary to send a report about his arrest, dated 18th January 1773, to the State War College.

Mutineers from the Yaik region were no rarity in those days, and so the Kazan authorities paid no particular attention to the offender sent to them. Pugachov was not confined with any greater strictness than other prisoners. Meanwhile his followers were not asleep. One day, escorted by two soldiers of the garrison, he was walking about town collecting alms. In Zamochnaya Reshotka (as one of the main streets of Kazan used to be called) stood a troika in readiness. Pugachov stepped up to it and, suddenly pushing one of his escorts aside, got into the covered wagon aided by the other, and the two of them went galloping out of town together. This happened on 19th June 1773. Three days later there was received in Kazan St Petersburg's confirmation of Pugachov's sentence – flogging and exile to Pelym for penal servitude.[3]

Pugachov turned up on the farmlands of a retired Cossack, Danila Sheludyakov, for whom he had previously worked as a farmhand. That is where the conspirators' deliberations took place.

At first the possibility of fleeing to Turkey – an idea long entertained by all discontented Cossacks – was discussed. Under the reign of the Empress Anna, as is well known, Ignaty Nekrasov put that idea into practice, drawing after him a large number of Don Cossacks.* Their descendants are still living in territories under Turkish rule, preserving in an alien country the faith, language and customs of their former homeland. In the last Turkish war they fought forlornly against us. Some of them came to the Emperor Nicholas after he had crossed the Danube in a Zaporozhian boat: like the remaining Zaporozhian Cossacks, they pleaded guilty in the name of their fathers and returned to the suzerainty of their legitimate monarch.*

But the Yaik conspirators were too strongly attached to their bountiful native riverbanks. Instead of fleeing, they decided on a fresh uprising. Imposture, they thought, would be a reliable motive force. All it required was a bold and resolute rascal not yet known to the people. Their choice fell on Pugachov.* It did not take long to persuade him. They immediately started recruiting followers.

The War College circulated information about the Cossack convict's escape in all the locations where it was thought he might be hiding. Lieutenant Colonel Simonov soon learnt that the fugitive had been seen on farmsteads around Yaitsk. Detachments were sent to capture Pugachov, but they had no success. Pugachov and his chief associates eluded their pursuers by moving from one place to another, all the while augmenting their band. In the meantime strange rumours were spreading... Many Cossacks were put under arrest. Mikhaylo Kozhevnikov was captured and brought to the commandant's chancery, where the following important testimony was extracted from him by torture:

> At the beginning of September he was on his farm when Ivan Zarubin came to him and told him confidentially that a highborn person was staying in their region. He asked Kozhevnikov to shelter this person on his farm. Kozhevnikov agreed. Zarubin left and returned that night just before dawn with Timofei Myasnikov and a stranger, all three on horseback. The stranger was of medium height, broad-shouldered, and lean. He had a black beard just beginning to turn grey. He wore a camel-skin coat and a blue Kalmyk hat, and was armed with a rifle. Zarubin and Myasnikov left for the town *in order to notify the people*, while the stranger, remaining at Kozhevnikov's, informed him that he was the Emperor Peter III, that the rumours about his death had been false, and that, with the help of the officer guarding him, he had escaped to Kiev, where he had remained in hiding for about a year.* Then he had spent some time in Constantinople and had served in the Russian army, under an assumed identity, during the last Turkish war. From there he had gone to the Don region; he had subsequently been captured in Tsaritsyn, but was soon liberated by his faithful Cossacks. He had spent the last year on the

Irgiz and in Yaitsk, where he had been arrested and subsequently taken to Kazan. Once again, he had been set free by his guard, who had been bribed with seven hundred roubles by an unknown merchant. After his escape, he had headed for Yaitsk, but, having heard from a woman that identity certificates were being very strictly demanded and scrutinized, he had turned back and had taken the highway towards Syzran. He had drifted about on this highway until at last being picked up by Zarubin and Myasnikov at the Talovin *umyot* and brought to Kozhevnikov.

Having told his preposterous story, the pretender began laying out his plans. In order to circumvent the garrison's resistance and to avoid *unnecessary bloodshed*, he would not reveal his identity until after the Cossack Host had left for the *surge* (the autumn fishing season). He would appear among the Cossacks during the fishing expedition, have the hetman tied up, head straight for Yaitsk, occupy it, and post guards on each highway, so that the news about him would not spread prematurely. Failing to accomplish this, he intended to *fall upon Old Russia*, win it all over to his side, appoint new judges everywhere (for in those presently in office he had observed, as he said, much injustice), and place the Crown Prince on the throne.* *As for myself*, he said, *I no longer wish to reign*. Pugachov spent three days at Kozhevnikov's farm, after which Zarubin and Myasnikov came to take him to Usikhina Rossash, where he was planning to hide until the fishing season. Kozhevnikov, Konovalov and Kochurov accompanied him.

The arrest of Kozhevnikov and of the Cossacks who were implicated by this testimony hastened the unfolding of events. On 18th September Pugachov made his way from the Budarino outpost[4] to the vicinity of Yaitsk with a mob numbering 300; he stopped at a distance of three kilometres from the town, beyond the Chagan River.

The town was thrown into confusion. Inhabitants, only recently pacified, began crossing over to the side of the new rebels. Simonov sent a force of five hundred Cossacks, reinforced by infantry and two pieces of artillery, and under the command of Major Naumov, to confront Pugachov. Two hundred of the Cossacks, with Captain Krylov in charge, were sent forward as a vanguard. They were met by a Cossack holding a seditious manifesto from the pretender* above his head. Krylov's Cossacks demanded that the manifesto be read aloud to them. Krylov refused. A mutiny followed, with half the detachment deserting to the pretender's side and dragging along fifty loyal Cossacks by the bridles of their horses. Seeing this treason among his troops, Naumov returned to the town. The Cossacks who had been seized were led before Pugachov, who ordered eleven of them hanged. These first victims of Pugachov's were: Lieutenants Vitoshnov, Chertorogov, Rainev and Konovalov; Sub-Lieutenants Ruzhenikov, Tolstov, Podyachev and Kolpakov; and Privates Sidorovkin, Larzyanev and Chukalin.

The next day Pugachov approached the town, but when he saw troops coming out to meet him, he began retreating, scattering his band across the steppe. Simonov did not pursue him because he did not wish to detach any Cossacks, fearing their betrayal, and he did not dare move the infantry any distance from the town, whose inhabitants were on the verge of revolt. He sent a report about all of this to the governor of Orenburg, Lieutenant General Reinsdorp, asking him for a troop of light cavalry that could pursue Pugachov. But direct communication with Orenburg had already been severed, and Simonov's report did not reach the governor for a whole week.

With his band multiplied by new rebels, Pugachov headed straight for Ilek,[5] sending its commandant, Hetman Portnov, an order to meet him outside the fort and join forces with him. He promised the Cossacks to grant them their cross and their beards (all the Ilek Cossacks, like their Yaik brethren, were Old Believers),* and their rivers, meadows, wages and provisions, lead and gunpowder, and freedom in perpetuity. In case of disobedience he threatened revenge. Faithful to his duty, the hetman tried to resist, but the Cossacks tied him up and received Pugachov with pealing bells and bread and salt. Pugachov hanged the hetman, celebrated his victory for three days; then, taking all the Ilek Cossacks and the garrison cannon with him, he marched on Fort Rassypnaya.[6]

The forts erected in that region were no more than villages enclosed by wattle or wooden fences. They were enough to safeguard a few aging soldiers and local Cossacks under the protection of two or three cannon from the arrows and lances of the nomadic tribes that roamed the steppes of Orenburg Province and its frontier lands. On 24th September Pugachov besieged Rassypnaya. The Cossacks deserted here too. The fort was taken. The commandant, Major Velovsky, a few officers and a priest were hanged; and the garrison platoon and 150 or so Cossacks joined the insurgents.

News of the pretender spread quickly. While still at the Budarino outpost, Pugachov had written to the Kyrgyz-Kazakh Khan, signing himself Emperor Peter III and demanding the Khan's son as a hostage along with an auxiliary corps of one hundred men. Nur-Ali Khan went to Yaitsk under the pretext of discussions with the authorities and offered them his services. They thanked him and answered that they hoped they could cope with the rebels without his help. The Khan sent the governor of Orenburg a copy of the pretender's letter in Tatar, in which he first announced his appearance. "We steppe-dwellers," Nur-Ali wrote to the governor, "do not know who this person is, riding about the riverbanks: is he an imposter or the real sovereign? Our envoy came back declaring he had learnt nothing except that the man had a light brown beard." Using this opportunity, the Khan demanded that the governor return the hostages he was holding, the cattle that had been driven off the Kyrgyz lands, and the slaves who had run away from the Horde. Reinsdorp hastened to reply that the death of the Emperor Peter III was common knowledge throughout the world and that he, Reinsdorp, had himself seen the Sovereign in his coffin and kissed his dead hand. He admonished the Khan to hand the pretender over to the government if he should happen to flee to the Kyrgyz steppes, assuring him of Empress's favour in return. The Khan's requests were complied with. Meanwhile Nur-Ali entered into friendly exchanges with the pretender, while ceaselessly assuring Reinsdorp of his loyalty to the Empress; at the same time the Kyrgyz were getting ready to attack.

Right after the communication from the Khan reached Orenburg, the report from the Yaik commandant, sent via Samara, was received. Soon Velovsky's report about the taking of Ilek arrived too. Reinsdorp hastened to take measures to put an end to the incipient disorder. He directed Brigadier Baron von Bülow to set out from Orenburg with four hundred infantry and horse and six field-pieces, and to head for Yaitsk, collecting more people from outposts and forts on the way. The commander of the Upper Ozyornaya fortified zone,[7] Brigadier Baron Korff, was ordered to come to Orenburg as fast as possible, and Lieutenant Colonel Simonov was to send Major Naumov with a field detachment and Cossacks to join Bülow. The chancery at Stavropol was instructed to supply Simonov with five hundred armed Kalmyks.[8] The Bashkirs and Tatars living in the vicinity were to assemble a corps of one thousand men with the greatest possible speed and to link up with Naumov. Not one of these orders was carried out. Bülow took charge of Fort Tatishcheva and was about to move on to Lower Ozyornaya, but on hearing some cannonade at night while he was still sixteen kilometres away from his destination he became frightened and retreated. Reinsdorp ordered him a second time to hasten to defeat the rebels, but Bülow paid no attention and stayed on at Tatishcheva. Korff tried to evade action under various pretexts. Instead of five hundred, fewer than three hundred armed Kalmyks were assembled, and even those ran off along the way. The Bashkirs and Tatars paid no heed to the instructions. Major Naumov and the Host elder, Borodin, left Yaitsk and trailed Pugachov at a distance; they arrived in Orenburg from the steppe side on 3rd October, bringing tidings of nothing but the pretender's triumphs.

From Rassypnaya Pugachov proceeded to Lower Ozyornaya.[9] On the way there, he crossed paths with Captain Surin, who had been sent to Velovsky's aid by the commander of Lower Ozyornaya, Major Kharlov. Pugachov hanged him, and his platoon joined the rebels. Having learnt of Pugachov's approach, Kharlov sent his young wife, the daughter of Yelagin, commander of Tatishcheva, to her father, while he himself made preparations for the defence of his fort. His Cossacks deserted to Pugachov's side. Kharlov was left with a handful of soldiers of advanced age. On the night before 26th September he took it into his head to raise his soldiers' morale by firing his two cannon* – occasioning the cannonade that scared Bülow and made him retreat. By the morning Pugachov had arrived at the fort. He rode at the head of his troops.

"Your Majesty, take care that they don't kill you with a cannon shot," an old Cossack said to him.

"Old age must have gone to your head," answered the pretender, "cannon are not forged to kill tsars."

Kharlov ran from one soldier to another, commanding them to fire. Nobody paid attention. He grabbed the fuse, fired one cannon, and dashed to the other one. While this was going on, the rebels occupied the fort, threw themselves on its single defender and covered him with wounds. Half-dead, he thought of ransoming himself, and led his attackers to his cottage, where his possessions were hidden. In the meantime the gallows were already being put up outside the fort; Pugachov sat in front of them, receiving oaths of allegiance from the fort's inhabitants and garrison. Kharlov, dazed by his wounds and bleeding profusely, was led before him, One of his eyes, poked out by a lance, dangled over his cheek. Pugachov ordered him executed, along with Ensigns Figner and Kabalerov, one clerk and a Tatar, Bikbay. The garrison troops started pleading for the life of their good-hearted commander, but the Yaik Cossacks leading the rebellion were implacable. Not one of the victims betrayed a faint heart. Bikbay, a Muslim, crossed himself as he mounted the scaffold, and put his neck in the noose himself.[10] The next day Pugachov set out for Tatishcheva.[11]

This fort was under the command of Colonel Yelagin. The garrison was augmented by Bülow's detachment, since he had sought refuge there. On the morning of 27th September Pugachov's troops appeared on the hills around the fort. All the inhabitants could see him placing his cannon there and aiming them at the fort with his own hands. The rebels rode up to the walls of the fort, trying to persuade the garrison *not to listen to the boyars* and to surrender voluntarily. They received fire in response. They retreated. Ineffectual shooting continued from noon till evening. At that point some haystacks close to the fort were set on fire by the besiegers. The flames soon reached the wooden breastwork. The soldiers rushed to put the fire out. Pugachov, taking advantage of the confusion, attacked from the other side. The Cossacks stationed in the fort defected to his side. The wounded Yelagin and even Bülow put up a desperate fight. At last the rebels charged into the fort's smoking ruins. The commanders were captured. Bülow was beheaded. Yelagin, a corpulent man, was skinned; the scoundrels cut his fat out and rubbed it on their wounds. His wife was hacked to pieces. Their daughter, Kharlov's wife, widowed the day before, was led before the victor as he was giving orders for the execution of her parents. Pugachov was struck by her beauty and decided to make the poor woman his concubine, sparing her seven-year-old brother for her sake. Major Velovsky's widow, who had escaped from Rassypnaya, was also there: they strangled her. All the officers were hanged. A number of regulars and Bashkirs were marshalled into a field and killed by grapeshot. The rest of the soldiers were shorn after the Cossack fashion and incorporated into the rebel forces. Thirteen cannon came into the victor's possession.

Reports of Pugachov's successes were reaching Orenburg one after the other. No sooner had Velovsky reported the taking of Ilek than Kharlov was reporting the fall of Rassypnaya; right afterwards Bülow reported from Tatishcheva that Lower Ozyornaya had been taken, and Major Kruse from Chernorechenskaya, that shooting had been heard at Tatishcheva. Finally (on 28th September) a troop of three hundred Tatars, assembled with great difficulty and dispatched to Tatishcheva, came back with the news of Yelagin's and Bülow's fate. Reinsdorp, alarmed by the speed with which the conflagration was spreading, convened a council of the leading officials of Orenburg, who approved the following measures:

1) All the bridges over the Sakmara to be dismantled and sent floating downstream.
2) Polish Confederates held in Orenburg* to be disarmed and conveyed to Fort Troitsk under the strictest supervision.
3) Commoners possessing arms to be assigned places for the defence of the city under the supervision of the commander-in-chief, Major-General Wallenstern; the remainder to keep themselves in readiness for fire-fighting under the command of the custom house director Obukhov.

4) The Seitov Tatars to be brought into the city and placed under the command of Collegiate Councillor Timashev.
5) The artillery to be commanded by Councillor of State Starov-Milyukov, who had at one time served as an artilleryman.

In addition Reinsdorp, concerned about the safety of Orenburg itself, ordered the senior commandant to repair the fortifications, making them ready for the city's defence. The garrisons of smaller forts not yet taken by Pugachov were ordered to come to Orenburg, either burying or throwing into the rivers whatever heavy equipment and gunpowder they had.

On 29th September Pugachov left Tatishcheva and marched on Chernorechenskaya.[12] In that fort there remained a few veterans under the command of Captain Nechayev, standing in for the commandant, Major Kruse, who had disappeared to Orenburg. They surrendered without resistance. Pugachov hanged the captain because of a complaint against him by one of his serf girls.

Pugachov, leaving Orenburg on his right, proceeded to Sakmarsk,[13] whose inhabitants were awaiting him impatiently. He went there on 1st October from the Tatar village Kargaly in the company of a few Cossacks. An eyewitness describes his arrival in the following words:[14]

> In the fort carpets had been spread out beside the Cossack command post, and a table laid with bread and salt. The priest was waiting for Pugachov with cross and holy icons. When he entered, the fort bells were rung and people bared their heads, and when he began to climb off his horse, two of his Cossacks supporting him by the arms, all prostrated themselves. He kissed the cross and the bread and salt. Seating himself in the chair provided for him, he said, "Rise, my children." Then they all came to kiss his hand. He inquired about the Cossacks of the town. He was told that some were away in state service; others had been ordered to Orenburg with their hetman, Danila Donskoy; only twenty men had been left behind for courier duties, but even they had vanished. He turned to the priest and sternly commanded him to

find the men, adding, "You are their priest; be their hetman, too. You and all who live here will answer for them with your heads." Then he went to the house of the hetman's father, where dinner had been prepared for him. "If your son were here," he said to the old man, "this dinner would be worthy and honourable, but as it is your bread and salt are tainted. What kind of a hetman is he, if he has deserted his post?" After dinner, drunk now, he was about to have the old man executed, but the Cossacks accompanying him dissuaded him; in the end the old man was just put in fetters and locked up at the Cossack command post for one night. The next day those Cossacks who had been tracked down were brought before Pugachov. He treated them kindly and took them with him. They asked him what provisions they should bring with them. "Just a hunk of bread," he answered. "You will accompany me only as far as Orenburg." Meanwhile, Bashkirs sent by the governor of Orenburg had surrounded the town. Pugachov rode out to meet them and without a gunshot attached them all to his own troops. On the bank of the Sakmara he had six people hanged.[15]

Thirty-two kilometres from Sakmarsk there was a fort called Prechistenskaya. The major part of its garrison had been taken by Bülow on his march to Tatishcheva. One of Pugachov's detachments occupied it without a fight. The officers and the garrison came out to meet the victors. The pretender, as usual, attached the soldiers to his own troops and, for the first time, disgraced the officers by sparing them.

Pugachov gathered strength: it had only been two weeks since he had arrived below Yaitsk with a handful of rebels, yet he now had as many as three thousand men, both infantry and cavalry, with more than twenty cannon. Seven forts had been taken by him or had surrendered. His army grew by the hour at an incredible pace. He decided to take advantage of his good luck, and during the night of 3rd October, crossing the river below Sakmarsk by a bridge that had been left standing despite Reinsdorp's orders, he marched on Orenburg.

Chapter III

MEASURES TAKEN BY THE GOVERNMENT – THE STATE OF ORENBURG – REINSDORP'S ANNOUNCEMENT ABOUT PUGACHOV – THE BANDIT KHLOPUSHA – PUGACHOV OUTSIDE ORENBURG – THE BERDA ENCAMPMENT – PUGACHOV'S COMPANIONS – MAJOR-GENERAL KAR – HIS FAILURE – THE DEMISE OF COLONEL CHERNYSHOV – KAR LEAVES THE ARMY – BIBIKOV

THE AFFAIRS OF ORENBURG PROVINCE were taking a turn for the worse. A general mutiny of the Yaik Host was expected at any moment; the Bashkirs, stirred up by their elders (whom Pugachov had already managed to suborn with camels and goods seized from Bukhara merchants), began to raid Russian villages and join the rebel forces in large numbers; Kalmyks on military duty at the outposts were deserting; the Mordva, the Chuvash and the Cheremis* no longer obeyed the Russian authorities; manorial serfs openly showed their allegiance to the pretender; and soon not only Orenburg Province, but other, adjacent provinces entered a state of alarming instability.

Various governors – von Brandt of Kazan, Chicherin of Siberia and Krechetnikov of Astrakhan, in addition to Reinsdorp – were sending reports to the State War College about events in the Yaik region. The Empress anxiously turned her attention to the emerging calamity. Conditions prevailing at the time strongly favoured disorder. Troops had been drawn away from every region to Turkey and to a seething Poland. The plague had only recently been raging, and the strict measures taken all over Russia to curb it had produced widespread discontent among the rabble. Recruiting levies added to the problems. Several platoons and squadrons from Moscow, St Petersburg, Novgorod and Bakhmut* were ordered to hasten to Kazan. They were put under the command of Major-General Kar, who had distinguished himself in Poland by an unwavering execution of the strict measures prescribed by his superiors. He was in St Petersburg at the time, enlisting new recruits. He was ordered to hand his brigade over to Major-General Nashchokin* and to hurry to the endangered regions. Major-General Freymann, who had already pacified the Yaik Host once and was familiar with the theatre of the new disturbances, was to be attached to his staff. The military commanders of neighbouring provinces were also ordered to take appropriate measures. On 15th October the government issued a proclamation announcing the appearance of a pretender and admonishing those deceived by him to renounce their criminal error before it was too late.[1]

Let us turn to Orenburg.

There were up to three thousand troops and seventy cannon in the city. With such resources the rebels could and should have been liquidated. Unfortunately, however, not one among the military commanders knew his business. Lacking in courage from the start, they gave Pugachov time to gather momentum and deprived themselves of the opportunity for offensive action. Orenburg endured a calamitous siege, of which Reinsdorp himself has left an interesting record.[2]

For some days Pugachov's arrival on the scene remained unknown to the citizens of Orenburg, but rumours about the taking of forts soon spread, and Bülow's hasty departure confirmed them.[3] There was unrest in Orenburg itself: the Cossacks grumbled menacingly, and the terrified citizens talked of surrender. An instigator of the disturbances, a retired sergeant sent by Pugachov,[4] was caught. He confessed during the interrogations that he had intended to assassinate the governor. Agitators began operating in villages around Orenburg. Reinsdorp published an announcement about Pugachov, revealing the pretender's true identity and earlier crimes.[5] The announcement, however, was written in a tangled, obscure style. It stated that "the one engaged in villainous acts in the Yaik quarter is rumoured to be of an estate different from the one to which he truly belongs," and that in fact he was the Don Cossack Yemelyan Pugachov, who had been flogged and had his face branded for previous crimes.

This allegation was incorrect.[6] Reinsdorp had given credit to a false rumour, thereby enabling the rebels triumphantly to accuse him of slander.[7]

It seemed that every measure Reinsdorp took worked against him. In the Orenburg prison there was at this time a villain kept in irons who was known by the name of Khlopusha. He had been committing robberies in those parts for twenty years, had been banished to Siberia three times, and had found a way to escape three times. Reinsdorp took it into his head[8] to use this sharp-witted convict to transmit some admonitory leaflets to Pugachov's band. Khlopusha swore he would fulfil his mission faithfully. Set free, he went directly to Pugachov and handed all the governor's leaflets to him.

"I know what's written on them, brother," said Pugachov, illiterate as he was, and presented Khlopusha with half a rouble and the clothes of a recently hanged Kyrgyz. Since Khlopusha was thoroughly familiar with the region, which he had so long terrorized with his robberies, he became indispensable to Pugachov. He was appointed to the rank of colonel and entrusted with pillaging and stirring up trouble at the factories. He lived up to Pugachov's expectations. He proceeded along the Sakmara River, inciting rebellion in the villages of the area. He descended on the landings at Bugulchan and Sterlitamak, and on factories in the Urals, whence he sent Pugachov cannon, cannon balls and powder. His band grew, swelled with factory serfs and Bashkirs – his accomplices in brigandage.

On 5th October Pugachov and his forces pitched camp on a Cossack pasture five kilometres from Orenburg. He immediately moved forward and set up, under gunfire, one battery on the portico of a church in a suburb and another at the governor's suburban house. The heavy cannonade, however, drove them back. That same day the suburb was burnt down at the governor's orders. The only two buildings left standing were a cottage and the church of St George. The inhabitants, who had been moved to the city, were promised full compensation for their losses. A start was made on cleaning out the moat that ringed the city and on lining the ramparts with protective spikes.

During the night stacks of hay laid up for the winter outside the city caught fire on every side. The governor had not had time to have them transferred within the city walls. The very next morning Major Naumov (who had only just arrived from Yaitsk) led an offensive against the incendiaries. He had 1,500 troops with him, both cavalry and infantry. Encountering artillery, they stopped, exchanged fire with the rebels for a while and eventually withdrew without any success. His regular soldiers were fearful, and he did not trust his Cossacks.

Once more Reinsdorp convened his council, now consisting of both military and civil officials, and asked them to submit written opinions on whether to attempt another offensive against the villain or to await the arrival of new troops under the protection of the city's fortifications. At this council meeting State Councillor Starov-Milyukov was the only one to voice an opinion worthy of a military man, namely "to march against the rebels". All the others, fearing that a new failure might throw the citizens into utter despondency, thought only of defence. Reinsdorp accepted the latter view.

On 8th October the rebels raided the barter market, three kilometres outside the city.[9] A detachment sent out against them routed them, killing two hundred people on the spot and taking 116 prisoners. Reinsdorp, wishing to take advantage of an event that had raised the morale of his troops a little, was minded to take the field against Pugachov the next day, but his senior officers unanimously reported that the troops could in no way be counted upon: the soldiers, disheartened and confused, were fighting unwillingly; and the Cossacks might cross over to the rebel side on the very field of battle, which could lead to the fall of Orenburg. Poor Reinsdorp was at a loss.[10] Eventually he managed to awaken his subordinates' conscience, and on 12th October Naumov made another sally out of the city with his unreliable troops.

A battle ensued. Pugachov's artillery pieces outnumbered those brought out of the city. The Orenburg Cossacks, intimidated by the unfamiliar cannon fire, stayed close to the city, under the protection of the cannon ranged on the ramparts. Naumov's detachment was surrounded by multitudes on all sides. He drew up his troops in square formation and began retreating while maintaining fire. The engagement lasted four hours. Naumov lost 117 men, dead, wounded and deserters.

Not one day passed without an exchange of fire. Mobs of rebels rode around the city ramparts attacking foraging detachments. Pugachov went right up to Orenburg with all his forces several times, but he had no intention of storming it.

"I will not waste men," he said to some Cossacks from Sakmarsk. "I'll wipe the city out by famine."

He found many an opportunity to get his inflammatory leaflets into the hands of Orenburg citizens. Several rascals sent by the pretender and equipped with explosives and fuses were caught in the city.

Orenburg was soon gripped by a shortage of fodder. All military and civilian horses that were emaciated and unfit for work were rounded up and send off, some to Iletskaya Zashchita, others to Upper Yaitsk Fort, still others to the Ufa district. But rebel peasants and Tatars captured the horses a few kilometres from the city and sent their Cossack drivers to Pugachov.

Cold weather set in earlier than usual that autumn. The first frost came on 14th October, and on the 16th it snowed. On the 18th Pugachov, having burnt his camp, left the Yaik with full train and headed for the Sakmara. He camped outside the village of Berda,[11] close to the summer road along the Sakmara, seven kilometres from Orenburg. His mounted units, based here, relentlessly harassed the city, attacking foraging detachments and posing a constant threat to the garrison.

On 2nd November Pugachov moved up to Orenburg with all his forces once more and, having positioned batteries all round the city, began a fearful bombardment. He was answered in kind from the city walls. In the meantime a thousand men from Pugachov's infantry crept into the burnt-out suburb from the river side and almost reached the rampart with its spikes. Hiding in cellars, they pelted the city with bullets and arrows. Pugachov himself led them. The chasseurs of the field command drove them out of the suburb. Pugachov was almost taken prisoner. The firing ceased in the evening, but all through the night the rebels answered the chiming of the cathedral clock, marking each hour with a burst of gunfire.

The next day the firing resumed despite the cold and a blizzard. The rebels took turns warming themselves by a campfire lit in the church and by the stove of the one cottage that had been left standing in the burnt-out suburb. Pugachov had one cannon placed on the portico of the church and another hoisted up to the bell tower. The rebels' main battery was positioned on top of a tall target that had been set up a kilometre away from the city for artillery practice. Both sides continued firing all day. At nightfall Pugachov drew back, having suffered some insignificant losses and having caused no harm to the troops under siege.[12] In the morning a group of convicts, guarded by Cossacks, was sent out of the city to raze the target and other barricades, and to demolish the cottage. In the chancel of the church, where the rebels had been bringing their wounded, there were puddles of blood. The frames of icons had been ripped off, and the altar cloth had been torn to pieces. The church had also been desecrated by horse dung and human excrement.

The frosts were intensifying. On 6th November Pugachov and his Yaik Cossacks moved from their new camp into the village of Berda proper. The Bashkirs, Kalmyks and factory peasants stayed at the camp, in covered sleighs and dugouts. The movement of mounted units, the raids and the skirmishes went on relentlessly. Pugachov's forces grew by the day. His army numbered 25,000 at this point. The Yaik Cossacks and the regular soldiers commandeered from forts formed its nucleus, but an unbelievable multitude of Tatars, Bashkirs, Kalmyks, rebellious peasants, escaped convicts, and vagabonds of all kinds gathered around the main body. All this rabble was armed in a makeshift fashion: some with spears, pistols, or officers' swords, others with bayonets stuck onto long staffs, still others with clubs. But a good many had no weapon at all. The army was divided into regiments of five hundred each. Only the Yaik Cossacks received regular pay; the rest had to content themselves with plunder. Liquor was sold from the "state treasury". Horses and fodder were obtained from the Bashkirs. Desertion, it was announced, would be punished by death. Each corporal answered for his men with his own head. Frequent patrolling and the posting of guards were instituted. Pugachov strictly supervised the guards, riding around to check them himself, sometimes even at night. Drills (especially in the artillery units) were held almost every day. There was a daily church service. During the intercessions prayers were offered for the Emperor Peter III and his wife, the Empress Catherine. Pugachov, a schismatic, never went to church. Riding around the market or the streets of Berda, he always scattered copper coins among the populace. He held court and pronounced judgment seated in an armchair in front of his cottage. On either side of him there sat a Cossack, one with a mace, the other with a silver axe in hand. Those approaching him had to bow to the ground, make the sign of the cross and kiss his hand. Berda was a veritable den of vice and murder. The camp was full of officers' wives and daughters, given over to the bandits to violate at will. There were executions every day. The ravines outside Berda were filled with the corpses of victims shot to death, strangled or quartered. Bands of marauders swarmed in all directions, carousing in the villages, and plundering public coffers and the possessions of the nobility, but never touching the property of peasants. Some daredevils would ride right up to the spikes on the Orenburg walls; others, sticking a hat on their spears, would shout: "Cossack sirs! It is time to come to your senses and serve your Emperor Peter!" Still others clamoured for the handing over of Martyushka Borodin (the Host elder who had come from Yaitsk to Orenburg with Naumov's detachment) or issued invitations to the Cossacks saying, "Our father-sovereign has liquor to spare!" Sorties were made against them from the city, resulting in skirmishes, at times quite hot ones. Pugachov himself was frequently there to show how plucky he was. Once he arrived drunk, hatless and swaying in his saddle; he was rescued by some Cossacks who grabbed his horse by the bridle and dragged him away.[13]

Pugachov did not have absolute authority. The Yaik Cossacks who had instigated the revolt controlled the actions of the vagabond, whose only merits were a degree of military know-how and exceptional daring. He never undertook anything without their consent, whereas they frequently acted without his knowledge and sometimes even against his wishes. Outwardly, they showed him respect, walking behind him with bared heads and bowing low down before him in public, but in private they treated him as a comrade, getting drunk with him, sitting in their shirtsleeves and with their hats on in his company, and singing barge haulers' songs. Pugachov chafed at their guardianship. "My path is narrow," he once said to Denis Pyanov, as they were feasting at the wedding of Pyanov's younger son.[14] Distrustful of outside influences on the tsar they had created, they did not allow him to have other favourites or confidants. At the beginning of the revolt Pugachov had made a Sergeant Karmitsky his secretary, having pardoned him under the very gallows. Karmitsky had soon become his favourite. The Yaik Cossacks strangled the man during the taking of Tatishcheva and threw him into the river with a rock tied to his neck. Pugachov inquired after him. "He left," they answered him "to visit his mother down the Yaik." Pugachov let the matter go without a word. Kharlov's young wife had the misfortune of winning the pretender's affection. He kept her at his camp near Orenburg. She was the only person allowed to enter his covered wagon at whatever time; and at her request he sent orders to Ozyornaya to bury the bodies of all those he had hanged there when the fort was taken. She aroused the jealous villains' suspicions, and Pugachov, yielding to their demand, gave his concubine up to them. Kharlova and her seven-year-old brother were shot. Wounded, they crawled up to each other and embraced. Their bodies, thrown into the bushes, remained there in each other's arms for a long time.

Most prominent among the leading rebels was Zarubin (nicknamed Chika), Pugachov's mentor and close associate from the very beginning of the revolt. He had the title of field marshal and held the highest office next to the pretender. Ovchinnikov, Shigayev, Lysov, and Chumakov commanded the army. They were all nicknamed after grandees surrounding Catherine's throne at the time: Chika was called Count Chernyshov, Shigayev Count Vorontsov, Ovchinnikov Count Panin, and Chumakov Count Orlov.[15] A retired artillery corporal, Beloborodov, enjoyed the pretender's full confidence; together with Padurov, he looked after all paperwork for the illiterate Pugachov and introduced strict order and discipline into the rebel bands. Perfilyev, happening to be in St Petersburg at the beginning of the uprising on Yaik Host business, had promised the government to bring the Cossacks under control and to hand Pugachov over to the legal authorities, but after he arrived in Berda he proved to be one of the most hardened rebels, linking his fate with that of the pretender. The brigand Khlopusha, flogged and then mutilated at the torturer's hand, with nostrils slit to the very cartilage, was one of Pugachov's favourites. Ashamed of his disfigurement, he either wore a loosely woven cloth over his face or held his sleeve over it as if protecting it from the frost.[16] These were the sort of people who rocked the state to its foundations!

In the meantime Kar arrived at the boundary of Orenburg Province. Before Kar's arrival the governor of Kazan had managed to assemble a few hundred soldiers, some retired, some brought in from garrisons and military settlements, and had deployed some of them near the Kichuyev entrenchment, and some along the Cheremshan River, halfway along the road from Kichuyev to Stavropol.* On the Volga there were about thirty regulars, commanded by one officer, whose task was to catch plunderers and to keep an eye on the rebels' movements. Brandt had written to the general-in-chief in Moscow, Prince Volkonsky, to ask for troops, but the whole Moscow garrison had been sent away to convoy recruits, and the Tomsk Regiment, which had been brought to Moscow, was manning the sentry posts around the city that had been set up in 1771 when the plague was raging. Prince Volkonsky was able to release only three hundred regulars and one fieldpiece, but he had these transported to Kazan without delay.

Kar instructed the commandant of Simbirsk, Colonel Chernyshov, who was proceeding up the Samara Line* towards Orenburg, to take Tatishcheva as soon as possible. Kar's intention was to reinforce Chernyshov's troops with those of Major-General Freymann as soon as the latter returned from Kaluga, where he had gone to receive new recruits. Kar had full confidence in victory. "The only thing I am afraid of," he wrote to Count

Z.G. Chernyshov, "is that as soon as these bandits get wind of the troops' approach they will flee to the places where they came from, not giving the troops an opportunity to get close to them." He foresaw difficulties in pursuing Pugachov only because of the winter and shortage of horses.

Kar began pressing forward at the beginning of November, without waiting for the artillery, for the 170 grenadiers sent off from Simbirsk, or for the armed Bashkirs and Meshcheryaks dispatched from Ufa to join him. On his way, just over one hundred kilometres from Orenburg, he learnt that the convicted robber Khlopusha, having cast some cannon at the Avzyano-Petrovsk ironworks,[17] and having rallied the factory peasants as well as the Bashkirs of the vicinity – all at Pugachov's behest – was returning to Orenburg. Anxious to cut Khlopusha off, Kar sent Second Major Shishkin on 7th November with four hundred regulars and two fieldpieces to the village of Yuzeyeva,[18] while he himself, accompanied by General Freymann and First Major F. Warnstedt who had both just come from Kaluga, set out from Sarmanayeva. Shishkin ran into six hundred rebels right outside Yuzeyeva. The Tatars and armed peasants who were with him defected immediately, yet Shishkin managed to disperse the whole mob with a few shots. He occupied the village, where Kar and Freymann also arrived towards four in the morning. The troops were so exhausted that it was impossible even to detail mounted patrols. The generals decided to wait until daylight to make their assault on the rebels. When dawn broke, they saw before them the same mob that had been dispersed the day before. An admonitory manifesto was delivered to the rebels; they took it, but rode off swearing and saying that their own manifestos were more trustworthy; they started firing from a cannon. They were dispersed once more... Then Kar heard four distant bursts of cannon fire in the rear of his position. He grew alarmed and began to beat a hasty retreat, supposing himself cut off from Kazan. At this point over two thousand rebels galloped up from all sides and opened fire from nine fieldpieces. Pugachov himself was leading them. He and Khlopusha had managed to join forces. Scattered about the fields, a cannon's range away, they were perfectly safe. Kar's cavalry was exhausted and small in number.

The rebels, who had good horses, fell back from the infantry charges, deftly hauling their fieldpieces from one hill to another. They accompanied the retreating Kar in this manner for eighteen kilometres. He returned fire from his five fieldpieces for a full eight hours. He abandoned his supply train; and lost (if his report is to be believed) not more than 120 of his men, killed, wounded or deserted. There was no sign of the Bashkirs expected from Ufa; and those under Prince Urakov's command, who were now not far away, took to their heels as soon as they heard the gunfire. Kar's soldiers, the majority of whom were either advanced in years or new conscripts, grumbled loudly and were ready to surrender; their young officers, who had never been under fire, did not know how to raise their morale. The grenadiers, who had been despatched from Simbirsk in horse-drawn sledges under Lieutenant Kartashov, had travelled in so lax a manner that they did not even have their guns loaded and were all sleeping as they rode. They surrendered after the rebels' first four cannon shots – the same shots that Kar heard that morning from Yuzeyeva.

Kar suddenly lost his self-assurance. Reporting his losses, he declared to the War College that in order to defeat Pugachov what was needed was not small detachments, but whole regiments, with reliable cavalry and strong artillery. He also hastily dispatched an order to Colonel Chernyshov not to leave Perevolotskaya but to try to fortify it while awaiting further instructions. The messenger was, however, too late to catch up with him.

Chernyshov left Perevolotskaya on 11th November and arrived at Chernorechenskaya on the night of the 13th. Here two Ilek Cossacks, brought to him by the hetman of Sakmarsk, informed him of Kar's defeat and of the capture of the 170 grenadiers. Chernyshov could not doubt the truth of this last report, since he himself had sent the grenadiers off from Simbirsk, where they had been stationed for convoying recruits. He did not know what to do: whether to draw back to Perevolotskaya or to hurry on to Orenburg, where he had sent notification of his approach just the night before. At this moment five Cossacks and one regular soldier presented themselves to him, claiming to have defected from Pugachov's camp. One of these people was a Cossack lieutenant, and another was Padurov, a former delegate to the Legislative Commission.[19] He assured Chernyshov of his loyalty, displaying his delegate's medal as proof, and advised the colonel to march to Orenburg immediately, offering to guide him by a safe route. Chernyshov trusted him and left Chernorechenskaya immediately, without drumbeat. Padurov led him across the hills, assuring him that Pugachov's advance patrols were far away, and that even if the patrols should catch sight of them at daybreak, by then they would be out of danger and would be able to get into Orenburg without hindrance. Chernyshov arrived at the Sakmara River by the morning and started crossing it on the ice at Mayak paddock, five kilometres from Orenburg. He had 1,500 regulars and Cossacks, five hundred Kalmyks, and twelve fieldpieces with him. Captain Rzhevsky crossed the river first with the artillery train and a light field detachment; reaching the other side, he immediately galloped into Orenburg in the company of just three Cossacks, and presented himself to the governor with the news of Chernyshov's arrival. At that same moment those in Orenburg heard cannon fire; it continued for a quarter of an hour, then ceased... A little later Reinsdorp received the intelligence that Chernyshov's entire battalion had been captured and was being taken to Pugachov's camp.

Chernyshov had been deceived by Padurov, who in fact led him straight to Pugachov. The rebels suddenly charged at his troops and seized his artillery. The Cossacks and Kalmyks defected. The infantry, exhausted from cold, hunger, and a night's march, was unable to put up any resistance. All were captured. Pugachov hanged Chernyshov,* together with thirty-six officers, an ensign's wife and a Kalmyk colonel[20] who had stayed loyal to his unfortunate commander.

Brigadier Korff was approaching Orenburg at the same time with 2,400 troops and twenty fieldpieces. Pugachov attacked him too, but was repulsed by Cossacks from the city.

The Orenburg authorities seemed witless from panic. On 14th November Reinsdorp, who only the day before had made no attempt to help the battalion of the unfortunate Chernyshov, took it into his head to make a strong sally. All the troops within the walls of the city (even those who had just arrived) were ordered to take the field under the leadership of the senior commandant. The rebels, true to their usual tactics, fought from a distance and from all directions, incessantly firing from their numerous fieldpieces. The garrison's emaciated cavalry could not even hope for success. Wallenstern, who had lost thirty-two men, was eventually forced to draw his troops into square formation and retreat.[21] That same day Major Warnstedt, dispatched by Kar along the New Moscow Road, ran into a strong rebel force and hastily retreated, losing some two hundred men killed.

When Kar learnt of Chernyshov's capture, he lost heart altogether, and from then on he was concerned, not with defeating a despicable rebel, but only with his own security. He reported all that had transpired to the War College, voluntarily resigned from the commandership under the pretext of illness, offered a few clever pieces of advice about how to operate against Pugachov and, leaving his army under Freymann's care, left for Moscow, where his arrival raised a general outcry. The Empress issued strict orders to discharge him from the service. He spent the rest of his life on his estate, where he died at the beginning of Alexander's reign.*

The Empress saw that strong measures were called for against the encroaching mischief. She looked for a reliable commander to succeed the runaway Kar, and settled on General-in-Chief Bibikov. Alexandr Ilyich Bibikov was one of the most illustrious personalities of Catherine's time, which abounded in remarkable people. While still in his youth he had distinguished himself both on the battlefield and in civic affairs. He served with honour in the Seven Years War, attracting the attention of Frederick the Great. Important tasks were assigned to him. In 1763 he was sent to Kazan to pacify the rioting factory peasants. By firmness and prudent moderation he soon managed to restore order. In 1766, when the Legislative Commission was initiated, he oversaw the election of delegates in Kostroma. He himself was elected a delegate and was later appointed leader of the whole assembly. In 1771 he replaced Lieutenant General von Weymarn as commander-in-chief in Poland, where he not only quickly introduced order into a disorganized state of affairs, but also won the love and trust of the vanquished.*

During the period under discussion he was in St Petersburg. Having recently yielded his commandership of Poland to Lieutenant General Romanius, he was preparing to leave for Turkey to serve under Count Rumyantsev. The Empress had been cool in her reception of him on this occasion, though heretofore she had always shown kindness towards him. It is possible that she was displeased with some indelicate expressions he had let fly in a moment of irritation, for Bibikov, though diligent in his assignments and sincerely devoted to the Empress, tended to be querulous, and bold in voicing his opinions. But Catherine was able to overcome personal grudges. At a court ball she approached him with her former affectionate smile and, while graciously conversing with him, gave him his new assignment. Bibikov answered that he had dedicated himself to the service of the fatherland and immediately cited the words of a folk song, applying them to his own situation:

My precious dress, my sarafan!
My dress, you're useful everywhere,
but if there is no need of you,
my dress, you lie beneath a chair.

He accepted this most arduous of tasks without demur and on 9th December set out from St Petersburg.

Arriving in Moscow, Bibikov found the ancient capital apprehensive and dejected. Its citizens, who had only recently witnessed riot and plague, trembled at the thought of a new calamity. Many noblemen whose homes had been ravaged by Pugachov or were threatened by the upheaval had fled to Moscow. The serfs they had brought with them filled the streets with rumours about the freeing of peasants and the extermination of landlords. Moscow's multitudinous rabble, getting drunk and staggering about the streets, awaited Pugachov with conspicuous impatience. The enthusiasm with which the citizens greeted Bibikov revealed the extent of the danger they felt themselves to be in. He soon left Moscow, hastening to justify the city's trust.

Chapter IV

THE REBELS' MOVEMENTS – MAJOR ZAYEV – THE TAKING OF FORT ILYINSKAYA – THE DEATH OF KAMESHKOV AND VORONOV – THE STATE OF ORENBURG – THE SIEGE OF YAITSK – THE BATTLE AT BERDA – BIBIKOV IN KAZAN – CATHERINE II AS A KAZAN LANDOWNER – THE OPINION OF EUROPE – VOLTAIRE – THE DECREE ABOUT PUGACHOV'S HOUSE AND FAMILY

THE DEFEAT of Kar and Freymann, the annihilation of Chernyshov and the unsuccessful sallies of Wallenstern and Korff increased the rebels' boldness and self-assurance. They surged in every direction, ravaging villages and towns and inciting people to rebellion, and they met no resistance. Tornov revolted at the head of six hundred men and ransacked the whole district of Nagaybak. Meanwhile Chika marched on Ufa with a 10,000-strong division and invested it at the end of November. The city lacked the kind of fortifications Orenburg had, but its commandant, Myasoyedov, together with the noblemen who had sought refuge there, resolved to defend themselves. Chika, not daring to mount a strong offensive, set himself up in the village of Chesnokovka, eleven kilometres from Ufa, rousing the neighbouring (mostly Bashkir) villages, and cutting the city off from all communication. Ulyanov, Davydov and Beloborodov were operating between Ufa and Kazan. At the same time Pugachov sent Khlopusha with five hundred troops and six fieldpieces to take the forts of Ilyinskaya and Upper Ozyornaya, situated to the east of Orenburg. The governor of Siberia, Chicherin, had detailed Lieutenant General Dekalong and Major-General Stanislavsky[1] to undertake the defence of this region. The former kept guard on the borders of Siberia, the latter stayed in Fort Orsk,[2] acting indecisively, losing heart at the approach of the slightest danger, and refusing to carry out his duty under various pretexts.

Khlopusha took Ilyinskaya, slaying its commandant Lieutenant Lopatin in the assault, but sparing its other officers and even leaving the fort standing. He marched on Upper Ozyornaya. The commandant of that fort, Lieutenant Colonel Demarin, repulsed the attack. On learning this, Pugachov himself hurried to Khlopusha's assistance and, joining forces with him on the morning of 26th November, laid siege to the fort. The bombardment lasted all day. Several times the rebels dismounted and assaulted the fort with lances, but were repulsed each time. In the evening Pugachov drew back to a Bashkir village thirteen kilometres from Upper Ozyornaya. Here he learnt that Major-General Stanislavsky had dispatched three platoons from the Siberian Line to Ilyinskaya. He set out to intercept them.

The commander of this detachment, Major Zayev, managed, however, to occupy Ilyinskaya (on 27th November). Khlopusha had not burnt the fort on vacating it. Its inhabitants had not been forced out. There were a few captive Polish Confederates among them. The walls and a few of the cottages had been damaged. All the garrison had been removed, except for one sergeant and a wounded officer. The storehouse had been left open: some quarter measures of flour and pieces of rusk were lying about the yard. A cannon was abandoned by the gate. Quickly making what arrangements he could, Zayev set up the three cannon he had brought with him on three of the bastions (there was none for the fourth), posted guards and sent out patrols, and started waiting for the enemy.

Pugachov appeared at the fort the next day when it was already getting dark. His men came right up to the fort and, riding around it, shouted to the guards, "Don't shoot; come out: the Emperor is here." A cannon was fired at them. The ball killed a horse. The rebels withdrew, but reappeared from behind a hill an hour later, and galloped pell-mell towards the fort under Pugachov's leadership. They were driven off by cannon fire. The soldiers and the captive Poles (especially the latter) fervently implored Zayev to let them make a sally, but he refused, fearing their defection. "Stay here and defend the fort," he said to them. "I have no orders from the general to make sallies."

Pugachov approached once more on the 29th, moving up two fieldpieces on sledges behind several wagonloads of hay. He launched an attack on the bastion that had no cannon. Zayev made a hasty attempt to set up two cannon there, but before the transfer could be accomplished, Pugachov's balls smashed through the wooden bastion. The rebels dismounted, surged forward, demolished what remained, and rushed into the fort with their usual battle cry. The soldiers broke ranks and fled. Zayev, almost all his officers, and two hundred of the rank and file were killed. The remaining soldiers were herded to a nearby Tatar village and lined up facing a loaded cannon. Pugachov, in red Cossack attire, rode up accompanied by Khlopusha. As soon as he appeared, the soldiers were ordered to kneel. He said to them, "The Lord God and I, your Emperor Peter III, grant you pardon. Arise." Then he gave orders to turn the cannon around and fire it into the steppe. Captain Kameshkov and Ensign Voronov were brought before him. These modest names must be recorded in history.

"Why did you fight against me, your Sovereign?" asked the victor.

"You're no sovereign to us," answered the captives; "we Russians have our Sovereigns, the Empress Catherine and the Crown Prince Paul. You are a bandit and an impostor."

They were hanged on the spot. Then Captain Basharin was led forth. Pugachov was about to have him hanged without addressing a word to him, but the captive soldiers began pleading with him for their captain's life. "If he's been good to you," said the pretender, "I'll grant him pardon." He ordered the captain, like his soldiers, to be shorn Cossack-fashion, and he had the wounded carried to the fort. The Cossacks of the detachment were greeted by the rebels as their comrades. When asked why they had not joined the besiegers sooner, they said they had been afraid of the regular soldiers.

From Ilyinskaya Pugachov turned towards Upper Ozyornaya once more. He was very eager to take it, the more so as Brigadier Korff's wife was there. He had threatened to hang her in revenge for her husband's having planned to trick him with false negotiations.[3]

On 30th November Pugachov invested the fort again, bombarding it by cannon all day and making attempts to storm it now from this, now from that side. Demarin, in order to keep up his garrison's spirit, stood on the rampart throughout the day, loading the cannon with his own hands. In the end Pugachov withdrew; he was going to march against Stanislavsky, but, having intercepted the Orenburg mail, he changed his mind and returned to Berda.

Reinsdorp wanted to make a sally during Pugachov's absence, and a detachment did indeed leave the city on the night of the 30th, but the emaciated horses collapsed and died in the effort to pull the artillery, and some Cossacks defected. Wallenstern was forced to withdraw behind the city walls.

The shortage of provisions was beginning to be felt in Orenburg. Reinsdorp requested some from Dekalong and Stanislavsky. Both found excuses for refusing him. He expected reinforcements to arrive hour by hour, but since he was cut off from communication on all sides except Siberia and the Kyrgyz-Kazakh steppes, he could receive no information about them. In order to catch one informant, he had to send out as many as a thousand men, and at times even such a great effort brought no results. On Timashev's advice he even resorted to setting up traps outside the ramparts in an attempt to catch night-roaming rebels like wolves. Even the besieged citizens laughed at this bit of military artfulness, though in general they were not much disposed to laughter. As for the rebels, Padurov in one of his letters sarcastically rebuked the governor for his unsuccessful stratagem, at the same time predicting his ruin and scornfully advising him to capitulate to the pretender.[4]

Yaitsk, that first hotbed of rebellion, remained loyal for a long time due to the intimidating presence of Simonov's troops. But Pugachov's followers in the town were emboldened by frequent communication with the rebels and a false rumour about the fall of Orenburg. Cossacks whom Simonov regularly sent out to patrol the environs and catch agitators from Berda began to disobey orders quite openly, letting the captured rebels go, tying up elders loyal to the government, and paying visits to the pretender's camp. A rumour spread about a rebel force approaching. On the night of 29th December the elder Mostovshchikov set out with a detachment to counter it. Within a few hours three of the Cossacks who had gone with him came back to the fort at a gallop, reporting that Mostovshchikov and his men had been surrounded at a place seven kilometres from the town and had all been taken prisoner by a huge band of rebels. There was great confusion in the town. Simonov lost his nerve, but fortunately there was a captain in the fort named Krylov, a resolute and level-headed man. From the first moment of the upheaval, he took over command of the garrison and saw to the necessary measures. On 31st December a rebel detachment led by Tolkachov entered the town. The citizens received him with enthusiasm and immediately joined his forces, arming themselves as best they could. They besieged the fort from all the side streets, took up positions in tall houses, and began shooting from windows. One witness tells that the hail of bullets that hit the fort sounded like the beating of ten drums. In the fort people died, not only if they stood in the open, but even if they happened to raise their heads momentarily from behind barriers. The rebels were safe at a distance of only twenty metres from the fort, and, being mostly hunters, they could hit even the slits through which the defenders were shooting. Simonov and Krylov tried to set the nearest houses on fire, but either the firebombs fell in the snow and fizzled out or else the attackers managed to pour water on them. Not one of the houses started burning. At last three regulars volunteered to set fire to the nearest homestead, and they succeeded. The flames spread quickly. The rebels came out; the cannon from the fort were fired at them; they withdrew carrying their dead and wounded. Towards evening the garrison, its spirit buoyed, sallied out and succeeded in setting several other houses on fire.

There were about a thousand garrison soldiers and obedient Cossacks within the walls of the fort; they had plenty of ammunition but not enough food. The rebels invested the fort; erected log barricades on the burnt-out square and across the streets and alleys leading to it; set up sixteen batteries behind the barricades; built double walls in front of the houses exposed to gunfire, filling the gap between them with earth; and began digging underground tunnels. The defenders, confining their efforts to keeping the enemy at a distance, periodically cleared the square and stormed the fortified houses. These dangerous sorties took place daily, sometimes even twice daily, and were always crowned with success: the regular soldiers were full of fury, and the obedient Cossacks could hope for no mercy from the rebels.

The situation in Orenburg was becoming terrible. Flour and groats were confiscated from the citizens, and a daily ration was introduced. The horses had been fed with brushwood for some time. Most of them died and were eaten. Hunger was intensifying. A sack of flour sold (even in the greatest secrecy) for twenty-five roubles. On the advice of Rychkov (an academician living in Orenburg at the time), the citizens started frying bull and horse hides, chopping them into small pieces, and mixing them in dough. People fell ill. The grumbling grew louder. It was feared that a mutiny might break out.

In this extreme situation Reinsdorp decided to try his luck at arms once more, and on 13th January all the troops stationed in Orenburg sallied out in three columns under the command, respectively, of Wallenstern, Korff and Naumov. But the darkness of the winter morning, the depth of the snow, and the exhaustion of the horses hindered the coordination of the troops. Naumov arrived at the designated place first. The rebels caught sight of him, which gave them time to take countermeasures. They prevented Wallenstern from occupying, as the plan called for, the hills near the Berda-Kargala road. Korff encountered heavy artillery fire; and bands of rebels were beginning to encircle the columns. The Cossacks, left in reserve, fled from the rebels to Wallenstern's column, causing general confusion. Wallenstern found himself under fire from three directions, and since his soldiers were beginning to flee, he beat a retreat; Korff followed suit; and Naumov, who had been operating quite successfully at first, rushed after them for fear of being cut off. The whole corps ran all the way back to Orenburg in disorder, losing some four hundred men killed or wounded, and leaving fifteen fieldpieces in the bandits' hands. After this fiasco Reinsdorp did not dare mount another offensive; he simply waited for liberation under the protection of the city walls and cannon.

Bibikov arrived in Kazan on 25th December. He found neither the governor nor the other leading officials in the city. The majority of the noblemen and merchants had fled to provinces not yet threatened. Brandt was in Kozmodemyansk. Bibikov's arrival revived the despondent city; citizens who had left began to return. On 1st January 1774, after public prayers and an address by Archbishop Veniamin of Kazan, Bibikov summoned the nobility to his house and made a clever and effective speech. After describing the widespread calamity and the government's efforts to bring it to an end, he addressed his appeal to the class that, no less than the government, faced disaster from the rebellion, requesting its cooperation out of patriotism and loyalty to the crown. His speech made a deep impression. The meeting resolved there and then to assemble and arm at their own expense a corps of cavalry, furnishing one recruit for each two hundred serfs. Major-General Larionov, a relative of Bibikov's, was elected commander of the legion. The nobility of Simbirsk, Sviyazhsk and Penza followed this example, assembling two more cavalry corps, placing them under the command of Majors Gladkov and Chemesov and Captain Matyunin. The Kazan council also outfitted a squadron of hussars at its own expense.

The Empress conveyed to the Kazan nobility her imperial favour, goodwill and patronage; and in a separate letter to Bibikov, which she signed as a Kazan landowner, offered to add her share to the common effort. Makarov, the marshal of the nobility, answered the Empress with an oration composed by Second Lieutenant of the Guards Derzhavin,* who was serving on the staff of the commander-in-chief at the time.[5]

Bibikov, in an attempt to raise the morale of the citizens and his subordinates, put on a show of equanimity and good cheer, but in fact worry, irritation and impatience were gnawing at him. The difficulty of his position is vividly described in his letters to Count Chernyshov, to Fonvizin and to his own family. On 30th December he wrote to his wife:

> *Now that I have become acquainted with all the circumstances here, I find the situation so appalling that I could not find the language to express it even if I wished to: I have quickly realized that my position is much worse and more vexing than it was on my arrival in Poland. I do everything in my power, writing day and night, never letting the pen out of my hand; and I pray to the Lord for His help. He alone in His mercy can set matters right. True, people have come to their senses late in the day. My troops began arriving yesterday: a battalion of grenadiers and the two squadrons of hussars that I ordered to be transported by post-horses, have come. But they will not suffice for stamping out the pestilence. The evil afflicting us is like the St Petersburg fire (you remember), which burnt in so many places at once that it was well-nigh impossible to keep pace with it. Despite all, I will do whatever is in my power, and place my hope in the Lord. Poor old Governor Brandt is so worn out that he can hardly drag himself about. The one who has confounded the affairs of this region so quickly and denuded it of troops will have to answer before God for innocent blood and the demise of many innocent people. Anyhow, my health is good; it's just that I have no appetite for food or drink, and I never even think about sweetmeats. The evil is great and daunting in the extreme. I beg my sire, whom I know to be the kindest of fathers, to offer his paternal prayers for me. I appeal frequently to the Blessed Yevpraxiya.*[6] *Ugh! It's a bad business!*

The situation was indeed terrible. A general uprising of Bashkirs, Kalmyks and other nationalities scattered about the region interrupted communication on all sides. The army was small and unreliable. Commanding officers deserted their posts, fleeing at the sight of a Bashkir with a bow and quiver or a factory serf with a club.[7] Winter exacerbated the difficulties. The steppes were blanketed with deep snow.[8] It was impossible to move forward unless one had a good supply not only of grain, but of firewood too.[9] The villages were deserted; the major cities either besieged or occupied by bands of rebels; the factories plundered and burnt. Mobs rampaged and wrought havoc everywhere. The troops dispatched from different regions of the country were slow in coming. The evil, unimpeded, spread far and wide with great speed. The Yaik Cossacks were in revolt from Ilek to Guryev. The provinces of Kazan, Nizhny Novgorod and Astrakhan[10] were brimming over with bands of brigands; the conflagration threatened to spread into Siberia itself; upheavals were commencing in Perm; Yekaterinburg was in danger. The Kyrgyz-Kazakhs, taking advantage of the absence of troops, began crossing over the unguarded border, pillaging hamlets, driving off cattle and taking captives.[11] The trans-Kuban peoples were stirring, incited by Turkey, and even some European powers considered taking advantage of the difficult situation in which Russia now found herself.[12] *

The instigator of this terrible upheaval attracted general attention. In Europe Pugachov was regarded as an instrument of Turkish policy. Voltaire, a typical representative of prevailing opinion, wrote to Catherine:

> *C'est apparemment le chevalier de Tott qui a fait jouer cette farce; mais nous ne sommes plus au temps de Demetrius, et telle pièce de théâtre qui réussissait il y a deux cents ans est sifflée aujourd'hui.* *

The Empress, irritated by European gossip, replied to Voltaire with a degree of impatience:

> *Monsieur, les gazettes seules font beaucoup de bruit du brigand Pugatschef, lequel n'est en relation directe ni indirecte avec m-r de Tott. Je fais autant de cas des canons fondus par l'un que des entreprises de l'autre. M. de Pugatschef et M. de Tott ont cependant cela de commun, que le premier file tous les jours sa corde de chanvre et que le second s'expose à chaque instant au cordon de soie.** [13]

Although the Empress despised the brigand himself, she seized every opportunity to bring the misguided mob to reason. Admonitory manifestos were widely distributed, and a reward of ten thousand roubles was offered for the pretender's capture.

There was a particular fear of contact between the Yaik and the Don. Hetman Yefremov was dismissed, and Semyon Sulin was chosen to replace him. Instructions were sent to Cherkassk to burn Pugachov's house and belongings, but to convey his family, *without insult or injury*, to Kazan, in order to identify the pretender if he was caught. The local authorities carried out Her Majesty's command to the letter. Pugachov's house in Zimoveyskaya had been sold by his impoverished wife a year before, dismantled and conveyed to another homestead; it was now transported back to its previous location and burnt in the presence of the clergy and the whole Cossack township. The executioners scattered the ashes to the winds, dug a trench, and erected a fence around the yard, for ever to be left desolate as an accursed place. The authorities, in the name of all the Zimoveyskaya Cossacks, sought permission to transfer the township to another site, *even if it were less advantageous*. The Empress did not agree to such a wasteful demonstration of zeal; she simply renamed the Zimoveyskaya township "Potyomkinskaya", erasing the gloomy remembrance of the rebel by the glory of a new name that was already dear to her and to the fatherland. Pugachov's wife and his son and two daughters (all three still minors) were sent to Kazan, together with his brother, who had served as a Cossack in the Second Army. Meanwhile the following detailed information was gathered about the villain who was rocking the foundations of the state.[14]

Yemelyan Pugachov of the village of Zimoveyskaya, a Cossack formerly in state service, was the son of Ivan Mikhaylov, long deceased. He was forty years old, and of medium height, had a dark complexion, and was lean; he had brown hair and a small black goatee beard. He had lost one upper front tooth in childhood, in a fist-fight. He had a white blemish on his left temple and on his chest traces of the so-called "black pox".[15] He was illiterate and crossed himself in the schismatics' manner. Ten years previously he had married a Cossack girl Sofya Nedyuzhina, who subsequently bore him five children. He joined the Second Army in 1770; participated in the taking of Bendery; and after a year was furloughed to the Don for reasons of ill health. He took a trip to

Cherkassk for treatment. When he returned to his native village, the hetman of Zimoveyskaya asked him at a communal meeting where he had obtained the chestnut horse on which he had ridden home. Pugachov replied that he had bought it in Taganrog; but the Cossacks, familiar with his unprincipled ways, did not believe him, and sent him back to fetch written proof. Pugachov left. While he was away, it became known that he had been inciting certain Cossacks who were living near Taganrog to flee beyond the Kuban. It was resolved that Pugachov should be handed over to the government authorities. When he returned home in December of that year he tried to hide on his farm, but was caught. He managed to escape, however, and roamed no one knew where for three months, until at last, during Lent, he came back to his house one evening and rapped on the window. His wife let him in and informed the other Cossacks of his arrival. Pugachov was taken into custody again and was conveyed under guard first to the police investigator, the elder Makarov, at Lower Chirsk township and then on to Cherkassk. On the way there he managed to escape once more, and after that he never again appeared in the Don region. It was already known from Pugachov's own testimony, given before the Court Chancery at the end of 1772, that after his escape he had gone into hiding beyond the Polish border, in the schismatic settlement of Vetka; that he then obtained an identity certificate at the Dobryanskoye frontier post, making himself out to be a refugee from Poland; and that he finally journeyed to the Yaik region, begging for food along the way. All this information was public knowledge, but in the meantime the government prohibited all talk about Pugachov because his name stirred up the rabble. This temporary police measure remained in force until the late Emperor's accession to the throne,* when permission was granted to write about Pugachov and publish materials relating to him.[16] Even today the aged witnesses of that upheaval who are still alive are reluctant to respond to enquirers' questions.*

Chapter V

BIBIKOV'S DISPOSITIONS – FIRST SUCCESSES – THE TAKING OF SAMARA AND ZAINSK – DERZHAVIN – MICHELSOHN – THE SIEGE OF YAITSK CONTINUED – PUGACHOV'S MARRIAGE – THE DESTRUCTION OF ILETSKAYA ZASHCHITA – LYSOV'S DEATH – THE BATTLE AT TATISHCHEVA – PUGACHOV'S FLIGHT – THE EXECUTION OF KHLOPUSHA – THE LIFTING OF THE SIEGE OF ORENBURG – PUGACHOV'S SECOND DEFEAT – THE BATTLE OF CHESNOKOVKA – THE LIBERATION OF UFA AND YAITSK – THE DEATH OF BIBIKOV

At last the various forces dispatched against Pugachov from different directions were approaching their destination. Bibikov directed them towards Orenburg. Major-General Prince Golitsyn's assignment was to secure the Moscow road, working from Kazan to Orenburg. Major-General Mansurov was entrusted with the right flank, providing coverage for the Samara Line, where Major Muffel and Lieutenant Colonel Grinyov had been sent with their detachments. Major-General Larionov was dispatched to Ufa and Yekaterinburg. Dekalong shielded Siberia and was ordered to send Major Gagrin with a field detachment to defend Kungur. Lieutenant of the Guards Derzhavin was dispatched to Malykovka to protect the Volga on the Penza and Saratov side. Success vindicated these dispositions. At first Bibikov had misgivings about the morale of his army. In one corps (the Vladimir Regiment) there was indeed some indication of the presence of Pugachov's followers. But the commandants of the towns through which the regiment passed were instructed to send officials disguised as peasants around the taverns, and with their help the agitators were discovered and apprehended. Thereafter Bibikov was satisfied with his regiments. "My affairs, thank God, are fast improving," he wrote in February. "The troops are approaching the robber's den. I see from all the letters that they are satisfied with me in St Petersburg; I only wish someone had asked the goose if its feet were cold."

On 29th December Major Muffel and his field detachment approached Samara, which had been occupied by a band of rebels the day before. The rebels came out to meet him, but he crushed them and chased them right back to the city. Once inside, they thought they could hold out under the protection of the city's cannon, but Muffel's dragoons cut their way into the city with their sabres, hacking at the fleeing rebels and trampling them underfoot. At this same moment some Stavropol Kalmyks,[1] coming to reinforce the rebels, appeared two kilometres outside Samara; they fled, however, as soon as they saw the cavalry detachment sent against them. The city was cleared of rebels. The victors took six cannon and two hundred prisoners. Lieutenant Colonel Grinyov and Major-General Mansurov arrived in Samara right after Muffel. Mansurov detached a troop to subdue the Kalmyks at Stavropol, but the Kalmyks scattered in all directions, and the detachment returned to Samara without a sight of them.

Colonel Bibikov* was detached from Kazan with four platoons of grenadiers and a squadron of hussars to reinforce Major-General Freymann, who had been staying entirely inactive in Bugulma. Bibikov proceeded to march on Zainsk, whose seventy-year-old commandant, Captain Mertvetsov, had received a band of the brigands deferentially and surrendered control of the town to them. The rebels strengthened their position as best they could; Bibikov heard their cannon fire when he was still five kilometres from the town. But the rebels' defensive spikes were smashed, their batteries wrested from them, and the outskirts of the town occupied: they all took to their heels. Twenty-five rebel villages were pacified in the area. Up to four thousand contrite peasants came to Bibikov each day; they were issued documents and allowed to go home.

Derzhavin, who commanded three platoons of musketeers, brought under control the schismatic settlements on the Irgiz and the nomadic hordes that roamed the region between the Yaik and the Volga.[2] Having heard on one occasion that a multitude of people had gathered in a village with the intention of joining Pugachov's forces, he rode with two Cossacks directly to the meeting place and demanded an explanation from the crowd. Two ringleaders stepped forward, declared their intentions, and started towards Derzhavin levelling accusations and threats. The whole crowd was ready to run riot. But Derzhavin, speaking in a tone of authority, ordered his Cossacks to hang both ringleaders.* His order was carried out immediately, and the mob scattered.

Major-General Larionov, the commander of the legion sponsored by the nobility, who had been sent to liberate Ufa, did not justify the general trust placed in him. "As a punishment for my sins," wrote General Bibikov, "this cousin of mine, A.L., has been foisted on me. He volunteered to command the special detachment himself, but now I can't get him to budge." Larionov stayed in Bakaly, taking no action. His inability to perform his duty forced the commander-in-chief to replace him with an officer who had at one time been wounded under Bibikov's eyes and had distinguished himself in the war against the Polish Confederates – Lieutenant Colonel von Michelsohn.

Prince Golitsyn assumed command of Freymann's troops. On 22nd January he crossed the Kama. On 6th February Colonel Bibikov joined him, and on the 10th Mansurov. The army advanced on Orenburg.

Pugachov was aware of its approach, but paid little attention. He trusted that the regulars would defect and the commanding officers would make blunders. "They'll fall into our hands of themselves," he kept telling his associates when they repeatedly advised him to meet the approaching troops midway. In case of a defeat he intended to flee, leaving his rabble to the mercy of fate. For this purpose he kept thirty horses, chosen for their speed, on the best fodder. The Bashkirs suspected what was on his mind, and grumbled. "You stirred us up," they said, "but now you want to leave us, and then they'll put us to death, like they put our fathers to death." (The executions of 1740 were still fresh in their memory.*)[3] The Yaik Cossacks, on the other hand, contemplated handing Pugachov over to the government, thus winning pardon for themselves. They guarded him as if he were a hostage. As the following remarkable lines written to Fonvizin show, Bibikov read both their minds and Pugachov's:

Pugachov is no more than a plaything in the hands of these Yaik Cossack scoundrels: he is not important; what matters is the general discontent.[4]

Pugachov left his camp near Orenburg for Yaitsk. His arrival put new life into the rebels' operations. On 20th January he himself led a memorable assault on the fortress. In the night part of the wall was blown off under the battery facing the "Staritsa" (the Yaik's former riverbed). The rebels, in full battle cry, rushed at the fortress through the smoke and dust, occupied the moat, and tried to scale the wall with ladders, but were toppled and driven back. All the townspeople, including women and children, gave them support. Pugachov stood in the moat with a spear in his hand, first cheering them on in an attempt to excite their fervour, later stabbing at those who tried to flee. The assault continued without a break for nine hours, to the incessant firing of cannon and musketry. At last Second Lieutenant Tolstovalov made a sortie with fifty volunteers, cleared the moat and drove off the rebels, killing some four hundred at the price of no more than fifteen of his own men. Pugachov ground his teeth. He swore to hang not only Simonov and Krylov themselves, but also Krylov's family, which was in Orenburg at the time. Thus a death sentence was pronounced on a four-year-old boy, who was later to become the famous Krylov.*

While in Yaitsk, Pugachov saw a young Cossack girl, Ustinya Kuznetsova, and fell in love with her. He went to ask for her hand. Her astonished mother and father replied, "Have mercy on us, Sovereign! Our daughter's not of princely or royal blood: how could she be your wife? And in any case, how could you marry while our Lady Sovereign and mother is still in good health?" Nevertheless, Pugachov married Ustinya at the beginning of February, naming her Empress and appointing Cossack women in Yaitsk as her ladies-in-waiting and maids of honour; and he wanted "his wife the Empress Ustinya" to be mentioned in church during the litany, after the Emperor Peter. His priests refused, saying they had not received permission from the Holy Synod. This annoyed Pugachov, but he did not press his request. His wife remained in Yaitsk, where he came to visit her every week. Each time he arrived there was a new attempt on the fortress. But the besieged did not lose heart. Their cannon never grew silent, and their sorties never ceased.

In the early hours of 19th February an under-age lad[5] came running into the fortress from the town and reported that a tunnel leading to the foundation of the bell tower had been completed the day before, and that over three hundred kilograms of gunpowder had been placed in it. Pugachov, he said, had chosen that very day for storming the fortress. The report did not seem credible. Simonov supposed that the urchin had been sent deliberately to cause groundless panic. The defenders, though they had engaged in countermining operations, had not heard any sound of excavations; and three hundred kilograms of powder seemed insufficient to blow up the tall, six-tiered structure. On the other hand, the fortress's whole powder supply was kept in the cellar under the tower (which the rebels could well have known). The defenders decided to bring the powder out at once; they also tore up the brick floor of the cellar and began countermining. The garrison was all prepared for an explosion and an assault. Two hours had scarcely passed when the mine was detonated. The bell tower began slowly to totter. Its lower chamber collapsed and the six upper tiers settled on it, crushing some people who had been standing close by. The stones of the structure, not having been blown apart, collapsed into a pile. The six sentries posted at a cannon on the top tier dropped down alive; one of them, asleep at the time, not only did not suffer any harm, but did not even wake up as he fell.

Even as the tower was still collapsing, the fortress's cannon were already being fired; the garrison troops, who had been standing under arms, immediately occupied the ruins of the tower and set up a battery amid the rubble. The rebels, who had not expected such a reaction, stopped in bewilderment; a few minutes later they issued their usual cry, but none went forward. In vain did the leaders shout, "Charge, brave hetmen, charge!" No assault transpired. The war cries continued until dawn, when the rebels dispersed, grumbling against Pugachov, who had assured them that when the bell tower blew up, it would shower stones on the fortress and crush the whole garrison.

The next day Pugachov received news from his Orenburg camp of Prince Golitsyn's approach. He hurriedly left for Berda, taking with him five hundred cavalrymen and a supply train of some 1,500 conveyances. The news reached the defenders of the fortress too. They rejoiced, calculating that a relief force would reach them in a couple of weeks. But the moment of their liberation was still far off.

During Pugachov's frequent absences, Shigayev, Padurov and Khlopusha directed the siege of Orenburg. Taking advantage of the leader's absence, Khlopusha concocted a plan for overrunning Iletskaya Zashchita[6] (where rock salt is mined), and at the end of February he stormed the outpost with four hundred men. He was able to occupy it with the help of convicts working there – his own family among them. All government property was plundered; all the officers, except for one saved at the convicts' request, were slaughtered; and the convicts were enlisted in the rebels' band. When Pugachov returned to Berda, he was piqued at the bold outlaw's insubordination and reproved him for the destruction of Zashchita as damage to state property. He took the field against Prince Golitsyn with ten thousand selected troops, leaving Shigayev at Orenburg with two thousand men. On the eve of his departure he gave orders to strangle one of his faithful followers, Dmitry Lysov. A few days earlier he and Lysov had been riding from Kargala to Berda; they were both drunk and had quarrelled on the way. Lysov had galloped at Pugachov from behind and struck him with his lance. Pugachov fell off his horse, but the coat of mail he always wore under his clothes saved his life. Subsequently their comrades reconciled them, and Pugachov even sat drinking with Lysov a few hours before the latter's death.

Pugachov took Forts Totskaya and Sorochinsk,[7] and with his usual boldness, attacked Golitsyn's vanguard at night in a heavy snowstorm. He was repulsed, however, by Majors Pushkin and Yelagin. The courageous Yelagin was killed in this battle. Just at this time Mansurov joined forces with Prince Golitsyn. Pugachov retreated to Novosergiyevskaya,[8] with no time to burn the forts he was vacating. Golitsyn, leaving his supplies at Sorochinsk under the protection of four hundred men and eight cannon, marched forward two days later. Pugachov at first moved towards Ilek, but then suddenly turned in the direction of Tatishcheva; he took up position there and started improving its defences. Golitsyn had earlier detached Lieutenant Colonel Bedryaga, with three squadrons of cavalry supported by infantry and artillery, to Ilek, while he himself advanced by a direct route to Perevolotskaya;[9] Bedryaga subsequently rejoined him there. Leaving their supply train under the protection of a battalion commanded by Lieutenant Colonel Grinyov, they advanced on Tatishcheva on 22nd March.

Pugachov had taken and burnt that fort the year before, but by now it had been restored. The burnt-down wooden palisades had been replaced by walls of snow. His preparations astonished Prince Golitsyn, who had not expected him to be so well versed in warcraft. Golitsyn at first detached three hundred men to reconnoitre the enemy.[10] The rebels hid, allowed the reconnoitrers to come right up to the fort, and then suddenly made a sally. Their thrust was checked, however, by two squadrons that had been sent forward to reinforce the reconnoitrers. Colonel Bibikov also threw into action his chasseurs, who, skiing fast on top of the deep snow, occupied all vantage points. Golitsyn arranged his troops in two columns, advanced on the fort, and opened fire, to which the fort responded in kind. The shooting continued for three hours. Seeing that his cannon alone could not overpower the enemy, Golitsyn threw Freymann with the left column into attack. Pugachov brought seven fieldpieces outside to counter him, but Freymann's forces overran these and stormed the frozen walls. The rebels put up a desperate defence but had to yield to the superiority of a properly trained army; they soon fled in all directions. The cavalry, which until then had been kept in reserve, pursued them along all the roads. The bloodshed was horrendous. Some 1,300 rebels were slaughtered at the one fort. Their bodies lay scattered around Tatishcheva for a radius of over twenty kilometres. Golitsyn lost about four hundred men killed or wounded, among them over twenty officers.[11] It was a decisive victory. The victor took thirty-six cannon and over three thousand prisoners. Pugachov broke through the enemy lines with sixty Cossacks; he galloped to Berda with four companions, bringing the news of their defeat. The rebels began to flee from the village, some on horseback, some on sledges. They piled their vehicles high with plunder. The women and children went on foot. Afraid of drunkenness and mutiny, Pugachov gave orders to smash the barrels of liquor standing near his house. The liquor poured out on the street. Shigayev, meanwhile, seeing that all was lost, schemed to earn himself a pardon: he held Pugachov and Khlopusha back,[12] and sent an emissary to the governor of Orenburg offering to hand over the pretender and asking the governor to signal his agreement with two shots from a cannon. The lieutenant Loginov, who had fled with Pugachov earlier, brought the offer to Reinsdorp. The poor governor could not believe his luck, and for two full hours could not make up his mind whether to give the required signal! In the meantime some convicts still in Berda released Pugachov and Khlopusha. Pugachov fled with ten fieldpieces, with his booty and with the remainder of his mob, numbering 2,000. Khlopusha galloped to Kargala hoping to save his wife and son. The Tatars tied him up and sent word to the governor. The famous outlaw was brought to Orenburg, where they finally beheaded him in June 1774.

The citizens of Orenburg, learning of their liberation, dashed out of the city in large crowds, close on the heels of the six hundred infantry soldiers Reinsdorp dispatched to the abandoned village of Berda, and helped themselves to provisions. Eighteen cannon, seventeen barrelfuls of copper coins,[13] and a large quantity of grain were found in the village. The people of Orenburg hastened to offer thanks to God for their unexpected liberation. Golitsyn was eulogized. Reinsdorp wrote to him to congratulate him on his victory, calling him the liberator of Orenburg.[14] Supplies began arriving in the city from all directions. Suddenly there was abundance, and the harrowing siege of six months was forgotten in one joyous moment. On 26th March Golitsyn came to Orenburg and was received with indescribable enthusiasm.*

Bibikov had been waiting for this turning point with impatience. He had left Kazan in order to speed up the military operations, but he had got only as far as Bugulma when news of the complete victory over Pugachov reached him. He could not contain his joy. He wrote to his wife on 26th March:

> *What a weight off my mind! My army will enter Orenburg today; I am hurrying there, too, to be able to direct the operations more easily. There are so many more grey hairs in my beard now, God is my witness, and the bald patch on my head has grown still bigger; but even so I go around without a wig in the freezing weather.*

In the meantime Pugachov, eluding all the patrols that had been sent out, reached the Seitov settlement on the 24th,[15] set it on fire and moved on to Sakmarsk township, collecting a new mob along the way. He evidently surmised that from Tatishcheva Golitsyn would turn towards Yaitsk with all his forces, so he suddenly came back to reoccupy Berda, hoping also to take Orenburg by surprise. Golitsyn, however, was advised of this bold move by Colonel Khorvat, who had been on Pugachov's tracks ever since he had left Tatishcheva. Reinforcing his troops with the infantry and Cossack detachments stationed in Orenburg – giving the Cossacks the last horses from under his own officers – Golitsyn set out against the pretender immediately, and made contact with him at Kargala. Pugachov, realizing he had miscalculated, beat a retreat, cleverly taking advantage of the topography of the area. He set up seven fieldpieces against Colonels Bibikov and Arshenevsky astride the narrow road and, under their protection, adroitly dashed off towards the Sakmara River. By now, however, Bibikov's fieldpieces had caught up with him; his men took a hill and set up a battery. Khorvat, on his part, attacked the rebels in the last defile, wrested their fieldpieces from them, routed them, and chased throngs of them for eight kilometres, riding into Sakmarsk along with them. Pugachov lost his last fieldpieces, four hundred men killed, and 3,500 taken prisoner. His chief followers – Shigayev, Pochitalin, Padurov and others – were among those captured. He fled with four factory serfs to Prechistenskaya, and from there to the Ural factories. The tired cavalry could not catch up with him. After this decisive victory, Golitsyn returned to Orenburg and detached

Freymann to pacify Bashkiria, Arshenevsky to clear the new Moscow road, and Mansurov to Ilek to clear that whole region and then proceed to rescue Simonov.

Michelsohn's manoeuvres were just as successful. Having taken command of his detachment on 18th March, he immediately set out for Ufa. Chika dispatched two thousand men with four fieldpieces to block his advance. They waited for him in the village of Zhukovo. Leaving them at his rear, Michelsohn headed straight for Chesnokovka, where Chika was waiting with ten thousand rebels. On his way he scattered a few smaller rebel detachments, and at dawn on the 25th he arrived at the village of Trebikova (five kilometres from Chesnokovka). Here a band of rebels with two fieldpieces engaged him, but Major Kharin crushed and scattered them while the chasseurs took possession of the fieldpieces. Michelsohn was able to move on. His supply train was protected by a hundred men with one fieldpiece, who also served as a rear guard in case of attack. He encountered more rebels at dawn on the 26th outside the village of Zubovka. Some of them sallied forth on skis or on horseback and, spreading out on either side of the highway, tried to encircle him, while a force of three thousand men, supported by ten fieldpieces, met him head-on. At the same time a battery inside the village opened fire. The battle lasted four hours. The rebels fought bravely. At last Michelsohn, seeing that a detachment of horsemen was arriving to reinforce the rebels, flung all his forces at their central corps and ordered his own cavalry, which had dismounted at the beginning of the engagement, to remount and rush to the charge with sabres. The first line of the enemy's defence took to flight, abandoning the fieldpieces. Kharin, hacking at them all the way to Chesnokovka, entered the village close on their heels. Meanwhile the cavalry detachment coming to reinforce them at Zubovka had been repulsed; its members, too, began to flee to Chesnokovka, were met by Kharin, and were captured to man. The skiers, who had managed to get around Michelsohn's main corps and cut off his supply train, were smashed by two platoons of grenadiers. They scattered into the woods. Three thousand rebels were taken prisoner. The factory and church serfs* were sent home to their villages. Twenty-five fieldpieces and a large quantity of munitions were captured. Michelsohn hanged two leading insurgents: a Bashkir elder and the elected head of Chesnokovka village. The siege of Ufa was lifted. Michelsohn, without stopping, proceeded to Tabynsk, where Ulyanov and Chika had escaped after the action at Chesnokovka. There they were seized[16] by some Cossacks and surrendered to the victor, who sent them to Ufa in fetters. Michelsohn detailed patrols in all directions and was able to restore order in most of the villages that had rebelled.

Ilek and the forts of Lower Ozyornaya and Rassypnaya, which had witnessed Pugachov's first successes, had by now been abandoned by the rebels. Their rebel commanders, Chuloshnikov and Kizilbashin, fled to Yaitsk. The day they arrived, news of the pretender's defeat at Tatishcheva reached them. Rebels fleeing from Khorvat's hussars galloped through the forts shouting, "Run for your lives, fellows, all is lost!" They hastily bandaged their wounds and hurried to Yaitsk. Soon the spring thaw set in, clearing the rivers of ice; the corpses of those killed at Tatishcheva floated downstream, past the forts. Wives and mothers stood on the riverbanks, trying to identify their husbands or sons among the corpses. An old Cossack woman wandered along the Yaik by Lower Ozyornaya every day,[17] drawing the floating corpses to the bank with a crooked stick and saying, "Is that you, my child? Is it you, my Stepushka? Are these your black curls, washed by the waves?" And when she saw an unfamiliar face she gently pushed the corpse away.*

On 6th and 7th April Mansurov occupied the abandoned forts and Ilek township, where he found fourteen cannon. On the 15th, as he was fording the swollen stream Bykovka under dangerous conditions, Ovchinnikov, Perfilyev and Degterev pounced on him. They were beaten back and scattered; Bedryaga and Borodin chased after them, but the bad condition of the roads saved the band's leaders.

The fortress at Yaitsk had been invested since the very beginning of the year.[18] Pugachov's absence had not cooled the rebels' fighting spirit. Crowbars and spades were forged at the smithies; new batteries were put up. The rebels assiduously continued their excavations, now digging a breach in the bank of the Chechora, thereby cutting off communication between the two parts of the town, now digging trenches in order to block sorties. They were planning to dig tunnels into the steep bank of the old river bed all the way around under the fortress, undermining the main church, the batteries, and the commandant's palace. The defenders found themselves in constant danger and were forced to dig counter-tunnels on all sides, working with great difficulty to break up ground that was frozen three quarters of a metre deep. They partitioned the inside of the fortress with a new wall and with barricades made of sacks filled with bricks from the blown-up bell tower.

At dawn on 9th March, 250 regulars sallied out of the fortress with the aim of destroying a new battery that had been severely harassing them. They reached the town barricades, but there they encountered strong fire. Their ranks were broken. The rebels caught them in the narrow passages between the barricades and the houses to which they had intended to set fire; they slaughtered those who were wounded or fell, chopping their heads off with axes. The soldiers beat a retreat. Some thirty were killed, and eighty wounded. Never had the garrison suffered so much loss from a sortie. All they had succeeded in doing was to burn down one battery, not the main one at that, and a few houses. The testimony they extracted from three rebels brought back as prisoners deepened the defenders' despondency, for the prisoners told them about the mines under the fortress and about Pugachov's expected arrival. The frightened Simonov gave orders to start new work in all directions: the ground around his house was constantly probed with drills, and digging of a new trench was begun. The men were exhausted, not only because of the hard work, but also because they got scarcely any sleep at night: half of the garrison always remained under arms, and the other half was only allowed to sleep sitting up. The hospital filled with invalids; the provisions left could not last more than ten days. The soldiers' daily ration was reduced to a quarter of a pound of flour, one-tenth of their regular allowance. They ran out of both groats and salt. The soldiers would boil some water in a common cauldron, whiten it with a little flour, drink a cupful – and that was their daily meal. The women, unable to endure the hunger any longer, began asking for permission to leave the fort, and they were told they could go. A few debilitated and sick soldiers followed their lead, but the rebels would not accept them. The women were kept under arrest for a night and then herded back to the fortress with the promise that any inmates let out would be received and fed provided that the rebels' comrades kept in the fortress were released. Simonov, wary of increasing the enemy's numbers, could not agree to that condition. The hunger became more and more horrible every day. The horsemeat, which had been rationed by weight, was all gone. Everyone began eating cats and dogs. Some dead horses thrown out on the ice at the beginning of the siege three months before were now remembered, and people eagerly gnawed at bones already stripped bare of their meat by the dogs. Finally even this supply ran out. New resources for sustenance were being invented. A kind of clay was found that was exceptionally soft and free of sand. People tried to cook it, making a kind of blancmange from it, and started eating it. The soldiers lost all their strength. Some could no longer walk. Infants of sick mothers wasted away. The women tried several times to touch the rebels' hearts, throwing themselves at their feet and begging to be allowed to stay in the town. They were chased back with the earlier demands. Only some Cossack women were admitted. The long-expected relief had not come. The defenders had to postpone their hopes from day to day, from week to week. The rebels shouted to the garrison that the government's troops had been crushed, that Orenburg, Ufa and Kazan had already bowed down before the pretender, and that he would soon be coming to Yaitsk, by which time there would be no mercy. On the other hand, they promised in his name that surrender would bring not only pardon but even rewards. They tried to impress the same on the minds of the poor women who were pleading to be allowed into the town. It was impossible for the commanding officers to give hope to the besieged that relief would arrive quickly, because nobody could even hear talk of it now without getting angry: so hardened were their hearts by long and futile waiting. What the commanders did try was to maintain the garrison's loyalty and obedience by emphasizing that no one could save his life by a shameful desertion, since the rebels, enraged by the garrison's long resistance, would not spare even those who renounced their oaths of allegiance. They tried to awaken in the souls of their unfortunate soldiers a trust in God, omnipotent and omniscient; and the sufferers, their spirits raised, would repeat that it was better to put one's fate into God's hands than to serve the impostor. Indeed no more than two or three men defected from the fortress during the whole of the harrowing siege.

Passion Week came. The defenders had been eating nothing but clay for fifteen days. None wanted to die of starvation. They decided that all of them (except those entirely incapacitated) would participate in a last sally. With no hope for victory (the rebels had erected such fortifications that they were unapproachable from the fortress on any side), they simply wanted to die the honourable death of soldiers.

On Tuesday, the day assigned for the sally, the sentries posted on the roof of the main church noticed that the rebels were running about town in confusion, saying goodbye to one another, congregating again, and riding out onto the steppe in large groups. The Cossack women were with them. The besieged suspected that something unusual was going on, and their hopes were raised once more. "All this buoyed our spirit as much," writes an eyewitness who had lived through all the horrors of the siege, "as if we had each eaten a piece of bread." But the confusion gradually abated, and everything seemed to have returned to normal. The defenders fell into even deeper despondency. In silence they fixed their gaze on the steppe, whence, only a short time before, they had expected their liberators to emerge… Then, suddenly, towards five o'clock in the afternoon, clouds of dust appeared in the distance, and great bands of people could be seen galloping in disarray, one after another, from behind a wood. The rebels rode in through various gates, each through the one closest to his house. The besieged realized that the insurgents had been beaten and were fleeing; but they still did not dare rejoice, fearing a last desperate assault. The townspeople ran up and down the streets as if the town were burning. Towards evening they rang the bells in the cathedral, gathered in a circle, and approached the fortress in one great throng. The defenders were getting ready to beat them back, but they noticed that the rebels were bringing their leaders, Hetmen Kargin and Tolkachov, tied up. The crowd came up close and loudly pleaded for mercy. Simonov admitted them, though he could hardly credit his deliverance. The garrison threw themselves on the loaves of bread brought by the townspeople. "There were still four days left until Easter Sunday," writes one eyewitness of these events, "but for us that day was already the festival of resurrection." Even those who had been bound to their beds by weakness or disease recovered on the instant. The whole fortress was in an uproar, with everybody giving thanks to God and congratulating each other; that night no one slept a wink. The townspeople told the defenders about the lifting of the siege of Orenburg and Mansurov's impending arrival. On 17th April he did arrive. The gates of the fortress, which had been locked and obstructed since 30th December, were opened. Mansurov assumed command of the city. The leaders of the rebellion, Kargin, Tolkachov and Gorshkov, as well as the pretender's illegitimate wife Ustinya Kuznetsova, were taken to Orenburg under guard.

Such was the success that crowned the measures taken by an experienced, intelligent commander-in-chief. But Bibikov did not have the opportunity to complete what he had begun: tired out by work, worry and troubles, taking little care of his already failing health, he developed a fever in Bugulma. Sensing that his end was approaching, he gave some final orders. He sealed all his confidential papers, with instructions to have them delivered to the Empress, and handed over command to his highest-ranking officer, Lieutenant General Shcherbatov. He still had time to send a report to the Empress about the liberation of Ufa, of which he had just received some oral reports, but soon after, on 9th April at 11 a.m., he died. He was in his forty-fourth year. His body had to remain on the bank of the Kama for several days, because it was impossible to cross the river at the time. Kazan wanted to inter him in their cathedral, erecting a monument to their deliverer, but at the insistence of Bibikov's family his body was taken to his estate. A ribbon of the Order of St Andrew, the title of senator and the rank of Colonel of the Guards were too late to reach him alive. On his deathbed he had said: "I do not feel sorry to leave my wife and children, for the Empress will look after them; I feel sorry to part with my fatherland."[19]

A rumour attributed his death to poisoning, supposedly by a Polish Confederate. Derzhavin wrote a poem about his demise. Catherine mourned him and showered his family with favours.[20] St Petersburg and Moscow were horror-stricken. Soon the whole of Russia was to realize what an irreparable loss had befallen her.[21]

Chapter VI

PUGACHOV'S NEW SUCCESSES – THE BASHKIR SALAVAT – THE TAKING OF SIBERIAN FORTS – THE BATTLE AT TROITSK – PUGACHOV'S RETREAT – HIS FIRST ENCOUNTER WITH MICHELSOHN – IN PURSUIT OF PUGACHOV – THE INACTIVITY OF GOVERNMENT TROOPS – THE TAKING OF OSA – PUGACHOV OUTSIDE KAZAN

Pugachov's position seemed desperate. He turned up at the Avzyano-Petrovsk metalworks. Ovchinnikov and Perfilyev, pursued by Major Shevich, galloped through the Sakmara Line with three hundred Yaik Cossacks and managed to join forces with Pugachov. The Stavropol and Orenburg Kalmyks wanted to follow them, and advanced, with six hundred covered wagons, towards Fort Sorochinsk. Retired Lieutenant Colonel Melkovich, an intelligent and resolute man, was in the fort at the time supervising provisions and fodder. He assumed command of the garrison, attacked the Kalmyks, and forced them to return to their respective homes.

Pugachov moved quickly from one place to another. Mobs started to gather around him as before; the Bashkirs, who had been almost entirely pacified, rebelled again. The commandant of the Upper Yaitsk Fort, Colonel Stupishin, penetrated Bashkiria and burnt down some deserted villages; he caught one of the rebels, had his ears, nose and right-hand fingers cut off, and let him go with the threat that he would do the same to all the other insurgents. But the Bashkirs did not relent. The old troublemaker Yulay, who had gone into hiding at the time of the executions of 1741,[1] reappeared among them with his son Salavat. The whole of Bashkiria rose up in arms, the conflagration spreading with even greater force than before. Freymann was supposed to pursue Pugachov, while Michelsohn made every effort to intercept him, but he was saved by the bad condition of the roads in spring. The highways were impassable, the men were mired in bottomless mud, rivers swelled to widths of several kilometres, and streams became rivers. Freymann stopped in Sterlitamak. Michelsohn, who had managed to cross the Vyatka while it was still iced over, and the Ufa River in eight boats, continued his forward march despite all the impediments, and on 5th March, near the Sim metalworks, caught up with a horde of Bashkirs under the command of the fierce Salavat. Michelsohn routed them, liberated the factory, and continued his advance the next day. Salavat took up position nineteen kilometres from the metalworks, waiting for Beloborodov. They subsequently joined forces and took the field against Michelsohn with two thousand rebels and eight fieldpieces. Michelsohn beat them once more, seizing their fieldpieces, slaying some three hundred of their numbers on the spot, and scattering the rest. He then hurried on to the Uyskoye metalworks in the hope of catching up with Pugachov himself, but soon learnt that the pretender was already at the Beloretsk plants.

Beyond the Yuryuzan River, Michelsohn succeeded in crushing another rebel horde, pursuing them all the way to the Satka works. Here he learnt that Pugachov, having rallied some six thousand Bashkirs and peasants, had advanced on Fort Magnitnaya. Michelsohn decided to move deeper into the Ural Mountains in the hope of joining forces with Freymann near the headwaters of the Yaik.

After plundering and burning down the Beloretsk metalworks, Pugachov quickly crossed the Ural Mountains, and on 5th May he set siege to Magnitnaya, even though he had no cannon with him. Captain Tikhanovsky defended the fort bravely. Pugachov himself took an arm wound from grapeshot and withdrew, having suffered considerable losses. It appeared that the fort had been saved, but it soon became evident that there was a traitor within: one night the fort's powder magazine was blown up, after which the rebels stormed it, tore down the palisades and rushed inside. Tikhanovsky and his wife were both hanged; the fort was plundered and burnt down. The same day Beloborodov joined Pugachov with a mob of four thousand rebels.

Lieutenant General Dekalong advanced from Chelyabinsk, which had recently been liberated from the rebels, in the direction of the Upper Yaitsk Fort, hoping to catch Pugachov still at the

Beloretsk works, but no sooner had he reached the line of defence than he received a report from Colonel Stupishin, the commandant at Upper Yaitsk, informing him that Pugachov was proceeding up the line from one fort to another, just as when he had made his first terrifying appearance. Dekalong hurried on towards Upper Yaitsk. As soon as he reached it, he heard of the taking of Magnitnaya. He set off towards Kizilskoye. He had already covered sixteen kilometres when he learnt from a captured Bashkir that Pugachov, having heard of the approach of government troops, was no longer heading for Kizilskoye but was taking a route straight through the Ural Mountains to Karagaysky. Dekalong turned around. Arriving at Karagaysky, he saw only smoking ruins: Pugachov had left the day before. Dekalong hoped to catch up with him at Petrozavodsk but missed him there, too. The fort had been ravaged and burnt, its church had been plundered, and the icons stripped of their frames and smashed to smithereens.

Dekalong left the line and took a shortcut straight to Fort Uyskoye. He was down to his last day's supply of oats. He thought he might be able to catch up with Pugachov at Fort Stepnoye if not before; but he soon learnt that even Stepnoye had already been taken; he rushed to Troitsk. On the way there, at Sanarka, he found a great many people who had escaped from the destroyed forts in the vicinity. Officers' wives and children, barefooted and in rags, were sobbing, not knowing where to seek refuge. Dekalong took them under his protection, entrusting them to the care of his officers. On the morning of 21st May, after a forced march of sixty-four kilometres, he drew near Troitsk and at last set eyes on Pugachov, who had pitched camp outside the fort, which he had taken the day before. Dekalong attacked immediately. Pugachov had more than ten thousand troops and some thirty cannon. The engagement lasted four long hours. Pugachov lay in his tent through it all, suffering from the wound he had received at Magnitnaya. Beloborodov was in charge of operations. At last the rebels' ranks were broken. Pugachov, his arm in a sling, got on his horse and rushed about in all directions trying to restore order, but his troops were all scattered and running. He got away along the Chelyabinsk road with one fieldpiece. It was impossible to pursue him; the cavalry was far too tired. Dekalong found some three thousand people of both sexes, of all ages, from all walks of life, at the camp: they had been rounded up by the pretender and were destined for execution. The fort was saved from fire and pillage, but its commandant, Brigadier Feyervar, had been killed in the previous day's assault, and his officers had been hanged.

Pugachov and Beloborodov, knowing that the exhaustion of Dekalong's troops and horses would not allow him to take advantage of his victory, reassembled their scattered hordes and began an orderly retreat, taking forts and mustering fresh forces along the way. Majors Gagrin and Zholobov, detached by Dekalong the day after the battle to pursue them, were unable to catch up with them.

Michelsohn, meanwhile, was advancing along little-known roads across the Ural Mountains. The Bashkir villages were deserted. It was impossible to obtain the necessary supplies. His detachment was in constant danger from the many bands of rebels swirling around it. On 13th May some Bashkirs under the leadership of a rebellious elder fell on him and fought desperately. Even when driven back into a swamp they would not surrender. All, except one, who was forcibly saved, were slain together with their leader. Michelsohn lost one officer and sixty men killed or wounded.

The captive Bashkir, whom Michelsohn treated with kindness, told him about the taking of Magnitnaya and the movements of Dekalong. Michelsohn, finding these reports consistent with his own suppositions, left the mountains and advanced on Troitsk in the hope of either being able to liberate that fort or encountering Pugachov, should he be retreating. He soon heard about Dekalong's victory and proceeded to Varlamovo with the intention of blocking Pugachov's way. And indeed, on the morning of 22nd May, as he approached Varlamovo, he ran into Pugachov's vanguard. Seeing an orderly troop, Michelsohn could not at first imagine this to be the remnant of the horde beaten the day before, and he took it (as he says wryly in his report) for the corps of Lieutenant General Cavalier Dekalong. He soon realized his mistake, however, and halted, retaining his advantageous position next to a forest that provided cover for his rear. Pugachov at first marched on him, but then suddenly turned off towards Fort Cherbarkul. Michelsohn cut across the wood and intercepted Pugachov. This was the first time the pretender came face to face with the man who was to strike so many blows at him and was to put an end to his bloody enterprise. Pugachov immediately attacked his left flank, threw it into disarray, and wrested away two fieldpieces. But Michelsohn bore down on the rebels with the whole of his cavalry and managed to scatter them in one minute, taking back his fieldpieces along with the last cannon that had remained in Pugachov's possession after his defeat at Troitsk. Some six hundred rebels lay slain on the field, five hundred were taken prisoner, and the rest pursued for several kilometres. Nightfall interrupted the chase. Michelsohn spent the night on the battlefield. In the next day's orders he severely reprimanded the platoon that had lost its fieldpieces, and he stripped the soldiers of their insignia buttons and brassards until such time as they merited them again. Indeed the platoon soon made amends for its dishonourable conduct.[2]

On the 23rd Michelsohn marched on Fort Cherbarkul. The Cossacks stationed there had mutinied, but Michelsohn administered a new oath to them, signing them into his own corps, and he never had cause to be dissatisfied with them thereafter.

Zholobov and Gagrin operated slowly and indecisively. Having informed Michelsohn that Pugachov had rallied his scattered horde and was mustering new forces, Zholobov refused to march against him under the pretext of flooding rivers and bad roads. Michelsohn complained to Dekalong. Although Dekalong promised to come forward to extirpate Pugachov's last remaining forces, he remained in Chelyabinsk and, to make matters worse, ordered Zholobov and Gagrin to join him.

Thus the task of pursuing Pugachov was left to Michelsohn alone. Having heard of the presence of some Yaik Cossack rebels at the Zlatoust metalworks, he went there, but the rebels learnt of his approach and escaped. The farther their traces led, the less distinct they became, and they finally disappeared altogether.

On 27th May Michelsohn arrived at the Satka works.[3] Salavat was ravaging the surrounding countryside with a fresh band. He had already plundered and burnt the Sim metalworks. Hearing of

Michelsohn, he crossed the Ay River and stayed in the mountains, where Pugachov, no longer pursued by Gagrin and Zholobov, managed to join him with a ragtag mob of two thousand.

At the Satka works, which had been saved thanks to his celerity, Michelsohn took his first rest since leaving the Ufa area. He set out against Pugachov and Salavat two days later and came to the bank of the Ay. The bridges had been dismantled. The rebels, seeing the small size of Michelsohn's detachment, felt safe on the other side of the river.

On the morning of the 30th, however, Michelsohn ordered fifty Cossacks to swim their horses across the river, each double riding with a chasseur behind him. The rebels were ready to fall on this group but were scattered by cannon fire from the other side. The chasseurs and Cossacks held the bridgehead as best they could while Michelsohn forded the river with the rest of the detachment: the gunpowder was carried by the cavalry, and the fieldpieces were sunk to the bottom and dragged across by ropes. Michelsohn quickly attacked the enemy forces, crushed them, and pursued them for twenty-one kilometres, killing some four hundred and taking a great many prisoners. Pugachov, Beloborodov and Salavat – the last one wounded – barely managed to escape.

The surrounding countryside was deserted. Michelsohn could find no one to tell him where the enemy had fled. He set out at random, and during the night of 2nd June Captain Kartashevsky, whom he had detached with a vanguard, found himself surrounded by Salavat's band. Towards morning Michelsohn reached him, in time to help. The rebels scattered and fled. Michelsohn pursued them with extreme caution: his infantry protected his supply train, and he himself rode at the head of the column, accompanied by some of the cavalry. This arrangement was what saved him. A large band of rebels suddenly surrounded his supply train and attacked his infantry. Pugachov himself led them: in a matter of six days he had gathered some five thousand rebels around the Satka works. Michelsohn galloped back to the supply train to help, and stayed there with the infantry, sending Kharin to bring the cavalry together. The rebels were beaten and took flight once more. Michelsohn learnt from captives that Pugachov intended to march on Ufa. He rushed ahead to intercept him and on June 5 encountered him again. An engagement was unavoidable; Michelsohn attacked quickly, defeating and driving away the enemy once more.

Despite all his successes Michelsohn realized that he needed to interrupt his pursuit of the enemy for a while. He had run out of both provisions and munitions. Each man had only two cartridges left. Michelsohn went to Ufa in order to stock up with everything he needed.

While Michelsohn rushed this way and that, striking at the enemy, the other leaders of the army remained immobile. Dekalong stayed put at Chelyabinsk and, out of jealousy of Michelsohn, positively refused to cooperate with him. Freymann, a personally courageous man but a timid and indecisive leader, stayed at Fort Kizilskoye, annoyed with Timashev for going off to Fort Zilair[4] with his best cavalry. Stanislavsky had already distinguished himself by cowardice in all the proceedings, but when he heard that Pugachov had gathered a significant mob and was near Fort Upper Yaitsk, he abandoned his post and fled to Fort Orsk, his favourite hiding place. Colonels Yakubovich and Obernibesov, together with Major Duve, were near Ufa, but they allowed the rebellious Bashkirs to assemble all around them undisturbed. Birsk was burnt down almost under their very eyes, but they marched from one place to another, avoiding the remotest danger and not thinking to coordinate their actions. On Prince Shcherbatov's instructions Golitsyn's troops remained in the vicinity of Orenburg and Yaitsk, where they were entirely useless since these places were already out of danger, while the region where the conflagration was spreading again was left defenceless.[5] Pugachov, driven away from Kungur by Major Popov, was about to advance on Yekaterinburg, but hearing of the troops stationed there, he turned off towards Krasnoufimsk.

The Kama valley was left open, and Kazan exposed to danger. Brandt hurriedly dispatched Major Skrypitsyn with a garrison detachment and armed peasants to the small town of Osa, and at the same time wrote to Prince Shcherbatov demanding immediate help. Shcherbatov, however, placed his hopes in Obernibesov and Duve, who were supposed to come to Major Skrypitsyn's assistance in case of danger, and he took no new measures.

On 18th June Pugachov appeared outside Osa. Skrypitsyn took the field against him, but on losing three cannon at the very beginning of the engagement he hastily withdrew into the fort. Pugachov ordered his men to dismount and to storm the fort. They entered the town and burnt it, but they were driven away from the fort itself by cannon fire.

The next day Pugachov and some of his chief associates rode over to the Kama, looking for a convenient place to cross it. He ordered his men to repair the highway and lay logs and brushwood over muddy patches. On the 20th he stormed the fort once more, and was driven back once more. After this, Beloborodov advised him to encircle the fort with wagons full of hay, straw and birch bark with which to set the wooden walls on fire. Fifteen wagons were drawn by horses to within a short distance of the fort, and then pushed forward by men who were safe behind them. At this juncture Skrypitsyn, who had already wavered somewhat, asked for a one-day truce, and on the following day he surrendered, receiving Pugachov on his knees, with icons and bread and salt. The pretender treated him kindly and allowed him to continue wearing his sword. The hapless major thought that in time he could vindicate himself, and, together with Captain Smirnov and Sub-Lieutenant Mineyev, he composed a letter to the governor of Kazan, which he carried around with him, waiting for an opportunity to send it off secretly. Mineyev told Pugachov about this. The letter was seized, Skrypitsyn and Smirnov were hanged, and the informer was promoted to colonel.

On 23rd June Pugachov crossed the Kama and advanced on the Izhevsk and Votkinsk distilleries. The director, Wenzel, was tortured to death, the plants were plundered, and the workers were signed into the villainous horde. Mineyev, who had earned Pugachov's trust by his treachery, advised him to march straight for Kazan. Informed as he was about the precautions the governor had taken, he offered to guide Pugachov, vouching for success. Pugachov did not vacillate for long: he marched on Kazan.

The news of the fall of Osa frightened Shcherbatov. He sent an order to Obernibesov to occupy the ferry at Shum and dispatched Major Mellin to the one at Shurma. Golitsyn was ordered to proceed to Ufa as fast as possible and to operate in that region according to his best judgment. Shcherbatov himself set out for Bugulma with a squadron of hussars and a platoon of grenadiers.

There were only 1,500 troops in Kazan, but six thousand of the local citizenry were armed in haste. Brandt and the military commandant, Banner, prepared to defend the city. Major-General Potyomkin,* chairman of the Secret Commission set up to investigate the Pugachov affair, helped them in every way he could. Major-General Larionov, on the other hand, did not wait for Pugachov's arrival: he and his men crossed the Volga and decamped for Nizhny Novgorod.

Colonel Tolstoy, commander of the Kazan cavalry legion, took the field against Pugachov and on 10th July made contact with him thirteen kilometres from the city. A battle ensued. The brave Tolstoy was killed, and his troops scattered. The next day Pugachov appeared on the left bank of the Kazanka and pitched camp near the Troitsk mill. In the evening he rode out, in plain view of all the inhabitants, to inspect the city, then returned to his camp, postponing the assault until the next morning.

Chapter VII

PUGACHOV IN KAZAN – THE CITY'S ORDEAL – MICHELSOHN'S ARRIVAL – THREE BATTLES – THE LIBERATION OF KAZAN – PUGACHOV'S ENCOUNTER WITH HIS FAMILY – REFUTATION OF A LIBEL – MICHELSOHN'S DISPOSITIONS

At dawn on 12th July the rebels, under Pugachov's command, advanced in a column from the village of Tsaritsyn across Arskoye Field, pushing their wagons loaded with hay and straw interspersed with fieldpieces. They quickly occupied the brick barns near the city outskirts, a coppice and Kudryavtsev's country residence; there they set up their batteries, sweeping aside the feeble detachment that guarded the highway. The detachment retreated in square formation, sheltering behind defensive spikes.

The city's main battery was positioned directly opposite Arskoye Field. Pugachov did not attack on that side, but sent a detachment of factory peasants from his right wing, under the command of the traitor Mineyev, towards the suburb. This herd of riff-raff, mostly unarmed and driven forward by the Cossacks' whips, nimbly ran from gully to gully and hollow to hollow, scrambling across ridges exposed to cannon fire, until it reached the ravines on the very edge of the suburb. This dangerous point was defended by grammar school students equipped with one cannon. Despite fire from this cannon, the rebels carried out to the letter the instructions Pugachov had given them: they clambered onto the high ground, chased the students away with their bare fists, took charge of the cannon, and occupied the governor's summer residence, which had a gate opening onto the suburb; they placed the cannon in that gate, started firing into the streets, and burst into the suburb in packs. On the other side, Pugachov's left wing assaulted the Drapers' Quarter. The quarter's inhabitants (of different classes, but most of them good fist fighters) armed themselves as best they could, under the encouragement of Archbishop Veniamin; they set up a cannon at Gorlov's tavern, and were ready to defend the area.[1] The Bashkirs released a volley of arrows at them from Sharnaya Hill and charged into the streets. The local people were about to beat them off with crowbars, spears and sabres, but their cannon blew up at the first shot, killing the cannoneer. At the same time Pugachov set up his fieldpieces on Sharnaya Hill and fired grapeshot at both his own men and the townsfolk. The quarter caught fire. The inhabitants fled. The rebels swept away the guards and defensive spikes and poured through the streets of the city. Seeing the flames, the citizens and the garrison left the cannon behind and dashed to the fortress as their last refuge. Potyomkin entered with them. The city became the rebels' booty. They rushed to plunder the houses and shops; burst into churches and monasteries, stripping the iconostases; and slew anyone they came across in western dress. Pugachov set up his batteries in the market hall's eating place, behind the churches and by the triumphal gates, and opened fire on the fortress, especially on the Monastery of the Saviour, whose ancient walls formed its right-hand corner and barely held together. On the other side, Mineyev pulled up a cannon onto the gates of the Kazan Monastery and another one onto the portico of a church and bombarded the fortress at its most vulnerable point. A cannon ball from the fortress, however, smashed one of his guns. The bandits decked themselves out in women's dresses and priests' surplices, and ran around the streets screaming, plundering and setting houses on fire. Those engaged in the siege of the fortress began to envy them, fearing to be left out of the booty... Suddenly Pugachov ordered them to withdraw. Setting fire to a few more houses, they returned to their camp. The wind rose. A sea of flames spread across the whole city. Sparks and charred pieces of wood were blown into the fortress and set several wooden roofs on fire. At this moment part of a wall collapsed with the boom of a thunderclap, crushing several people. The besieged, huddled in the fortress, sent up a wail, believing that the villain had burst in and their last hour had struck.

Those who had been captured were herded out of the city, and the loot was carted away. The Bashkirs, disregarding Pugachov's strict orders to the contrary, kept lashing the people with whips and jabbing pikes at the women and children who fell behind. A great many drowned while fording the Kazanka River. When the captives had at last been driven to the camp, they were lined up on their knees in front of cannon. The women burst into a howl. It was announced that they were pardoned. They all shouted "Hurrah!" and rushed to Pugachov's tent. Seated in an armchair, he was receiving gifts from the Kazan Tatars who had ridden in to do obeisance to him. Then the question was put, "Who wishes to serve the Emperor Peter III?" – Many were the volunteers.

During the entire siege, Archbishop Veniamin[2] stationed himself inside the fortress, at the Cathedral of the Annunciation, praying on his knees with the citizenry for the deliverance of the faithful. The cannonade had hardly ceased when he raised the miracle-working icons and, defying falling beams and the unbearable heat of the conflagration, processed around the inside of the fortress with all his clergy, accompanied by the citizenry, to the chanting of prayers. Towards evening the storm abated and the wind changed direction. Night set in – a night of horror for the citizens! Kazan, reduced to heaps of burning embers, smoked and glowed in the dark. No one could sleep. At dawn the citizens hurried onto the battlements and fixed their gaze on the side from which a new assault was expected. But instead of Pugachov's hordes they beheld, to their amazement, Michelsohn's hussars galloping towards the city under the command of an officer sent from him to the governor.

Nobody knew that Michelsohn the previous afternoon had fought a ferocious battle with Pugachov seven kilometres from the city and that the rebels had retreated in disorder.

Last time we mentioned Michelsohn he had been doggedly tracking Pugachov's precipitate onrush. He left his sick and wounded in Ufa, attached Major Duve to his own corps and by 21st June arrived in Burnovo, a few kilometres from Birsk. The rebels had put up a new bridge to replace the one Yakubovich had burnt. About one thousand rebels came out to counter Michelsohn, but he crushed them. He detached Duve against a band of Bashkirs gathered nearby: Duve scattered them. Michelsohn advanced towards Osa, and on 27th June he learnt from a group of Bashkirs and Tatars whom he had subdued along the way that Pugachov had taken Osa and crossed the Kama. Michelsohn followed in his tracks. There were no bridges standing over the Kama, nor were there any boats available. The cavalry swam across, and the infantry made rafts. Michelsohn, leaving Pugachov to his right, headed straight for Kazan; by the evening of 11th July he was only fifty-three kilometres away.

His detachment moved on during the night. In the morning, at a distance of forty-eight kilometres from Kazan, cannon fire was heard. By noon a thick crimson cloud of smoke announced the fate of the city.

The midday heat and the exhaustion of his troops forced Michelsohn to take an hour's rest. In the meanwhile he learnt that there was a group of insurgents nearby. He attacked them and took four hundred prisoners; the rest fled to Kazan and informed Pugachov of the enemy's approach. It was then that Pugachov, fearing a sudden assault, withdrew from the fortress and ordered his troops to vacate the city as soon as possible. He took up an advantageous position near Tsaritsyn, seven kilometres from Kazan.

Having received information about this, Michelsohn set off through the forest in a single column. When he came out into open country he was confronted by the rebels arrayed in battle formation.

Michelsohn sent Kharin against their left flank and Duve against the right, while he himself advanced directly on the enemy's main battery. Pugachov's men, buoyed by their victory and strengthened by the cannon they had captured, countered the attack with heavy fire. In front of the main battery there was a marsh: Michelsohn had to cross this, while Kharin and Duve tried to turn the enemy's flank on either side. Michelsohn overran the main battery, and Duve, too, was able to wrest away two cannon on the right flank. The rebels now divided into two groups. One advanced towards Kharin; halting in a defile behind a ditch, they set up batteries and opened fire; the other tried to circle around to the rear of the government troops. Michelsohn left Duve to his own devices and went to reinforce Kharin, whose men were passing through the gully under enemy fire. At length, after five hours of stubborn fighting, Pugachov was beaten and put to flight, at a cost of eight hundred men killed and 180 captured. Michelsohn's losses were insignificant. The darkness of night and the exhaustion of his troops prevented him from pursuing Pugachov.

Having spent the night on the field of battle, Michelsohn proceeded to Kazan just before dawn. As he approached the city he kept coming across groups of looters, who had been carousing among the charred ruins of the city all night. They were slain or taken prisoner. As he arrived at Arskoye Field, Michelsohn caught sight of the enemy approaching: realizing how small Michelsohn's detachment was, Pugachov had hurried to prevent him from joining forces with the garrison. Michelsohn sent warning of this to the governor, then opened up his cannon on the mob charging towards him, yelling and shrieking; he forced them to retreat. Potyomkin arrived with the garrison in good time. Crossing the Kazanka, Pugachov withdrew to the village of Sukhaya Reka, sixteen kilometres from the city. Michelsohn was unable to pursue him, for he had fewer than thirty sound horses in his detachment.

Kazan was liberated. The citizens thronged to the battlements to take a look from a distance at their deliverer's camp. Michelsohn stayed where he was, expecting a new assault. Indeed Pugachov, provoked by his failures, had his heart set on subduing Michelsohn at last. He rallied new mobs on all sides, gathered in his various detachments, and on the morning of 15th July, after having a manifesto read to his troops in which he declared his intention to advance on Moscow, he charged at Michelsohn for the third time. His army was a ragtag band of twenty-five thousand. These multitudes advanced up the same highway along which they had twice fled. Clouds of dust, wild shrieks, clatter and rumble announced their approach. Michelsohn took the field against them with eight hundred carabineers, hussars and Chuguyev Cossacks. He occupied the site of the earlier battle near Tsaritsyn, dividing his troops into three detachments though keeping them in close proximity. The rebels charged at him. The Yaik Cossacks brought up the rear, with orders from Pugachov to skewer anyone who turned back. But Michelsohn and Kharin mounted counterattacks on two sides, drove the rebels back and chased them away. It was all accomplished in a moment. In vain did Pugachov try to rally his scattered hordes, initially at his first campsite, then at the second. Kharin pursued him briskly, giving him no time to pause. At these camps they found some ten thousand Kazan citizens of both sexes, from all walks of life. They were now liberated. The Kazanka was dammed with corpses; the victor took five thousand prisoners and nine cannon. Up to two thousand men, mostly Tatars and Bashkirs, were killed in the engagement. Michelsohn lost about a hundred troops killed or wounded. He entered the city to the shouts of its enraptured inhabitants, witnesses of his victory. The governor, debilitated by an illness that was to kill him in another two weeks, met the victor at the gate of the fortress accompanied by the nobility and clergy. Michelsohn went straight to the cathedral, where Archbishop Veniamin celebrated a thanksgiving mass.

Kazan was in a terrible state: 2,057 of its 2,867 houses had burnt down. Twenty-five churches and three monasteries had also been destroyed in the conflagration. The market hall and those houses, churches and monasteries left standing had all been plundered. Some three hundred inhabitants were found either dead or wounded; about five hundred were missing without a trace. Among those killed were the principal of the grammar school, Kanitz, several teachers and students, and Colonel Rodionov. Major-General Kudryavtsev,[3] aged one hundred and ten, had refused to seek shelter in the fortress, disregarding all attempts to persuade him. He was on his knees in prayer in the Kazan Convent. When some pillagers burst in, he started admonishing them; the scoundrels butchered him on the portico of the church.

Thus had the wretched convict celebrated his return to Kazan, whence he had escaped only a year before! The prison where he had been waiting for a sentence of lashes and forced labour had now been burnt down by him, and the prisoners, his former comrades, had been released. The Cossack woman Sofya Pugachova and her three children had been held in a Kazan barracks for several months. The pretender is said to have burst into tears when he saw them, but he did not betray his identity. Some accounts claim that he gave orders to transfer them to his camp, saying, "I know this woman: her husband has done me a great favour."[4] The traitor Mineyev, chief instigator of Kazan's catastrophe, was taken prisoner at the time of Pugachov's first defeat and sentenced by a military tribunal to run the gauntlet to his death.*

The Kazan authorities took measures to rehouse the inhabitants in the buildings left standing. The citizens were invited to the rebels' camp to sort out the booty captured from Pugachov and take back what belonged to them. The goods were divided up hastily and at random. People who had been rich became poor, and those who had been indigent ended up wealthy!

History must refute a libel that was irresponsibly bandied about in society: it was asserted that Michelsohn could have prevented the sack of Kazan but deliberately gave the rebels time to plunder the city so that he could lay hands on a rich booty – as if he could have preferred profit of any kind to the fame, honour and imperial favours that awaited the liberator of Kazan and the pacifier of the revolt! We have seen how speedily and how persistently Michelsohn had been pursuing Pugachov. Had Potyomkin and Brandt done their duty and held the city for just a few more hours, Kazan would have been saved. Certainly, Michelsohn's soldiers did enrich themselves; but it would be shameful of us to level an unsubstantiated accusation at a worthy old warrior, who spent all his life on the field of honour and who was to die as commander-in-chief of a whole Russian army.* [5]

On 14th July Lieutenant Colonel Count Mellin* arrived in Kazan and was detached by Michelsohn to pursue Pugachov. Michelsohn himself remained in the city in order to replenish his cavalry and reprovision. The other commanders hastened to make some military dispositions, realizing by now how dangerous the active and enterprising Pugachov still was, despite his defeat. His movements were so fast and unpredictable that there was no way to pursue him; in any case the government cavalry was completely worn out. There were attempts to block his advance, but the troops, dispersed over large areas and unable to change direction speedily, could not get to the right places at the right time. It must also be stated that few of the military leaders of the time had the capacity to master Pugachov or his less famous accomplices.*

Chapter VIII

PUGACHOV ACROSS THE VOLGA – A GENERAL UPRISING – GENERAL STUPISHIN'S LETTER – CATHERINE'S PLAN – COUNT P.I. PANIN – TROOP MOVEMENTS – THE TAKING OF PENZA – VSEVOLOZHSKY'S DEATH – DERZHAVIN'S DISPUTE WITH BOSHNYAK – THE TAKING OF SARATOV – PUGACHOV AT TSARITSYN – THE DEMISE OF THE ASTRONOMER LOWITZ – PUGACHOV'S DEFEAT – SUVOROV – PUGACHOV HANDED OVER TO THE AUTHORITIES – HIS CONVERSATION WITH COUNT PANIN – THE VERDICT ON PUGACHOV AND HIS FOLLOWERS – THE EXECUTION OF THE REBELS

Pugachov fled along the highway towards Kokshaysk in the company of three hundred Yaik and Ilek Cossacks, periodically changing horses. At last they reached a forest. Kharin, who had been chasing after them for a full thirty-two kilometres, was forced to stop. Pugachov spent the night in the forest. He had his family with him. There were two new faces among his followers. One of them was the young Pulaski,* brother of the renowned Polish Confederate.[1] He had been living in Kazan as a prisoner of war and joined Pugachov's band out of hatred for Russia. The other one was a protestant pastor. He had been brought before Pugachov during the burning of Kazan, and the pretender recognized him as a person who had given him alms at the time he had been led about the streets of Kazan in fetters. The poor minister had been expecting his last hour, but Pugachov received him with kindness and appointed him a colonel. The colonel-minister was subsequently placed on a Bashkir horse, and accompanied Pugachov in his flight for several days, until at last he dropped behind and returned to Kazan.[2]

For two days Pugachov wandered in one direction and another, thereby misleading his pursuers. His mobs, scattering about, carried on their usual depredations. Beloborodov was caught on the outskirts of Kazan, flogged, then conveyed to Moscow and executed. Several hundred fugitives joined Pugachov. On 18th July he suddenly descended on the Volga, at the Kokshaysk ferry, and crossed the river with five hundred of his better troops.

Pugachov's river-crossing caused a general commotion. The whole region to the west of the Volga rose up in arms and joined the pretender. The manorial serfs rebelled; non-Christians and new converts started killing Russian priests. Regional administrative officials began to flee from the cities, and landowners from their estates; the mob captured many of both and brought them before Pugachov from every side. He proclaimed freedom for the people, extermination of the nobility, remission of compulsory levies, and free distribution of salt.[3] He marched on Tsivilsk, pillaged the town and hanged the head of the regional administration. Dividing his band into two, he sent one division along the road to Nizhny Novgorod and the other towards Alatyr, thereby cutting communications between Nizhny and Kazan. The governor of Nizhny Novgorod, Lieutenant General Stupishin, wrote to Prince Volkonsky that his city awaited the fate of Kazan and that he could not even vouch for Moscow. All the military units stationed in Kazan and Orenburg provinces were mobilized and dispatched against Pugachov. Shcherbatov from Bugulma and Prince Golitsyn from Menzelinsk each hurried to Kazan; Mellin crossed the Volga and on 19th July set out from Sviyazhsk; Mansurov advanced from Yaitsk to Syzran; Muffel went to Simbirsk; and Michelsohn rushed from Cheboksary to Arzamas to block Pugachov's path to Moscow.

But Pugachov no longer had any intention of attacking the old capital. Surrounded by government troops on all sides and having no faith in his followers, he turned his attention to his own safety. His plan was to force his way either to the trans-Kuban region or to Persia. The chief rebels, on their part, could tell that their undertaking was doomed and were ready to strike a bargain for their leader's head. Perfilyev, in the name of all the guilty Cossacks, sent a secret emissary to St Petersburg with a proposal to hand over the pretender. The government, which he had already deceived once, was disinclined to trust him, but nevertheless entered into negotiations.[4] Pugachov was fleeing, but his flight seemed like an invasion. Never had his victories been more horrifying; never had the rebellion raged with greater force. The insurrection spread from village to village, from province to province. Only two or three villains had to appear on the scene and whole regions revolted. Separate bands of plunderers and rioters were formed, each having its own Pugachov...

This grim news made a deep impression in St Petersburg, overshadowing the joy there over the end of the Turkish war and the conclusion of the famous Peace of Kuchuk-Kainarji. The Empress, dissatisfied with Prince Shcherbatov's procrastination, had resolved as early as the beginning of July to recall him and to put Prince Golitsyn in command of the army. The courier conveying this order, however, was held up in Nizhny Novgorod due to the hazardous conditions lying ahead. When the Empress subsequently learnt of the fall of Kazan and the spread of the rebellion to the west of the Volga, she contemplated coming to this region of calamity and danger in order to lead the army in person. Count Nikita Ivanovich Panin managed to dissuade her. The Empress did not know whom to entrust with the saving of the homeland. At this time an aristocrat, who had withdrawn from court and was, like Bibikov, in disfavour, himself volunteered to complete the noble deed left unfinished by his predecessor. This was Count Pyotr Ivanovich Panin.[5] The Empress was grateful to see her noble subject's zeal, and Count Panin, just as he was setting out from his village to march against Pugachov at the head of his armed peasants and domestic serfs, received her order to assume command over the provinces where the rebellion raged and over the troops sent there. Thus the conqueror of Bendery was to wage war against the simple Cossack who had served under his command, unnoticed by him, four years previously.

On 20th July Pugachov's forces swam across the Sura close to Kurmysh. The gentry and government officials fled. The mob greeted the pretender on the banks of the river with icons and bread. A subversive manifesto was read to them. A troop of veterans was brought before Pugachov. Its commander, Major Yurlov, and a non-commissioned officer whose name, unfortunately, has not been recorded, were the only ones who refused to swear allegiance to the pretender and accused him of imposture to his face. They were hanged and, already dead, lashed with the whip. Yurlov's widow was saved by her domestics. Pugachov gave orders to distribute liquor from the state warehouse among the Chuvash; he hanged several noblemen who had been brought before him by their peasants; and he set out for Yadrin, leaving the town under the command of four Yaik Cossacks and putting at their disposal sixty serfs who had joined the rebels. He also left behind a small band to slow down Count Mellin. Michelsohn, who was heading for Arzamas, sent a detachment under Kharin towards Yadrin, to which Count Mellin's troops were also hastening. When Pugachov learnt of this, he turned around towards Alatyr, but sent the small band on to Yadrin in order to secure his rear. This band was first beaten back by the head of the regional administration and the local citizenry; then it ran into Count Mellin and was finally dispersed. Mellin hurried off towards Alatyr, but first, on his way, he liberated Kurmysh, hanging several rebels and taking with him as an informant the Cossack whom they called their commander. The officers of the troop of veterans who had sworn allegiance to the pretender justified themselves by claiming that their oath had "not come sincerely from the heart, but to further Her Imperial Majesty's interests." In their letter to Stupishin they wrote:

> *We repent as Christians of having broken our oath before God and Her Most Gracious Majesty, and of having sworn allegiance to that impostor; we beg with tears in our eyes to be forgiven for this involuntary sin, committed with no other motive than fear of death.*

Twenty men signed this shameful apology.

Pugachov was moving with exceptional speed and sending bands off in all directions. His pursuers could not tell which of these bands was his own. It was impossible to catch up with him, because he galloped along country roads, seizing fresh horses and leaving behind agitators who rode around the towns and the villages unopposed in groups of two, three, rarely more than five, and gathered new bands. Three such agitators turned up on the outskirts of Nizhny Novgorod, but Demidov's peasants trussed them up and handed them over to Stupishin. He ordered them to be hanged on gallows erected on barges and left to float down the Volga, past the rebellious shores.

On 27th July Pugachov entered Saransk. He was received not only by the rabble, but also by the clergy* and the merchants… Three hundred nobles of both sexes and of various ages were hanged by him here; peasants and house serfs flocked to him in droves. He left the town on the 30th. The next day Mellin reached Saransk; he arrested Ensign Shakhmametev, who had been appointed commander by the pretender, as well as a number of other traitors from among the clergy and nobility, and ordered common people to be flogged beneath the gallows.

Michelsohn set out from Arzamas to race after Pugachov. Muffel hurried from Simbirsk to meet him head-on, while Mellin pursued him from behind. Thus three detachments were encircling the pretender. Prince Shcherbatov, impatiently waiting for the arrival of troops from Bashkiria to reinforce the detachments already in action, intended to hurry after them himself, but on receiving the Empress's order of 2nd July he handed over command to Golitsyn and left for St Petersburg.

Meanwhile Pugachov drew close to Penza. Vsevolozhsky, the regional administrator, managed to keep the rabble under control for a while, which gave the gentry an opportunity to escape. Pugachov appeared outside the city. The inhabitants came out to greet him with icons and bread, and knelt before him. He entered Penza. Vsevolozhsky, whose garrison had deserted, locked himself in his house with twelve noblemen, resolved to defend himself. The house was set on fire; the brave Vsevolozhsky and his comrades all perished; government buildings and noblemen's houses were plundered. Pugachov appointed a manorial serf commander of the city and proceeded towards Saratov.

Hearing of the fall of Penza, the authorities at Saratov began taking measures.

Derzhavin was there at the time. As we have seen, he had been detached to the village of Malykovka in order to bar Pugachov's way in case he should flee to the Irgiz valley. Having learnt of

Pugachov's contacts with the Kyrgyz-Kazakhs, he succeeded in cutting them off from the nomadic tribes roaming the region of the two Uzen rivers, and he was intending to march on to liberate Yaitsk, but General Mansurov anticipated him. At the end of July he arrived in Saratov, where his rank as lieutenant of the guards, his keen intelligence, and his ardent nature earned him considerable influence over public opinion.

On 1st August Derzhavin, together with the head of the Board of Protection of Foreign Colonists, Lodyzhinsky, requested the military commander of Saratov, Boshnyak, to hold consultations about measures to be taken under current circumstances. Derzhavin urged that the centre of the city, around the state warehouses, be fortified and all government goods be transferred there; that the boats on the Volga be burnt, batteries arrayed along the bank, and an offensive mounted against Pugachov. Boshnyak would not hear of leaving his fortress, and proposed to stay on outside the city. The argument became heated; Derzhavin lost his temper and began to suggest putting the commander under arrest. Boshnyak remained steadfast, repeating that he would not expose to plunder the fortress and holy churches of God entrusted to him. Derzhavin walked out and rode to the city council; he proposed that all the inhabitants to a man should report for digging at a place designated by Lodyzhinsky. Boshnyak complained, but no one listened to him. Derzhavin's vitriolic letter to the obstinate commander has been preserved as a memento of this dispute.[6]

On 4th August word reached Saratov that Pugachov had set out from Penza and was approaching Petrovsk. Derzhavin requested a detachment of Don Cossacks and rushed to Petrovsk to salvage government property, gunpowder and cannon. As he drew close to the town, however, he heard bells ringing and saw the vanguard of the rebel forces marching into town, and the clergy coming out to greet the invaders with icons and bread. He rode on with a Cossack captain and two other Cossacks, but realizing there was nothing he could do, he galloped back towards Saratov with his three men. The rest of his detachment remained on the highway, waiting for Pugachov. The pretender, accompanied by his associates, rode up to the detachment. The Cossacks received him on their knees. Hearing them speak of an officer of the Guards, Pugachov immediately changed horses, seized a javelin, and chased after him with four Cossacks. He slew one of the Cossacks accompanying Derzhavin, but Derzhavin himself managed to get back to Saratov. The next day both he and Lodyzhinsky left the city, leaving its defence to Boshnyak, the man he had ridiculed.[7]

On 5th August Pugachov marched on Saratov. His army consisted of three hundred Yaik Cossacks and one hundred and fifty Don Cossacks – the latter having joined him the day before – as well as some ten thousand Kalmyks, Bashkirs, Tatar tributaries, manorial peasants, serfs and other riff-raff. About two thousand carried armament of some sort; the rest marched with axes, pitchforks and clubs. They had thirteen fieldpieces.

On the 6th Pugachov approached Saratov and stopped at a distance of three kilometres from the city.

Boshnyak detached some Saratov Cossacks to capture an informant, but they defected to Pugachov. In the meantime the citizenry had sent a secret emissary, the merchant Kobyakov, to the pretender with proposals for changing sides. The rebels rode right up to the fortress, engaging the garrison in conversation. Boshnyak gave orders to fire at them. At that time, however, the citizens led by the mayor Protopopov openly defied his authority: they confronted him and demanded that there be no hostilities until Kobyakov's return. Boshnyak asked them how they had dared enter into negotiations with the pretender without his knowledge. They continued to raise a clamour. In the meanwhile Kobyakov returned with a letter inciting rebellion. Boshnyak snatched it from the traitor's hand, tore it up and trampled on it, and gave orders for Kobyakov's arrest. The merchants, however, pressed him with pleas and threats, so that he was forced to give in to them and release Kobyakov. Nevertheless, he made preparations for the city's defence. In the interim Pugachov occupied Sokolov Hill dominating Saratov, set up a battery there and opened fire on the city. The first shot sent the inhabitants and the Cossacks stationed in the fortress scurrying in all directions. Boshnyak gave orders to fire the mortar, but the shell dropped to the ground only a hundred metres away. Going around to inspect the troops, he found defeatism everywhere, but he did not lose heart himself. The rebels stormed the fortress. Boshnyak opened fire and had already succeeded in driving the rebels back when suddenly three hundred of his gunners pulled the wedges from under their cannon, snatched up the fuses and ran out of the fortress to surrender. At this point Pugachov himself led an attack on the fortress from the hill. Boshnyak decided to cut his way through the throngs of rebels with the garrison battalion alone. He ordered Major Salmanov to sally forth with the first half of the battalion; but, noticing the man's fright and suspecting him of treason, he removed him from command. However, when Major Butyrin interceded on Salmanov's behalf, Boshnyak, once again showing weakness, agreed to leave Salmanov in his post after all. Turning to the second half of the battalion, Boshnyak gave order to unfold the banners and march out from behind the fortifications. At this moment Salmanov surrendered, and Boshnyak was left with sixty men, officers included. The brave Boshnyak sallied out of the fortress with this handful of followers and spent a full six hours fighting his way through innumerable rebel hordes. Nightfall put an end to the fighting. Boshnyak reached the bank of the Volga. He sent his state funds and chancery papers to Astrakhan by boat, and he himself managed to reach Tsaritsyn* on 11th August.

As soon as the rebels captured Saratov, they liberated prisoners, opened up grain and salt warehouses, broke into taverns and plundered houses. Pugachov hanged all the noblemen who fell into his hands and forbade their burial. He appointed a Cossack lieutenant, Ufimtsev, local commander, and at noon on 9th August set out from Saratov. Muffel arrived in the ravaged city on the 11th, Michelsohn on the 14th. Joining forces, they hastened after Pugachov.

The pretender followed the course of the Volga. The foreigners who had settled in this region, mostly vagabonds and scoundrels, all joined his forces at the instigation of a Polish Confederate (not identified by name; certainly not Pulaski because he had already left Pugachov, disgusted by his bestial atrocities). Pugachov formed them into a hussar regiment. The Volga Cossacks also came over to his side.

Thus Pugachov mustered greater forces by the day. His army already consisted of twenty thousand men. His bands spread over the provinces of Nizhny Novgorod, Voronezh and Astrakhan. A fugitive serf Yevstigneyev, also calling himself Peter III, took Insar, Troitsk, Narovchat and Kerensk, hanged the regional administrators and gentry, and set up his own administration everywhere. The bandit Firska marched on Simbirsk, and in the fray killed Colonel Rychkov, successor of the Chernyshov who had perished near Orenburg at the beginning of the uprising. The garrison betrayed him. But Simbirsk was saved by the arrival of Colonel Obernibesov. Firska engulfed the outlying areas in murder and plunder. Upper Lomov and Lower Lomov were ravaged and burnt by other villains. The state of this whole region was horrifying. The nobility seemed doomed to extinction. The bodies of landowners or their stewards hung on the gates of manor houses in every village.[8] The rebels and the detachments pursuing them confiscated the peasants' horses, supplies and last belongings. Law and order were suspended everywhere. The simple people did not know whom to obey. If asked, "To whom do you give allegiance, Peter III or Catherine II?" peaceable people dared not answer, not knowing to which side their questioners belonged.

On 13th August Pugachov approached Dmitriyevsk (Kamyshin). He was countered by Major Dietz at the head of a five-hundred-strong garrison, one thousand Don Cossacks, and five hundred Kalmyks under the command of Princes Dundukov and Derbetev. An engagement ensued. The Kalmyks scattered at the first cannon shot. The Cossacks fought bravely and were pressing close to the cannon, but when they found themselves cut off they surrendered. Dietz was killed. The garrison and all the cannon were captured. Pugachov pitched camp for the night on the battlefield; the next day he took Dubovka and moved on towards Tsaritsyn.

That well-fortified city was under the command of Colonel Tsypletev. The brave Boshnyak had joined him. On 21st August Pugachov laid siege to Tsaritsyn with his usual daring. He was driven back with losses, and retreated to a distance of eight kilometres from the fortress. Fifteen hundred Don Cossacks were sent out against him, but of these only four hundred came back: the rest had defected to his side.

The next day Pugachov made a new assault on the city, this time from the Volga side, but he was again repulsed by Boshnyak. He also received news of the approach of government troops and hurriedly backed off towards Sarepta.

Michelsohn, Muffel and Mellin arrived at Dubovka on the 20th, and entered Tsaritsyn on the 22nd.

Pugachov fled along the Volga. On the riverbank he chanced on the astronomer Lowitz and asked him who he was. Hearing that Lowitz observed the movement of heavenly bodies, he ordered him hanged "a bit closer to the stars". Lowitz's assistant Inokhodtsev, who was there too, managed to escape.

Pugachov rested in Sarepta a full twenty-four hours, secluded in his tent with two concubines.[9] His family were also at the camp. Then he set off down towards Chorny Yar. Michelsohn was on his heels. At length, at dawn on the 25th, he caught up with Pugachov 111 kilometres from Tsaritsyn.

Pugachov had occupied a height between two roads. During the night Michelsohn bypassed him and took up his position against the rebels. In the morning Pugachov once again faced his formidable pursuer, but he remained undaunted: he marched boldly on Michelsohn, throwing his pedestrian rabble into combat against the Don and Chuguyev Cossacks, who were stationed on both wings of the detachment. The engagement did not last long. A few cannon shots were enough to break the rebels' ranks. Michelsohn counterattacked. The rebels fled, leaving their cannon and the whole of their supply train behind. Pugachov, having crossed a bridge, tried to hold his men back, but all in vain: he had to flee with them. They were battered and chased for forty-two kilometres. Pugachov lost some four thousand men dead and seven thousand captured. The rest of his horde dispersed. Just above Chorny Yar, seventy-four kilometres from the field of battle, he crossed the Volga in four boats and went off into the grasslands with no more than thirty Cossacks. The cavalry pursuing them arrived a quarter of an hour late. The runaways who had not managed to get across in boats plunged into the river to swim and were drowned.

This defeat was the final and decisive one. Count Panin, who had just arrived in Kerensk, was able to send the joyous news to

St Petersburg, paying full tribute in his report to Michelsohn for his speed, skill and courage. Meanwhile a new important personage appears on the scene: Suvorov arrived in Tsaritsyn.

Bibikov was still alive when the State College, realizing the seriousness of the rebellion, had attempted to recall Suvorov, who was at the walls of Silistra at the time; but Count Rumyantsev refused to let him go, lest Europe attach too much significance to Russia's internal troubles. So great was Suvorov's fame!* When the war came to an end, he received orders to proceed to Moscow immediately and report to Prince Volkonsky for further instructions. He joined Count Panin on his estate and reached Michelsohn's troops a few days after their last victory. He brought with him an order from Count Panin enjoining both the military leaders and the governors of the region to obey all his commands. He assumed command of Michelsohn's troops, mounted the infantry on the horses captured from Pugachov, and crossed the Volga at Tsaritsyn. In a village that had participated in the rebellion he confiscated fifty yoke of oxen as a punishment; and with these for victuals, he plunged deep into the steppe, where there is neither forest nor water, and where he had to orient himself by the sun during the day and by the stars at night.

Pugachov meandered about the same steppe. Troops were encircling him on all sides: Mellin and Muffel, who had also crossed the Volga, cut off the routes to the north; a light field detachment approached the rebel from the direction of Astrakhan; Prince Golitsyn and Mansurov barred the way to the Yaik; Dundukov was crisscrossing the steppe with his Kalmyks; patrol lines were set up from Guryev to Saratov and from Chorny Yar to Krasny Yar. There was no way for Pugachov to slip through the net tightening around him. His followers, seeing inescapable doom on the one hand and hope for a pardon on the other, put their heads together and finally resolved to deliver him to the authorities.

Pugachov intended to head towards the Caspian Sea, hoping somehow to get through to the Kyrgyz-Kazakh steppes. The Cossacks pretended to agree, but, saying that they wished to take their wives and children with them, they drew him to the

Uzen region – the usual refuge of criminals and fugitives. On 14th September they arrived at the settlements of Old Believers in that area. Here the Cossacks held their last council. Those not willing to surrender to the authorities dispersed; the others went to Pugachov's tent.

Pugachov was sitting by himself, deep in thought. His weapons were hanging up at the side. Hearing the Cossacks enter, he raised his head and asked what they wanted. They started talking about their desperate situation, at the same time slowly moving closer in order to get between Pugachov and his weapons. Once more he tried to persuade them to go to Guryev. The Cossacks answered that they had been following him for a long time, and now it was time for him to follow them.

"What?" asked Pugachov. "Are you going to betray your Sovereign?"

"What else is there to do?" answered the Cossacks, throwing themselves on him. He managed to fight free. They drew back a few steps.

"I've been aware of your treason for a long time," said Pugachov. Then he called forth his favourite among them, the Ilek Cossack Tvorogov, and held his hands out to him: "Tie them!"

Tvorogov wanted to tie his arms behind his back, but Pugachov would not let him, asking angrily, "What am I? A bandit?" The Cossacks put him on a horse and led him to Yaitsk. All along the way he threatened them with the Tsarevich's revenge. Once he managed to free his hands; he grabbed a sword and a pistol, wounded one of the Cossacks, and shouted for the traitors to be tied up. But nobody listened to him any more. The Cossacks rode up to Yaitsk and sent word to the commandant. The Cossack Kharchev and Sergeant Bardovsky were dispatched to meet them; they took charge of Pugachov, put him in foot stocks and had him carried into town, straight to Lieutenant Captain of the Guards Mavrin, who was a member of the investigating commission.[10]

Mavrin interrogated the pretender. The latter revealed his true identity from the very beginning. "It was God's will," he said, "to punish Russia through my devilry."

The citizens were ordered to gather in the town square, and the rest of the rebels were brought out, clamped in irons; Mavrin led Pugachov forth and showed him to the people. Everyone recognized him; the rebels cast their eyes down. Pugachov began loudly to accuse them, saying, "You were the ones who led me to ruin: you begged me for several days to assume the name of the late great Sovereign; I refused for a long time, and even after I agreed, I did everything according to your will and with your consent, while you often acted without my knowledge, and sometimes even against my will."

The rebels did not have one word to say.

In the interim Suvorov arrived in the Uzen region and learnt from the hermits that Pugachov had been tied up by his followers and carried off to Yaitsk. Suvorov hurried after them. At night he lost his way and stumbled on the campfires that some Kyrgyz freebooters had lit in the steppe. Suvorov set on them and chased them off, but not without losing some of his men, his adjutant Maximovich among them. A few days later he arrived in Yaitsk. Simonov handed Pugachov over to him. Suvorov questioned the famous rebel with curiosity about his military manoeuvres and plans. He had him transported to Simbirsk, where Count Panin was due to arrive.

Pugachov sat in a wooden cage placed on a two-wheeled cart. A large detachment, supported by two pieces of artillery, surrounded him. Suvorov did not leave his side. In the village of Mosty (148 kilometres from Samara) a fire broke out close to the cottage where Pugachov was spending the night. He was taken out of the cage and tied to the cart, together with his son, a lively, bold little fellow. Suvorov himself guarded them all night. He crossed the Volga by night in rough weather from Samara to Kosporye, and arrived in Simbirsk at the beginning of October.

The pretender was brought straight to the courtyard of the house occupied by Count Panin. The latter came out on the porch accompanied by his staff.

"Who are you?" he asked the pretender.

"Yemelyan Ivanov Pugachov" was the answer.

"How did you dare call yourself sovereign, you jailbird?"

"I'm no bird," responded Pugachov in the figurative manner customary with him. "I'm only a fledgling; the real bird is still flying about."*

It should be mentioned that the Yaik rebels, to subvert the prevailing story, had spread the rumour that though there had indeed been a certain Pugachov among them, this person had nothing to do with the Emperor Peter III who was their leader. Noticing that Pugachov's impudent reply had made an impression on the common people who were crowding around the courtyard, Panin struck him in the face, enough to draw blood, and tore out a tuft of his beard. Pugachov fell on his knees and asked for mercy. He was placed under heavy guard, with his hands and feet in fetters and an iron loop, chained to the wall, fastened around his waist. The academician Rychkov, father of the murdered commandant of Simbirsk, saw him and left a record of their encounter. Pugachov was eating fish soup from a wooden bowl. Seeing Rychkov enter, he bade him welcome and invited him to share his dinner. "This," writes Rychkov, "revealed to me his base mind." Rychkov asked him how he had dared commit such crimes. Pugachov answered, "I am guilty before God and Her Majesty, but I will try to make amends for all my sins." And he kept adding oaths to his words for greater emphasis ("revealing his base nature," Rychkov remarks again). Speaking about his son, Rychkov could not refrain from tears; Pugachov, looking at him, also burst into tears.

At last Pugachov was despatched to Moscow, where his fate was to be decided.[11] He was conveyed in a covered sleigh drawn by horses hired locally at each stage. His escorts were Captain Galakhov and Captain Povalo-Shveykovsky – the latter having been his prisoner a few months before. He was kept in irons. The soldiers fed him with their own hands, and kept telling children who crowded around his sleigh, "Remember, children, you have seen Pugachov". Old people still tell stories about how boldly he responded to the questions of gentlefolk who drove past him on the road. He was cheerful and calm all along the way.

In Moscow he was met by a large crowd, which only recently had been looking forward impatiently to his arrival and who had barely been held in check by the dreaded villain's arrest. He was kept at the Moscow Mint, where from morning till night, for two whole months, the curious could see the famous rebel, chained to the wall, still fearsome even in his powerlessness. It is said that many women fainted on meeting his fiery glance and hearing his menacing voice. Before the court he betrayed an unexpected feebleness of spirit.[12] He had to be prepared gradually for hearing his death sentence. He and Perfilyev were condemned to be quartered; Chika to be beheaded; Shigayev, Padurov* and Tornov to be hanged, and another eighteen men to be flogged and exiled to penal servitude.

The execution of Pugachov and his associates took place in Moscow on 10th January 1775. From early morning an immense crowd stood gathered on the Marsh,* where a tall scaffold had been erected. The executioners sat on the scaffold, drinking liquor while they waited for their victims. Three gallows stood next to the scaffold. Infantry regiments were lined up on all sides. The officers wore fur coats because of the severe cold. The roofs of neighbouring houses and stores were covered with people; the low-lying open space and adjacent streets were full of carriages and barouches. Suddenly there was a general commotion, followed by a roar and shouts of, "Here they come! They're bringing him!" Behind a detachment of cuirassiers came a sledge with a tall platform where Pugachov sat bareheaded, facing a priest. An official of the Secret Commission rode in the same conveyance. As he was driven along, Pugachov kept bowing to both sides. Behind the sledge more cavalry followed, and a group of the other condemned men on foot. An eyewitness (then barely more than an adolescent, now a venerable old man, crowned with the fame of both poet and statesman) describes the bloody spectacle in the following words:

> The sledge halted before the steps leading up to the place of execution. Pugachov and his favourite, Perfilyev, accompanied by a priest and two officials, had hardly mounted the scaffold when the command "Present arms!" was heard, and one of the officials began reading the sentence. I could hear almost every word.

When the official read the chief villain's name and full identification, including the name of the Cossack settlement where he had been born, the chief of police asked him in a loud voice:

"Are you the Don Cossack Yemelka Pugachov?"

"Yes, sir, I am Yemelka Pugachov, Don Cossack from the settlement of Zimoveyskaya," he answered in an equally loud voice.

Afterwards, all through the reading of the sentence, he fixed his gaze on the cathedral and frequently crossed himself, while Perfilyev, a man of considerable height, with bent back, pockmarked face and fierce countenance, stood motionless, looking at the ground. When the reading of the sentence was over, the priest addressed a few words to them, blessed them, and descended from the scaffold. The official who had read the sentence followed suit. Pugachov, crossing himself, bowed to the ground facing the cathedrals; then with a hurried air he turned to the crowd to say farewell, and bowed to all sides, uttering in a breaking voice: "Farewell, Orthodox people: forgive me if I have done harm in your sight; farewell, true believers!"

At this moment the official in charge gave a signal, and the executioners rushed forward to undress Pugachov: they pulled off his white sheepskin coat and started ripping apart the sleeves of his crimson silk jacket. Then he threw up his hands and fell backwards, and a minute later a head dripping with blood was raised high.[13]

The executioner had received secret orders to curtail the offenders' sufferings. The headsmen cut off the corpse's arms and legs and carried them to the four corners of the scaffold; straight after this they displayed the head, stuck on the end of a long stake. Perfilyev, making a sign of the cross, prostrated himself on the floor and remained motionless. The headsmen lifted him up and executed him the same way as Pugachov. Meanwhile Shigayev, Padurov and Tornov were already in their last convulsions on the gallows... At that point the jingle of a bell was heard: Chika was carried off to Ufa, where his execution was to take place. Then the public floggings began, and the crowd dispersed; only a small group of the curious remained around the post to which those sentenced to be flogged were tied one after the other. The dismembered rebels' severed limbs were taken around to the city gates, and a few days later were burnt together with their torsos. The executioners scattered the ashes to the winds. Those rebels who were granted pardon were lined up before the Granovitaya Palace the day after the executions. The amnesty was announced to them, and their shackles were taken off in front of the people.

Thus ended the rebellion that had begun at the instigation of a handful of insubordinate Cossacks, had gathered strength through the inexcusable negligence of the authorities, and had rocked the foundations of the state from Siberia to Moscow and from the Kuban to the forests of Murom. Complete tranquillity could not be restored for a long time. Panin and Suvorov stayed in the pacified provinces a whole year, bolstering enfeebled local administrations, rebuilding cities and forts, and eradicating the last remnants of the quashed rebellion. At the end of 1775 a general amnesty was announced, and it was decreed that the whole affair should be consigned to eternal oblivion. Catherine, wishing to obliterate the memory of that terrible epoch, abolished the ancient name of the river whose banks had first witnessed the insurgence. The Yaik Cossacks were renamed Ural Cossacks, and their town became Uralsk. But the name of the dreaded rebel still resounds in the regions where he wrought havoc. People still clearly remember the bloody episode that they have so aptly dubbed the *pugachovshchina*.

Pushkin's Notes to *A History of Pugachov*

NOTES TO CHAPTER I

1 Some of the educated Yaik Cossacks regard themselves as descendants of *streltsy*. This view is not without foundation, as we shall see below. We find the most satisfactory study of the Yaik Cossacks' original settlement in *A Historical and Statistical Survey of the Ural Cossacks*, a work by A.I. Lyovshin, outstanding (as are the author's other publications) for its genuine erudition and sound critique. According to the author* –

> The passage of time and the nature of Cossack life have deprived us of accurate and reliable information on the origins of the Ural Cossacks. All the surviving historical data about them is based solely on quite late traditions that are less than definitive and await critical analysis.
>
> The most ancient, but at the same time the briefest, account of these traditions is to be found in a report of the Yaik village hetman Fyodor Rukavishnikov to the government's College of Foreign Affairs dated 1720.
>
> A supplement and sequel to that document is provided by – 1. The report of the Orenburg governor Neplyuyev to the War College of 22nd November 1748. 2. Rychkov's *History of Orenburg*. 3. The same author's *Topography of Orenburg*. 4. A quite interesting manuscript journal by the former Yaik Host hetman Ivan Akutin. 5. Some more recent documents that are preserved in the archives of the Ural Host Chancery and of the Orenburg Frontier Commission. These are the best, and virtually the only, sources for the history of the Ural Cossacks.

The writings of non-Russian authors on this subject are not worthy of inclusion here. Most of such works are based on conjectures that are unproven, frequently at odds with the truth, and absurd. So, for example, the author of the commentary on Abu al-Ghazi Bahadur Khan's *Genealogical History of the Tatars* maintains that the Ural Cossacks were descended from the ancient Kipchaks; that they became Russian subjects immediately after the subjugation of Astrakhan; that they have a special hybrid language that they use with all the neighbouring Tatars; that they can field thirty thousand armed fighters; that the town of Uralsk stands forty-two kilometres from the mouth of the Ural where it flows into the Caspian Sea; et cetera. These absurdities are not worthy of refutation among Russians, but are taken as correct in the rest of Europe. De Guignes and the illustrious Puffendorf have unfortunately incorporated them in their works.

If we return now to our above-mentioned five sources and compare them with each other, we observe in all of them one principal fact – that the Yaik or Ural Cossacks originated with those of the Don. But as to the time of their settlement of the lands they now occupy we find no positive or unanimous information.

Rukavishnikov, writing as we said in 1720, suggested that his forebears came to the Yaik "perhaps around two hundred years ago" – i.e. in the first half of the sixteenth century.

Neplyuyev repeats Rukavishnikov's words.

Rychkov in his *History of Orenburg* writes: "This Yaik Host, according to information from the Yaik elders, dates from about 1584." In his *Topography*, however, written after the *History*, he writes that the first Cossack settlement on the Yaik took place in the fourteenth century. He based this last statement on a tradition received in 1748 from the Yaik Host hetman Ilya Merkuryev. Ilya's father Grigory had also been Host hetman, had lived for one hundred years, had died in 1741 and had heard in his youth from his grandmother, also a centenarian, that she, at the age of twenty, had known a very old Tatar woman, Gugnikha by name, who had told her the following: "At the time of Tamerlane, a Don Cossack named Vasily Gugna, together with thirty Cossack companions and one Tatar, left the Don on a plundering raid to the east, built boats, sailed in them down to the Caspian Sea, reached the mouth of the Ural, and, finding its shores uninhabited, settled there. Several years later this band came up against three Tatar brothers hiding in the forests near their own habitation. The youngest of the three was married to her, Gugnikha (the narrator). They had broken away from the Golden Horde, which was in any case scattered because Tamerlane, returning from Russia, was intending to attack it. The Cossacks slaughtered these three brothers, but they took Gugnikha prisoner and presented her to their hetman." Later, after some unimportant details, the same narrator had told how "her husband had heard of the Russian city of Astrakhan in his childhood", how "in her time many Tatars from the Golden Horde and many Russians had joined up with the Cossacks that had taken her prisoner" and how "they used to kill their own children", et cetera.

The rest of the old woman's stories are close to what we shall be relating as the truth; but the earlier part that we have just set out, in spite of Rychkov's famed erudition, valuable research and extensive knowledge of Central Asia and the Orenburg region, is chronologically impossible and at odds with many undisputed historical facts. So, because this tale has been accepted as the sole and entirely accurate source for the history of the Ural Cossacks, and because it has been repeated over and over again in the latest Russian and foreign works, we consider it essential to go into some, albeit tedious, detail in order to refute it.

i. If the hetman Grigory Merkuryev, who lived to be about one hundred, died in 1741, then he was born in 1641 or thereabouts. His centenarian grandmother, who passed on to him such circumstantial narratives that have such significance for every Cossack, cannot have died before he was fifteen years old – that is, around 1656 – and must therefore have been born in 1556 or, if you like, in 1550. She met Gugnikha when she was twenty – that is, around 1570. Now, supposing that Gugnikha was ninety at that time and so was born in 1480 or, in round terms, at the end of the fifteenth century, how could she have remembered events that took place in the fourteenth century, that is almost a hundred years before her birth – for Tamerlane arrived in Russia in 1395?

ii. Gugnikha's husband "had heard from old folk as a small child that not very far from the River Yaik were the Russian cities of Astrakhan and others". It is well known that Astrakhan was captured in 1554, and so do we not have to assume, on this basis, that Gugnikha and her husband lived in the sixteenth century? Such an assumption is closer to the truth and is also, as we shall now see, consistent with other data about the origin of the Ural Cossacks.

iii. Gugnikha and Rukavishnikov and Rychkov in his *History of Orenburg* and the traditions that I myself picked up in Uralsk and Guryev, are all unanimous that the Ural Cossacks originate from those of the Don. But at the time of Tamerlane the Don Cossacks did not yet exist, and history nowhere speaks to us of them before the sixteenth century. Even if we accept that the Don Cossacks constitute one and the same nation as the Azov Cossacks, even the latter (as Mr Karamzin writes) are only recorded for the first time in 1499 – that is, more than one hundred years after the incursions of Tamerlane.

iv. In the fourteenth century Russia had yet to shake off the Tatar yoke. At that time her frontiers were more than one thousand kilometres distant from the Caspian Sea, and vast areas of steppe, stretching from the Don, across the Volga to the Yaik, were occupied by Mongol-Tatar tribes. How could a handful of adventurous Cossacks not only find their way across such a large distance and through thousands of foes, but even settle among them and plunder them? Müller, well known for his researches and expertise in our history, says: "For as long as the Tatars ruled the southern lands of the Russian state, there was no record of Russian Cossacks."

Now that we have demonstrated the inaccuracy of the tale included by Rychkov in his *Topography of Orenburg*, we shall take his earlier data about the Ural Cossack Host published in his *History of Orenburg*; we shall supplement that with the information contained in Rukavishnikov's and Neplyuyev's reports already referred to, and with the traditions I myself collected by the Ural River; we shall combine those with the works of the most eminent writers; and we shall present to our readers the *Historical Survey of the Ural Cossacks* that follows.

2 On Gugnikha, see Rychkov's full account of the legend in his *History of Orenburg*.

3 This charter has not been preserved. Elderly Cossacks used to tell Rychkov that it had been destroyed by fire at the time of an earlier conflagration. Mr Lyovshin says –

> Without this charter it is impossible to fix the exact date when the Ural Cossacks first became subjects of Russia. Not only this charter but many others too granted them by Tsars Mikhail, Alexei, and Fyodor III have been incinerated. The oldest document – the only one of its kind – that Neplyuyev found in the Yaik Host's headquarters was a charter of Tsars Peter I and Ivan V of 1684, in which mention is made of past military service provided by the Host since the time of Tsar Mikhail.
>
> From 1655 – that is, from the Ural Cossacks' first service against the Poles and Swedes – to 1681 there is no information about their campaigns. In 1681 and 1682 three hundred Cossacks served under Chigirin. In 1683 five hundred of their men were sent to Menzelinsk to pacify rebellious Bashkirs, in return for which, besides wages in the form of money and cloth, an order was issued to provide them with artillery shells. From the time of Peter the Great they were employed in many of the principal Russian military engagements, such as in 1689 at Azov; in 1701, 1703, 1704 and 1707 against the Swedes; in 1708, 1,225 Cossacks were again sent to pacify the Bashkirs; in 1711, 1,500 men went to the Kuban; in 1717, 1,500 Cossacks marched with prince Bekovich-Cherkassky to Khiva; and so on.

4 Mr Lyovshin correctly remarks that the Tsar's *streltsy* most likely prevented the Yaik Cossacks from taking part in Razin's uprising. However that may be, the Ural Cossacks of today cannot abide his name, and the words "Razin's brood" are regarded among them as the most offensive abuse.

5 From the *Topography of Orenburg*:

At the same period a Cossack of the Yaik Host named Nechay gathered together a band of five hundred men and thought up a plan to march on Khiva, in the expectation of finding great wealth there and of winning valuable booty. He set out with his men up the Yaik River, and when he got to the hills now called the Dyakovs, thirty-two kilometres up the Yaik from today's town, he halted and, in accordance with the Cossack custom, held a council, or "circle", to discuss this expedition of his and choose a man to guide them there by the shortest and easiest route. When the plan was presented to the council, his *dyak*, or clerk, stepped forward and began to argue that the proposed expedition was foolhardy and unrealistic. He explained that their route was an unknown one across the steppe, the provisions they had brought were insufficient, and there were too few men for such a big undertaking. Nechay was so angry at the clerk's criticisms and got into such a temper that, without adjourning the council, he ordered the man to be hanged; so hanged he was there and then, and those hills were named after him and are called the Dyakovs to this day.

Nechay set off on his journey with the Cossacks and reached Khiva successfully. He advanced on the city at a time when the Khan of Khiva with all his army was at war elsewhere in those parts and there was almost nobody in the town but children and old folk. So Nechay seized control of the city and all its wealth without any trouble or resistance. He captured all the Khan's wives, taking one for himself and keeping her as his mistress. After this lucky conquest Nechay and the Cossacks with him stayed on for a time in Khiva, amusing themselves in all kinds of ways. They gave very little thought to the danger they were in; but the Khan's wife, who had fallen seriously in love with Nechay, kept warning him that, if he wanted to save his skin, he should withdraw from the city with all his men in good time, to avoid the Khan and his army catching him there. Nechay finally listened to the Khan's wife, but he did not leave Khiva soon enough and, encumbered as he was with the quantity of valuable booty, was unable to make a speedy retreat. The Khan soon afterwards returned from his campaign. Seeing that his city had been plundered, he set off instantly with all his army in pursuit of Nechay. After three days he caught up with him on the river called Syr Darya, which the Cossacks had crossed at its mouth, and attacked them with such force that Nechay with his Cossacks, though putting up a brave defence and killing many Khivans, was eventually slaughtered with all the men he had with him; only for three or four escaped from the carnage and on their return to the Yaik Host told the story of his destruction. The hetmen of the Host's account also included the statement that after that time the Khivans blocked the channel leading from the Aral Sea into the Caspian at the Caspian end, so that in future there should be no passage for ships from one sea to the other. But in the absence of more trustworthy information I do not vouch for this last matter; I simply record it as it was related to me by the Host's hetmen.

Some years later the Yaik Cossacks transferred their settlement to the mouth of the river Chagan, its third site, where the Yaik Cossacks' town is now situated. As the settlement became established the population greatly increased. Then a Cossack called Shamay picked himself a band of up to three hundred men and came up with the same plan as Nechay, namely to attempt a further campaign against Khiva to commandeer the wealth of the place. They reached agreement on this and set off up the Yaik to the River Ilek, on the banks of which, having travelled on upstream for several days, they settled for the winter. In spring they set off again. When they were near the Syr Darya, they espied two Kalmyk lads on the steppe who were out hunting and digging holes to trap animals (at that time Kalmyk nomads were still roaming near the Syr Darya). The Cossacks seized the Kalmyk boys intending to use them as guides to show them the way across the steppe. The Kalmyks demanded that the Cossacks return the boys, but the Cossacks refused. The Kalmyks took umbrage at this and adopted the following stratagem. A large number of them assembled and hid in a well-concealed low-lying spot. They sent two Kalmyks on ahead of them to some high ground and told them, when they saw the Yaik Cossacks, to start digging the earth and, by throwing it in the air, to make it appear that they were digging animal traps again. The Cossacks at the front saw them and thought that some more wandering Kalmyk herdsmen were digging traps. They told their hetman Shamay; then the whole party left their baggage train and galloped after them. The two nomads ran away from the Cossacks as fast as they could towards the places where the Kalmyk troops lay hidden and so brought them to the Kalmyks, who all at once fell upon them. They seized Shamay and several of the Cossacks, but took only the hetman prisoner, simply in order to secure thereby the release of the Kalmyks the Cossacks had seized earlier. The Kalmyks, in setting free the other Cossacks, did indeed demand the return of their youngsters. The deputy hetman, however, replied that they had plenty of hetmen, but without guides it was impossible for them to proceed. With that the Cossacks went on their way. But they failed to find the spot where Hetman Nechay's Cossacks had previously crossed the mouth of the Syr Darya and, forging on, they came up against the Aral Sea, where their supplies ran out. To make matters worse winter weather arrived, and for this reason they were forced to spend the winter by the Aral Sea. They became so terribly famished that they started killing and eating one another; others died of hunger. The survivors sent to the Khivans, asking them to take them in and so to rescue them from death. The Khivans accordingly rode up and took them all to the city. In this way all the Yaik Cossacks, three hundred men, disappeared. The elected hetman Shamay, however, was brought back by the Kalmyks several years later and restored to the Yaik Host.

6 See Mr Sukhorukov's article 'On the Internal Condition of the Don Cossacks at the End of the Sixteenth Century', published in *Sorevnovatel Prosveshcheniya* (*Champion of Enlightenment*) in 1824. Here is what Mr Lyovshin writes about the Cossack "circles" –

In the past, as soon as any decree was received or any event that concerned the Host as a whole took place, then they would ring a tocsin or summons in the cathedral bell tower, so as to get all the Cossacks to come together to the place of assembly at the Host's office or *prikaz* (now the Host's chancery), where the Host's hetman would be awaiting them. When a sufficiently large number of people had assembled, the hetman would come out to them onto the steps of the headquarters with his mace of gilt silver. Behind him came the Cossack captains with staffs in their hands: they would walk immediately into the middle of the assembly, lay their staffs and hats on the ground, recite a prayer, and bow deeply, first to the hetman, and then to the Cossacks surrounding them on every side. After that they would pick the staffs and hats up again in their hands, approach the hetman to receive his instructions, and then turn back to the people, greeting them loudly with these words: "Silence, brave hetmen and all the great Yaik Host!" Finally, once they had explained the business for which the assembly had been convened, they would put the question: "To your pleasure, brave hetmen?" Then on all sides either there would be shouts of "Yes!", or a chorus of grumbling and cries of "No!" In the latter case the hetman himself would begin to urge the dissenters, explaining the proposition and enumerating its benefits. If the Cossacks were content with him, then his appeal would usually be acted upon; if to the contrary, then no one would listen to him, and the will of the people would take effect. (*Historical and Statistical Survey of the Ural Cossacks*)

7 From the *Historical and Statistical Survey of the Ural Cossacks*:

The Ural Cossack Host is like all Cossacks in not paying taxes to the government. But they are liable for military service and are under an obligation at any time on demand to provide at their own expense a stipulated number of mounted soldiers, uniformed and equipped; and in case of emergency all those registered for service have to take the field. Today there are twelve regiments of serving Cossacks in the Ural Host. Of these, one is at the Ilek and one at the Sakmarsk settlements. Both these regiments, because they have no part in the rich Ural fishing enterprises, are also exempted from the Cossacks' liability for army service; but they do perform "line duties", i.e. they protect the frontier from the Kyrgyz. The remaining ten regiments that are registered for service but not actually serving provide troops for the army at their own expense and frontier defence across the whole extent of their territory as far as the Caspian Sea. Both kinds of service are provided not by fixed rotation but for hire, in return for payment. When the government first orders the mobilization of one or more regiments, an assessment takes place: one armed conscript has to be provided per so many men registered for service; each group then hires one Cossack at its joint expense, on the basis that he provides his own uniform and weaponry. His pay amounts to one thousand roubles, one thousand five hundred roubles or more. For a ten-month expedition to Bukharia, to escort the mission we sent there, each Cossack was paid two thousand or even three thousand roubles because of the unfamiliarity of the country. Any Cossack who, on the occasion of the assessment, cannot pay his share of the joint levy volunteers himself for hire for the campaign. Some who offer themselves for hire then pass the obligation on to someone else, sometimes at a profit to themselves. The pay for those who hire themselves out for frontier defence duty is the lowest, because they have their own homes, cattle, merchandise and entire property in the forts and outposts, and have an interest themselves in going about protecting the frontier – though, as a matter of fact, this need deprives them of the right to take part in the communal fishing enterprises.

The custom of providing military service for hire seems on the one hand unfair, because a wealthy Cossack is always exempt from the duty to serve, while a poor one is always liable. On the other hand it has its benefits:

i. As it is, every Cossack that goes on campaign has the wherewithal to clothe and arm himself well.
ii. When leaving his family he is able to allocate them enough money to support them for the duration of his absence.
iii. A man who is engaged in work or in an enterprise of some sort and is of value to himself and to the community is not compelled to give up his activities and go off against his will to military service, which he would then discharge with the utmost indifference.

> Cossacks who are unfit no longer undertake any kind of service, and consequently are not allowed to go on fishing expeditions without payment.

We cite from the same book a vivid and interesting description of fishing on the Ural River:

> Let us now turn our attention to the Ural Host's fishing industry and examine it in more detail, partly because it constitutes the major and almost the sole source of wealth for the inhabitants thereabouts, and partly because the various forms that industry takes are interesting in themselves. So first of all let us note that opposite the town of Uralsk after the spring floods they construct across the Ural a weir or permeable barrier of thick logs, called an *uchug*, that stops the fish that come up from the sea and prevents them from swimming farther upstream. (Old folk tell that in earlier times there were so many fish in the Ural that the pressure of them used to cause the *uchug* to break and the fish had to be chased back by cannon fire from the bank.)
>
> The principal modes of fishing (none of which may be commenced before the day prescribed by the Host's chancery) are –
>
> *i.* Gaffing, subdivided into "minor" and "major". Minor gaffing commences around 20th or 18th December and does not go on beyond 25th. Major gaffing begins around 6th January and finishes the same month. They gaff fish only from Uralsk downstream for just over two hundred kilometres; they do not go on beyond that because that is where the autumn fishing takes place.
>
> The gaffing procedure is as follows: At the appointed day and hour the "gaffing hetman" (appointed each time by the chancery from among the staff officers) appears on the Ural, together with all those Cossacks with the right to gaff, each on small one-man, one-horse sledges; they bring a pickaxe, a shovel, and several gaffs; the steel tips of these gaffs are fastened by cords to a ferrule attached to the shaft, and their wooden poles, made in sections, to a length of six, eight or

sometimes twenty-five metres trail behind through the snow. When the hetman arrives at the assembly point, he takes his stand in front surrounded by several mounted Cossacks to keep order; all those who have ridden out for gaffing fall in behind him in rows. Their number always reaches several thousand. If any of them dares break rank and gallop off alone, the constables break up his gaffs and harness.

This strict but fair measure forces the Cossacks to keep rank, despite the impatient desire to dash forward straightaway written on almost all their faces. And more than that: you can even see in the eyes of the horses, trained up as they are for this activity, an impatience to gallop off. The hetman, watched intently by everyone, walks around his own sledge, approaches it as though to get in, and then walks away again, repeatedly giving them false signals; then finally he jumps on board the sledge in earnest, gives the sign and gallops off at full speed, with all the assembled Host dashing after him. At this stage there is no order, and no quarter given to anyone. They all try to get ahead of each other, and woe to the one unlucky enough to be thrown from his sledge. If he is not trampled to death (they recall few cases of this), he may well be maimed for life.

When the sledges reach the place designated for fishing (these places are called *yetovy* and are identified in autumn by the multitude of fish, which, having found somewhere to spend the winter, appear on the surface of the water at sunrise and sunset), the Cossacks all stop. Each rider jumps out with all possible haste, breaks a small hole in the ice and immediately lowers his gaff into it. The scene presented at this moment to spectators on the banks of the Ural is fascinating. The speed with which the Cossacks race each other, the general commotion that engulfs everything on their arrival at the place of fishing, and the forest of poles that sprouts up in a few minutes on the ice is a striking and extraordinary sight. No sooner are the gaffs lowered than the fish, disturbed by the noise of the galloping horses, rise up from their place, thrash around and impale themselves on the gaffs which are held at a depth of several centimetres from the bottom. In an abundant spot it is sometimes less than a quarter of an hour from the start of the catch before there are twitching sturgeon of all kinds to be seen all over the ice. If a fish caught on a gaff is so large that one man cannot land it, he immediately calls for help, and his friends or neighbours "sub-gaff" for him. There is a boundary set each day for gaffing, beyond which no one may go.

After the minor gaffing each year a quantity of the best caviar and fish is sent on the Host's behalf to the Imperial court. This offering, a long-established token of loyalty, is called a "present" or first-fruit. For catching this "present" a specially good spot, or *yetov*, is normally designated; and if on that occasion they gaff little, then the shortfall of fish is purchased at the expense of the Host chancery. But if at the gaffing for the court they catch more fish than are needed, then the remainder may not be sold for a period of time, to avoid it reaching St Petersburg before what has been sent from the Host. Those officers that are despatched with the "present" receive a cash award from the court for their travelling expenses, for a liquor bowl and for a sabre.

ii. The second mode of fishing is the "spring surge" or "sevruga catch", so called because at that time the sevruga sturgeon are almost the only ones to be caught. It begins in April immediately after the ice breaks up below Uralsk, and continues for about two months along the whole stretch of the Ural to the sea. For this, as for all the other modes of fishing, a day is fixed, a hetman is chosen, and he is given a cannon. When the gun is fired, all the Cossacks who have assembled for the enterprise launch themselves out from the place in small boats that take no more than one man. Each man then begins to let out a net of predetermined length. The nets used on this occasion consist of two panels, one coarse-meshed and the other fine-meshed, so that the fish that usually travel up the Ural River from the sea in spring get trapped between them. One end of the net is fastened to a cask or a bit of timber floating in the water; the other end the Cossack holds with two cords. An area is set aside for resting, and in front of it, on the bank, is the hetman's tent, beside which everyone has to terminate their fishing. The close of fishing is announced every evening, again by the firing of the gun. Any common or beluga sturgeon that are caught on this occasion must by regulation be thrown back into the water: in the first place they are still small at that season, and secondly they are too cheap. Those who infringe this regulation are punished by having all the fish they have caught confiscated.

iii. Third is the "autumn surge" that begins on 1st October and finishes in November. It differs from the spring surge in that, first, nets of a completely different type are used; that is, they are woven like a sack and the fish are, as it were, scooped up with them (because the fish at this time of year have chosen a place to winter); secondly, with each of these nets (called *yarygas*) there are two men in separate boats on each side. The autumn fishing expedition, like the others, is commenced from a designated site under the authority of a special hetman. To prevent one man using a larger net or *yaryga* to commandeer a bigger stretch, and therefore more fish, than another with a smaller net, the length of all the nets has been fixed once and for all. When they have caught all the fish in one spot, they assemble again where the hetman is and ride on to the next site, or (to use the Cossacks' language) they make another "strike".

The autumn surge only takes place beyond the spot where the gaffing finishes, i.e. from just over two hundred kilometres from Uralsk down to the sea. (Each Cossack takes with him for this catch a mate, to whom he has to pay between seventy and a hundred roubles for one-and-a-half or two months' work.)

iv. A different kind of fishing net is used. The catch begins in winter, again as directed by the chancery; but the fishing is not done communally but individually, wherever anyone wishes. The net is passed below the ice on a pole, which the fisherman manoeuvres wherever he wants through holes in the ice.

v. *Akhan* fishing, or fishing with *akhans* – that is, with nets of a special kind. It takes place around the middle of December and only at sea, i.e. in the vicinity of Guryev. On the day fixed for the beginning of this activity, the officer in charge allocates sectors by lot to all those who want to fish and have the right to do so. The sectors are all equal, i.e. each Cossack is assigned an equal area for a specific number of *akhans* of a specific size. Officials get two, three or more sectors, according to rank.

The *akhan* is let down into the sea under the ice. It is suspended in a position perpendicular to the surface and fastened at the two corners and in the middle by cords or loops; three ice holes are made to let these through, and sticks or poles that rest on the ice above the holes are fed through the loops.

The *akhans* held fast in this way require only that the fisherman goes up to them from time to time, lifts each *akhan* by the middle through the middle hole (or, as they say here, "sounds it out"). Then, if he feels by the weight that a fish is entangled in it, he just needs to pull it out, extract his catch and then make the net fast again as before. This type of fishing is extremely profitable for those that engage in it, but, because it stops the fish from swimming up the Ural, it is detrimental to the gaff-fishers.

vi. *Kurkhay* fishing happens normally in spring, and only at sea or, more correctly, along the seashore. It is carried out by means of nets that are fastened perpendicularly at the ends and middle to three posts that have been driven into the seabed. Any fish coming from the sea and entangling themselves in these nets are hauled up into the boats in which the fishery men make the rounds of their tackle.

vii. This mode of fishing is with hooks suspended on a line that is similarly held in position under the ice by three loops. It is of less significance than any of the other modes described.

Other kinds of fishing with rods and lines et cetera are unimportant and there is nothing to be said about them.

Beginning this year 1821 the Cossacks have for the first time, by permission of the highest authority, begun to fish in Lake Chalkar (or "the little sea", as it is called locally), which lies eighty-five kilometres from Uralsk in the Kyrgyz steppe.

Fish that are caught in the Ural in the greatest quantities are: various kinds of sturgeon (osyotr, beluga, ship, sevruga), whitefry, zander, bream, pike, perch, carp, catfish and chub. Osyotr are sometimes landed at 115, 130 or even close to 150 kilograms; beluga at 300, 500 or even (rarely) close to 650 kilograms. With osyotr, the bigger they are, the better and the dearer; with beluga, the bigger they are, the worse and the cheaper. But in general all the fish now have become smaller than previously because of the declining water levels in the sea and in the Ural. The prices for caviar and fish at the gaffing season bear no comparison with the prices for the spring catch. During the spring catch prices go down by three quarters, because the time of year does not permit the fish to be preserved except by salting.

The Ural Cossacks get salt either from the Inder and Gryaznoye salt lakes, which lie not far from the frontier in the Kyrgyz steppe, or from the lakes that lie along the banks of the Emba. There are also some small salt lakes near the Uzen rivers.

8 For the most reliable and objective information about the migration of the Kalmyks we are obliged to Father Iakinf, whose deep knowledge and conscientious labours have shed such a bright light on our relations with the East. We are grateful to quote here an extract provided by him from his as yet unpublished book about the Kalmyks –

> There is no doubt that Ubashi and Seryn embarked on the return to their fatherland by previous arrangement with their fellow tribesmen in the Altai, who were full of hatred for China. They probably considered, too, that that empire, after its conquest of Dzungaria, had recalled its armies from there, leaving weak garrisons in Ili and Tarbagatay that would easily be driven out by their combined forces. Indeed, in their passage across the Kyrgyz-Kazakh lands they anticipated danger all the less because those brigands, bold as they were in the face of merchant caravans, had always trembled at the very sight of armed Kalmyks. In a word, the Kalmyks imagined in their minds that this trek would be for them, as it had always been in the past, a pleasant stroll from the sandy plains of the Volga and Ural to the mountain peaks of the

Irtysh. But what happened was just the opposite: they encountered circumstances that were entirely beyond their expectations.

The Dzungarian Confederation in the East, once the terror of northern Asia, no longer existed, and the Volga Kalmyks, who had long lived under Russian suzerainty, were regarded as deserters once they had set out across the frontier. The Russian government pursued them with its own weaponry, and sent messages to the Kyrgyz-Kazakhs ordering them to obstruct the Kalmyks at every step, as it were, by force of arms. The Chinese frontier authorities for their own part, at the first report of the eastward march of the *Torgots*, took all necessary precautionary measures; they also ordered the Kazakhs and Kyrgyz not to let them pass through areas with pasturage, and in the event of their resistance to counter force with force. Could any Kyrgyz or Kazakh remain passive in the face of such an unlooked-for opportunity for plunder with impunity?

The Russian detachments that had been detailed to pursue the deserters were unable – for various reasons to do mainly with season and terrain – to catch up with them. The former Yaik Cossacks had already at this very time became restive and refused to obey orders. The Orenburg Cossacks, although they had marched out in the middle of February and had joined Nur-Ali, Khan of the Lesser Kazakh Horde, had soon been compelled by the shortage of green pasture to turn back to the frontier. After the usual exchanges of letters, which took up plenty of time, it was not until 12th April that a detachment of regular troops set out from Fort Orsk and managed to join Khan Nur-Ali. But the Kalmyks in the meantime had moved southwards and were so far ahead that this detachment was only able for a short time, and then from a distance, to harass their rear. Near Ulu-Tag, the soldiers and horses being now in no condition to go farther through hunger and thirst, the detachment commander Traubenberg was forced to turn north and return to the frontier via Fort Uyskoye.

The Kyrgyz-Kazakhs, however, took up arms regardless, with the utmost zeal. Their Khans, Nur-Ali in the Lesser Horde, Ablay in the Middle Horde, and Er-Ali in the Great Horde, one after the other fell upon the Kalmyks from every side; and the deserters had to spend a whole year on their journey fighting continuously to defend their families from capture and their herds from pillage. In spring of the following year (1772) the Kyrgyz (Buruts) completed the discomfiture of the Kalmyks by driving them into the vast sandy steppe that extends to the north of Lake Balkhash, where large numbers of them, humans and cattle, perished from hunger and thirst.

After enduring incredible hardships and undergoing countless troubles the Kalmyks at last drew near to the longed-for borders of their ancient country. But here they were faced with a new misfortune. The cordon of Chinese frontier guards formed a fearsome barrier to their entering their former homeland, and the Kalmyks had no choice but to sacrifice their independence to gain entry. The people's extreme exhaustion compelled Ubashi along with the other princes to submit unconditionally to Chinese suzerainty. He had left Russia with 33,000 wagons, carrying approximately 169,000 souls of both sexes. On arriving in Ili not more than 70,000 souls remained of the former number. In the course of one year the Kalmyks had lost 100,000 people who had fallen victim to the sword and to disease, and were left behind in the deserts of Asia as carrion for wild beasts, or else they had been taken prisoner and sold into slavery in distant countries.

The Chinese emperor gave orders that these unhappy wanderers and new subjects of his should be given a notably humane reception. The Kalmyks were quickly provided with aid in the form of yurts, cattle, clothing and grain. After they had been assigned to nomadic encampments, a further distribution of necessities was made to them:

Horses, horned cattle and sheep	1,125,000 head
Brick tea	20,000 cases
Wheat and millet	20,000 quarts
Fleeces	51,000
Lengths of cotton cloth	51,000
Raw cotton	25,000 kilos
Yurts	400
Silver	6,500 kilos (approximately)

In the autumn of the same year Ubashi and Princes Tsebok-Dortszi, Seryn, Gunghe, Momyntu, Shara-Keukyn and Tsile-Mupir were dispatched to the Chinese court, which was residing at Chengde. These princes, apart from Seryn, were very close relatives of Khan Ubashi, descendants of Chakdor-Chzhaba, elder son of Khan Ayuki. Only Tsebok-Dortszi was great-grandson of Gun-Chzhaba, Khan Ayuki's younger son. Ubashi received the title of Chzhoriktu Khan, while the other princes, including those who stayed behind in Ili, were awarded various other princely titles. On their departure from Chengde these lords were loaded with presents, and after their return to Ili three divisions of the Torgots were stationed in Tarbagatay or in Khur-Khara-Usu, while Ubashi with four divisions of the Torgots, and Gunghe with the Khoshuts, were settled at Karashahr along the sides of the Great and Small Yulduz valleys, where part of the population were obliged to engage in grain cultivation under the supervision of Chinese officials. The Kalmyks who went over to the Chinese side are split into thirteen divisions.

The Russian government made representations to Chinese ministers that, by virtue of the treaties in force between Russia and China, they should send back the runaway Volga Kalmyks; but they received an answer to the effect that the Chinese court could not comply with this request for the same reasons that had led the Russian court to refuse to surrender Seryn when he left Dzungaria for the Volga to take refuge from legal prosecution.

However, the Volga Kalmyks themselves apparently soon regretted their precipitate adventure. In 1791 various reports were received from the Chinese side that the Kalmyks were intending to return from Chinese jurisdiction and place themselves once more under Russian suzerainty. In the light of these reports an order was issued to the authorities in Siberia to grant them asylum in Russia and settle them initially in Kolyvan province.

However, it seems that the Kalmyks, surrounded as they were by Chinese guards and scouts, and separated from each other by significant distances, had no opportunity to put their plan into effect.

9 Field detachments consisted of five hundred infantry, cavalry and artillerymen. In 1775 they were replaced by provincial battalions.

10 *Umyot* – a wayside inn.

NOTES TO CHAPTER II

1 Pugachov used to mow hay on Sheludyakov's farm. In Uralsk there is still living an old Cossack woman who wore boots made by him. Once, when he had been hired to dig over beds in the vegetable garden, he dug out four graves. This incident was interpreted later as a portent of his destiny.

2 A memorandum from the Malykovka office of court affairs to the commandant's chancery in the town of Yaitsk, dated 18th December 1772, submitted by Superintendent Ivan Rastorguyev:

> The parish clerk of Malykovka Trofim Gerasimov, the superintendent of the Mechetnaya settlement Fedot Fadeyev and Lieutenant Sergei Protopopov (who was staying in Mechetnaya at the time) made the following statement in writing: "A peasant of the Mechetnaya settlement, Semyon Filippov, was in Yaitsk to buy grain; he travelled on from there with a schismatic Yemelyan Ivanov. While in Yaitsk this man kept inciting the Cossacks to abscond to the river Loba, to the territory of the Turkish Sultan, promising each man a wage of twelve roubles and declaring that he had 200,000 roubles waiting for him at the frontier and goods to the value of 70,000 roubles; moreover, on their arrival a pasha would allegedly give them up to 5,000,000. Some of the Cossacks wanted to tie him up and take him off to the commandant's chancery, but he evidently escaped and is probably now in the village of Malykovka."
>
> Further to this, the schismatic Yemelyan Ivanov (who had crossed the Polish frontier with an identity certificate issued by the Dobryanskoye control post authorizing residence on the Irgiz River) has been traced and brought to the administrative office by Deputy Mitrofan Fyodorov, by the monk Filaret of the Filaretov schismatic community and by a peasant of the Mechetnaya settlement Stepan Vasilyev and friends. *Being deemed suspicious, he has been flogged.* Under questioning he has made the following statement: that he is

> Yemelyan Ivanov Pugachov, a Cossack from Zimoveyskaya eligible for military service, forty years old; during Lent of this year 1772 he decamped from that settlement to the village of Vetka across the frontier, he stayed there about fifteen weeks and then turned up at the control post of Dobryanskoye, where he claimed to be a refugee from Poland; having completed six weeks there in quarantine, he arrived in Yaitsk in August and stayed for a week or so with the Cossack Denis Stepanov Pyanov; whatever he had said there he had said when drunk; he had not spoken of giving allegiance to the Sultan, of meeting a pasha or of any five million; but he did have the intention of presenting himself at the *Simbirsk provincial* chancellery to get authorization to take up residence on the Irgiz River. By decision of the office of court affairs he has been dispatched under guard together with the peasants from Malykovka. Reported to the commandant's chancery at Yaitsk on 19th December 1772.

The peasant Semyon Filippov was held under guard right until 1775. After the end of investigations over Pugachov and his accomplices the order was given for his release, and in addition for the Senate then in session to be asked to consider a reward for him as the one who had given information in Malykovka of the villain Pugachov's first attempts at sedition. (See court decision of 10th January 1775)

3 From *Notes on the Life and Career of A.I. Bibikov*:

> The said Pugachov, for escaping across the frontier into Poland, for concealing his true name after his return from there to Russia, and the more so for making seditious and dangerous statements about the escape of all the Yaik Cossacks into Turkish territory, to be punished with the lash and to be sent to the town of Pelym, as a vagrant and one accustomed to a life of idleness and insolence, where he should be put to forced labour. Sixth of May 1773.

4 The outpost of Budarino is eighty-four kilometres from Yaitsk.

5 Ilek (Iletsky Township) is 154 kilometres from Yaitsk and 131 from Orenburg. Up to three hundred Cossacks were based there. The Ilek Cossacks had been settled there by State Councillor Kirillov, first administrator of Orenburg Province.

6 Fort Rassypnaya was built at the spot where the Kyrgyz customarily forded the Yaik. It lies twenty-six kilometres from Ilek and 107 kilometres from Orenburg.

7 In 1773 Orenburg Province was divided into four regions: Orenburg, Isetskoye, Ufa and Stavropol. To the first belonged the district (*uyezd*) of Orenburg and Yaitsk, with all its outposts and Cossack settlements right down to Guryev, also the Bugulma administrative office. Isetskoye Region included trans-Ural Bashkiria and the districts of Isetskoye, Shadrinsk and Okunevo. Ufa Region included the districts of Osa, Birsk and Menzelinsk. Stavropol Region consisted of a single extensive district. In addition, Orenburg Province was further divided into eight *lines of defence* (a series of forts built along the Rivers Volga, Samara, Yaik, Sakmara and Uy). These Lines came under the jurisdiction of the military authorities, who exercised the powers of regional governors. (See Bisching and Rychkov.)

8 The Stavropol chancery dealt with the affairs of the Christianized Kalmyks who had settled in Orenburg Province.

9 Lower Ozyornaya lies twenty kilometres from Rassypnaya and eighty-seven from Orenburg. It is built on a bluff above the Yaik.

The memory of Captain Surin is preserved in the soldiers' song:

> Out from Fort Ozyornaya
> to reinforce Rassypnaya
> Captain Surin, only he,
> marched out with his company [...]

10 The anonymous author of a short historical monograph – *Histoire de la révolte de Pougatschef* – relates the death of Kharlov in the following manner:

> *Le major Charlof avait épousé, depuis quelques semaines, la fille du colonel Iélagin, jeune personne très aimable. Il était dangereusement blessé en défendant la place et on l'avait rapporté chez lui. Lorsque la forteresse fut prise, Pougatschef envoya chez lui, le fit arracher de son lit et emmener devant lui. La jeune épouse, au désespoir, le suivit, se jeta aux pieds du vainqueur et lui demanda la grâce de son mari. – Je vais le faire pendre en ta présence, – répondit*

le barbare. À ces mots la jeune femme verse un torrent de larmes, embrasse de nouveau les pieds de Pougatschef et implore sa pitié; tout fut inutile, et Charlof fut pendu, à l'instant même, en présence de son épouse. À peine eut-il expiré que les cosaques se saisirent de la femme et la forcèrent d'assouvir la passion brutale de Pougatschef.

[Major Kharlov had several weeks earlier married Colonel Yelagin's daughter, a very charming girl. He had been seriously wounded during the defence of the fort and had been carried back to his house. Pugachov sent for him there and had him hauled from his bed and brought before him. The young wife, in despair, followed him, threw herself at the victor's feet and begged him to spare her husband. "I shall have him hanged in front of you," the savage replied. At these words the young woman burst into floods of tears, put her arms once more round Pugachov's feet and besought his mercy. It was all futile: Kharlov was hanged that very instant in front of his wife. He had hardly breathed his last when the Cossacks seized the woman and forced her to satisfy Pugachov's brutish lust (French).]

The author finds this improbable and sets out to explain it all away.

Les peuples les plus barbares respectent les mœurs jusqu'à un certain point, et Pougatschef avait trop de bon sens pour commettre devant ses soldats, etc.

[Even the most savage nations have a certain respect for morality, and Pugachov had too much good sense to commit, in front of his troops, etc. (French).]

That is nonsense; but for the most part the whole monograph is noteworthy and was probably written by a diplomat stationed at that time in St Petersburg.

11 Fort Tatishcheva, which stands at the mouth of the Kamysh-Samara River, was founded by Kirillov, first administrator of Orenburg Province, and named by him Kamysh-Samara. Kirillov's successor

Tatishchev called it after his own name *Tatishcheva Landing*. It is situated thirty kilometres from Lower Ozyornaya and fifty-seven (by direct route) from Orenburg.

12 Chernorechenskaya is thirty-eight kilometres from Tatishcheva and nineteen from Orenburg.

13 Sakmarsk town, founded on the River Sakmara, is situated thirty-one kilometres from Orenburg. It had up to three hundred Cossack inhabitants.

14 Deposition by the peasant Alexei Kirillov dated 6th October 1773 (from the Orenburg archives).

15 Those hanged were: two couriers who had been riding to Orenburg, one from Siberia and the other from Ufa; a corporal from the garrison; a Tatar interpreter; an old gardener who had formerly been in St Petersburg and had known the Emperor Peter III; and an office-clerk from the Tverdyshev mines.

NOTES TO CHAPTER III

1 [Pushkin refers the reader to the text of the proclamation in his Volume Two, not included in this edition.]

2 A diary of the siege, maintained in the governor's office, is included in an interesting manuscript of the academician Rychkov's, which the reader will find in the appendices [i.e. in Pushkin's Volume Two, not included in this edition]. Three copies have passed through my hands, obtained for me by Messrs Spassky, Yazykov and Lazhechnikov.

3 Bülow set out from Orenburg on 24th September. On that day the governor gave a ball at his residence. The news about Pugachov circulated at the ball.

4 The name of this sergeant was Ivan Kostitsyn. His fate is unknown. His interrogator was Lieutenant Colonel V. Mogutov.

5 [Pushkin refers the reader to the text of the announcement in his Volume Two, not included in this edition.]

6 In a memorandum from the Malykovka court office it was said of Pugachov: "*Being deemed suspicious, he has been flogged.*" See note 2 to Chapter Two.

7 Padurov, who was subsequently hanged, wrote to Martemyan Borodin, urging him to submit to Pugachov: "And you people are

now calling him (the pretender) the Don Cossack Yemelyan Pugachov, and claiming that he has had his nostrils torn off and has been branded. But I have seen him for myself and he has none of these scars."

8 On the advice of one of his officials (according to Rychkov).

9 *The topography of Orenburg Province*:

> At the barter market, trade and barter are carried on with Asiatic peoples for the whole summer right till autumn. The market is built on the steppe side of the Yaik River, within sight of the city, at a distance of about two kilometres from the river bank. It could not be built nearer because the whole area was low-lying and liable to flooding. The frontier customs office is situated there. Surrounding the market there are about 246 stalls and 140 storerooms. Inside, a special market has been built for the Asiatic merchants with ninety-eight stalls and eight storerooms. In 1762 market dues amounted to 4,854 roubles. The barter market is fortified with gun emplacements.

10 Letter from Reinsdorp to Count Chernyshov of 9th October 1773:

> *Der kläglichste Zustand des Orenburgischen Gouvernments ist weit kritischer als ich ihn beschreiben kann; eine reguläre feindliche Armee von zehntausend Mann würde mich nicht in Schrecken setzen, allein ein Verräter mit 3000 Rebellen [Pushkin's note: Reinsdorp does not count the Bashkirs in this number.] macht ganz Orenburg zittern [...] Meine aus 1200 Mann bestehende Garnison ist noch das einzige Kommando worauf ich mich verlasse, durch die Gnade des Höchsten haben wir 12 Spione aufgefangen, etc.*

> [The lamentable state of Orenburg Province is far more critical than I can describe. An enemy army of 10,000 regular soldiers would not alarm me; but a traitor with 3,000 rebels causes the whole of Orenburg to tremble... My current garrison of 1,200 men is still the only unit on which I can rely; by the grace of the Almighty we have caught twelve spies, etc. (German).]

11 The Cossack settlement of Berda is on the Sakmara River. It had been encircled with ramparts and defensive spikes. There were gun emplacements at the angles. It contained about two hundred households and about one hundred paid Cossack soldiers. They had their own hetman and their own elders.

12 In the city seventeen people were killed, including one old peasant woman going to fetch water.

13 On another occasion Pugachov, lying drunk in a covered sleigh, lost his way during a storm and rode into the gates of Orenburg. The sentries challenged him. The Cossack Fedulev, who was driving the horses, turned round without answering and managed to gallop off. Fedulev, who died not long ago, was one of the Cossacks who handed the pretender over to the government.

14 I heard this from the son Dmitry Denisovich Pyanov himself, who flourishes to this day in Uralsk.

15 Pugachov and his accomplices did not apparently take this masquerade seriously. They also jokingly called the Berda settlement "Moscow", Kargala village "St Petersburg", and Sakmarsk "Kiev".

16 So said Kar in a letter of 11th November 1773 to Count Chernyshov.

17 The Avzyano-Petrovsk works belonged to the merchant Tverdyshev, an enterprising and clever man. He acquired his huge fortune in the course of seven years. His heirs' descendants are still among Russia's wealthiest people.

18 The village of Yuzeyeva is 127 kilometres from Orenburg.

19 That is, a delegate to the Commission for the drafting of a New Legal Code.* There were 652 delegates. Each was awarded an oval medallion of gold on a gold chain, to be worn in the buttonhole; it displayed on one side Her Imperial Majesty's initials and on the other a pyramid wreathed with the imperial crown, with the inscription "The well-being of one and all" and below "The 14th day of December 1766".

20 This Kalmyk colonel got turned into "Captain Kalmykov".

21 In this engagement Danila Sheludyakov, one of the first instigators of the revolt, was captured. The old horseman mistook the Orenburg Cossacks for his own and galloped towards them, giving orders. One Cossack seized him by the collar. Pugachov, who had

once lived with him when they were labourers, was fond of him and used to call him his father. The next day, large numbers of rebels, not finding him among the dead, rode up to the city and demanded his release. A couple of days later three men rode up to the city wall before dawn and again asked for Sheludyakov. They were told, "Bring us his son (Pugachov) as well," and they were promised five hundred roubles reward if they did so. They rode away in silence. Sheludyakov was tortured and died about five days later.

NOTES TO CHAPTER IV

1 Dekalong and Stanislavsky together had around five thousand troops. But they were all spread out over a wide area from Upper Yaitsk Fort to Orsk. Dekalong refused to concentrate them, for fear of leaving the forts of the Line without protection.

2 Fort Orsk, on the steppe side of the Yaik River and two kilometres from the River Or, was built in 1735 under the name of Orenburg. It possessed adequate earthen fortifications. The commander of the Orsk line of defence was always stationed here, with a garrison of double the usual number because of the propinquity of the nomadic hordes.

3 After the engagement on 14th November Korff had sent a Cossack to Pugachov with proposals for the surrender of Orenburg and with an undertaking to come out to meet him. Pugachov began riding cautiously towards Orenburg, but, doubting the sincerity of the proposals, soon turned back to Berda.

4 Reinsdorp, having given up hope of defeating Pugachov by force of arms, launched into a not altogether seemly war of words. In reply to the pretender's insolent admonitions he sent him a letter with the following preamble:

> *To the quintessential rogue, the apostate from God, the scion of Satan, Yemelka Pugachov...*

Pugachov's secretaries were not behind the game. We cite here a letter of Padurov's, as a specimen of his "officialese":

To the Orenburg governor, scion of Satan, son of the Devil: Your fouler than foul admonition has been received here, for which we thank you, foulest of enemies that you are to the public peace. But however much, with Satan's aid, you play your tricks, you will not outsmart the might of God. Be sure of this, you swindler: it is well known (and you above all, knave, must be aware of it) that, however far you push your all-foul luck, even so this luck of yours works only to the benefit of Satan your father. Understand this, you knave: even though with Satan's aid you set your wolf-traps in many places, even so your labours will remain in vain; and even though we may be short of nooses of rope with which to hang you, we shall buy string for ten kopecks from the Mordva people, and we can twist cord to hang you. So do not doubt, you swindler, son of a whore. Our most all-gracious Sovereign, like an eagle beneath the heavens, visits all armies in a single day, and is present with us always. So we would give you this advice: leave your stronghold and come to our Father who loves his children, our most all-gracious Sovereign: and if you come in submission, whatever enragements you have caused him, not only does he most graciously pardon you in all your excusings, but more than that – he does not strip you of your former honour; and it is not beyond our knowledge here that you now gladly eat dead flesh; and in notifying you thus, let us stay ready at your service according to your pleasure. The 23rd day of February 1774.

5 I have not had the opportunity to read this oration. Let us cite a letter, also composed by Derzhavin, on the same subject:

Most wholly august Sovereign Lady, most wise and invincible Empress!

Hearing a word most precious to us and beyond price to our descendants, scenting this fragrance so soothing especially to this present generation of Kazan's nobility, hearing this voice of gladness, of our eternal glory, of our eternal joy, through Your Imperial Majesty's supreme goodwill towards us, which of us would not sense rapture in his soul, which heart would not dance for the great happiness it feels? You have poured down the light of your grace upon us in our grief and sorrow! Wherefore, if any of us were not now rejoicing, then he would in truth have inadequately displayed his devotion to the fatherland and to Your Imperial Majesty by the granting of some portion of his property for the formation of our corps. As it is, our sacrifice has been pleasing to you; this is our happiness, this is the ecstasy of our souls!

But, most all-gracious Sovereign Lady, Your Imperial Majesty has deigned to accustom yourself to look upon small tokens of devotion as on great ones; and as you shed the bounties of your mercy around your throne, you shed them also on distant regions. As you illumine all people together with the rays of your grace, you also grace all people everywhere with your philanthropy; and this is clearly why, Your Imperial Majesty, you have so graciously and condescendingly deigned to accept from us the gift, such as it is, of the duty that we ourselves cannot in truth withhold.

"This is quite clearly the embodiment of noble thoughts," Your Imperial Majesty was generously pleased to tell us. What, then, should we infer from this sublime word of acknowledgement to us? Is it not just in truth a maternal prompting to the fulfilment of our duty? Is it not graciousness alone? We are receiving praise for that which is our essential business! Consider a priest: apart from the special respect in which he is held, exceeding what he deserves, does a priest earn praise for the prayers he offers before the congregation? Apart from Your Imperial Majesty's indescribable favour towards us, do noblemen deserve any special praise for wanting to shield their fatherland? They are its shield; they are the support on which the tsars' throne rests. The ashes of our ancestors cry out to us and summon us to defeat the pretender. The voice of posterity is already rebuking us for allowing this evil to emerge in the era of Catherine the great and glorious. The blood of our brethren, still steaming, impels us to annihilate the villain. Then why have we delayed? What has held us back so long from facing up together to the marauder? If a nobleman has one serf, then he has all that is necessary for army service. So what has been missing? Not, surely, our devotion? No! We have long been ablaze with it, we have long been preparing, we have long been wanting to risk our lives. But now, by the grace of Your

Imperial Majesty, there is one who shares our aspirations. By his leadership our corps has been formed. Its chosen commander is at work, his comrades are eager, all is in order. Our goods are ready to be sacrificed; our blood is ready to be shed; our lives are ready to be laid down; let us die – whoever does not have these thoughts is not a nobleman.

But however great is our enthusiasm for duty, however fervent is the ardour of our hearts, our forces would still be inadequate for crushing our vile foe, had Your Imperial Majesty not hastened to our defence with your troops and above all by sending us His Excellency Alexandr Ilyich Bibikov. Maybe we should even now be hesitating over the formation of our corps, had he not offered us his wise advice. By his arrival he has dispersed the cloud of despair that was drifting above our city. He has emboldened our spirits. He has stiffened those hearts that were wavering in their loyalty to God, to the fatherland and to you, most all-gracious Sovereign Lady: in a word, he has brought life to a land that was near to death. The greatness of our monarch is discernible in this: that this man has the wisdom to understand people and to make use of them opportunely; so in this too Your Imperial Majesty's most acute perceptiveness has not failed. The crisis here demands a statesman, a warrior, a judge and a devotee of the Holy Faith. Through Your Imperial Majesty's percipience and goodwill we behold all this in Alexandr Ilyich Bibikov. For all this we write to express from the bottom of our hearts our gratitude to your discerning spirit.

But, most all-gracious Sovereign Lady, we have scarcely managed to tell Your Imperial Majesty of our feelings of deepest devotion in recognition of your mercies; we have scarcely managed to set alight the censer of our hearts, great Empress, before the image of you that we worship and adore in recognition of your kindnesses, when already we hear a new report, new joyful tidings from you of your generosity and condescension towards us. Why do you concern yourself with us? Holding dominion in three regions of the world, renowned at the ends of the earth, honoured among tsars, treasured among crowned heads for the divine beauty of your majesty, for the radiance of your glory, you condescend to name yourself "Kazan landowner", one of us! Oh, our unspeakable joy, our boundless happiness! Such a path straight to our hearts! Such a glorious exaltation of the dust that we are, we and our descendants! She, who gives laws to half the world, submits to our rules! She, who holds dominion over us, follows our lead! And in doing so you make yourself still greater, still more majestic!

So although by fulfilling our duty we do not merit any special recognition from Your Imperial Majesty, any kindly and priceless comradeship towards us, nonetheless we accept your sublime will with open hearts and count it a blessing; with veneration we inscribe on our memories the priceless words of your benevolence. We acknowledge you as our fellow-landowner; we welcome you into our society. If this is pleasing to you, we accept you on our level. But in return intercede with us yourself at the throne of your majesty. If ever our strength proves too feeble to carry through our earnest intentions, come to our help and speak for us in your presence. We place greater confidence in you than in ourselves.

Great Empress! What are we to render up to you in return for your maternal love to us, for these your inexpressible favours to us? Let us fill our hearts with still greater zeal to uproot from the world the malice that is unworthy of your dominions. Let us ask the King of kings to grant us in this his succour, and to grant Your Imperial Majesty, true mother of the fatherland, together with Your Imperial Majesty's dear son, our priceless hope, and his most precious spouse, many years of prosperity in an untroubled empire.

6 The nun Yevpraxiya Kirilovna was Bibikov's grandmother. She brought him up. Within her family she was regarded as a near-saint.

7 [Pushkin refers the reader to the text of Bibikov's letter to Count Chernyshov of 21st January 1774 in his Volume Two, not included in this edition.] On 5th January the same year Bibikov had written to Filosofov:

My patience is getting shorter by the hour as I wait for the regiments; for I receive terrible news each hour [...], and, on the other side, that the Bashkirs and all sorts of riff-raff are riding around in bands, plundering factories and villages, and committing murders. Commanders and senior officers are fleeing in terror on every side, while the foolish rabble, bewitched by the villain, runs eagerly to meet the man. I cannot describe to you in detail, my friend, the suffering and devastation in this part of the country, so judge my predicament from that very fact. The garrison troops here, shameful oafs, are frightened of everything, dare show their noses nowhere, sit tight at their posts like marmots, and do nothing but send alarmist dispatches. Pugachov's outrages, and those of his accomplices, have gone beyond all bounds; they send manifestos and edicts everywhere. I work day and night like a galley-slave, I push myself, I strain myself, I burn myself up as though in hell-fire; but I do not yet see any variation in the barbarity of their treacheries and in their villainy, nor does the spite and savagery abate, and I wonder if it is possible to defend ourselves adequately against a domestic enemy – at their gatherings everything makes for betrayal, villainy and rebellion. God alone is almighty, and will turn all this round for the better. In all my anxieties I do not cease to beseech Him… etc.

8 Snow in Orenburg Province sometimes reaches a depth of over two metres.

9 [Pushkin refers the reader to the text of Bibikov's letter to Count Chernyshov in his Volume Two, not included in this edition.]

10 One must not lose sight of the delegation of governmental powers at that period to provinces and districts.

11 In 1774 some 1,380 persons were carried off as captives by the Kyrgyz.

12 See, in Khrapovitsky's memoirs (for 1791), the Sovereign's particularly interesting remarks about Gustav III.

13 See Voltaire's correspondence with the Empress.

14 We cite here the testimony of Pugachov's wife Sofya Dmitriyeva in the form in which it was submitted to the War College.

DESCRIPTION OF THE NOTORIOUS VILLAIN AND PRETENDER, HIS CHARACTER AND PARTICULARS, DRAWN UP FROM THE DEPOSITION OF HIS WIFE SOFYA DMITRIYEVA:

i. Her husband, a Cossack eligible for military service, belonging to the Don Host from the Zimoveyskaya settlement, is named Yemelyan, son of Ivan, and surnamed Pugachov.

ii. His birth father was an eligible Cossack from the same Zimoveyskaya settlement, Ivan, son of Mikhail, Pugachov, who died many years ago.

iii. The said husband will now be about forty years old, lean in the face, with one upper tooth missing in the front of his mouth, which he broke through a blow to the jaw when playing as a child, but which from that time till now has not regrown. On the left temple there is a round white mark the size of a two-kopeck piece caused by an illness, which contrasts sharply with his complexion. On both breasts for the last two years or more he has had pockmarks, which she thinks must also have been caused by an illness. He has yellow streaks on his face, though his natural colour is dark; the hair on his head is dark brown, cut in the Cossack manner; he is of medium height; he used to have a small black pointed beard.

iv. He was a true Orthodox believer; he used to attend church, go to confession and partake of the sacred mysteries; his confessor was Fyodor Tikhonov, priest in the same Zimoveyskaya settlement. He made the sign of the cross with the thumb joined to the last two fingers.

v. The said husband married her, and she him, both for the first time, about ten years ago; together they had five children, of whom two have died and three are still living. The first, a son Trofim, is ten; the second, a daughter Agrafena, is six; and the third, a daughter Khristina, is three.

vi. The said husband was sent three years ago to serve in the Second Army, where he spent two years; at the end of spring, over a year ago now, he was discharged on account of the chest disorder mentioned above. For this reason he spent one summer at home, during which period he hired a Cossack to serve in his place in Bakhmut on the Donets; but what the man's name is or his surname or where he is now she does not know. And after that –

vii. In October 1772, he left her with the children and ran off to places unknown, and where he was and what activities he was engaged in, since he told her nothing, she herself did not know; but –

viii. In Lent 1773 the said husband came secretly to their farmhouse window one evening, and she let him in; but that same hour she informed the Cossacks; and they arrested him and took him to the hetman of the settlement, and he, she says, sent him to the Upper Chirsk settlement to an elder, but she does not recall his name, and from there to Cherkassk, but they did not get him that far: at the Tsimlyanskaya settlement he escaped, and so where he is now she does not know.

ix. At the time of her husband's arrest he kept telling the hetman and all the Cossacks at the assembly that he had been in Mozdok, but what he had been doing, for the same reason she does not know.

x. He never sent her any letters, neither when he was on army service nor when he was on the run; and whether he wrote to their settlement or to anyone else she does not know; the fact is that he is completely illiterate.

xi. That her husband is indeed the Yemelyan Pugachov in question, quite apart from her own personal knowledge and that of her children, can be confirmed as true both by his birth brother Dementy, son of Ivan, Pugachov, a Cossack also of Zimoveyskaya (who is currently serving in the First Army), and by his birth sisters, of whom the first is Ulyana Ivanova, who is now married to a Cossack Fyodor Grigoryev, surnamed Brykalin, of the same settlement, and the second is Fedosya Ivanova, who is also married to a Cossack Simon Nikitin, whose surname she does not know, from Prusaki, who now has a dwelling in Azov: all these also know her husband quite well.

xii. Her husband's language and manner of speaking were the usual for a Cossack; he knew no foreign languages.

xiii. The house where they lived in Zimoveyskaya settlement was their own property. After her husband had gone on the run (because there was nothing for her or her children to live on from day to day) she sold it for twenty-four roubles and fifty kopecks to a Cossack, Yerema Yevseyev of the Yesaulovskaya settlement, for dismantling, and after dismantling it he transported it to Yesaulovskaya. It has now by special order been transported back to Zimoveyskaya and, on the very spot where it used to stand and where they lived, it has been incinerated; and their farmhouse, which stands not far from Zimoveyskaya, has also been incinerated.

xiv. Pugachov's wife herself is a Cossack's daughter; her father Dmitry was a Cossack of Yesaulovskaya eligible for army service; his surname was Nedyuzhin, but she does not know his patronymic because she lost him as a child. He was survived by children who are still alive – namely, her birth sisters: first, Anna Dmitriyeva, married to a Cossack of the Yesaulovskaya settlement, Foma Andreyev, surname Pilyugin, who has been serving for over seven years, in which army she does not know; second, Vasilisa Dmitriyeva, also married to a Cossack of the Yesaulovskaya settlement, Grigory Fyodorov, surnamed Makhichev; and the third child, son of her father and birth brother to herself, Ivan Dmitriyev, surname Nedyuzhin, a Cossack eligible for army service, who also lives in the Yesaulovskaya settlement and who has since her departure for this place been at his home and in readiness for call-up to the army.

I append a no less interesting excerpt from a deposition made by the retired Cossack Trofim Fomin, who had been hetman of Zimoveyskaya in 1771:

> In 1771, in the month of February, Yemelyan Pugachov left for the town of Cherkassk, with an official permit obtained from me, to get treatment for an illness, and after a month he returned on a bay horse. When I asked him where he had got it, he answered in front of our Cossack assembly that he had bought it in the Taganrog fortress from a Cossack of the cavalry regiment called Vasily Kusachkin. But the Cossacks did not believe him and sent him to get documentary evidence from the company commander. Pugachov rode off accordingly; but before his return his brother-in-law Prusak, who had been a Cossack at the Zimoveyskaya settlement but is now in the Taganrog Cossack regiment, came before us and stated at the settlement assembly that he and his

wife and Vasily Kusachkin and a third man had been persuaded by Pugachov to escape beyond the Kuban to the Kuma River, where he (Prusak) stayed for a short time, then he left them and returned to the Don. On account of their unauthorized absence I therefore dispatched Prusak (together with his wife and mother-in-law) to Cherkassk with an official report from us. In December of the same year Pugachov was apprehended in his farmhouse and held under guard. It was my intention to hand him over, as a vagrant, to elder Mikhaylo Makarov, who happened at that time to be engaged in the pursuit and transportation of runaways from all walks of life. But Pugachov slipped his guards and escaped from the settlement office. He was then caught three months later at the same farmhouse and stated before the settlement assembly that he had been in Mozdok. I therefore sent him with a report to Elder Mákarov at the Lower Cherkassk settlement, and he sent him with a report to Cherkassk by way of our settlement. When they brought him through, I saw from his transportation papers that he had been dispatched in leg irons, which he was no longer wearing, so I gave orders to clamp another set on him and sent him off to the Upper Kurmoyarskaya settlement, from which I received a written receipt for his delivery. A couple of weeks later a notice was sent by elder Makarov to all the Cossack settlements announcing that this Pugachov had escaped along the way and that as soon as he appears anywhere, he is to be caught; but how he escaped I do not know.

Signed by Vasily Yermolayev,
by reason of the illiteracy of the informant.

15 Mr Lyovshin writes that the pretender used to show these scars to his credulous companions and pass them off as some kind of tokens of tsarship. That is not altogether right: the pretender used to display them boastfully as the marks of wounds that he had received.

16 Many did avail themselves of this permission; but even so the history of the Pugachov uprising is little known. We find the most detailed information about it in the *Notes on the Life and Career of A.I. Bibikov*, but the author has taken his narrative only as far as

Bibikov's death. The booklet published under the title *Michelsohn in Kazan* is nothing other than an extremely interesting letter from Archimandrite Platon Lyubarsky, printed almost without alteration, but with the addition of some unimportant depositions. Mr Lyovshin in his *Historical and Statistical Survey of the Ural Cossacks* has touched but lightly on Pugachov. This bloody and fascinating episode of Catherine's reign remains too little known.

NOTES TO CHAPTER V

1 The Christianized Kalmyks living in Orenburg Province were split between the Orenburg Kalmyks and the Stavropol Kalmyks. See Rychkov (in his *Topography of Orenburg*) for detailed information.

2 Derzhavin in the commentary to his works states that he had the good fortune to rescue about 1,500 captive settlers from the Kyrgyz. Derzhavin wrote his memoirs, which are sadly as yet unpublished.

3 The rebellious Bashkirs had been cruelly suppressed by Lieutenant General Prince Urusov, who was, like Sulla,* nicknamed "the Lucky", because everything used to go well for him.

4 [Pushkin refers the reader to the text of Bibikov's letter to Fonvizin in his Volume Two, not included in this edition.] Fonvizin's relatives and heirs made this letter, together with other valuable papers, available to Prince Vyazemsky, who has been engaged on a biography of the author of *The Young Hopeful*. This work, remarkable in every respect, we hope before long to publish.

5 An under-age lad: i.e. one who has not yet reached the age of fourteen.

6 Iletskaya Zashchita ("the Ilek defence post") is situated in the steppe beyond the River Ural, sixty-six kilometres from Orenburg, in the very place that produces the famous Ilek salt. Rychkov writes:

> The extraction of this salt has been carried out in this locality for a long time, first by the Bashkirs, but subsequently also by serfs living there. The instruction to build this fort was given only last year, on 26th October 1753, in accordance with a decree of the Senate promulgated the same year, on 24th May 1753. By this decree government salt stores were to be established in Orenburg and in

the new forts and villages administered by it; Ilek and Ebeley salt was to be sold at the then stipulated price of thirty-five kopecks a pood*; for this reason a Salt Board, too, was established at the same time in Orenburg city. A contractor then came forward, Alexei Uglitsky, a lieutenant of the Orenburg Cossacks, who undertook to procure at his own expense, and supply to the Orenburg store for four years, fifteen thousand poods of this salt, and if necessary even more, at a price of six kopecks a pood. What is more, in the summer of the following year 1754, again at his own expense, he would construct, to the specification of the Engineering Corps, a small defence post in the form of a rampart with emplacements for cannon and, inside, several living quarters and a barracks for the garrison and a store for provisions; and he would furnish firewood for all the living quarters during autumn and winter seasons; and, whatever the size of the contingent stationed there, he would transport provisions there from Orenburg in his own vehicles. All this has come to pass; one company of the Alexeyev infantry regiment in full strength has been detailed for garrison duty at the fort; and sometimes, when necessary, further military personnel are despatched there. For these soldiers, as well as for those who work on the extraction of salt (of whom there are normally two hundred or more), there is a church together with a priest and church servitors. (*Topography of Orenburg*)

7 Fort Totskaya, at the mouth of the River Soroka, is 218 kilometres from Orenburg. It was built under Kirillov in 1736. Sorochinsk is the main fort on the Samara Line of Defence; it is 187 kilometres from Orenburg and 32 from Totskaya.

8 Fort Novosergiyevskaya is 42 kilometres from Sorochinsk and 144 from Orenburg. It was built in the time of Privy Counsellor Tatishchev under the name "Tevkelev Ford" and was renamed Novosergiyevskaya under Neplyuyev.

9 Perevolotskaya is 83 kilometres from Orenburg by the main road, but only 64 directly across the steppe. It was built at the headwaters of the River Samara.

10 From the *Histoire de la révolte de Pougatschef*:

Les rebelles restèrent si tranquilles à Tatitscheva, que le Prince lui-même doutait qu'ils fussent dans cette place. Pour en apprendre des nouvelles, il envoya trois cosaques qui s'approchèrent de la forteresse, sans rien apercevoir. Les rebelles leur envoyèrent une femme, qui leur présenta du pain et du sel, selon l'usage des Russes, et qui, interrogée par les cosaques, les assura que les rebelles, après avoir été dans la place, en étaient tous sortis. Lorsque Pougatschef crut avoir trompé les cosaques par cette ruse, il fit sortir de la forteresse quelques centaines d'hommes pour s'emparer d'eux. L'un des trois fut tué et le second pris; mais le troisième s'échappa et vint render compte à Galitzin de ce qu'il venait de voir. Aussitôt le Prince résolut de marcher sur la place dans le jour même et d'attaquer l'ennemi dans ses retranchements.

[The rebels stayed so quiet at Tatishcheva that the Prince himself doubted that they were there. To obtain information he sent three Cossacks, who approached the fort without noticing anything. The rebels sent a woman out to them, who presented them with bread and salt according to the Russian custom and who, when questioned by the Cossacks, assured them that the rebels, though they had been in the fort, had subsequently all left. When Pugachov believed that the Cossacks had fallen for this trick, he sent several hundred men out of the fortress to seize them. One of the three was killed and the second captured; but the third escaped and came to give Golitsyn an account of what he had just witnessed. The Prince immediately resolved to march on the fort that very day and attack the enemy in his stronghold (French).]

11 Bibikov wrote in a letter of 26th March:

We have lost: 9 officers and 150 soldiers killed; 12 officers and 150 soldiers wounded. That's what kind of a party it was! But my poor Koshelev has been badly wounded in the leg. I fear for his life, though Golitsyn actually writes that it's not dangerous.

12 Rychkov writes that Shigayev gave orders for Pugachov and Khlopusha to be tied up. The statement is implausible. We shall see that Pugachov

and Shigayev acted in concert shortly after their flight from near Orenburg.

13 Contrary to widespread belief, Pugachov never struck coinage bearing the image of Tsar Peter III and the superscription "*Redivivus et ultor*" ["He who comes back to life and avenges" (Latin) (Ed.)] (as foreign writers assert). The illiterate and semi-literate rebels were not up to devising clever Latin superscriptions and were content with the money already in circulation.

14 From a letter of Reinsdorp's to Prince Golitsyn of 24th March 1774:

> *La victoire que Votre Altesse vient de remporter sur les rebelles rend la vie aux habitants d'Orenbourg. Cette ville bloquée depuis six mois et réduite à une famine affreuse retentit d'allégresse, et les habitants font des vœux pour la prospérité de leur illustre libérateur. Un poud de farine coûtait déjà 16 roubles, et maintenant l'abondance succède à la misère. J'ai tiré un transport de 500 четвертъ de Kargalé et j'attends un autre de 1000 d'Orsk. Si le détachement de Votre Altesse réussit de captiver Pougatschef, nous serons au comble de nos souhaits, et les Baschkirs ne manqueront pas de chercher grâce.*

> [The victory that Your Highness has just won over the rebels brings life back to the people of Orenburg. This city, blockaded for six months and reduced to an appalling famine, is now resounding with joy, and the inhabitants are offering prayers for the well-being of their distinguished deliverer. One pood of flour was already costing sixteen roubles, and now plenty has taken the place of destitution. I have obtained a cargo of 500 *chetverts** from Kargala, and I am awaiting another 1,000 from Orsk. If Your Highness's division succeeds in capturing Pugachov, we shall have all that we could wish for, and the Bashkirs will not fail to beg for mercy (French).]

15 The settlement of Seitov (also called Kargala), frequently mentioned in this *History*, is situated twenty-one kilometres from Berda and nineteen from Orenburg. It was named after Seit-Khayalin, a Tatar from Kazan, who was the first to apply to the chancellery at Orenburg for

an allotment of lands for settlement. The number of souls in the Seitov settlement was reckoned at about 1,200; they enjoyed special rights.

16 After his defeat, Chika, together with Ulyanov, stopped to spend the night at the Bogoyavlensk copper-smelting works. The manager entertained them and plied them with drink till they were intoxicated; he then tied them up during the night and presented them at Tabynsk. Michelsohn awarded five hundred roubles to the manager's wife, who had suggested getting the runaways drunk.

17 The woman was called Razina.

18 The interesting particulars that follow I have taken from a most remarkable article ('Defence of the Yaitsk Fortress against a Detachment of Rebels'), printed in P.P. Svinyin's *Memoirs of the Fatherland*. For some of the narrative I have followed Simonov's daily record, presuming a greater reliability in an official document than in the recollections of an old man. But in general the little-known eyewitness's article bears the precious stamp of an unadorned and unaffected authenticity.

19 These words were preserved by Derzhavin in his ode on the death of Bibikov. The final stanza should have been engraved on his tomb:

> A leader of great skill in war was he,
> man of good counsel, lover of the arts,
> a steadfast bulwark for the fatherland,
> a guardian of the faith, a friend of truth,
> esteemed by Catherine for his loyal service,
> for his fine mind, for his nobility,
> and for the genuineness of his heart.
> He died defending the imperial throne.
> Stay traveller, stay and venerate this spot –
> here the remains of Bibikov lie buried.

20 The Empress instructed that the deceased's widow be asked what she desired personally for herself. Bibikov's wife asked that one of her husband's relatives who had served under his command should have his future secured.

21 Derzhavin continued to the end of his life to honour the memory of his first patron. When he learnt that A.I. Bibikov's son was intending

to publish a memoir of his father's life and career, he wrote to him the following lines:

> *Alexandr Ilyich Bibikov's life was short, but filled with glorious deeds. He dedicated it to the service of his fatherland. He has in all justice earned the respect and recognition of his compatriots, who will not cease to remember with veneration the achievements, so beneficial to society, of this illustrious man and to bless his memory.*
>
> *As everyone reads about the career of this exemplary public servant and of the changes of fortune that he encountered, they will readily discern his exceptional qualities – bravery, foresight, enterprise, alertness – that led to his being employed with distinction and trustworthiness in all the various duties that were laid upon him. Throughout he displayed his skill and zeal, not only earlier, in the reign of the Empress Elizabeth, but also in the many assignments he received from Catherine the Great – skill and zeal that were marked by successes. He was a good general; far-sighted, upright and honourable in his private affairs; a shrewd politician, gifted with a mind that was enlightened, wide-ranging, flexible, but always noble. His kindly heart was ready to give help and assistance to his friends, even to the detriment of his own interests. His strength of character, reinforced as it was with faith and piety, won him the trust of all, in upholding which he never faltered. He loved literature, and wrote very well himself in his own language; he knew German and French, and not long before his death he learnt English. He was a good judge of people; he was accessible and affable to everyone, but nonetheless he was wise enough, by his grave but pleasant bearing, to keep his subordinates in due subservience. In him gravity did not diminish good humour, nor did straightforwardness impair gravity. Every official, of low rank or high, held him in love and awe. Having accomplished his final task of defending the throne and saving the fatherland, he crowned with his demise a life of integrity that was now cut short to the grief of the whole empire.*

NOTES TO CHAPTER VI

1 See Rychkov's *History of Orenburg*.
2 *Histoire de la Révolte de Pougatschev*.
3 The Troitsko-Satkinsky ironworks, one of the most important in Orenburg Province, lies on the Satka River, 269 kilometres from Ufa.
4 Fort Zelair is situated at the very centre of Bashkiria, 243 kilometres from Orenburg. It was built in 1755 after the last Bashkir uprising (the last before Pugachov's).
5 Derzhavin, in the commentary to his works, states that Prince Shcherbatov, Prince Golitsyn and Brandt quarrelled, refused to link up with each other, let themselves be neutered in dealing with the scoundrel's new forces and squandered the victories that had begun to be won.

NOTES TO CHAPTER VII

1 In the indictment it was stated that Pugachov broke into the city through the treachery of people in the Drapers' Quarter. The investigation showed that the inhabitants of the quarter were not traitors; on the contrary, they were the last to abandon their weaponry and give way to overwhelming force.
2 Subsequently Veniamin was slandered by one of the rebels (Aristov) and found himself for some time in disgrace. The Empress, having satisfied herself of his innocence, rewarded him with the rank of metropolitan and sent him a white hood with the following letter:

> *Most Reverend Metropolitan, Veniamin of Kazan!*
>
> *After my arrival it was my first concern to review the proceedings in respect of the rogue Aristov; and I realized, to my extreme pleasure, that Your Reverence's innocence has been completely vindicated. Cover your venerable head with this personal mark of honour, and may it be for everyone a perpetual reminder of your triumphant goodness. Forget the distress and sorrow that have been tormenting you. Ascribe this message to God's dispensation, whereby he deigns to exalt you after the unhappy and troublous circumstances that have afflicted your region. Bring prayers to the Lord God.*

With the greatest benevolence, I am,
Catherine

The reply of Veniamin, Metropolitan of Kazan:

Most All-Gracious Sovereign Lady!

The unexampled mercy and judgement of Your Imperial Majesty have been bestowed on me to the wonder of the whole world; they have raised me from the tomb and have restored to me the life which from childhood, so far as in me lies, I have dedicated to God's service in unshakeable loyalty to your royal throne and to the good of the fatherland – this life that has lasted now for fifty-three years, but which slander, insolence and malice, unconscionable and inhuman, have attempted to destroy. This priceless token of your royal generosity, which with inexpressible heartfelt emotion I have been deemed worthy to take upon my head, has covered and removed my disgrace, my disgrace in the eyes of humanity. What then am I to render to you in return, Sovereign Lady unequalled in justice in the world, so solicitous as you are of my renewed well-being? The pouring out in gratitude of this life bestowed upon me by your sublimely regal magnanimity will not suffice, unless I unceasingly beseech the Most High day and night, until my dying breath, that, in return for so compassionate a preservation of my own life, He preserve your own most precious life to the longest span of years possible for a human being; and that He send down from His sacred and sublime abode onto your crowned head every blessing with which in times of old He blessed King Solomon. For all the days of your life may the strong right hand of the Lord's power safeguard your most prized good health from disease, your unsleeping labours from weariness, and your burgeoning and blossoming glory from envy and malice; and may your house, your empire and your throne be as the days of Heaven.

With such devotion and all-submissive loyalty, as long as I have breath, I remain,

Your Imperial Majesty's all-submissive slave and intercessor,
the lowly Veniamin, Metropolitan of Kazan.

3 An extract from the unpublished *Historical Dictionary* compiled by D.N. Bantysh-Kamensky:

> Major-General Nefed Nikitich Kudryavtsev, son of the Nikita Alferyevich who enjoyed the confidence of Peter the Great, took part in the first Persian War in the rank of lieutenant of the guards in the Preobrazhensky Regiment. In the reign of the Empress Anna he fought against the Turks and Tatars; and under the Empress Elizabeth against the Prussians. He took retirement under the Empress Catherine II. His body is buried in the church where he was killed.

4 This is related by the author of the historical memoir *Histoire de la révolte de Pougatschev*. I have found nothing about it in the official documents that have passed through my hands. It is indisputable, however, that Pugachov's family were with him until 24th August 1774.

5 Ivan Ivanovich Mikhelson [i.e. Johann von Michelsohn (Ed.)], cavalry general and commander-in-chief of the army in Moldavia, was born around 1735 and died in 1809 [actually 1807 (Ed.)]. Prince Varshavsky served under his command at the outset of his distinguished career. Even in advanced old age Michelsohn preserved a youthful alacrity, he loved the dangers of battle and still used to visit forward operations within range of enemy fire.

NOTES TO CHAPTER VIII

1 There were three Pulaski brothers. The eldest won notoriety for his daring attempt on the person of King Stanislaw Poniatowski; the youngest had been a prisoner from 1772 and lived in the house of the governor, by whom he was treated as a member of the family.

2 This I heard from K.F. Fuchs, doctor and professor of medicine at Kazan University, a man as learned as he is generous and approachable. I am obliged to him for many interesting pieces of information relating to the period and region here described.

3 Before this the price of salt, fixed by Pugachov, had been five kopecks a pood, and the poll tax three kopecks a head. He promised to triple army pay and to carry out recruitment levies only every five years.

4 For the sharing of documents that expose Perfilyev's dealings with the government – a circumstance previously quite unknown – we are gratefully indebted to A.P. Galakhov, grandson of the Captain of the Guards to whom important duties were entrusted by the government at the time.

5 Count Pyotr Ivanovich Panin, general-in-chief, chevalier of the orders of St Andrew and St George first degree, et cetera, son of Lieutenant General Ivan Vasilyevich, was born in 1721. He began his army service under the command of Field Marshal Count Münnich; in 1736 he was present at the capture of Perekop and Bakhchisaray. During the Seven Years War he served as Major-General and was primarily responsible for the success of the Battle of Frankfurt. In 1762 he was made a senator. In 1769 he was appointed commander-in-chief of the Second Army. In 1770 he captured Bendery, and in the same year retired from the service. The Pugachov insurrection summoned Panin back from retirement to the field of political endeavour. He died in Moscow in 1789, in his sixty-ninth year.

6 [Pushkin refers the reader to the text of Derzhavin's letter in his Volume Two, not included in this edition.]

7 Statements by the Cossacks Fomin and Lepelin. They show no knowledge of the name of the guards officer who was sent to Petrovsk with them, but Boshnyak names Derzhavin in his report.

8 At the time a list (still far from complete) was published of the victims of Pugachov and his associates. We include it here:

A register, compiled up to the present time from the reports of various towns, of the number of churches desecrated and plundered by the pretender and rebel Yemelka Pugachov and his villainous associates, and of the number of nobles, clergy, citizens and people of other classes killed, identifying names and places.

[Pushkin's note then continues with the full register, which lists some sixty-three churches that were desecrated, plundered or burnt in the provinces covering the Yaik valley and the middle and lower Volga region; and some 1,342 men, women and children that were killed in the towns and districts of the same area.]

9 See Benjamin Bergmann's *Nomadische Streiferein u.s.w.*

10 Mavrin had been with Bibikov from 1773. He had been sent from the Secret Commission to Yaitsk, where he was conducting enquiries. Mavrin was a man of conspicuous moderation and good sense.

11 On 22nd October 1774 the Empress wrote to Voltaire:

> *Volontiers, monsieur, je satisferai votre curiosité sur le compte de Pougatschef: ce me sera d'autant plus aisé, qu'il y a un mois qu'il est pris, ou pour parler plus exactement qu'il a été lié et garrotté par ses propres gens dans la plaine inhabitée entre le Volga et le Jaïck, où il avait été chassé par les troupes envoyées contre eux de toutes parts. Privés de nourriture et de moyens pour se ravitailler, ses compagnons excédés d'ailleurs des cruautés qu'ils commettaient et espérant obtenir leur pardon, le livrèrent au commandant de la forteresse du Jaïck qui l'envoya à Simbirsk au général comte Panine. Il est présentement en chemin pour être conduit à Moscou. Amené devant le comte Panine, il avoua naïvement dans son interrogatoire qu'il était cosaque du Don, nomma l'endroit de sa naissance, dit qu'il était marié à la fille d'un cosaque du Don, qu'il avait trois enfants, que dans ces troubles il avait épousé une autre femme, que ses frères et ses neveux servaient dans la première armée, que lui-même avait servi, les deux premières campagnes, contre la Porte, etc., etc.*
>
> *Comme le général Panine a beaucoup de cosaques du Don avec lui, et que les troupes de cette nation n'ont jamais mordu à l'hameçon de ce brigand, tout ceci fut bientôt vérifié par les compatriotes de Pougatschef. Il ne sait ni lire, ni écrire, mais c'est un homme extrêmement hardi et déterminé. Jusqu'ici il n'y a pas la moindre trace qu'il ait été l'instrument de quelque puissance, ni qu'il ait suivi l'inspiration de qui que ce soit. Il est à supposer que M. Pougatschef est maître brigand, et non valet d'âme qui vive.*
>
> *Je crois qu'après Tamerlan il n'y en a guère un qui ait plus détruit l'espèce humaine. D'abord il faisait pendre, sans rémission ni autre forme de procès, toutes les races nobles, hommes, femmes et enfants, tous les officiers, tous les soldats qu'il pouvait attraper; nul endroit où il a passé n'a été épargné, il pillait et saccageait ceux même, qui pour éviter ses cruautés cherchaient à se le rendre*

favorable par une bonne réception: personne n'était devant lui à l'abri du pillage, de la violence et du meurtre.

Mais ce qui montre bien jusqu'où l'homme se flatte, c'est qu'il ose concevoir quelque espérance. Il s'imagine qu'à cause de son courage je pourrai lui faire grâce et qu'il ferait oublier ses crimes passés par ses services futures. S'il n'avait offensé que moi, son raisonnement pourrait être juste et je lui pardonnerais. Mais cette cause est celle de l'empire qui a ses lois.

[I shall gladly satisfy your curiosity, sir, on the subject of Pugachov: this will be all the easier because he was captured one month ago – or, to put it more precisely, he was tied up and taken into custody by his own people in the uninhabited steppe between the Volga and the Yaik, where he had been pursued by the troops that had been sent against them from all sides. Deprived of food and of the means of reprovisioning themselves, his companions, who were also by now surfeited with the cruelties they were perpetrating and hoping to win their pardon, delivered him to the Yaitsk fortress commandant, who sent him to General Count Panin in Simbirsk. He is currently in the process of being conveyed to Moscow. When he was brought before Count Panin, he admitted ingenuously at his interrogation that he was a Don Cossack, he gave the name of his place of birth, and he said that he was married to the daughter of a Don Cossack, that he had three children, that during the troubles he had married another woman, that he had brothers and nephews serving in the First Army, that he himself had served in the first two campaigns against the Turk, etc., etc.

As General Panin has plenty of Don Cossacks with him, and as the troops of that nation have never nibbled at the brigand's bait, all these particulars were soon verified by Pugachov's compatriots. He is unable to read or write, but he is an extremely audacious and determined man. So far there is not the least evidence that he has been the tool of any foreign power, or that he has been acting under the influence of anyone else at all. The assumption must be that monsieur Pugachov is a master brigand, and no one's lackey.

I do not believe that there has been anyone since Tamerlane that has wrought more destruction on the human race. First of all, he ordered the hanging, without mercy or any other kind of procedural restraint, of all those of noble birth – men, women and children – all officers and all soldiers that he could lay hands on: nowhere that he has visited has been spared: he looted and despoiled even those who, to escape his atrocities, tried to win his favour by welcoming him: no one he encountered was safe from looting, violence and murder.

An excellent demonstration, however, of the extent of the man's self-delusion is the fact that he dares to harbour some hope. He imagines that his courage will enable me to forget his past crimes through the prospect of his future services. If I were the only one that he had offended, then his reasoning might be correct and I would pardon him. But his case concerns the whole empire, and the empire has its laws (French).]

12 From a letter from the Empress to Voltaire of 29th December 1774:

Le marquis de Pougatschef, dont vous me parlez encore dans votre lettre du 16 décembre, a vécu en scélérat et va finir en lâche. Il a paru si timide et si faible en sa prison qu'on a été obligé de le préparer à sa sentence avec précaution, crainte qu'il ne mourût de peur sur le champ.

[The great lord Pugachov, of whom you continue to talk in your letter of 16th December, has lived as a criminal and will end as a coward. He has appeared so faint-hearted and feeble in prison that we have been obliged to prepare him for his sentence with care, for fear he might die of fright straight away (French).]

13 From the unpublished memoirs of I.Ya. Dmitriyev:

Soon after our arrival in Moscow I witnessed an ugly spectacle that was extraordinary for everyone and, for me in particular, new – an execution. Pugachov's fate had been determined. He had been condemned to be quartered. The place of execution was on the so-called Marsh.

Throughout the city, in streets and houses, there was talk of nothing else but the awaited spectacle. I and my brother desperately wanted to be among the spectators; but for a long time my mother would not agree to it. In the end, at the urging of one of our relatives, she entrusted us to him on the strict injunction that we move not one step away from him.

That event has so etched itself on my memory that I hope even now to describe it with all possible fidelity, at least as it presented itself to me at the time.

On the tenth day of January in the year one thousand seven hundred and eighty-five, at eight or nine in the morning, we drove onto the Marsh. In the centre had been erected a scaffold, or place of execution, around which regiments of infantry were drawn up. The senior officials and army officers wore their insignia and sashes over fur coats because of the intense frost. The chief of police Arkharov was there too, surrounded by his functionaries and aides. On a high spot, or platform, at the place of execution I saw with a shudder for the first time those who would carry out the sentence. Behind the lines of soldiers the whole expanse of the Marsh, or – to put it better – of the low-lying flat ground, and all the roofs of the houses and shops on the high ground on either side of it, were thick with people of both sexes and various classes. Curious onlookers were even jumping up onto the boxes and footboards of coaches and carriages. Suddenly there was a general commotion and a roar and cry of "Here they come! They're bringing him!" Soon a detachment of cuirassiers appeared, and behind it a sledge of unusual height; on the sledge sat Pugachov, opposite him his confessor and another official of some kind, probably the secretary of the Secret Commission; and behind the sledge followed another detachment of cavalry.

Pugachov, bareheaded, kept bowing on both sides as he rode along. I did not observe any fierceness in his facial features. By appearance he was about forty, of medium build, swarthy but pasty in the face, with eyes that flashed. He had a rather bulbous nose, hair that was black, I seem to remember, and a small, pointed beard.

The sledge halted before the steps leading up to the place of execution. Pugachov and his favourite, Perfilyev, accompanied by a priest and two officials, had hardly mounted the scaffold when the command "Present arms!" was heard, and one of the officials began reading the sentence. I could hear almost every word.

When the official read the chief villain's name and full identification, including the name of the Cossack settlement where he had been born, the chief of police asked him in a loud voice, "Are you the Don Cossack Yemelka Pugachov?"

"Yes, sir, I am Yemelka Pugachov, Don Cossack from the settlement of Zimoveyskaya," he answered in an equally loud voice.

Then, all through the reading of the sentence, he fixed his gaze on the cathedral and frequently crossed himself, while Perfilyev, a man of considerable height, with bent back, pockmarked face and fierce countenance, stood motionless, looking at the ground. When the reading of the sentence was over, the priest addressed a few words to them, blessed them, and left the scaffold. The official who had read the sentence followed suit. Pugachov, crossing himself, bowed to the ground facing the cathedrals; then with a hurried air he turned to the crowd to say farewell, and bowed to all sides, uttering in a breaking voice: "Farewell, Orthodox people: forgive me if I have done harm in your sight; farewell, true believers!"

At this moment the official in charge gave a signal, and the executioners rushed forward to undress Pugachov: they pulled off his white sheepskin coat and started ripping apart the sleeves of his crimson silk jacket. Then he threw up his hands and fell backwards, and a minute later a head dripping with blood was raised high. The executioner was waving it by the hair. The same happened with Perfilyev.

The details of this execution are strikingly reminiscent of the execution of another Don Cossack, who led a violent uprising a hundred years before Pugachov in almost the same localities and with almost the same horrific successes. See *Relations des particularités de la rebellion de Stenko-Razine contre le Grand Duc de Moscovie. La naissance, le progrès et la fin de cette rebellion; avec la manière dont fut pris ce rebelle, sa sentence de mort et son exécution, traduit de l'anglais par C. Desmares MDCLXXXII.* [*Account of the details of the rebellion of Stenka Razin against the Grand Duke of Muscovy. The origin, course and ending of this rebellion; with the manner in which the rebel was captured, his death sentence and his execution – translated from the English by C. Desmares, MDCLXXXII* (French).] This book is exceedingly rare; I have seen a single copy of it in the library of A.S. Norov; it now belongs to Prince N.I. Trubetskoy.

Notes to
A History of Pugachov

p. 163, *The future historian… correct and augment my work*: Pushkin received permission to open the sealed "Pugachov file" only in the summer of 1835, after the publication of his monograph. Access to this material and new information from other sources prompted him to plan a second edition of *A History of Pugachov*, but the first edition had not sold well and he did not live to carry out his plan.

p. 165, *Archimandrite Platon Lyubarsky*: Archimandrite Platon Lyubarsky (1738–1811) was rector of the Kazan seminary and superior of the Monastery of the Saviour in Kazan at the time of the Pugachov Rebellion. His manuscript, entitled 'A Brief Account of the Villainous Acts of the Outlaw Pugachov Against Kazan' (1774), was one of Pushkin's source documents that he included in the second volume of the *History*.

p. 167, *Khvalynian Sea*: The Caspian Sea.

p. 168, *streltsy*: See note to page 78.

p. 169, *Stenka Razin*: Stenka (or Stepan) Razin (1630–71) was a notorious seventeenth-century Don Cossack raider and peasant leader, who led a serious rebellion against the Russian government in the Volga region from 1670 to 1671. Earlier, from 1667 to 1668, Razin had invaded the Yaik valley and briefly occupied Yaitsk.

p. 169, *Khiva*: An ancient trading city of Central Asia, in what is now Uzbekistan.

p. 171, *Kizlyar*: A town in Daghestan, to the west of the Caspian Sea, then on the southern frontier of the Russian Empire.

p. 174, *Malykovka (today's Volgsk)*: While in Pushkin's time the settlement of Malykovka had been renamed Volgsk, later in the nineteenth century it came to be known as Volsk, and has remained so since.

p. 175, *Under the reign of the Empress Anna… Don Cossacks*: Pushkin later acknowledged that this sentence was inaccurate, and that the

Don Cossack Nekrasov, having rebelled unsuccessfully against Peter the Great in 1708, left the Don with his followers to settle on the Kuban shortly afterwards; the *nekrasovtsy*, however, only left the Kuban for Turkish territory on the Danube in 1775, in the reign of Catherine II.

p. 175, *like the remaining Zaporozhian Cossacks... legitimate monarch*: The Zaporozhian Cossacks ("the Cossacks from beyond the rapids") were Cossacks who had settled on the lower Dnieper River. Their semi-independent status was abolished by Catherine II in 1775, partly to punish them for harbouring Pugachov supporters who had taken refuge there after his defeat. Some of the Zaporozhians also then emigrated to Turkish territory and settled in the Danube delta, where they remained for many years, preserving their Cossack identity. In 1828, during one of the Russo-Turkish wars, these Zaporozhians renewed their allegiance to the Tsar and were given new lands in southern Russia.

p. 176, *Imposture... Pugachov*: In an unpublished note for Nicholas I Pushkin wrote: "Pugachov was already the fifth pretender to have assumed the name of the Emperor Peter III. Not only among the ordinary people but among the upper classes too the view persisted that the sovereign was alive and remained in confinement. The Crown Prince Paul himself for a long time believed, or wanted to believe, this rumour. After his accession to the throne the Sovereign's first question to Count Gudovich was: 'Is my father alive?'"

p. 176, *remained in hiding for about a year*: In an unpublished note for Nicholas I Pushkin wrote: "Pugachov used to say that the Empress herself had helped him to hide."

p. 177, *Crown Prince*: Pugachov is referring to the Grand Prince Paul, son of Peter III and Catherine II, born in 1754 and therefore about twenty at this time. Paul and his mother were constantly on bad terms, but he eventually succeeded Catherine and reigned from 1796 to 1801.

p. 178, *seditious manifesto from the pretender*: In an unpublished note for Nicholas I Pushkin wrote: "Pugachov's first seditious appeal to the Yaik Cossacks is a remarkable example of native eloquence, despite being ungrammatical. It was all the more effective because the announcements (or "publications") put out by Reinsdorp were written as feebly as they were correctly, in the form of lengthy circumlocutions with verbs at the end of long sentences."

p. 178, *their cross and their beards... Old Believers*: Two of the differences that marked off the Old Believers from Orthodox Russian Christians were in the manner of holding the fingers when making the sign of the cross and in the wearing of untrimmed beards (compulsory for Old Believers).

p. 180, *On the night before... cannon*: In an unpublished note for Nicholas I Pushkin wrote: "On the eve of the capture of the fort poor Kharlov was drunk; but I decided not to mention this out of respect for his bravery and noble death."

p. 182, *Polish Confederates held in Orenburg*: The so-called Bar Confederation was an alliance of conservative Polish patriots who had fought between 1768 and 1772 to defend Poland against Russian influence and territorial expansion. Defeated by Russia in 1772, many of the Confederates were captured and exiled to remote parts of Russia.

p. 185, *the Mordva, the Chuvash and the Cheremis*: The Mordva (Mordvins), Chuvash, and Cheremis (Mari) are non-Slavonic peoples inhabiting parts of the Volga and Ural regions of Russia.

p. 185, *Bakhmut*: Modern Artemivsk, a city in Ukraine on the Bahmutka River, a tributary of the Donets.

p. 186, *Major-General Nashchokin*: In an unpublished note for Nicholas I Pushkin wrote: "This Nashchokin was the same one who gave Suvorov a box on the ears (after that Suvorov, whenever he saw him, always used to hide and say: "I'm frightened, I'm frightened: he's a brawler!"). Nashchokin was one of the oddest people of that epoch. His son wrote his memoirs, and I have never in my life read anything funnier. The Emperor Paul was fond of him and on his accession to the throne kept trying to enlist him in the service. Nashchokin would reply to the Emperor: 'You are hot-tempered, and I am hot-tempered. To serve you won't do me any good.' The Emperor awarded him estates in Kostroma Province, to which he retired. He was a godson of the Empress Elizabeth and died in 1809."

p. 193, *Stavropol*: I.e. Stavropol-on-the-Volga, not the now better known city in southern Russia north of the Caucasus. Stavropol-on-the-Volga was inundated in the 1950s by the construction of the

Kuybyshev Dam and Reservoir. It was rebuilt on higher ground and renamed Togliatti, after the Italian Communist leader.

p. 193, *the Samara Line*: The Samara Line, a string of forts and redoubts, stretched southeastward from Samara on the Volga up the Samara River to link up with the Orenburg Line at Fort Tatishcheva.

p. 196, *Chernyshov*: In an unpublished note for Nicholas I Pushkin wrote: "Chernyshov (the same one that the Empress Catherine II mentions in her memoirs) had once held a junior post at court. He was banished from St Petersburg at the order of the Empress Elizabeth. When the Empress Catherine came to the throne, she showered him and his brother with her favours. The elder brother died in St Petersburg while commandant of the fortress."

p. 197, *When Kar... Alexander's reign*: In an unpublished note for Nicholas I Pushkin wrote: "Kar had before this been employed on matters that required firmness and even cruelty (which is no indicator of bravery, as Kar demonstrated). Defeated by a couple of jailbirds, he ran away on the pretext of feverishness, aching bones, a fistula and an inflammation. On reaching Moscow he wanted to present his excuses to Prince Volkonsky, who did not receive him. He drove to the Assembly of Nobility, but his appearance called forth such a commotion and such catcalls that he was obliged hurriedly to withdraw. Nowadays public opinion, if it exists at all, is much more apathetic than it used to be in days of old. This man, who sacrificed honour to personal safety, nonetheless met a violent death: he was killed by his serfs, who had been driven beyond endurance by his cruelty."

p. 197, *The Empress saw... vanquished*: In an unpublished note for Nicholas I Pushkin wrote: "The Empress respected Bibikov and was convinced of his devotion, but she did not like him. At the beginning of her reign he was sent to Kholmogory, where the family of the unfortunate Ivan VI were being held for secret negotiations. Bibikov returned having fallen madly in love with the Princess Catherine (which certainly did not endear him to the Empress). Bibikov was suspected of favouring the party that would like to have elevated the Crown Prince to the throne. The Empress was constantly haunted by this nightmare, and it poisoned relations between mother and son: the latter was infuriated and embittered by the petty vexations and mean insults inflicted daily by her powerful favourites. More than once Bibikov acted as a mediator between the Empress and the Crown Prince. Here is one of a thousand examples: the Crown Prince, chatting once about military logistics, summoned Colonel Bibikov (Alexandr Ilyich's brother) and asked how much time it would take his regiment (in an emergency) to march quickly to Gatchina. The next day Alexandr Ilyich learnt that the Crown Prince's question had been reported and that his brother was being relieved of his regiment. Alexandr Ilyich, after questioning his brother, rushed to the Empress and explained to her that the Crown Prince's remarks were simply part of a logistical discussion and not a plot. The Empress calmed down, but said: 'Tell your brother that in an emergency his regiment is to march to St Petersburg, not to Gatchina.'"

p. 205, *Derzhavin*: Gavrila Romanovich Derzhavin (1743–1816), a native of Kazan, was later regarded as the greatest Russian poet of the 18th century.

p. 207, *European powers... Russia now found herself*: In an unpublished note for Nicholas I Pushkin wrote: "Gustav III, when stating all his complaints in 1790, claimed credit for the fact that, disregarding all suggestions put to him, he had refrained from taking advantage of the unrest occasioned by Pugachov. The Empress exclaimed: 'There's something to brag about – that the king's not allied himself with an escaped jailbird who hangs women and children!'"

p. 207, *C'est apparemment... aujourd'hui*: "It must be the Baron de Tott who has staged this farce. But we are no longer living in the age of Dimitry, and the sort of drama that succeeded two hundred years ago is hissed off the stage today" (French). An extract from Voltaire's letter to Catherine II of 2nd February 1774. Baron de Tott (Ferenc Tóth, 1733–93) was a French aristocrat and military engineer of Hungarian descent who served for some years in the late 1760s and early 1770s in the Crimea and in Turkey assisting the Turks in their wars with Russia. Dimitry was an earlier pretender to the Russian throne, who led an uprising against Tsar Boris Godunov in 1604–05 and briefly usurped the Russian throne.

p. 207, *Monsieur... cordon de soie*: "Monsieur, it is only the newspapers that make a lot of noise about that brigand Pugachov – who has nothing to do, directly or indirectly, with Monsieur de Tott. I attach as much importance to the cannons cast by the one as I do to the machinations of the other. Pugachov and de Tott do, however, have this in common, that the first is each day spinning his rope of hemp, while the second is every moment risking a cord of silk" (French). From Catherine's letter to Voltaire of 4th March 1774. Baron de Tott (see previous note) was a controversial figure in Constantinople and might well have expected strangulation by silk cord (which was the way the Sultan disposed of high-ranking officials who had displeased him). Tott, as it turned out, was not strangled, but he was forced to leave Turkey in 1776.

p. 209, *the late Emperor's accession to the throne*: The reference is to Alexander I.

p. 209, *Even today... enquirers' questions*: In an unpublished note for Nicholas I Pushkin wrote: "The Ural Cossacks (especially the old folk) are to this day loyal to Pugachov's memory. 'I'm sorry to tell you,' an eighty-year-old Cossack woman told me, 'we've no complaint against him; he didn't do us any harm.' 'Explain to me,' I said to D. Pyanov, 'how Pugachov was a father-figure to you.' 'For you he's Pugachov,' the old man answered angrily, 'but to me he was the great sovereign Peter III.' Whenever I mentioned Pugachov's bestial cruelty, the old people used to defend him, saying: 'It wasn't his intention; our drunkards made him confused.'"

p. 211, *Colonel Bibikov*: This is Yury Bogdanovich Bibikov (1743–1812), no relation to the general.

p. 212, *hang both ringleaders*: In an unpublished note for Nicholas I Pushkin wrote: "I.I. Dmitriyev asserted that Derzhavin hanged these two peasants more out of poetic curiosity than from actual necessity."

p. 212, *The executions of 1740... memory*: In an unpublished note for Nicholas I Pushkin wrote: "The executions carried out in Bashkiria by General Prince Urusov are implausible. About 130 men were put to death, having been subjected to all imaginable tortures. 'Of the rest, about a thousand,' writes Rychkov, 'were pardoned after having their noses and ears cut off.' Many of these so pardoned must still have been alive at the time of the Pugachov rebellion."

p. 213, *the famous Krylov*: The reference is to the poet and fabulist Ivan Andreyevich Krylov (1769–1844).

p. 217, *Golitsyn... indescribable enthusiasm*: In an unpublished note for Nicholas I Pushkin wrote: "Prince Golitsyn, who delivered the first blow to Pugachov, was a young man, and a handsome one. The Empress noticed him at a ball in Moscow (in 1785) and said: 'How good-looking he is, a real doll!' This remark was fatal to him. Shepelev (who later married one of Prince Potyomkin's nieces) challenged Golitsyn to a duel, and ran him through – by foul play, so it is said. Rumour blamed Potyomkin..."

p. 219, *church serfs*: These are peasants who had belonged to the Church and monasteries until 1764, after which they were put under the authority of the College of the Management of Ecclesiastic Affairs.

p. 220, *An old Cossack woman... pushed the corpse away*: As Pushkin points out in his note (17) the woman's name was Razina, recalling that of the notorious Don Cossack Stenka Razin (see note to page 169). Nicholas I, seeing in these two sentences a possible reference to Stenka Razin, had Pushkin delete them from the text of the first edition on the grounds that they were irrelevant to Pugachov.

p. 234, *Major-General Potyomkin*: This is Pavel Sergeyevich Potyomkin (1743–96), cousin of Catherine II's favourite, the much more famous Grigory Alexandrovich Potyomkin.

p. 241, *The traitor Mineyev... death*: In an unpublished note for Nicholas I Pushkin wrote: "The distinction that the government made between those who were nobles in a personal capacity and the hereditary nobility was remarkable. Sub-Lieutenant Mineyev and several other officers were made to run the gauntlet, beaten with rods, etc. Shvanvich, on the other hand, was only disgraced by the breaking of a sword over his head. Catherine was already preparing to exempt the noblility from corporal punishment. Shvanvich was the son of a commandant of Kronstadt, who once cut open Alexei Orlov-Chesmensky's cheek with a sabre in a tavern brawl."

p. 241, *a venerable warrior... Russian army*: Michelsohn was to command the Dnieper Army against Turkey in 1806; he died in Bucharest during the ensuing campaign.

p. 241, *Lieutenant Colonel Count Mellin*: Mellin was in fact a major, as Pushkin correctly describes him in the antepenultimate paragraph of Chapter 6.

p. 241, *Pugachov or his less famous accomplices*: In an unpublished note for Nicholas I Pushkin wrote: "Who were those clever accomplices that masterminded the pretender's activities? Perfilyev? Shigayev?... This must be clear from the Pugachov file, but, regrettably, I have not read that, not having dared unseal it without permission from the highest quarters."

p. 242, *young Pulaski*: In an unpublished note for Nicholas I Pushkin wrote: "Young Pulaski was having an affair with the wife of the elderly governor of Kazan."

p. 246, *the clergy*: In an unpublished note for Nicholas I Pushkin wrote: "In Saransk Archimandrite Alexander greeted Pugachov with cross and gospel, and during a thanksgiving service made mention of Empress Ustiniya in the intercessions. The Archimandrite was brought before the civil court in Kazan. At midday on 13th October 1774 he was led into the cathedral in chains. He was taken to the altar and dressed in full vestments. Soldiers with fixed bayonets were standing at the north doors. The Dean and Archdeacon stood him in the middle of the church, in all his vestments and chains. After mass he was led out onto the square; his offences were read out to him. After that his robes were taken off him, his hair and beard were shorn, he was given a peasant's overcoat to wear and sent to prison for life. The people were appalled and felt sorry for the offender. Under the sentencing order Alexander was to have been brought out in monks' garb, but Potyomkin (Pavel Sergeyevich) had departed from that, 'for greater effect'."

p. 249, *Tsaritsyn*: This Tsaritsyn, not to be confused with the village near Kazan mentioned in Chapter Seven, was an important fortress and trading centre on the west bank of the lower Volga. It later developed into a major industrial city, renamed Stalingrad in 1925 and Volgograd since 1961.

p. 252, *Suvorov's fame*: In an unpublished note for Nicholas I Pushkin wrote: "The real reason why Rumyantsev did not want to release Suvorov was jealousy. He had been jealous of Bibikov, as generally of all those whose rivalry seemed a threat to him."

p. 255, *jailbird... flying about*: In the original the pun involves *vor* ("thief" or "impostor"), *voron* ("raven") and *voronyonok* ("raven fledgling").

p. 256, *Padurov*: In an unpublished note for Nicholas I Pushkin wrote:

"Padurov, as a delegate to the Legislative Commission and by virtue of the privileges granted him under the Sovereign's edict, could in no circumstances be subjected to the death penalty. I do not know whether he appealed for protection under that law; possibly he was unaware of it; possibly his judges gave it no thought. Nonetheless, the execution of this villain was illegal."

p. 256, *on the Marsh*: The Marsh (*Boloto*, in Russian) was the name of a low-lying open space on the island in the Moscow River directly opposite the Kremlin, used in the 18th century and earlier for markets, public gatherings and executions.

p. 259, The following passage omits Lyovshin's footnotes on references and other points of detail.

p. 284, *Commission for the drafting of a New Legal Code*: Proposed by Catherine II towards the end of 1766 for the purpose of considering reforms and inaugurated the following year.

p. 295, *like Sulla*: Lucius Cornelius Sulla (*c.*138–78 BC) was a successful Roman general under the Roman Republic who was awarded the title *Felix* ("the Lucky"); he later seized power and had himself appointed dictator.

p. 296, *pood*: A pood is an old Russian measure of weight equivalent to 16.36 kilograms.

p. 298, *chetverts*: A chetvert was an old Russian measure equivalent to about eight bushels or three hundred litres.

Note on the Texts

Professor Debreczeny translated the works in this volume from the Russian texts as given in the Soviet Academy's ten-volume collected works of Pushkin (B.V. Tomashevsky, ed., *Polnoye sobraniye sochineniy*, Moscow: *Akademiya Nauk SSSR*, 1962–66) collated with the large, seventeen-volume edition (V.D. Bonch-Bruyevich et al., eds., *Polnoye sobraniye sochineniy*, Moscow: *Akademiya Nauk SSSR*, 1937–59).

The text of Pushkin's notes to *A History of Pugachov* (not included in Professor Debreczeny's original edition) has been taken from the two-volume *Polnoye sobraniye sochineniy* of Pushkin's works, published in Moscow in 1999 by the *Klassika izdatelsky tsentr*. The contents of Volume Two of *A History of Pugachov* have been taken directly from Pushkin's own edition published in St Petersburg in 1834.

Appendix I

Omitted Chapter from *The Captain's Daughter*

Editor's note

In a draft dated spring 1836 Pushkin included the following passage after the words "Zurin received orders to cross the Volga" in the middle of Chapter 13 (page 128). Pushkin dropped almost all this section from the final draft, but preserved it in manuscript under the title "Omitted Chapter". Pushkin's reasons for the excision are not known for certain. The omitted chapter does not contain material any more likely to offend the censorship than the published version of the novel. Maybe Pushkin felt that the section slowed the pace of the novel unnecessarily, or that it contained a little too much melodramatic improbability. More likely, he realized that the older Grinyov's appalled reaction to news of his son's arrest, conviction and sentence in Chapter 14 was inconsistent with his having had the opportunity of an earlier visit to give them a first-hand account of his doings.

Between the spring draft and the final version Pushkin changed the names of some of the characters: Grinyov himself was originally "Bulanin", and Zurin was "Grinyov". In this edition, to avoid confusion, I have, where appropriate, replaced the names in the early draft with those in the final version, enclosing them in square brackets.

WE WERE APPROACHING the banks of the Volga. Our regiment entered the village of —— and took up quarters there for the night. The village elder told me that on the other side of the river all the villages had risen in rebellion, and Pugachov's bands were roaming everywhere. This news made me very anxious. We were supposed to cross the river the next morning. Impatience seized me. My father's estate lay thirty versts away, on the other side of the river. I enquired if it would be possible to find a boatman who would take me across. All the peasants were fishermen: there were plenty of boats about. I went to [Zurin] to inform him of my intention.

"Take care," he said to me. "It is dangerous to go by yourself. Wait until morning. Our detachment will be the first to cross, and we'll bring fifty hussars to lodge with your parents, just in case."

I insisted on going immediately. The boat was ready; I got into it with two oarsmen. They pushed the boat off and started rowing vigorously.

The sky was clear. The moon shone. The weather was calm. The Volga flowed smoothly and serenely. The boat, gently rocking, glided over the dark waters at a good pace. I gave myself over to the fancies of my mind. About half an hour passed. We had already reached the middle of the river... Suddenly the oarsmen began to whisper to one another.

"What's the matter?" I asked, waking from my reveries.

"We can't tell, God knows," answered the oarsmen, glancing to one side.

I turned my eyes in the same direction and saw in the dark something floating down the Volga. The indiscernible object was coming closer to us. I ordered the boatmen to stop and wait for it. The moon went behind a cloud. The floating apparition became even more indistinct. It was already quite close to me, yet I still could not make it out.

"What could it be?" the oarsmen were saying. "Might be a sail, but it isn't. Might be masts, but it isn't."

Suddenly the moon emerged from behind the cloud and lit up a horrifying spectacle. What was floating towards us was a gallows mounted on a raft, with three bodies hanging from the crossbeam. A morbid curiosity seized me. I wanted to look into the hanged men's faces.

On my orders the oarsmen snagged the raft with the boathook, and my boat knocked against the floating gallows. I jumped out and found myself between the dreadful posts. The bright moon illuminated the victims' disfigured faces. One of them was an old Chuvash; another a Russian peasant, a robust, sturdy fellow of about twenty. But it was the third one that shocked me to the core and made me cry out with pity when I looked up at it: it was Vanka, my poor Vanka, who in his foolishness had joined Pugachov. [Vanka is not a character that appears in the final version of the novel (Ed.).] A black board was nailed to the crossbeam above the corpses, on which was written in large white letters: "Brigands and rebels." The oarsmen looked on impassively and waited for me, holding the raft fast with the boathook. I got back into the boat. The raft floated on downstream. For a long time the gallows showed black in the darkness. At last it disappeared, and the boat came aground against the high, steep river bank...

I rewarded the oarsmen generously. One of them took me to the head man of the village near the ferry. We entered the hut together. When the chief heard that I wanted horses, he at first received me quite rudely; but my guide whispered a few words to him, and the chief's surliness at once turned into bustling solicitude. A team of three horses was ready in one minute; I sat down in the cart and gave orders to be driven to our estate.

I galloped along the main highway, past sleeping villages. The one thing I feared was to be stopped on the road. If my nocturnal encounter on the Volga indicated the presence of rebels, it also served as a proof of strong countermeasures by the government. For all eventualities I had in my pocket both the pass Pugachov had given me and the order Colonel [Zurin] had issued. But I did not run into anybody, and towards morning beheld the river and fir wood behind which our estate was situated. The driver lashed the horses, and in a quarter of an hour I rode into our village.

The manor house stood at the other end of the village. The horses were racing along at full speed. Suddenly, in the middle of the street, the driver started to pull them up.

"What's the matter?" I asked impatiently.

"A checkpoint, sir," the driver answered, stopping his frenzied horses with difficulty.

Indeed I beheld a barricade and a sentry with a wooden cudgel. The peasant came up to me and, doffing his hat, asked for my identity papers.

"What is the meaning of this?" I asked him. "Why is there a barricade here? And who are you holding under guard?"

"We're in revolt, so please Your Honour," he answered, scratching himself.

"And where are your master and mistress?" I asked with a sinking heart.

"Our master and mistress?" repeated the peasant. "Our master and mistress are in the grain store."

"What do you mean, in the grain store?"

"Well, you see, Andryukha, the parish clerk, has put them in fetters and wants to take them to the Tsar Our Father."

"My God! Open the barricade up quickly, you idiot; why don't you get a move on?"

The sentry refused to hurry. I jumped out of the cart, cuffed him (I confess) on the ear, and moved the barricade aside myself. My peasant gazed at me in stupid bewilderment. I got back into the cart and ordered the driver to the manor house at a gallop. The grain store was situated in the courtyard. At its locked door there stood two peasants, also with cudgels. My cart stopped right in front of them. I jumped out and rushed up to them.

"Open the doors," I told them.

I must have looked frightening: at any rate, they both dropped their cudgels and ran away. I tried to knock off the lock and break down the doors, but the doors were made of oak and the huge lock held firm. At this moment a self-important-looking young peasant came out of a servants' hut and asked me haughtily how I dared disturb the peace.

"Where's the parish clerk, Andryushka?" I shouted at him. "Call him to me at once."

"Andrei Afanasyevich, that's who I am, not Andryushka," he answered proudly, with his hands on his hips. "What do you want?"

Instead of replying, I grabbed him by the collar and, dragging him to the store doors, ordered him to open them. The clerk tried to be obstinate, but a fatherly chastisement had its effect on him too. He pulled out the key and opened the grain store. I dashed across the threshold and caught sight of my father and mother in a dark corner, feebly lit through a narrow slit in the ceiling. Their hands were tied and their feet were in fetters. I rushed to embrace them, unable to utter a word. They both looked at me with astonishment: three years of military life had changed me so much that they could not recognize me. Mother gasped and burst into tears.

Suddenly a sweet, familiar voice caught my ear.

"Pyotr Andreich! It's you!"

I stood dumbfounded... When I looked around, I saw in another corner Marya Ivanovna, also tied up.

My father was looking at me in silence, not daring to believe his own eyes. His face beamed with joy. I hurried to cut through the knots of their ropes with my sword.

"Hello, hello, Petrusha," Father said, pressing me to his heart. "Thank God we've lived to see you."

"Petrusha, my dearest," said Mother, "so the Lord has brought you! Are you all right?"

I was in a hurry to get them out of their imprisonment – but when I went to the door, I found it locked again.

"Andryushka," I shouted, "open up!"

"Not likely," answered the clerk from behind the door. "You just stay in there yourself. We'll teach you to disturb the peace and pull state officials about by the collar!"

I went around inspecting the grain store, looking for some way to break out.

"Don't trouble with it," said my father. "I'm not the kind of landowner to leave holes in his store room for thieves to go in and out."

My dear mother, who had been momentarily cheered by my arrival, now fell into despair, seeing that I was to perish with the rest of the family. But I felt calmer now that I had joined them. I still had a sabre and two pistols with me and was quite capable of holding out against a siege. [Zurin] was bound to arrive by the evening and set us free. I communicated all this to my parents and managed to calm Mother down. They gave themselves up to the joy of reunion.

"Well, Pyotr," Father said to me, "You've been up to enough tricks, and I've been thoroughly angry with you. But there is no need to dwell on the past. By now, I hope, you've finished with your devilry and reformed. I know you've served as an honest officer should. I thank you for that. You have been a comfort to your old father. If I owe my rescue to you, life will be doubly sweeter to me."

My eyes full of tears, I kissed his hand and glanced at Marya Ivanovna, who was so glad of my presence that she seemed entirely calm and cheerful.

Around noon we heard an extraordinary noise and shouting.

"What does this mean?" said Father. "Could it be that your colonel has made it here?"

"Impossible," I answered. "He won't be here before evening."

The noise intensified. The alarm was sounded. Horsemen were galloping across the yard. At that moment my poor attendant Savelich thrust his grey head through a chink in the wall and announced in a pitiful tone:

"Andrei Petrovich, Avdotya Vasilyevna, young master Pyotr Andreich, young mistress Marya Ivanovna, bad news! The villains have entered the village. And who do you think has brought them here, Pyotr Andreich? Alexei Ivanych Shvabrin, the devil take him!"

Hearing that odious name, Marya Ivanovna clasped her hands and froze to the spot.

"Listen," I said to Savelich, "send someone on horseback to the ferry at —— to meet the hussar regiment, and get them to tell the colonel of the danger we're in."

"But who can I send, sir? All the boys are in revolt, and all the horses are taken. Aah! They're already in the yard. They're heading for the store."

Several voices could now be heard beyond the door. I signalled silently to Mother and Marya Ivanovna to retire into a corner and, baring my sabre, hugged the wall by the door. Father took the two pistols, cocked them and placed himself beside me. The lock rattled, the door opened, and the clerk's head appeared. I struck it with my sabre, and he fell down, blocking the entrance. At the same time Father fired through the doorway. The mob laying siege to us pulled back with curses. I dragged the wounded man across the threshold and fastened the door on the inside with a knotted cord . The yard was full of armed people. Among them I recognized Shvabrin.

"Don't be afraid," I said to the women. "There is hope. And you, Father, don't shoot any more. Let's save the last of our ammunition."

Mother prayed silently to God; Marya Ivanovna stood by her and awaited our fate with angelic calm. From behind the doors threats, abuse and curses could be heard. I stood in my place, ready to cut down the first intruder. Suddenly the villains grew silent. I could hear Shvabrin's voice, calling me by name.

"I am here; what do you want?"

"Surrender, [Grinyov], there is no point in resisting. Take pity on your old ones. You can't save yourself by obstinacy. I'll get you, all of you!"

"Try it, traitor!"

"I'm not going to force my way in to no purpose, nor sacrifice my men. I'll give orders to set the grain store on fire, and then we'll see what you can do, you Don Quixote of Belogorsk. Right now it's time for dinner. In the meantime, sit there and take time to think. Goodbye, Marya Ivanovna. I won't apologize to you; I'm sure you're having a fine time in the dark with your cavalier."

Shvabrin moved away, leaving the store under guard. We were silent. We each kept our thoughts to ourselves, not daring to communicate them to the others. I imagined all the things that an enraged Shvabrin was capable of doing. About myself I hardly worried at all. Shall I confess it? Even the fate of my parents did not terrify me as much as the thought of what would become of Marya Ivanovna. I knew that all the peasants and house servants adored my mother; and my father, despite his strictness, was also well liked because he was fair and knew what the people under his authority truly needed. Their rebellion was an aberration, a temporary bout of drunkenness, and not an expression of resentment. For both of my parents mercy was likely. But what about Marya Ivanovna? What fate was this corrupt and unscrupulous man preparing for her? I dared not dwell on this horrible question; God forgive me, I was ready to kill her sooner than see her once more in the hands of her cruel enemy.

Another hour or so went by. Drunken singing could be heard in the village. Our guards, jealous of their comrades and annoyed with us, shouted abuse and tried to intimidate us with talk of torture and death. We awaited the sequel to Shvabrin's threats. At length a great commotion arose in the yard, and we heard Shvabrin's voice once more.

"Well, have you made up your minds? Will you give yourselves up to me voluntarily?"

Nobody answered him. Having waited a little, Shvabrin gave orders to bring some straw. In a few minutes a fire flared up, illuminating the dark grain store; smoke began to seep through the crevices under the threshold. At that moment Marya Ivanovna came up to me and, taking my hand, said quietly, "Enough, Pyotr Andreich! Don't destroy yourself as well as your parents for my sake. Let me out. Shvabrin will listen to me."

"Not for anything!" I cried with fury. "Do you realize what would happen to you?"

"I'll not outlive dishonour," she answered calmly. "But perhaps I shall be able to save my deliverer and the family that has given such generous support to a poor orphan. Farewell, Andrei Petrovich. Farewell, Avdotya Vasilyevna. You have been more than benefactors to me. Give me your blessing. And fare you well too, Pyotr Andreich. You can be assured that... that..." With these words she burst into tears and covered her face with her hands. I thought I would lose my mind. My mother wept.

"Enough of that talk, Marya Ivanovna," said my father. "As if any of us would let you go out to the brigands by yourself! Sit here with us and be quiet. If we're to die, we'll die together. Listen, what's that they're saying now?"

"Will you surrender?" Shvabrin was shouting. "Don't you realize? Within five minutes you'll be roasted alive."

"We'll not surrender, villain!" Father replied in a firm tone.

His face, covered with wrinkles, was animated with amazing vigour, and his eyes flashed menacingly from under his white brows. Turning to me, he said, "Now, now!"

He opened the doors. The flames burst in and whirled upwards over rafters stuffed with dry moss. Father fired his pistol and stepped across the flaming threshold shouting, "Everyone follow me!"

I seized Mother and Marya Ivanovna by the hand and quickly led them out into the open air. By the threshold lay Shvabrin, shot through by my father's frail hand; the crowd of brigands, which had fled at our unexpected sally, quickly gathered courage and began to encircle us. I managed to land a few more blows, but a well-aimed brick caught me straight in the chest. I fell down and lost consciousness for a moment. When I came to, I saw Shvabrin sitting on the bloodied grass, with my whole family in front of him. I was hauled up by the arms. A crowd of peasants, Cossacks and Bashkirs surrounded us. Shvabrin was terribly pale. He was pressing one hand to his wounded side. Pain and malice were written on his face. He slowly raised his head, looked at me, and uttered in a weak, indistinct voice, "Hang him... hang them all... except her..."

The crowd of villains immediately closed in on us and, shouting, dragged us towards the gate. But suddenly they let go of us and ran off: [Zurin], with a whole squadron of hussars behind him, rode in through the gate, sabres bared.

* * * * * * *

The rebels took off in all directions; the hussars pursued them, cutting them down and taking prisoners. [Zurin] leapt off his horse, bowed to the parents and shook me warmly by the hand.

"I've just come in time," he said to us. "Ah, and here is your fiancée!"

Marya Ivanovna blushed to her ears. Father went up to him and thanked him, looking calm but also moved. Mother embraced him, calling him "angel of deliverance".

"Please do us the honour," Father said to him, and led him into our house.

As he passed Shvabrin, [Zurin] stopped.

"Who is this?" he asked, looking at the wounded man.

"This is the chief, the leader of the gang himself," replied my father, now without a note of pride, betraying the old soldier in him. "God gave my frail old hand strength to punish the young villain and avenge my son's wound.

"It's Shvabrin," I told [Zurin].

"Shvabrin! Delighted! Hussars, take him! And tell our surgeon to bandage his wound and look after him like the apple of his eye. It is absolutely essential to bring him before the Secret Commission in Kazan. He is one of the chief offenders, and his testimony is bound to be important."

Shvabrin opened his weary eyes. All that was expressed in his face was physical suffering. Some hussars carried him off in a cloak.

We entered the house. I looked around with emotion, remembering my childhood years. Nothing had changed in the house; everything was in its former place. Shvabrin had not allowed it to be plundered, preserving, for all his degradation, an instinctive aversion to dishonest greed. The servants gathered in the entrance hall. They had not participated in the uprising and were sincerely glad at our deliverance. Savelich was triumphant. It must be mentioned that during the turmoil caused by the brigands' attack he had run to the stables where Shvabrin's horse was standing, saddled it, quietly led it out and, thanks to the commotion, galloped off unnoticed to the ferry. He met the regiment as it rested after crossing to this side of the Volga. [Zurin], hearing from him of the danger we were in, gave orders to mount and advance – advance at a gallop – and, thank God, arrived in time.

The hussars returned from pursuing the rebels and brought back several captives. They were locked up in the same grain store in which we had withstood the memorable siege.

[Zurin] insisted on displaying the clerk's head on a pole by the tavern for several hours.

We each retired to our rooms. The old folk needed a rest. I had not slept all night, and I threw myself on the bed and fell into a deep sleep. [Zurin] went off to make his dispositions.

In the evening we gathered in the drawing room by the samovar, merrily chatting about the danger that had passed us by. Marya Ivanovna poured out the tea; I sat down beside her and gave her all my attention. My parents seemed to be looking favourably on the intimacy of our relationship. That evening has remained fresh in my memory to this day. I was happy, completely happy; and how many such moments are granted in a man's paltry life?

The next day my father was informed that the peasants had gathered in the courtyard to make apology. Father went out onto the porch to see them. When he appeared, the peasants fell to their knees.

"Well, fools," he said to them, "what put it into your heads to rebel?"

"We're at fault, master," they started answering together.

"You *are* at fault, yes! Folk go on a spree, but it brings them no glee. I'll forgive you this time, out of joy that the Lord's let me see my son Pyotr Andreich once more."

"We're at fault! At fault, that's for sure!"

"Well, all right: if the head repents the sword relents. God's given fine weather: it's time to bring the hay in; but you, blockheads, what have you been doing for three whole days? Elder! Organize them for the hay mowing, everyone of them! And see to it, you red-haired rascal, that all my hay's in stacks by Saint Ilya's day. [2nd August in the Russian Orthodox calendar (Ed.).] Off with you."

The peasants bowed and went off to do service for their master as though nothing had happened.

Shvabrin's wound turned out not to be fatal. He was dispatched to Kazan under guard. From a window I saw them laying him in a cart. Our eyes met: he lowered his head and I hastily left the window. I was loath to appear to be exulting in my enemy's misfortune and humiliation.

[Zurin] had to continue his advance. I decided to go with him despite my desire to spend a few more days in the midst of my family. On the eve of my departure I went to my parents and, as was the custom in those days, bowed down to the ground before them, asking them to give their blessing to my marriage to Marya Ivanovna. They raised me up and gave their consent with joyous tears in their eyes. I brought Marya Ivanovna, pale and trembling, before them. They blessed us... What I felt I will not attempt to describe. Those who have been in my position will understand me, and those who have not I can only pity; I would advise them to fall in love and obtain parental blessing while there is still time.

The next day the regiment was ready to leave. [Zurin] said farewell to my family. We were all convinced that the military operations would soon come to an end; I hoped I would become a husband in another month. As Marya Ivanovna said goodbye to me, she kissed me in front of everybody. I mounted my horse. Savelich once more followed behind me, and the regiment set off.

For a long time I kept looking back at the country house that I was leaving once again. A gloomy premonition tormented me. A voice was whispering to me that not all my misfortunes were yet past. My heart felt the approach of a new storm.

I will not go into the details of our campaign and of the end of the war. We passed through villages ravaged by the rebels and had no alternative but to requisition from the poor villagers whatever the brigands had left them.

People did not know whose authority they should recognize. Law and order had broken down everywhere. Landowners were hiding in the forests. Bands of brigands were committing atrocities on every side. The commanding officers of various government detachments sent in pursuit of Pugachov (who was then already fleeing towards Astrakhan) arbitrarily dealt out punishment on guilty and innocent alike... Conditions were terrible in the whole region engulfed in the conflagration. May the Lord save us from another such senseless and merciless Russian rebellion! Those who conspire to bring about radical changes in Russia that cannot succeed are either young and ignorant of our people, or heartless men who set no value on others' heads or their own necks.

Pugachov fled, pursued by Johann von Michelsohn. Soon afterwards we learnt of his total defeat. Finally [Zurin] received from his general news of the pretender's capture, and at the same time orders to proceed no farther. I could at last return home. I was in raptures; yet a strange emotion overshadowed my joy.

Appendix II

Extra Material by Pushkin Relating to *A History of Pugachov*

Pushkin's Unpublished Notes to *A History of Pugachov*

[In December 1834, in the same month that A History of Pugachov *was published, Pushkin wrote some further notes that were not for publication but were sent privately, the following month, to Count Benckendorff for Tsar Nicholas I's information. Where these notes refer to specific passages of* A History *I have incorporated them among the editors' endnotes. Pushkin ended however, with a few brief general observations, a translation of which I give below (Series Editor).]*

GENERAL COMMENTS

All the lower classes were for Pugachov. The clergy wished him well, not only priests and monks, but also archimandrites and bishops. Only the nobility was clearly on the side of the government. Pugachov and his accomplices wanted at first to bring the nobility too round to their side, but their interests were too much in conflict. (NB The class of clerks and officials was still small in number and its allegiance was decidedly with the common people. The same thing can be said of those officers who had risen from the ranks. There were many of these in Pugachov's bands. Shvanvich was the only one from the true nobility.)

All the foreigners serving in the middle ranks did their duty honourably: Michelsohn, Muffel, Mellin, Dietz, Demorin, Duve, etc. But all those who were brigadiers and generals performed feebly and timidly, without commitment: Reinsdorp, Brandt, Kar, Freymann, Korff, Wallenstern, Bülow, Dekalong, etc. When one analyses the measures taken by Pugachov and his accomplices, it has to be admitted that the rebels chose the surest and most effective means for the achievement of their aim. The government, for its part, acted feebly, sluggishly and blunderingly.

There is no evil without good. The Pugachov rebellion demonstrated to the government the necessity for many changes, and in 1775 provincial administration was put onto a new basis. The power of the state was centralized; the provinces, too large before, were divided up; communication between all parts of government was made speedier, etc.

Pushkin's Volume Two

[The second volume of Pushkin's A History of Pugachov, *published in 1834, consisted of extensive extracts from his source material. Because of the amount of this material, because Pushkin himself relegated it to a second volume, and because none of it is Pushkin's own writing, it is not included in this edition. However, so that the reader may have an idea of its scope, we set out below Pushkin's contents list for this second volume.]*

CONTENTS OF THE SECOND VOLUME

I. PROCLAMATIONS, ORDERS AND RESCRIPTS RELATING TO THE PUGACHOV REBELLION

8. Sovereign's order, issued on 29th July 1774 to the War College, about the appointment of Count Panin as commander of the armies stationed in the Provinces of Oryol, Kazan and Nizhny Novgorod;
9. Instruction, issued over Her Majesty's autograph signature on 8th August 1774, to Captain Galakhov of the Preobrazhensky Guards Regiment;
10. Proclamation of 19th December 1774 about the offences of the Cossack Pugachov;
11. Senatorial order of February 1775 about the sending of reports to the Senate from city chanceries concerning those people implicated in Pugachov's rebellion, through the normal post and not by special couriers;
12. Sovereign's rescript, issued to Count Panin from the settlement of Tsaritsyn on 9th August 1775.

II. RESPONSE OF COUNT RUMYANTSEV TO THE WAR COLLEGE; AND LETTERS FROM NUR-ALI KHAN, BIBIKOV, COUNT PANIN AND DERZHAVIN

1. Response of Count Rumyantsev about Lieutenant General Suvorov, sent to the War College on 15th April 1774;
2. Translation of a letter in Tatar from the Kyrgyz-Kazakh Khan Nur-Ali, sent to Orenburg with his man Yakishbay, and received on 24th September 1773;
3. Letters from A.P. Bibikov;
4. Letters from Count P.I. Panin;
5. Letters from Lieutenant Derzhavin of the Life Guards to Colonel Boshnyak.

III. NARRATIVES BY CONTEMPORARIES

1. *The Siege of Orenburg* (Rychkov's chronicle), followed by:

   First supplement to the description of the six-month siege of Orenburg by the pretender and public malefactor and rebel Pugachov, from the time of that villain's defeat at Fort

Tatishcheva up to the date when the said villain was completely crushed at the Kargala settlement and at Sakmarsk township, leading to the liberation of the city of Orenburg from the aforementioned siege;

Second supplement, containing a brief account of the villainies of the pretender and rebel Pugachov, perpetrated by him and his accomplices in various places after their defeat at Sakmarsk township up to his, Pugachov's, capture, that is up to 18th September 1774;

Third supplement, containing a brief account of what happened on the transference of this villain Pugachov to Simbirsk and on his onward transference from there to Moscow, and of the nature of the execution administered to this enemy of the fatherland.

2. Extract from the record kept by the Commander of Her Imperial Majesty's Forces, Major-General and Cavalier Prince Pyotr Mikhaylovich Golitsyn, concerning the units sent on detachment to various places to seek out and destroy the malefactors, and the whereabouts and manner of their operations and successes;
3. Brief account of the villainous acts of the outlaw, traitor and rebel, Yemelka Pugachov, against Kazan, compiled by Platon Lyubarsky, Archimandrite of the Monastery of the Saviour in Kazan, 24th August 1774.

Appendix III

Extra Material

Reigns of Tsars of the Romanov Dynasty up to the Time of Pushkin

Mikhail	1613–45
Alexei	1645–76
Fyodor III	1676–82
Ivan V and Peter I (joint rulers)	1682–96
Peter I, the Great (sole ruler)	1696–1725
Catherine I	1725–27
Peter II	1727–30
Anna	1730–40
Ivan VI	1740–41*
Elizabeth	1741–61
Peter III	1761–62
Catherine II, the Great	1762–96
Paul	1796–1801
Alexander I	1801–25
Nicholas I	1825–55

* (*deposed; died in prison* 1764)

Alexander Pushkin's Life

Family, Birth and Childhood

Alexander Sergeyevich Pushkin was born in Moscow in 1799. He came of an ancient, but largely undistinguished, aristocratic line. Some members of his father's family took a part in the events of the reign of Boris Godunov (r. 1598–1605) and appear in Pushkin's historical drama about that Tsar. Perhaps his most famous ancestor – and the one of whom Pushkin was most proud – was his mother's grandfather, Abram Petrovich Gannibal (or Annibal) (*c.*1693–1781), who was an African, most probably from Ethiopia or Cameroon. According to family tradition he was abducted from home at the age of seven by slave traders and taken to Istanbul. There in 1704 he was purchased by order of the Russian foreign minister and sent to Moscow, where the minister made a gift of him to Tsar Peter the Great. Peter took a liking to the boy and in 1707 stood godfather to him at his christening (hence his patronymic Petrovich, "son of Peter"). Later he adopted the surname "Gannibal", a Russian transliteration of Hannibal, the famous African general of Roman times. Peter sent him abroad as a young man to study fortification and military mining. After seven years in France he was recalled to Russia, where he followed a career as a military engineer. Peter's daughter, the Empress Elizabeth, made him a general, and he eventually died in retirement well into his eighties on one of the estates granted him by the crown.

Pushkin had an older sister, Olga, and a younger brother, Lev. His parents did not show him much affection as a child, and he was left to the care of his grandmother and servants, including a nurse of whom he became very fond. As was usual in those days, his early schooling was received at home, mostly from French tutors and in the French language.

School

In 1811 at the age of twelve Pushkin was sent by his parents to St Petersburg to be educated at the new Lyceum (Lycée, or high school) that the Emperor Alexander I had just established in a wing of his summer palace at Tsarskoye Selo to prepare the sons of noblemen for careers in the government service. Pushkin spent six happy years there, studying (his curriculum included Russian, French, Latin, German, state economy and finance, scripture, logic, moral philosophy, law, history, geography, statistics and mathematics), socializing with teachers and fellow students, and relaxing in the palace park. To the end of his life he remained deeply attached to his memories and friends from those years. In 1817 he graduated with the rank of collegial secretary, the tenth rank in the civil service, and was attached to the Ministry of Foreign Affairs, with duties that he was allowed to interpret as minimal. While still at the Lyceum Pushkin had already started writing poetry, some of which had attracted the admiration of leading Russian literary figures of the time.

St Petersburg 1817–20

Pushkin spent the next three years in St Petersburg living a life of pleasure and dissipation. He loved the company of friends, drinking parties, cards, the theatre and particularly women. He took an interest in radical politics. And he continued to write poetry – mostly lyric verses and epigrams on personal, amatory or political subjects – often light and ribald, but always crisply, lucidly and euphoniously expressed. Some of these verses, even unpublished, gained wide currency in St Petersburg and attracted the unfavourable notice of the Emperor Alexander I.

Pushkin's major work of this period was *Ruslan and Lyudmila*, a mock epic in six cantos, completed in 1820 and enthusiastically received by the public. Before it could be published, however, the Emperor finally lost patience with the subversiveness of some of Pushkin's shorter verses and determined to remove him from the capital. He first considered exiling Pushkin to Siberia or the White Sea, but at the intercession of high-placed friends of Pushkin's the proposed sentence was commuted to a posting to the south of Russia. Even so, some supposed friends hurt and infuriated Pushkin by spreading exaggerated rumours about his disgrace.

Travels in the South

Pushkin was detailed to report to Lieutenant General Ivan Inzov (1768–1845), who was at the time Commissioner for the Protection for Foreign Colonists in Southern Russia based at Yekaterinoslav (now Dnepropetrovsk) on the lower Dnieper. Inzov gave him a friendly welcome, but little work to do, and before long Pushkin caught a fever from bathing in the river and was confined to bed in his poor lodgings. He was rescued by General Nikolai Rayevsky, a soldier who had distinguished himself in the war of 1812 against Napoleon. Rayevsky, who from 1817 to 1824 commanded the Fourth Infantry Corps in Kiev, was travelling through Yekaterinoslav with his younger son (also called Nikolai), his two youngest daughters Maria and Sofya, a personal physician and other attendants; they were on their way to join the elder son Alexander, who was taking a cure at the mineral springs in the Caucasus. General Rayevsky generously invited Pushkin to join them, and Inzov gave his leave.

The party arrived in Pyatigorsk, in the northern foothills of the Caucasus, in June. Pushkin, along with his hosts, benefited from the waters and was soon well again. He accompanied the Rayevskys on long trips into the surrounding country, where he enjoyed the mountain scenery and observed the way of life of the local Circassian and Chechen tribes. In early August they set off westwards to join the rest of the Rayevsky family (the General's wife and two older daughters) in the Crimea. On the way they passed through the Cossack-patrolled lands on the northern bank of the Kuban river and learnt more about the warlike Circassians of the mountains to the south.

General Rayevsky and his party including Pushkin met up with the rest of the family at Gurzúf on the Crimean coast, where they had the use of a villa near the shore. Pushkin enjoyed his time in the Crimea, particularly the majestic coastal scenery, the southern climate, and the new experience of living in the midst of a harmonious, hospitable and intelligent family. He also fell in love with Yekaterina, the General's oldest daughter, a love that was not reciprocated. Before leaving the Crimea Pushkin travelled with the Rayevskys through the coastal mountains and inland to Bakhchisaray, an oriental town which had till forty years before been the capital of the Tatar khans of the Crimea and where the khans' palace still stood (and stands).

After a month in the Crimea it was time for the party to return to the mainland. During the summer General Inzov had been transferred from Yekaterinoslav to be governor of Bessarabia (the northern slice of Moldavia, which Russia had annexed from Turkey only eight years previously). His new headquarters was in Kishinyov (modern Chişinău, capital of Moldova), the chief town of Bessarabia. So it was to Kishinyov that Pushkin went back to duty in September 1820. Pushkin remained there (with spells of local leave) till 1823.

Bessarabia 1820–23

Kishinyov was still, apart from recently arrived Russian officials and soldiers, a raw Near-Eastern town, with few buildings of stone or brick, populated by Moldavians and other Balkan nationalities. Despite the contrast with St Petersburg, Pushkin still passed a lot of his time in a similar lifestyle of camaraderie, drinking, gambling, womanizing and quarrelling, with little official work. But he wrote too. And he also, as in the Caucasus and Crimea, took a close interest in the indigenous cultures, visiting local fairs and living for a few days with a band of Moldavian gypsies, an experience on which he later drew in his narrative poem *Gypsies*.

In the winter of 1820–21 Pushkin finished the first of his "southern" narrative poems, *A Prisoner in the Caucasus*, which he had already begun in the Crimea. (The epilogue he added in May 1821.) This poem reflects the experiences of his Caucasus visit. The work was published in August 1822. It had considerable public success, not so much for the plot and characterization, which were criticized even by Pushkin himself, but rather, as he himself acknowledged, for its "truthful, though only lightly sketched, descriptions of the Caucasus and the customs of its mountain peoples".

Having completed *A Prisoner in the Caucasus*, Pushkin went on to write a narrative poem reflecting his impressions of the Crimea, *The Fountain of Bakhchisaray*. This was started in 1821, finished in 1823 and published in March 1824. It was also a great popular success, though again Pushkin dismissed it as "rubbish". Both poems, as Pushkin admitted, show the influence of Lord Byron, a poet whom, particularly at this period, Pushkin admired.

Just before his departure from Kishinyov in 1823, Pushkin composed the first few stanzas of Chapter One of his greatest work, the novel in verse *Eugene Onegin*. It took him eight years to complete. Each chapter was published separately (except Chapters Four and Five, which came out together) between the years 1825 and 1832.

Odessa 1823–24

In the summer of 1823, through the influence of his friends in St Petersburg, Pushkin was posted to work for Count Mikhail Vorontsov, who had just been appointed Governor General of the newly-Russianized region south of the Ukraine. Vorontsov's headquarters were to be in Odessa, the port city on the Black Sea founded by Catherine the Great thirty years previously. Despite its newness Odessa was a far more lively, cosmopolitan and cultured place than Kishinyov, and Pushkin was pleased with the change. But he only remained there a year.

Pushkin did not get on well with his new chief, partly because of temperamental differences, partly because he objected to the work Count Vorontsov expected him to do, and partly because he had an affair with the Countess. Vorontsov tried hard to get Pushkin transferred elsewhere, and Pushkin for his part became so unhappy with his position on the Count's staff that he tried to resign and even contemplated escaping overseas. But before matters came to a head the police intercepted a letter from Pushkin to a friend in which he spoke approvingly of the atheistic views of an Englishman he had met in the city. The authorities in St Petersburg now finally lost patience with Pushkin: he was dismissed from the service and sent into indefinite banishment on his mother's country estate of Mikhaylovskoye in the west of Russia. He left Odessa for Mikhaylovskoye on 1st August 1824; he had by now written two and a half chapters of *Eugene Onegin*, and had begun *Gypsies*.

Exile at Mikháylovskoye

Pushkin spent more than two years under police surveillance at Mikhaylovskoye. The enforced leisure gave him a lot of time for writing. Within a couple of months he had completed *Gypsies*, which was first published in full in 1827. *Gypsies* is a terser, starker, more thoughtful and more dramatic work than *A Prisoner in the Caucasus* or *The Fountain of Bakhchisaray*; along with *Eugene Onegin* it marks a transition from the discursive romanticism of Pushkin's earliest years to the compressed realism of his mature style. At Mikhaylovskoye Pushkin progressively completed Chapters Three to Six of *Eugene Onegin*, many passages of which reflect Pushkin's observation of country life and love of the countryside. He also wrote his historical drama *Boris Godunov* at this period and his entertaining verse tale *Count Nulin*.

The Decembrist Revolt 1825

In November 1825 Alexander I died. He left no children, and there was initially confusion over the succession. In December some liberal-minded members of the army and the intelligentsia (subsequently known as the "Decembrists") seized the opportunity to attempt a *coup d'état*. This was put down by the new Emperor, Nicholas I, a younger brother of Alexander's. Among the conspirators were several old friends of Pushkin, and he might well have joined them had he been at liberty. As it was, the leading conspirators were executed, and many of the rest were sent to Siberia for long spells of hard labour and exile. Pushkin feared that he too might be punished.

Rehabilitation 1826–31

The following autumn Pushkin was summoned unexpectedly to Moscow to see the new Emperor. Nicholas surprised Pushkin by offering him his freedom, and Pushkin assured Nicholas of his future good conduct. Pushkin complained that he had difficulty in making money from his writing because of the censorship, and Nicholas undertook to oversee Pushkin's work personally. In practice, however, the Emperor delegated the task to the Chief of the Secret Police, and, despite occasional interventions from Nicholas, Pushkin continued to have difficulty with the censors.

After a few months in Moscow Pushkin returned to St Petersburg, where he spent most of his time in the coming years, though he continued periodically to visit Moscow, call at the family's estates and stay with friends in the country. In 1829 he made his only visit abroad, following the Russian army on a campaign into north-eastern Turkey. During the late 1820s he made several attempts to find a wife, with a view to settling down. In 1829 he met Natalya Goncharova, whom he married early in 1831.

It was during the four years between his return from exile and his marriage that he wrote Chapter Seven (1827–28) and most of Chapter Eight (1829–31) of *Eugene Onegin*. In 1828 he also wrote *Poltava* (published in 1829), a kind of historical "novella in verse". This seems to have been the first attempt in Russian at a work of this kind based on the study of historical material. In its application of the imagination to real events, it prefigured Pushkin's later novel in prose *The Captain's Daughter* and helped to set a pattern for subsequent historical novels in Russia. It is also notable for the terse realism of its descriptions and for the pace and drama of its narratives and dialogues. It was during this period, too, that Pushkin began to write fiction in prose, though it was not till late in 1830 that he succeeded in bringing any prose stories to completion.

In the autumn of 1830 a cholera epidemic caused Pushkin to be marooned for a couple of months on another family estate, Boldino, some six hundred kilometres east of Moscow. He took advantage of the enforced leisure to write. This was when he virtually completed Chapter Eight of *Eugene Onegin*. He also composed at this time his collection of short stories in prose *The Tales of Belkin*, another verse tale, *The Little House in Kolomna*, and his set of four one-act dramas known together as *The Little Tragedies*.

The Final Years 1831–37

The 1830s were not on the whole happy years for Pushkin. His marriage, it is true, was more successful than might have been expected. Natalya was thirteen years his junior; her remarkable beauty and susceptibility to admiration constantly exposed her to the attentions of other men; she showed more liking for society and its entertainments than for intellectual or artistic pursuits or for household management; her fashionable tastes and social aspirations incurred outlays that the pair could ill afford; and she took little interest in her husband's writing. Nonetheless, despite all this they seem to have remained a loyal and loving couple; Natalya bore him four children in their less than six years of marriage, and she showed real anguish at his untimely death.

But there were other difficulties. Pushkin, though short of money himself and with a costly family of his own to maintain, was often called upon to help out his parents, his brother and sister and his in-laws, and so fell ever deeper into debt. Both his wife and the Emperor demanded his presence in the capital so that he would be available to attend social and court functions, while he would much have preferred to be in the country, writing. Though Nicholas gave him intermittent support socially and financially, many at court and in the government, wounded by his jibes or shocked by his supposed political and sexual liberalism, disliked or despised him. And a new generation of writers and readers were beginning to look on him as a man of the past.

In 1831 Pushkin at length completed *Eugene Onegin*. The final chapter was published at the beginning of 1832, the first complete edition of the work coming out in 1833. But overall in these years Pushkin wrote less, and when he did write he turned increasingly to prose. In 1833 he spent another productive autumn at the Boldino estate, producing his most famous prose novella, *The Queen of Spades*, and one of his finest narrative poems, *The Bronze Horseman*. He also developed in these years his interest in history, already evident in *Boris Godunov* and *Poltava*: Nicholas I commissioned him to write a history of Peter the Great, but alas he left only copious notes for this at his death. He did, however, write in 1833 his *A History of Pugachov*, a well-researched account of the 18th century Cossack and peasant uprising under Yemelyan Pugachov, which Nicholas allowed him to publish in 1834. He built on his research into this episode to write his longest work of prose fiction, *The Captain's Daughter* (1836). Over these years too he produced his five metrical fairy stories; these are mostly based on Russian folk tales, but one, *The Golden Cockerel* (1834), is an adaptation of one of Washington Irving's *Tales of the Alhambra*.

Writings From his schooldays till his death Pushkin also composed well over six hundred shorter verses, comprising many lyrics of love and friendship, brief narratives, protests, invectives, epigrams, epitaphs, dedications and others. He left numerous letters from his adult years that give us an invaluable insight into his thoughts and activities and those of his contemporaries. And, as a man of keen intelligence and interest in literature, he produced throughout his career many articles and shorter notes – some published in his lifetime, others not – containing a wide variety of literary criticism and comment.

It is indeed hard to name a literary genre that Pushkin did not use in his lifetime, or it would be truer to say that he wrote across the genres, ignoring traditional categories with his characteristic independence and originality. All his writing is marked by an extraordinary polish, succinctness and clarity, an extraordinary sense for the beauty of sounds and rhythms, an extraordinary human sympathy and insight, an extraordinary feel for what is appropriate to the occasion and an extraordinary directness and naturalness of diction that is never pompous, insincere or carelessly obscure.

Death Early in 1837 Pushkin's career was cut tragically short. Following a series of improper advances to his wife and insults to himself, he felt obliged to fight a duel with a young Frenchman who was serving as an officer in the Imperial Horse Guards in St Petersburg. Pushkin was fatally wounded in the stomach and died at his home in St Petersburg two days later. The authorities denied him a public funeral in the capital for fear of demonstrations, and he was buried privately at the Svyatye Gory monastery near Mikháylovskoye, where his memorial has remained a place of popular pilgrimage.

Select Bibliography

THE CAPTAIN'S DAUGHTER AND A HISTORY OF PUGACHOV

Russian texts are available in the collections of Pushkin's works published in the Soviet Union and in Russia during the last half-century and more, for example:

Sobraniye Sochineniy Pushkina, (Moscow: Gosudarstvennoye Izdatelstvo Khudozhestvennoy Literatury, 1959–1962). Volume V contains *The Captain's Daughter*, and Volume VII contains *A History of Pugachov*.

This ten-volume collection of Pushkin's works is also available on-line in Russian through the *Russkaya virtualnaya biblioteka* at www.rvb.ru/pushkin/toc.htm.

Alexander, John T., *Emperor of the Cossacks: Pugachov and the Frontier Jacquerie of 1773–1775* (Lawrence, Kan.: Coronado Press, 1973)

Blok, G.P., *Pushkin v rabote nad istoricheskimi istochnikami* (Moscow: Akademiya Nauk SSSR, 1949)

Chkheidze, A.I., *'Istoriya Pugachova' A.S. Pushkina* (Tbilisi: Izd. SSR Gruzii "Literatura i iskusstvo", 1963)

Dubrovin, N.F., *Pugachov i yego soobshchniki*, 3 vols. (St Petersburg: I.N. Skorokhodov, 1884)

Golubtsov, S.A., ed., *Pugachovshchina*, 3 vols. (Moscow: Gosizdat, 1926–31)

Mavrodin, V.V., et al., *Krestyanskaya voina v 1773–1775 gg. Vosstaniye Pugachova*, 3 vols. (Leningrad: Leningradsky gos. univ., 1961–70)

Ovchinnikov, R.V., *Pushkin v rabote nad arkhivnymi dokumentami ('Istoriya Pugachova')* (Leningrad: Nauka, 1969)

Pushkin, A.S., *The Captain's Daughter*, translated by Robert and Elizabeth Chandler (London: Hesperus Classics, 2007)

Pushkin, A.S., *The History of Pugachov*, translated by Earl Sampson (London: Phoenix Press, 2001)

BIOGRAPHIES OF PUSHKIN

Binyon, T.J., *Pushkin: a biography* (London: HarperCollins 2002)

Lotman, Yu.M., *Alexandr Sergeyevich Pushkin: biografiya pisatelya* (St Petersburg: Iskusstvo-SPB, 1995)

OTHER BOOKS ABOUT PUSHKIN AND HIS WORK

Bayley, Professor John, *Pushkin: a Comparative Commentary* (Cambridge University Press 1971)

Briggs, Professor A.D.P., *Alexander Pushkin: a Critical Study* (Croom Helm 1983)

Tomashevsky, B.V., *Pushkin*, (Moscow-Leningrad: Izdátelstvo Akademii Nauk USSR, 1956)

Wolff, Tatiana, ed., *Pushkin on literature* (London: The Athlone Press, 1986)

1. James Hanley, *Boy*
2. D.H. Lawrence, *The First Women in Love*
3. Charlotte Brontë, *Jane Eyre*
4. Jane Austen, *Pride and Prejudice*
5. Emily Brontë, *Wuthering Heights*
6. Anton Chekhov, *Sakhalin Island*
7. Giuseppe Gioacchino Belli, *Sonnets*
8. Jack Kerouac, *Beat Generation*
9. Charles Dickens, *Great Expectations*
10. Jane Austen, *Emma*
11. Wilkie Collins, *The Moonstone*
12. D.H. Lawrence, *The Second Lady Chatterley's Lover*
13. Jonathan Swift, *The Benefit of Farting Explained*
14. Anonymous, *Dirty Limericks*
15. Henry Miller, *The World of Sex*
16. Jeremias Gotthelf, *The Black Spider*
17. Oscar Wilde, *The Picture Of Dorian Gray*
18. Erasmus, *Praise of Folly*
19. Henry Miller, *Quiet Days in Clichy*
20. Cecco Angiolieri, *Sonnets*
21. Fyodor Dostoevsky, *Humiliated and Insulted*
22. Jane Austen, *Sense and Sensibility*
23. Theodor Storm, *Immensee*
24. Ugo Foscolo, *Sepulchres*
25. Boileau, *Art of Poetry*
26. Kaiser, *Plays Vol. 1*
27. Émile Zola, *Ladies' Delight*
28. D.H. Lawrence, *Selected Letters*
29. Alexander Pope, *The Art of Sinking in Poetry*
30. E.T.A. Hoffmann, *The King's Bride*
31. Ann Radcliffe, *The Italian*
32. Prosper Mérimée, *A Slight Misunderstanding*
33. Giacomo Leopardi, *Canti*
34. Giovanni Boccaccio, *Decameron*
35. Annette von Droste-Hülshoff, *The Jew's Beech*
36. Stendhal, *Life of Rossini*
37. Eduard Mörike, *Mozart's Journey to Prague*
38. Jane Austen, *Love and Friendship*
39. Leo Tolstoy, *Anna Karenina*
40. Ivan Bunin, *Dark Avenues*
41. Nathaniel Hawthorne, *The Scarlet Letter*
42. Sadeq Hedayat, *Three Drops of Blood*
43. Alexander Trocchi, *Young Adam*
44. Oscar Wilde, *The Decay of Lying*
45. Mikhail Bulgakov, *The Master and Margarita*
46. Sadeq Hedayat, *The Blind Owl*
47. Alain Robbe-Grillet, *Jealousy*
48. Marguerite Duras, *Moderato Cantabile*
49. Raymond Roussel, *Locus Solus*
50. Alain Robbe-Grillet, *In the Labyrinth*
51. Daniel Defoe, *Robinson Crusoe*
52. Robert Louis Stevenson, *Treasure Island*
53. Ivan Bunin, *The Village*
54. Alain Robbe-Grillet, *The Voyeur*
55. Franz Kafka, *Dearest Father*
56. Geoffrey Chaucer, *Canterbury Tales*
57. A. Bierce, *The Monk and the Hangman's Daughter*
58. F. Dostoevsky, *Winter Notes on Summer Impressions*
59. Bram Stoker, *Dracula*
60. Mary Shelley, *Frankenstein*
61. Johann Wolfgang von Goethe, *Elective Affinities*
62. Marguerite Duras, *The Sailor from Gibraltar*
63. Robert Graves, *Lars Porsena*
64. Napoleon Bonaparte, *Aphorisms and Thoughts*
65. J. von Eichendorff, *Memoirs of a Good-for-Nothing*
66. Adelbert von Chamisso, *Peter Schlemihl*
67. Pedro Antonio de Alarcón, *The Three-Cornered Hat*
68. Jane Austen, *Persuasion*
69. Dante Alighieri, *Rime*
70. A. Chekhov, *The Woman in the Case and Other Stories*
71. Mark Twain, *The Diaries of Adam and Eve*
72. Jonathan Swift, *Gulliver's Travels*
73. Joseph Conrad, *Heart of Darkness*
74. Gottfried Keller, *A Village Romeo and Juliet*
75. Raymond Queneau, *Exercises in Style*
76. Georg Büchner, *Lenz*
77. Giovanni Boccaccio, *Life of Dante*
78. Jane Austen, *Mansfield Park*
79. E.T.A. Hoffmann, *The Devil's Elixirs*
80. Claude Simon, *The Flanders Road*
81. Raymond Queneau, *The Flight of Icarus*
82. Niccolò Machiavelli, *The Prince*
83. Mikhail Lermontov, *A Hero of our Time*
84. Henry Miller, *Black Spring*
85. Victor Hugo, *The Last Day of a Condemned Man*
86. D.H. Lawrence, *Paul Morel*
87. Mikhail Bulgakov, *The Life of Monsieur de Molière*
88. Leo Tolstoy, *Three Novellas*
89. Stendhal, *Travels in the South of France*
90. Wilkie Collins, *The Woman in White*
91. Alain Robbe-Grillet, *Erasers*
92. Iginio Ugo Tarchetti, *Fosca*
93. D.H. Lawrence, *The Fox*
94. Borys Conrad, *My Father Joseph Conrad*
95. J. De Mille, *A Strange Manuscript Found in a Copper Cylinder*
96. Émile Zola, *Dead Men Tell No Tales*
97. Alexander Pushkin, *Ruslan and Lyudmila*
98. Lewis Carroll, *Alice's Adventures Under Ground*
99. James Hanley, *The Closed Harbour*
100. T. De Quincey, *On Murder Considered as One of the Fine Arts*
101. Jonathan Swift, *The Wonderful Wonder of Wonders*
102. Petronius, *Satyricon*
103. Louis-Ferdinand Céline, *Death on Credit*
104. Jane Austen, *Northanger Abbey*
105. W.B. Yeats, *Selected Poems*
106. Antonin Artaud, *The Theatre and Its Double*
107. Louis-Ferdinand Céline, *Journey to the End of the Night*
108. Ford Madox Ford, *The Good Soldier*
109. Leo Tolstoy, *Childhood, Boyhood, Youth*
110. Guido Cavalcanti, *Complete Poems*
111. Charles Dickens, *Hard Times*
112. Baudelaire and Gautier, *Hashish, Wine, Opium*
113. Charles Dickens, *Haunted House*
114. Ivan Turgenev, *Fathers and Children*
115. Dante Alighieri, *Inferno*
116. Gustave Flaubert, *Madame Bovary*
117. Alexander Trocchi, *Man at Leisure*
118. Alexander Pushkin, *Boris Godunov and Little Tragedies*
119. Miguel de Cervantes, *Don Quixote*
120. Mark Twain, *Huckleberry Finn*
121. Charles Baudelaire, *Paris Spleen*
122. Fyodor Dostoevsky, *The Idiot*
123. René de Chateaubriand, *Atala and René*
124. Mikhail Bulgakov, *Diaboliad*
125. Goerge Eliot, *Middlemarch*
126. Edmondo De Amicis, *Constantinople*
127. Petrarch, *Secretum*
128. Johann Wolfgang von Goethe, *The Sorrows of Young Werther*
129. Alexander Pushkin, *Eugene Onegin*
130. Fyodor Dostoevsky, *Notes from Underground*
131. Luigi Pirandello, *Plays Vol. 1*
132. Jules Renard, *Histoires Naturelles*
133. Gustave Flaubert, *The Dictionary of Received Ideas*
134. Charles Dickens, *The Life of Our Lord*
135. D.H. Lawrence, *The Lost Girl*
136. Benjamin Constant, *The Red Notebook*
137. Raymond Queneau, *We Always Treat Women too Well*
138. Alexander Trocchi, *Cain's Book*
139. Raymond Roussel, *Impressions of Africa*
140. Llewelyn Powys, *A Struggle for Life*
141. Nikolai Gogol, *How the Two Ivans Quarrelled*
142. F. Scott Fitzgerald, *The Great Gatsby*
143. Jonathan Swift, *Directions to Servants*
144. Dante Alighieri, *Purgatory*
145. Mikhail Bulgakov, *A Young Doctor's Notebook*
146. Sergei Dovlatov, *The Suitcase*
147. Leo Tolstoy, *Hadji Murat*
148. Jonathan Swift, *The Battle of the Books*
149. F. Scott Fitzgerald, *Tender Is the Night*
150. A. Pushkin, *The Queen of Spades and Other Short Fiction*
151. Raymond Queneau, *The Sunday of Life*
152. Herman Melville, *Moby Dick*
153. Mikhail Bulgakov, *The Fatal Eggs*
154. Antonia Pozzi, *Poems*
155. Johann Wolfgang von Goethe, *Wilhelm Meister*
156. Anton Chekhov, *The Story of a Nobody*
157. Fyodor Dostoevsky, *Poor People*
158. Leo Tolstoy, *The Death of Ivan Ilyich*
159. Dante Alighieri, *Vita nuova*
160. Arthur Conan Doyle, *The Tragedy of Korosko*
161. Franz Kafka, *Letters to Friends, Family and Editors*
162. Mark Twain, *The Adventures of Tom Sawyer*
163. Erich Fried, *Love Poems*
164. Antonin Artaud, *Selected Works*
165. Charles Dickens, *Oliver Twist*
166. Sergei Dovlatov, *The Zone*
167. Louis-Ferdinand Céline, *Guignol's Band*
168. Mikhail Bulgakov, *Dog's Heart*
169. Rayner Heppenstall, *Blaze of Noon*
170. Fyodor Dostoevsky, *The Crocodile*
171. Anton Chekhov, *Death of a Civil Servant*

www.almaclassics.com